The Contest

Stevanne Auerbach

Miriam

an adventure to

share with you.

love

Stevanne Auerbach.

Dedication

To my husband Ralph, and daughter Amy Beth, who both love me unconditionally, and to all single moms who struggle daily to manage the challenges of life.

Acknowledgements

Author greatly appreciates the... Inspiration of Roy Fairfield and Joe Bologna

Editing of Jim Dugan, Virginia Davis, Kathryn Lance and Adele Horowitz.

Feedback of Alan Kishbaugh, Amy Auerbach, Arline Zatz , Deborah Boldt, Elaine Bull, Jeane Stockheim, Jerry Kamstra, Judith Schwartz, Nancy Birnbaum, Pamela Drake, Rhona Hartman, Dee Copley and Suzanne Arms.

Graphic Design of Sherry Bloom

Published by ICR
268 Bush St. San Francisco, CA 94104 USA

ISBN: 978-0-9785540-2-6

Game Plan

High risks
Are gambled at high cost
To gain something beyond
No easy answers or smooth rules
To insure the risks
Discover exhilaration
At winning something special,
Unknown when the game begins

The author, **Petals 1962-1974 Collected Poems**

Contents

Prologue

Shelly bundles warmly against the unexpected chill falling swiftly over the darkened city, along familiar streets of North Beach, as she walks quickly along Columbus Avenue, she turns left on Vallejo. She stops on the corner of Grant at the door of her favorite respite, the Caffé Trieste, and enters the warm, noisy cafe, as she happily greets friends while unwrapping the bright red wool scarf from around her neck, hurrying to stand in line to order a latte.

A quiet, winter night settles softly over the narrow streets of North Beach. The holiday shopping frenzy has passed into oblivion. Now, the storied streets are still.

With only a few days left to signal the end of a decade, Shelly will say "Good-bye" to a difficult year, full of challenges, as most of her years seem to go.

Balancing the tall, hot, foam-topped glass, wrapped in a napkin, she takes a seat near the door facing outside, before taking a sip to relax and warm her body against the chill, as the cold, dark evening deepens on the outside.

She smiles at her girlfriend sitting across from her. Mona has been her friend for many years and they have had lots of good times together,

Quizzically, Shelly asks, "What are you doing New Year's Eve?"

Mona laughs, showing the laugh lines around her bright blue eyes that match the soft, blue sweater she is wearing. She says, "Who wants to go out? I'm happy to celebrate at home. Besides, who's around that's sexy, satisfying, and safe?"

Shelly nods her agreement, as she recalls vivid pictures of the past: How many years ago was it that she watched the glowing ball on the New York Times building slowly falling down along with the snowflakes over 42nd Street as the crowd shouted the "countdown" in unison...10, 9, 8, 7...?

She remembers all too well the chill of the night, and the "klutz" that made her body feel even colder. A big wet tongue kiss had broken the warm romance of the moment.

She recalls a party in Washington D.C. close to midnight, as she is given a cold glass of champagne, with a crisp toast wedge of caviar, and a light kiss on the hand, there among beautiful, bright and powerful people. There was some expression of passion, but not much. Those moments flickered out with the candles, along with faded memories of discarded 45-rpm records.

Mona quickly brings her back to the moment as she asks, "What do you want in the New Year?"

Shelly, stops, quickly makes a funny face, throws up her hands, and laughs.

"Something new!" and suddenly she turns to her right.

She sees a face, but it does not register. She stares quizzically into very familiar eyes.

"Hello," says the silver-haired, handsome man smiling back from the next table.

She looks again, not seeing him. She is puzzled. Then, as she recognizes him, she tries to shield her feelings. How could he be here at this very moment?

No, He can't be here. Not this ghost from years past. The Prince of the years she had lived in Camelot and eagerly waited for the dragon slayer.

The Prince came to her on his white horse, but instead of slaying dragons, his sword had deeply pierced her heart, and never again would the world of Camelot exist. She would not ride away on the back of his white horse or live in his castle.

Cinderella's slipper had fit too tightly and shattered along with her dreams of a fairytale existence in a magical land where many believe fairytales really do come true.

Shelly gathers her courage, as memories of the past fly in like bats released from a cave, and casting a chill over the already frosty night…

"Don't you recognize me?" asks the silver haired man, noting her surprised look.

He could always read the truth in her face, if he only took the time to look. She catches herself, holding back a tidal wave of feeling, not wanting him to see any of it.

"Oh! Hello. I was just not expecting…to see you here. How are you, Doug?"

"Fine," he replies. "I was just out taking a long walk, and decided to come in. I haven't been here for years. It's a good place to sit and people watch, but I hardly have much time to do that anymore."

"No, I guess you don't."

She gathers herself internally into a smooth ball, wanting to remain calm and cool on the outside, but her stomach is churning so much, her mind is blank for a moment.

As he gets up for coffee he asks, "Can I get you something?"

"Yes please, a bottle of sparkling water."

She hopes she appears calm as a pool of water with not even a tiny ripple shimmering on its shining surface.

She turns to Mona with a searching look for some support, but her friend is busy talking to a couple at the next table, unaware of Shelly's dilemma. Doug had happened long before she and Shelly met.

Doug returns shortly with his hot coffee, and her bottle of bubbling mineral water with lemon. She alternates between sips of coffee and water attempting to maintain a modicum of composure, as she takes quiet, deep breaths.

Doug smiles as they look at each other, pausing and collecting thoughts.

Composed and sure of himself, Doug fires the first round.

Casual conversation passes between them as if volleying balls on a tennis court. The balls include "people, work, children, the city and other casual comments about the cafe, opera music on Saturdays, the mutual friend who plays piano, and how much and how fast the City they both love is changing. They avoid conversation about deeper personal matters.

Finally Doug asks, "Would you like to take a walk?"

Shelly nods, leans over and tells Mona, "I'll call you. Have fun. Happy New Year! Hope all your dreams come true."

Mona looks up and gives Shelly a wink, thinking Shelly has found someone 'new.'

"Bye!" She says as they turn to the door.

As they leave the cafe Shelly throws her scarf around her neck wanting to create a soft shield of protective armor, but it is bogus.

Across the street at the Ace Hardware store Doug searches for an apple cutter. The store does not have one, so they continue down the street to Figoni, the oldest hardware store in the City. They find many household treasures, including the last two apple cutters to be had in North Beach that night. She decides she also needs one, because she just might want to cut an apple into nine even wedges.

He does not offer to buy her the apple cutter, so she pulls $2 from her pocket.

She thinks to herself, "This must be the modern version of the consolation prize Eve wins after losing Adam and Paradise. "Yes!" Even Eve is liberated today. The tempting apple will now be cut into perfectly even pieces, but it's too late because we already lost the 'Garden of Eden'—she just wondered where this curious unexpected synchronicity of their meeting again would lead. He was the last person she expected or wanted to see.

They continue up Grant Avenue past familiar, now-closed shops, and quaint, quiet restaurants, to the French-Italian bakery, where Doug buys a loaf of still warm, fresh, sweet bread. He breaks off a piece and offers it to her.

She thinks, how 'civilized' we both are. How 'generous' he is with offerings of 'bread and water.' After all the years, all the tears, all the time lost in a dark, painful prison of lost illusions, empty feelings, loneliness and struggle. She mutters her thanks, as she takes a bit of bread, but it sticks in her throat. The clerk hands her a cup of water as she smiles and sips weakly.

How odd was this chance meeting after all these years, an unplanned coincidence coming just at the end of the year, and the start of a new decade. Perhaps this was a sign, an omen, or finally a chance to let go of old memories, and gaping wounds that had been festering for more than ten years. Precious time was still needed to heal the still tender cuts not at all visible to the naked eye. Now, Doug calmly offers her a ride home, as he opens the door to his late-model dark-gray BMW, and continues chatting. She replies politely and simply "fine" to each question.

"How is your mother?

How is your sister?

How is your daughter?"

"How are your children?" asks Shelly.

Doug shares immediately news about his older son, "Andy is now gaining fame as a 'go-for-the-jugular' divorce lawyer." He adds, "Of course, he had the chance to gain all that experience first-hand at home."

"Yes," she replies softly, thinking to herself, "How clever the 'big-mouthed kid' was to capitalize on his natural talents of being a slick, obnoxious manipulator, and slide into the perfect readymade profession capitalizing on the undigested decomposition of relationships."

Doug continues, oblivious to her thoughts, "He observed, listened, and missed nothing. Did you realize how much fodder we gave him to prepare for his future career?"

"No, I guess I never thought about it at the time," Shelly replies, shrugging her shoulders. But, there were Doug's series of marriages, and divorces, and plenty of feisty drama to learn firsthand about what can be right, and what can go very wrong.

As they pulled up in front of her apartment, Shelly turned full face to Doug and asked him quietly,

"Is it true you and Beryl are separating?"

"Yes, we will be divorced in a few months." Doug replies, closing his eyes for a moment.

Shelly actually thought she saw a nanosecond of discomfort.

"I'm sorry to hear it." Shelly responds trying to be civil, but inside, Shelly feels relieved. The woman she has hated for years was finally getting what she deserved. Beryl finally was caught in the inevitable Venus flytrap set for her.

In a barely audible voice, she says as she got out of the car, "Well, a very happy New Year!" then trying to be flippant, she reaches out to shake his always sure, steady, cool, doctor's hand. "May acquaintance never be forgotten or never brought to mind?"

He says, "Happy New Year to you, too!" and adds, "Take care of yourself!"

Then she hurries to get inside before he can see her wet eyes streaming tears.

Shelly sits quietly in her dark apartment for a long while, to try to regain her composure. She needs to think, feel, and remember. It felt as if ten years had simply dissolved into a recently released feature length full-color film.

Mentally, she rewinds the reel back to the beginning. She wants to replay everything, all the frames, as if now, after seeing him again, she could finally make some sense of the whole challenging saga.

The past comes swiftly flowing into her 'projector of the mind,' full-flooding her abundant mental reservoir, and overflowing the fragile container. The details are still deeply etched into her memory. Years fall away, as she listens to her mental radio as if hearing her story told by the "Let's Pretend" radio show narrator. It was after all her strongest childhood memory, living out the lives of princesses' adventures in days gone by complete with sound effects, galloping horses, and the excitement of anticipation being swept off one's feet by Prince Charming.

When did it all begin? How could anything have been different? Could she have somehow saved herself? Could she have known in advance how it would turn out? Why didn't she listen to her "all-knowing mother" who foretold her well in advance how it was all going to end? Why, if she knew from childhood about wicked spells, dangerous witches, and evil villains, did she not protect her most prized possession, her hopeful and trusting heart, from being broken? How could she have saved her precious dreams from being consumed by fire?

Shelly watches the film in her mind, but this time, for the first time, without any tears. The "Let's Pretend" narrator's voice, the flashes of stored images from the projector, and lack of resistance to recall are flowing into her mind, all running simultaneously. The drama is rewinding, but this time shown in surround sound, with the full cast of characters and in full-blown color.

Only a few days left to the end of the year, but it would be a new beginning if she could finally forget, or better yet, just let go of the past, and release the spell cast over her memories. She needs to find some magic to break the spell. She had to live it all again this time also from his point of view and hers so she could better and more fully understand what might have been different. Was it a lifetime mistake or merely a life lesson?

Doug had never said he was sorry for anything, but that was only one of the problems. Shelly was not sorry they met. If only he had stopped the destruction, before it was too late, and not broken her heart. She wishes she had known critical answers before it was too late. It seems, but a few days ago, when the story began. This time she wants a new clear perspective.

Maybe this time something might be different. "What could have been different?"

Could she have stopped before burning her dreams? She sits back and closes her eyes and listens as her pretend narrator takes her into the past…

Chapter 1

Time for a Change

January is here with eyes that keenly glow-a frost
mailed warrior striding a shadowy steed of snow.
Edgar Fawcett, American poet (1847-1904)

The TWA jet dived directly toward the runway of the well-illuminated curve of Dulles Airport, touched down, and roared to a stop in front of the mobile lounge. Doug Fine grabbed his brown leather attaché case from under his seat, rose quickly to find his jacket in the overhead compartment, and joined the queue. It was icy cold outside. The waiting ground transport bus carried the passengers swiftly to the terminal.

Dr. Fine moved with the throng of fast-moving people toward the down escalator. While waiting for his bag in the baggage claim area, he opened the red, white and blue package and took out and lit a cigarette. What did he know, he was only a doctor? He liked the taste of a cigarette, especially when he felt stressed

With bag in hand, he put out the half smoked cigarette in a nearby sand receptacle and went quickly up the ramp to a waiting shuttle bus that would take him the rest of the way into Washington, D.C. During the familiar ride along the Expressway, and while the bus stopped at various hotels, he reflected on how often he had made this trip in the past few years

More and more he enjoyed travel. He found the time away from home and hospital usually gratifying. He closed his eyes as he thought about how much his life had changed over the past five years. He felt cold inside his heart despite all the work activity that filled his daily appointment book.

Time meant nothing. Discontent did. He was ready to start a new journey. He was bored with the daily routine, pressures at the hospital, and life at home. He wondered what was happening. The inner spark was gone.

He was certain it was not the flight. He felt he didn't have a destination even though he had a reservation. He felt he was without an itinerary or map.

Suddenly, he felt very tired. Yet another meeting lay ahead. This time, the respite from the pressures he faced was only four days, then back to the same worn out groove. He hoped the time away would last as long as possible. He needed a change, but he did not know what form it would take.

Finally, the bus arrived at the sprawling, red-bricked Sheraton Park Hotel. He walked out to catch the night air and clear his head. The cold stung against his ears. He shivered, turned and walked quickly inside to the hotel's expansive lobby, crossed the newly laid Oriental carpets, with the brand new carpet smell, to the large carved desk to register.

From across the lobby a familiar voice rang out, a fellow doctor signaled friendly recognition. It was true, he was better known than two years before. The rise from obscurity made him feel a little less empty inside. He was becoming more self-assured. But, what did it matter? Who could he really share his feelings of emptiness with?

Robert Mendel, his old friend from Chicago, came over to talk as Doug registered.

"Hi Doug, How are things? What's happening in 'Frisco? Sorry, I'm not supposed to call it that, or am I?"

They both laughed.

"Bob, you old rascal! Great to see you! You look as young as ever. Chicago winters must be keeping you young. Or is it chasing a large patient load that keeps you so trim?"

As he spoke to Bob, Doug finished registering. He put his credit card away in his wallet and invited Bob to meet him at the lobby bar in 20 minutes. Doug went to his room and quickly unpacked.

He returned to the lobby and found Bob at the bar. There was a loud, talkative crowd filling the place. The talk was full of Washington gossip, politics and the latest "buzz" about "Federal regulations," "program priorities," and the other usual "buzz words…hew, oeo, pdq, opd, doc, dol, doe, regs, rfp, and stats." "Buzz" is code that permeates typical Washington conversations. The "alphabet soup of the nation" spread out in the bowl of "Fedshorthand," a special language, extruding from one end of town to the other, from Capitol Hill to Georgetown, for the all-consuming verbiage of feds and lobbyists, the well fed-fund chasers.

This time the meeting was "Head Start," the still growing program for poor preschool children that was a "political football" once too often, but it managed somehow to survive, sustain support and grow stronger each year despite the politics that were not supportive of children. The annual event was vital to all participants. It was now time to gather, to plan strategy, and move forward.

The meeting attracted parents, teachers, social workers, community leaders, enthusiastic poverty workers, and pediatricians from all over the country. They came together with greater diversity and more determination every year. This year, 1968, was no different than any other year, just more stressful than usual due to great deal of shifting political turf. Richard Nixon had been elected by a margin of 500,000 votes. Times were changing. War and protests were mounting while communities struggled with tumultuous changes

Doug merged right into the conclave. He was congenial, professional, a representative of the new elite, the dedicated socially responsible doctor. He was one of the more liberal physicians who actually cared about honest delivery of health care services to poor people. He wanted to accomplish something real and make a difference. People were becoming concerned about the delivery of services for poor children. Health care would be important. All children would ultimately benefit from increased attention to the importance of early education, nutrition and health care. He believed in the goals of the program, and was there to prove it.

Doug was a handsome man with salt-and-pepper hair, who was friendly, outgoing, and had always done well. He possessed a drive and a concern that always pushed him to work hard. Yet, he felt personally incomplete. Suddenly, he was experiencing the feelings of excitement and a renewed sense of making new things happen. His drive had lain dormant for too long. Still, he felt something major was missing in his life.

Doug and Robert Mendel, an old professional friend from the University of Chicago, who for years was his mentor in Head Start, and other social causes, resumed their earlier conversation. They hoped to plan an effective strategy before the major meeting in the morning.

"Bob, is the weather in Chicago as cold as I remember?"

Bob laughed, "Worse, but that's no excuse for you to live in California. You are missed. I saw your dad not long ago. He is sure you will still open a practice with him in Chicago."

"He is still waiting? Doug asked wryly. I don't think I could ever do that now," he said softly.

They ordered drinks and settled back.

"Yes, the same old grind!" Bob said, "But, it's getting a little easier. I brought in a young associate who is willing to work those extra hours, nights, and weekends to cover for me while I do the 'socially correct' thing in D.C. I actually get to take a weekend off once in a while, so I started a new book to take care of my free time. This one is going to blow the lid off the medical profession, warts and all."

"Bob…you old goat! You will never slow down. I take my hat off to you." Doug replied. They both laughed.

They talked about their work and old friends. Bob had the opportunity earlier in the day to talk briefly with other physicians, who had come to Washington, from other parts of the country. He wanted to brief Doug on their agenda.

It was a smoky, noisy, active evening. They spent most of the time discussing the meetings. Afterwards, over drinks, Doug told Bob how he felt about the issues. They exchanged ideas.

"Bob, everything is going as we planned. The guidelines seem to be ready to be adopted. Do you think there will be any hang-ups?"

"No," replied Bob. "We've got the entire country represented now with our delegation from the Academy of Pediatrics. It's a good thing you got here or we would have been one member short from the west. There are a few problems with budget allocations, but it will get cleared by Congress. I'm sure the President will go along with it. It's good politics after all. But, you know 'Tricky Dick'; anything can happen, and it usually does."

Bob told Doug about a meeting he had attended earlier in the day at the headquarters of Health, Education & Welfare.

Bob said, "I spent a few hours with Marvin Felder, who is working for James Allen, who, you may recall, is the well-respected Commissioner of the Office of Education, and the former Commissioner of the New York State Department of Education."

Bob continued, "Marv is energetic, smart and impressed me with his new visionary ideas about the importance of early learning. He shares our views about how vitally children need the new, proposed community medical services.

Bob continued as he told Doug, "Marv shared with me his visions for childcare, and the growing need of working mothers that would help to break the cycle of poverty, especially with on-going talk about "Welfare Reform."

Bob enthusiastically revealed, "He shares our view that more medical people need to be involved. In the meeting, we discussed existing plans for a new national childcare system. The plan is being studied by Congress. It could become a vital program similar to Head Start."

Bob went on to explain, "They are trying to figure out how to administer plans and what role pediatricians would have." He added as Doug listened intently, "I shared our breakout of the proposed budget to show how involving pediatricians right in the programs would save money in the long run, and be cost effective." Bob added, "Marv likes the idea and saw many advantages. He thinks like we do!"

Bob continued, "Doug, listen, this plan is really timely. Marv wants us to meet with his staff to talk with them about specifics tomorrow. Can you get free and join us?"

Doug enthusiastically said, "Sure, I am interested. I have followed you into every other community health program you asked me to so far. I am still alive and none the worse for it." They both laughed.

Doug continued, "We have made a difference and, despite the politics, maybe we can still make a dent. What time and where?"

Bob replied, "They arranged for us to meet for lunch at the Embassy Restaurant. It's a nice place, they said, a converted Victorian-style house right down from here, on Calvert Street, off Connecticut Avenue, not far from the hotel. It's just before the Calvert Street Bridge. We can easily walk over there together after our morning session. Hey, maybe this is the start of something brand new!"

Doug relished the idea of new starts. He liked the beginnings of things a lot—the excitement, newness, the unknown excited his well-worn mid-western sensibilities. He was a top student at the University of Chicago, and continued doing well at the University of California. The 'docs' in his residency and in the administration saw something special in Doug: dedication and diplomacy. They wanted him to join them. He knew how to handle issues and find ways to solve them. After a few years in private practice specializing in pediatric allergies, he was ready for the challenges of the University system and take on more.

Bob continued, "The meeting is very important since we are all here to talk about the current issues and to see what is needed to launch the plans. It can make a big difference if the initiatives are successfully legislated. We have enough lead-time to get agreement from APA (American Pediatric Association) members.

Bob added, "Doug, this program could become another 'Head Start.'"

"How?" asked Doug?

"Well, for one thing," Bob continued, laying out the plan, "the kids of working mothers need to see pediatricians for primary care during the day when their mothers are away at work. So let's start the discussion with how to deliver health care services right at the childcare center directly to children the way visiting nurses used to do during, and for a while after, World War II. That should get their attention!

"This would save a lot of time for moms, not having to go to yet another doctor's appointment, and taking more time from work. Family practice trained nurses could do the follow up services. The docs can come in, supervise, and review 'paper clipped cases' that need more attention and referrals. The nurses could do initial screenings and manage health maintenance. They can even do 'house calls,' like visiting nurses used to do. Now that's a great idea. Think of ID'ing more babies at risk, helping to save lives. It's beneficial, sensible, responsible and cost effective. Except nurses may have something to complain about: The workload. We may need to train nurse's aides. He looks to see if Doug agrees.

Bob is thinking about practical implementation as Doug injects his thoughts,

"Great concept," Doug agrees. "But, who's going to pay for it?"

"That's what we'll be talking about at the meeting. The details on delivery we feel can be worked out. It's the costs that are the hang up." Bob quickly added.

"Okay, count me in, it sounds like the right way to go," replied Doug. "The plan should be expanded to provide a health support system for the new comprehensive childcare program."

Bob added, "What you might not have heard yet is Congress has just put together a new childcare legislation package that looks a lot like Head Start. The parents will be able to get trained, participate as they can and work while their kids get education, health care, meals, and lots of other benefits. This seems to be the best way we've heard of yet to help moms be independent, earn money, cut down on welfare costs, and give the benefits directly to kids."

Doug answered, "Sounds too good to be true. I'll bet it will be hard to get the whole package passed by Congress. Let's be realistic, it's a long shot. But, you never know. Stranger things have happened. Hey, just look at the Peace Corps."

"That passed under JFK. Kennedy was young and had small children himself. He would pass this package for kids too, because he invented the Peace Corp to do original thinking to solve problems in Third World countries, so he would say how come we don't try applying some of that brain power right here to solve problems for millions of our own poor families? But Nixon is another story his thoughts are on a war in a jungle called Vietnam. Is he really concerned about poor kids in this country?" They shook their heads and laughed.

From their combined experience as medical professionals in touch with community concerns, they understood the deeper complexities involved. They sensed a fresh and yet realistic model for the delivery of health care services was greatly needed especially for children. .

Doug confirmed his interest. "Bob, I will be glad to join you tomorrow to add my two cents into the discussion."

Doug felt good that Bob included him in what promised to be exciting plans. He knew that the new programs he put into place at the University of California Community Medicine Program would be helpful. He had learned a lot about cultural diversity, administration of community services, and about mistrust.

Bob smiled at Doug and said, "Ok! Let's meet in the lobby at noon and head over."

They quickly finished their drinks, stood up, shook hands, and adjourned for the night each seeking some much-needed rest.

Chapter 2

Cold Capitol

If one advances confidently in the direction of his dream and endeavors to lead a life which he has imagined, he will meet with a success unexpected in common hours.
Henry David Thoreau

On the same bitterly cold evening that Doug and Bob were warm inside at the bar of the hotel drinking their iced drinks while talking freely about social theories, the politics of children, welfare mothers, and old colleagues; across town in the shadow of the Capitol a very tired woman, Shelly Stern, was getting ready to finish a long day of work. She held a high-pressure job in the southwest Washington headquarters of the Office of Education, Department of Health, Education, & Welfare (HEW).

As Shelly prepared to leave her small, windowless, "faded, lime-green" office, she carefully filled her rapidly expanding briefcase with various reports on the need for childcare and proposals from deserving groups around the country seeking federal support. There was never enough time to do everything during the already too full workday.

She was hopeful that she would have some quiet time later that night at home after her two-year-old daughter Alison was asleep to make a dent in the increasing flow of incoming documents.

She carefully cleared her desk, put on her winter coat, and placed a copy of the Washington Post on the top of her bulging briefcase. She glanced at the headlines. War as usual.

Then, she looked in the mirror behind the door and arranged her soft, green, felt hat over her dark brown, wavy hair. She could see small dark circles under her eyes from lack of sleep and hoped they were not that noticeable to anyone else.

As she walked quietly toward the elevator she thought about work, her principal preoccupation. She was trying her utmost to keep up with the deluge of reports, proposals, and the unending mass of information coming in from concerned communities throughout the country now actively seeking more federal assistance to create new, local childcare services. The reports were based on ten regions, and the stacks grew larger each week. This proposed national childcare initiative was to be her new responsibility; and it matched her personal and professional mission.

Shelly felt tired, as she rode down in the dark elevator, and stepped outside into the cold night air. She had just completed one of the busiest days on her job. She headed toward the D.C. Transit bus stop, feeling revived by the cold.

It was very chilly, yet she felt warm inside, and proud of herself, as she thought about all the tremendous changes. She felt exhilarated, stimulated, and satisfied with her many contributions. She was delighted that "Sesame Street" was launched with her recommendation for support and it would make a big difference. She liked the challenges of her new job, but she was also struggling to make ends meet economically and to handle the endless daily challenges of being a single mom.

She was totally responsible for the well being of her young child, their home, and their future. There was little left in her checking account at the end of each month. She had little energy after work except to go home and attend to Alison, the house, and the basics.

Worried and alone with her thoughts late at night, as her daughter slept peacefully in the next room, Shelly often felt scared, frustrated, and lonely. She realized despite her best effort to preserve her marriage, what happened was inevitable considering everything, but the realities of the results were difficult to swallow. She did not set out down the most difficult path, nor want to enter a struggle, but the challenges found her.

Shelly boarded the bus, and mused on the trip home about the inevitable conclusion of a marriage gone sour:

Her ex-husband Arnold had more income, much more freedom, but instead of more, he got much less responsibility. He could go out, with no baby sitters to worry about, or no diapers to change, while Shelly was at home with their baby. His meager support of $200 a month barely covered the babysitter's salary. Shelly had to provide everything else, because now she was the sole "bread-winner." While she had "freedom," along with it came the undeniable stress of having to manage many roles. She had worked hard over the past few years to move up the rungs of government hierarchy.

When Shelly had time to check, she saw in her mirror an attractive, tall woman, trim, energetic, poised, and proud of all she had done. She was known for being thorough, responsible, punctual, and capable of handling everything—work, her child, and home.

As a working mother, she was sensitive to the needs of other working mothers, who shared the same pressures she faced every day. Friends said she radiated inner warmth when she smiled; so she tried hard to present a friendly smiling face, even though there were many days she was tired, her feet hurt, and personal concerns almost got the best of her positive nature.

As the bus traveled slowly across the Mall, her thoughts drifted back to early 1961, just as John F. Kennedy became President. Washington was a bee-hive of activity and inspiration. Shelly watched the new dynamic president on TV during press conferences and was motivated by JFK. She wanted to respond to his challenge and make a special contribution. She worked hard at work, career, on her marriage to Arnold, and made efforts to save money. She wanted to please Arnold, succeed in her work, be practical and prove herself.

She worked steadily and waited anxiously to become pregnant. However, her dreams were shattered like a broken vase when Arnold told her abrupt-ly that he was not interested in being a father. He had sadly waited until she proudly told him she was actually pregnant. She had thought they were both committed to their marriage, and to having a family. Isn't that why they bought the house, had a dog, baby birds, and an extra bedroom? Shelly thought they were living the perfect dream together and building a future when suddenly, instead of it being bliss, the dream turned into a nightmare. Shelly woke up to reality very fast.

She realized after her divorce that she would never be able to support herself and her daughter on a Washington, D.C. teacher's salary. Nor could she afford to continue educational work in the theatre… as much as she loved its creative freedom.

She sought a job with greater potential and security. Eventually, she went to work in the government agency responsible for the nation's education.

As she wiped away the condensation from the steamed windows of the bus, she thought about her challenging new work at the agency. She realized that she was not alone, as she juggled responsibilities, her child, her home, her social life, and new job, she listened to the problems of other single mothers.

One day during lunch in the employee dining room she had a revela-tion. She looked around, at the many other single mothers, with even fewer resources, trying to cope with the same predicament. They all needed child-care just to survive each day. Male supervisors in the government bureaucracy, especially those without children, were unaware of the daily problems faced by single female employees with children. No one in authority thought about how hard it was for all the working mothers to get to work on time every morning. Working mothers had the constant concerns: "Will the baby sitter show up, or not?" or "Can I get my child to the childcare center on time and still make it to the office?"

They were all dependent on the irregular, often-late, public transportation system, the often-malfunctioning childcare system, and the gnawing concerns for their children's welfare, education and nutrition. Women with children were fast becoming the most vulnerable class of citizens: the people with little resources, little help, and even less clout. Shelly found only a few administrators even remotely sensitive. She knew most did not even try to understand. Why should they? They had wives at home handling their responsibilities for their children.

Shelly's own experiences with the challenges of childcare created within her a hundred percent total commitment. She wanted to help other women, who, like her, were in the same situation. Determined, she made up her mind to work to be a catalyst, to make quality childcare services a reality. She smiled as she remembered her early vow. She would start within the government with the employees who needed childcare. She would find a way to expand greatly needed childcare services to public companies, communities, and municipalities. She just knew it could be done if Congress would take the same initiative it had with Head Start. The Federal Government could respond if it realized how much the future depended on its choices, so she optimistically thought.

She looked out the bus window and again moved her hand to clear the fogged window as if to clear her thoughts. Changes were taking place so rapidly. Minnesota's Senator, Walter Mondale, and Indiana's Congressman, John Brademas, had recently introduced legislation for childcare in Congress. Shelly knew that Congressional attention and the right legislation were the essential first big steps. She knew that this was an important recognition of the growing problems and a positive response to the huge, unmet needs. As soon as she heard the legislative plans she resolved to do whatever she could to work for bipartisan support in order to enact what might become landmark legislation.

For months Shelly had been organizing parents who worked in the Office of Education. They had formed a diversified network—parents, supervisors, and many staff members who believed a childcare center in the building was an "idea whose time had come." Finally, she got approval from the Commissioner himself to create a greatly needed "in-house" model childcare center. She was certain the new center would have lasting benefits that would ripple out well beyond the agency.

Shelly remembered when Commissioner Allan called her into his office not long ago and said, "I think that the childcare center is a good idea. Just last week my secretary did not show up because she lost her baby sitter. Maybe the new center could have space for emergency care. Not only do I think it is a good idea, but it is long overdue. But to make this final, you have to take the paperwork over to the HEW secretary's office and get their approval and 'sign off.' Then GSA can move ahead." He explained quickly the tangled loops of red tape involved. He then added his support letter to the top of the papers. "Think this letter will give it the plan the boost it needs" He smiled and added, "Everything helps!"

Shelly smiled at him and nodded. "Commissioner Allan, thank you so much for your enthusiastic endorsement. I think it's wonderful that you understand the enormous problems. I knew we could count on your support."

Shelly remembered as she left his office how happy she felt at the thought that the concept might soon be a reality. There were just a few hundred more hurdles through all the "red tape" ahead. A lot of hard work was still necessary.

Shelly still had to perform her regular job: evaluating Title I school programs throughout the country. When the Secretary of HEW approved the new and unique childcare center to be located in the Office of Education changes could happen, but to transform an executive dining room into a childcare center was unheard of.

Unfortunately, the Secretary, head of the entire HEW Agency, might not be as easy to convince as the secretary who worked for him, as she struggled every day to get to work after dropping her two kids off at the baby sitter's house. Shelly viewed the childcare program as one of the unfinished battles left over from the Kennedy's "War on Poverty."

Shelly vowed to respond when she heard JFK's challenge, "Ask not what your country can do for you, but what you can do for your country!"

"Does anyone have the name of a good babysitter so I can go out and work for my country?" she asked her friends as they sat together listening to his speech.

They laughed.

Childcare was an idea that Shelly thought made sense, and she could not understand why anyone would be opposed. How could anyone not respond or not help a mother from working, or going to school, to help she and her child have a better life? She thought it hypocritical that those who seemed to appreciate the needs of children never spoke about how they would support fiscal, social and personal responsibility for low income children without the resources for quality care, education, braces, health care, recreation, toys, summer camp, and childhood essentials. She never heard talk about assuming "bills for braces, summer camp, clothes, and food" or anything else. She wondered a lot about responsibility…her own, her ex-husband, government, family, and society. Roles and duties in government, communities and families were not so clear.

She packed into her already full schedule, additional daily meetings, parent surveys, and obtaining approvals needed from all the Department Heads, Personnel, and the Employees' Union. She needed the final approval from the Secretary. Shelly worked on a myriad of details. This process went on for almost two years. She knew that when she finally met with the final obstacle she needed to have all the solidified support she could fully muster behind the plan for the model childcare center.

Once, naively, she thought it would happen overnight, but it hadn't. She assumed it would be met with enthusiasm. With the final approval from the HEW Secretary and clearance from General Services Administration (GSA) they would be able to transform the seldom-used Executive Dining Room into vibrant fully utilized "Model Childcare Center" for federal workers' children.

Every time she looked out into the now empty space in the area just outside the employee dining room, she saw the playground, full of laughing children:

"Hi, mommy, look at me climb in the play gym."

"Mommy, look, I drank all my milk!"

"Mommy, I didn't wet my pants!"

"Mommy, can you play a game with me?"

"Mommy, I learned the alphabet today! Now I can read!"

Shelly saw and heard real activity alive and well in her mind. She felt it was worth all the extra effort she put forth. She felt certain the HEW Secretary would finally agree. She was excited thinking about the meeting she had earlier that day with Dr. Mendel and Marvin Felder. She liked Marvin. The Commissioner brought him in from his work in New York City to shake things up. He had the energy of a New Yorker (even though he was from Los Angeles). He had spent a lot of time working on educational programs, in areas like Bedford-Stuyvesant, and New York energy rubs off. He immediately understood the possibilities of her plans, saw their value, and was supportive of her action.

Marvin said in response to the plan, "I think it's sensible if Congress authorizes direct program grants for childcare. We will be able to fund specific pilot projects, and see about children's health services"

Then he added, "Shelly, you will learn more details in your meeting tomorrow with the Head Start Doctors who are giving us some essential guidance.

She confirmed to Marvin and Julie, another staffer, "I am sure Congress will see this is a sensible program. It will help reduce the national cry for help."

Marvin nodded his head. It was 1969, and they were still feeling the tragic losses of the Kennedys and Martin Luther King.

Every moment, Shelly focused on surviving, learning, and doing her best each day to handle reality. She was a young, single mother juggling too many fast flying balls. She tried to keep up at work, read, listen and follow the news, but the sixties whizzed right past her. Shelly learned what was going on, and wanted to participate more, but she did not have the extra money, nor could she get a sitter to attend peace rallies, or travel to Woodstock that summer. Instead, Shelly stayed in synch, focused on her career, motherhood, and trying to recover her personal balance. Maybe it was the start of new consciousness. No matter how much you try, she thought, you cannot "please the man all the time," and romantic dreams can turn into nightmares.

The bus was slow due to traffic, but her mind was moving faster than the wheels on the bus.

Since her divorce, Shelly grappled with pressures that sometimes were too heavy, as there was always just too much to do, and never enough time. She had a full-time job, a daughter, a house to take care of, a sitter, nursery school, carpools, shopping, appointments for medical check-ups, dental work, paying bills, and the usual errands like shopping for food and buying essentials for Alison. She also did her best to keep in touch with her family in New York. They still could not understand even years later how she could possibly leave "The Big Apple."

Shelly had little energy left to even think about a social life, or "the dating game," putting it all together, and keeping it that way, was a daily major challenge.

Finally, after a challenging teaching assignment the opportunity for a better paying job with more responsibility in the federal agency for education came along. The new job was a lot more work than teaching, but offered greater satisfaction as she found herself embroiled in trying to organize for unheard of childcare services for the agency. This goal was more important than anything else she had ever thought about. The purpose of her work made all of the pressures she experienced more bearable. She was moving in the right direction!

Shelly was lost in her thoughts, as the slow moving, crowded bus wound around the city, passed the White House, traversed downtown, and crossed the bridge over Rock Creek Park towards Connecticut Avenue. It was almost at her stop.

Despite not knowing what would happen next, life began to feel good. She was excited. Maybe the divorce had been the right thing after all. She wanted to make the most of every day.

So many doubts had filled that first year.

Could she really make it on her own with a baby? Would she ever find a fulfilling and permanent relationship? Would Arnold share any responsibility? Would she ever find someone who accepted her young child? Would she ever meet "Mr. Right" and have another child? Would she ever find the right reasons for working and leaving Alison every day with someone else and find a way not to have doubts? Her mind raced as she thought of the stressful first year after the divorce.

She finally got off the crowded bus. She felt the cold again as she started to cross the street and walk up Woodley Road. She thought about her own home as she walked past the Sheraton Park, or as it was known in earlier times, the Wardman.

Shelly was glad that she insisted they move into the city instead of staying in the suburbs, as Arnold demanded. She insisted they consider living in town, because she still felt like a New Yorker and she missed the excitement. Suburban living was out of the question. After much searching throughout the Northwest, the Adams Morgan area, Cleveland Park, Georgetown, and beyond, they found an available and affordable fixer upper townhouse built in 1920, by Wardman, a Washington, D.C. developer.

The first time they stood in the house. Arnold said, "There is a lot of work needed on this house, but, I can see it has "potential." He thought it would be a good investment, and he liked the idea of remodeling the older, worn out house.

Shelly nodded her head "What do you think of white for the walls? She asked.

Arnold said "We should do them off-white!"

Shelly smiled in agreement as they imagined how nice the place would be with a fresh look.

The house was part of a block-long stretch of brick townhouses on a pleasant, oak-lined street. The houses were set back from the sidewalk by sloping lawns with steps leading up to the front porches. Upon entering, one went down a hall that led directly into the kitchen. The floor plan was similar for each of the houses on the block. The staircase was to the left of the hallway. The living and dining rooms were off to the right of the hallway. There were three bedrooms upstairs, an attic, and a basement. Best of all there was a fireplace, and a patio. Everything needed work, but that was a challenge, and the reason for the low price.

Shelly and Arnold had spent months, of hard work, renovating, but it was worth all the effort. Shelly tried to block out the heated discussions, the fights, and the daily power struggles that they had. She just wanted to let her mind wander over the events now that had been pleasant, and not dwell on their arguments. They had agreed to open the fireplace wall to expose the original brick. Everything was painted off-white, transforming the once drab walls. They installed French louvered doors across the sun porch, insulated the floors, and made the new room in the back into a sunlit comfortable study.

They divided the pantry into two parts, so it also became a small bathroom opening in the study. She thought that was a very practical addition to the first floor that her next-door neighbor had suggested.

Shelly had found a brown refrigerator insulation that was perfect for making great cork-like walls. They hung a modern brass chandelier from the dining room ceiling that set off the dark walnut, Scandinavian-styled, Dux furniture. Arnold got all the furniture wholesale after he entered the office furniture business.

"What a deal!" he proudly exclaimed as each piece was unpacked.

Shelly was feeling the excitement of having her first real home.

"Arnold," she said to him, "this was the right choice to make. It's really perfect!"

They improved the kitchen with new appliances, cabinets, and a double sink. Shelly loved filling up and organizing the deep little pantry shelves where she finally had enough shelves to hold everything she had gathered to be a more artful and accomplished cook, including a collection of gadgets (melon scoop, peach pitter, skewers, garlic press, peeler, apple cutter, fondue forks, whisk, snail holders, and a set of spaghetti servers). She could also easily store her quiche pan, fondue pot, assorted casseroles, colanders, mixing bowls, spice bottles, egg ramekins, and serving plates. She was ready to entertain and had all the gadgets and accessories to prove it.

Shelly replaced the worn out appliances with new ones, but she still selected white ones like the ones that had been in the kitchen when they bought the house.

The sale clerk had tried to temp her with the new fashion colors, by saying, "No one is using white these days. How about this lovely Harvest gold or this bright turquoise those are the two most popular colors although some are choosing pink, but most males think that is too feminine."

"I'm into modern things, but not colored appliances." Shelly thought of what her mother's reaction would be a turquoise kitchen and smiled.

The backyard, once a tangle of weeds and overgrowth, was soon neatly landscaped. Fieldstone and sand were laid out to create a pleasant patio, perfect for summertime parties. They planted thick bamboo in raised containers on the patio.

Shelly found the bamboo while she was out walking "Friday," their newly acquired Collie dog, near Rock Creek Park. The neighbor had too much bamboo, and was only too happy to find someone who wanted the excess. They worked hard in the house – hauled, cleaned, sanded, painted, rebuilt, electrified, plumbed, decorated, planted, and refinished every nook and cranny.

Shelly painted the louvered doors in the bedroom. Arnold did not want anything to look "feminine", so they compromised on colors, and when they were "unisex" he was satisfied.

The second bedroom became her office at home.

Shelly put their first pets, a pair of Zebra Finches, Anthony (Tony) and Cleopatra (Cleo), in that room. She found the birds a large cage, and added a little wooden house, that she attached to the cage by cutting the wire so they could enter the door to the house. She fed them special items to help stimulate them to mate – millet spray (hardboiled egg yolk, cod liver oil, grapes, vitamins and Cuttle -bone) – and she left straw, string and leaves on the bottom of the cage. Soon, the birds were nesting, too.

When everything was finally ready they decided to throw their first big open house party. They invited Arnold's two bosses, the brothers who owned the office furniture business, their wives, salesmen, friends, and new neighbors. The crowd spilled out everywhere, even into their next-door neighbor's yard.

"Oh, this is just great. Look, Tom, how nicely they fixed up the powder room! Isn't this clever?" Debra pointed to old prints in restored frames in the small powder room on the first floor.

"What a wonderful use of a broom closet." Tom nodded his head. "I can't believe you tore out this whole wall!"

Peggy admired the fireplace workmanship. "What a fantastic find, all this wonderful brick hidden behind plaster."

"This cork…where did you get it? What is it? I have never seen anything like it before," Harry asked closely examining the wall.

"Oh! How sweet! Look! It's a nest for birds!" The box filled with four tiny white eggs was a big attraction.

Comments flowed throughout. The party was a success.

After the house was finished, Shelly returned to graduate school at George Washington University for her Master's degree. She did her best to expand her professional training.

Arnold didn't care about her education, but he enjoyed the friendly, casual parties, and that Shelly was learning to cook by watching Julia Child, on GWETA, the educational television station. The friendly neighbors congregated for wonderful gourmet meals. The wives shopped, talked, and prepared the meals, while the men talked business or politics. Sometimes later they washed the dishes, but not often. That was the job of the new dishwasher. Arnold, in his usual methodical way showed Shelly the "right way to stack it."

Women took care of the kids, the house, and arranging social activities. What else? Oh, yes they also managed to juggle careers and everything else. Some of them did not work, and they had time for hair, nails, shopping, lunch, and gossip. Shelly gave little thought to those things. She had a practical haircut, completed her degree, and still managed to prepare gourmet meals for Arnold every night. She had enough energy left for sex and romance, but Arnold was indifferent. So she held in her frustration and channeled her energy into work. She found their wonderful collie dog to walk, nurture, train and play with, and that helped to channel her frustration. Her affection for the dog was reciprocated with a wagging tail, attention and enthusiastic greetings.

She found she had a lot of energy, and felt happy most of the time. She did her best to make her husband happy. But, soon she found Arnold became more absorbed in business, and was very tired when he got home. He ate, but barely had the energy to recognize a gourmet meal, let alone talk.

Arnold preferred staying home, fixing a drink, lighting a fire, and talking shop. Tickets to the theater would go unused.

He was not affectionate, and barely touched her. He felt threatened by her education. Wives, according to the "Laws of Arnold," were expected to be home when their husbands came home from working all day, have a good meal ready, be there to listen, go to bed when they did, not talk much, and certainly never complain. That's what Arnold's mother had done. That's what the wives of his buddies did. Shelly was different. She stayed up late studying, her collie and the chirping birds kept her company.

Arnold thought, "That's what I get for marrying a New Yorker."

Ice built up between them, cooling rapidly whatever remnants of warmth were left.

When she learned she was pregnant Shelly felt happy. She wanted to attend childbirth classes, decorate the baby's room, and get to better know the neighbors with children. Despite Arnold's reluctance to go to childbirth classes, nothing melted between their cordial but icy connection during the entire nine months of her pregnancy except their marriage. Shelly thought having a baby would change everything, and it did, but not in the way she had dreamed. When she learned that she was pregnant she was happy, but Arnold grimaced.

"We are not ready to have a kid." He complained.

"But, we've been married six years. When will we be ready?" Shelly asked.

"Who says a kid is necessary? We have to save money for the future." Said Arnold, loudly determined to make his point.

His response was not what she hoped. She tried to stay in a good frame of mind. She felt that it was the right decision, regardless of his negativity. She thought his attitude would pass.

Shelly happily went on to fix up the third bedroom for the baby. She decorated the room with a circus motif: bright balloons trimmed the wallpaper, shelves held a variety of toys, the curtains added life. She placed the bear, doll and small kitty cat on the shelves. Finally it was all finished. The furniture was moved in–dresser and crib. Everything looked fantastic!

By the time the house was finished, the collie well trained, the pair of Zebra finches feeding the tiny baby birds in their nesting box, —everything was ready, except for them. The baby birds hatched as Shelly and Arnold's marriage shell cracked apart. A beautiful baby girl was born; Shelly was thrilled about being a mother, yet the joy was short-lived.

Chapter 3

Climbing Stairs

You don't have to see the whole staircase, just take the first step.
Martin Luther King.
Planning the future happens when there is a firm footing you can depend on.
(Author)

Shelving memories of Arnold, the painful divorce, the fear and loneliness that followed. Shelly slowly climbed the steps on that bitter cold evening after a long day. She had to quickly clear her head, drop the past, think about next steps and muster needed energy as plenty of work was left to do. She quietly walked to the front door, as the briefcase full of papers grew heavier, and peered in the window.

Alison was playing happily. "The little rascal," thought Shelly," she's always happy, and then when I walk in she will start to fuss. I'm not going to feel guilty anymore."

She opened the door. Alison careened down the hall calling, "Mommy! Mommy! I missed you!"

Shelly picked her up, held her close, with tears suddenly filling her eyes. She felt so glad to be home with Alison, yet she also felt chilled and lonely. If only there were someone to care about her, how she looked, and how she felt. She wanted to be hugged by a man who loved her and Alison. She had, out of necessity, re-learned a limited version of her five years of study of high school-college Spanish over the past year. Finding the "right" person to be with Alison while she worked, a person who would really care, had been incredibly difficult. She needed someone upon whom she could depend every day. From the beginning of the first year after her divorce it became increasingly frustrating, until she found Flora.

There were no childcare programs anywhere in her area. She had no choice. She had no family in the city, and her friends with children were in the same boat as she. Everyone was caught up in his or her own social whirl.

It was impossible to find a volunteer to help out a friend with a child, even if they were sympathetic. Washington was full of cocktail parties, opening nights at the theatre or art galleries, attending concerts or a political soiree, being seen at Duke Zeibert's or the Monocle, and being with the right people on the right night. Gossip was the main course, politics, the dessert.

Shelly thought about writing an article for the "Washingtonian Magazine" about the anguish of searching for a caregiver in Washington. But she had no time to write on spec, what with her workload and all the needs that had to be dealt with every day.

She thought about all the different sitters who showed up for the interview (with and without experience, references, or common sense). She laughed out loud as she hugged Alison.

The perspective sitters were each characters forever detailed in her memory: The first girl was very young, very quiet, and without stability, childcare references, or experience.

"I want to try this. I don't like working as a salesgirl." She said. "It's too hard on the feet!" I have no place to live right now. She looked around and smiled nervously.

Another one was somewhat edgy, and who took out a cigarette to smoke in the middle of the interview.

"You don't mind if I have one bad habit do you? I will try to remember not to smoke around the baby," she reassured Shelly, blowing smoke away from her face. Shelly recoiled at the smell.

Another was a recovering alcoholic.

"I need to attend AA meetings every night. I hope you will be home in time for me to go to them," she requested. And then she added, "I stopped drinking three months ago. I am doing my best not to fall back into the trap!"

Another older woman needed care herself, and seemed too frail to lift a hefty toddler much less keep up with play or personal needs.

"I can't live with my daughter-in-law anymore. I don't want to go to a home so I think this is the best choice," she said timidly. She needed help to get up from the chair. Shelly assisted her up and out the door.

Finally the "baby sitter angels" brought Flora Sanchez to her door. Flora had left a convent in Spain to move to Washington, D.C., to be near her distant cousin. Flora had lived in a convent since her own mother left her there when she was ten. She grew up and cared for children at the convent school. Coming to Washington, and the job caring for Alison was a big change. She spoke no English. She explained to Shelly as best as she could that she wanted a job caring for one child, to gain experience, and to learn English. A neighbor who knew her cousin had introduced Flora. Shelly dredged up five years of Spanish study muy pronto.

"Si Yo pienso es possible. Cada dia nosotros hablan Ingles and Espanol Si? Que es mas importante es la nina." Yes, I think it's possible. We can both learn.

She decided to give Flora the job. Flora seemed sincere, sensitive, and was certainly honest. She was timid, but she smiled, and was enthusiastic when she met Alison and immediately began to warmly play with her. She was the first one of the applicants to actually appear motivated or show an interest in the child.

The toddler happily responded, and Shelly felt she could trust her with Alison all day. They would all learn to communicate. Why not encourage Alison to be bi-lingual? The three of them would help each other. Alison immediately liked Flora.

Flora laughed with joy as she played with the toddler, glad to be learning English, to be caring for a child, and to be an important part of the family. Shelly fervently hoped that Flora would stay, adjust and continue to give Alison the attention and affection she needed, when Shelly went to work in her new job. She was going to work to create better childcare for other families. Now she didn't need to worry about her own arrangements, and she crossed her fingers as she hoped for the best.

As she entered the kitchen Flora and Shelly exchanged the news of the day, information exchanged both in Spanish and English.

"Senora, La Nina, muy Buena nina. Good girl. We go park. Ella come mucho. She ate a lot. Ella le gusta la comida. She liked her food. Senora por favor llame el senor, el numero sobre la mesa. Please call man on phone"

"Gracias, Flora. Muy bueno. Very good. Me apprecio muchos todas. I appreciate everything and I am hungry. Yo tengo hambre," Shelly said as she crossed the room.

Flora was chattering.

"Alison es una buena nina toda la dia. Ella come eat "una buena comida, a big meal un gran almuerzo. A big lunch Por favor, please Shelly, show Alison's rash to el Doctor."

Shelly appreciated Flora's concern for Alison. She would take Alison to the doctor. She needed to go also, but she barely had the time. Flora probably needed a check-up too. They would just have to work it all out.

Alison played nearby with her toys. Shelly thought about making out the grocery list as she went to look for the senor's number.

After she made the call, she would eat. They communicated, if not smoothly, they covered essentials.

She turned to sit at the hall table so she could take off her shoes, as her feet were cold, and they hurt. She wrote down some items needed as she took off her shoes with her left hand. Then she dialed the phone with her right hand, as always juggling a few things at a time. The number was all too familiar.

A person, who had been her teacher, friend, and lover, answered the phone. Nick Gilmore, a director at Arena Stage, steadily advancing in his theatrical career, missed the good times he had with Shelly. They had met on a warm summer evening at The Olney Theater. That night in the light of the full moon in the garden near the backstage door, Nick sat across from Shelly and stared at her. They sensed each other's kindred spirits. They began an emotionally-charged dialogue about theater, education, and life in and out of the theatre that ran non-stop for six months. When it did stop, Shelly was filled with frustration. She could not stop the feelings that flowed between them, but there was no future in the relationship. Nick was much too involved with himself and his latest conquests. But, she wanted to forgive him and still remain friends if possible.

Shelly had learned as a child that it seemed necessary to accept emotional hurt, and even sometimes physical abuse, along with what she thought was love. She loved her father despite pain he had inflicted on her as a child. She learned about rejection, and understood verbal, emotional, and physical abuse. She accepted those realities as part of what unconditional love seemed to be about. Pain can be inflicted without obvious bruises and hurt just as much or even more.

She learned that lesson when Nick left her for another woman, who was a good friend. She had trusted him and, of course, she had trusted her friend. How foolish she felt. She thought all she had to do was to be trustworthy and others would be too. She did not think they would ever speak again, or certainly ever be friends again. She was now all the more protective of herself. She held up her guard even though he tried to pry open the door to her heart again. His affair was over, but she did not want to resume being lovers. She knew it would be a big mistake.

After she put the phone down she walked over to the dining table where Flora had placed her share of a casserole. Flora was a good cook, excellent with Alison, and was trying hard to learn English. She was really sensitive to Shelly's work and needs. As soon as she could, she took Alison upstairs for a bath as Shelly had her dinner. Now Alison rushed downstairs ready for a story before bed. She carried her favorite book.

The doorbell rang. Nick walked in. He did not wait for Shelly to come to the door, but made his entrance. Alison ran over to him in her floppy slippers.

"Hi, Kiddo! Remember me? What a big girl you are!" He raised her up on his shoulders. Alison, freshly powdered and sweet after her bath, loved his attention.

Her slippers flew off as he whirled her around. His few words and hugs communicated easy affection. Alison squealed, and Shelly laughed. Nick was certainly great with kids.

He carried Alison upstairs as Shelly followed. Nick decided to read her a story and improvise all the voices in her favorite Dr. Seuss book, "The Cat and the Hat." Alison was effortlessly asleep just as the last hat was taken off.

Nick and Shelly went downstairs and talked. They sat in front of the fire. Shelly found him to be a most interesting and complex man, with a deep voice, ready smile, acerbic wit, and unique approach to life. He always kept her riveted.

She looked into his engrossing deep brown eyes, noted his dark curly hair, and strong physique. But, she would not succumb to her desires. He had provoked her to make so many changes. She wondered how they could have gone through so much. Finally, in spite of the emotional upheavals he had caused her, they became friends again. They picked up where they had left off before his affair, but Shelly did not want to reconnect with her former girlfriend.

They laughed a lot now without any pressure or romantic illusions. It was easier to be together now. Shelly remained emotionally detached, safe, on guard, and she intended to stay that way. "Who wants the pain?" she thought to herself.

"Nick," Shelly asked, "What's happening at the theatre?"

He replied, "I am busy directing, teaching, and being part of a new program that's just been created. I do miss your energy and, as he winked at her, "hot sex." He scanned her face looking for clues, but found none.

She enjoyed his attention, their mutual physical and creative attraction. She was ready for something new, but he also stimulated uncomfortable feelings in her. Nick pushed her limits.

That is, until she woke up on the sofa one morning having drunk too much wine after they had gone to visit Ellen, her trusted girlfriend. She found Nick and Ellen in the aftermath of sex on the landing of the upstairs hall. Shelly left the house, feeling betrayed and wounded.

It was not until after Nick and Ellen's serious car crash a few months later that Shelly felt feelings of empathy and forgiveness. She sent cards to express "get well" greetings. She tried to understand what had happened.

Nick was no angel, and she had known it. When they saw each other again over the wine table at an opening at Arena Stage, their relationship began again, even if only politely. Nick said he was okay; he did care about her, and Alison. He wanted to see Alison. He was, after all, there the day she walked for the first time. He wanted to be friends. The dalliance with Ellen was over. Her friendship with Ellen was over.

"Do you want to have dinner sometime?" Nick asked.

"Yes, sure, whenever you have time," replied Shelly, sipping her wine to calm her slight nervousness. Shelly and Nick had a pleasant conversation despite her restlessness.

"Let's do it soon," said Nick. "I'll call you."

"Sure. Why not?" replied Shelly.

Nick could see right through her, there was no fooling him. She did not feel secure about the next steps. She did feel horny and wanted so much to be held, but she thought about the consequences, and was glad when Nick left early.

She thought that she would throw herself more into her work, mothering, and maybe even resume acting lessons if she could only find time. She felt ready to do more discovery of herself. She wanted to find whatever new aspects of talent she didn't yet know she possessed. She wanted to feel that life was going to be fun again, and not only hard work.

When they met next time, a week later, at their favorite restaurant on a boat, near the Theater, she told Nick, "I am willing to 'forgive and forget.' "

"Nick, you have been such a real positive influence on my life. I will not forget easily what you have done for me and for Alison. I just want to protect myself."

"What's the matter?" He asked, "Can't you just live in the 'now,' and enjoy the 'anything goes' attitude?"

She looked at him. She said, "I will always be glad to have you as my friend, Nick, and only as a friend. You will always be welcome in our lives."

He kissed her. She felt glad that she could be clear and honest with him.

She had survived a divorce, jealousy, rejection, and healing again. "What's next?" she thought.

Nick managed to retain his job at the theater despite painful funding cutbacks. Shelly recalled, as she cleaned up the living room, that despite all the creative fun and satisfaction of the theatre, she had to find more consistent work to support herself and Alison.

She searched to find a job with the Office of Education. It was definitely a very different atmosphere from the loose, freewheeling, tumultuous ambiance of the theater.

Nick's freewheeling spirit had little tolerance for the indifferent bureaucracy; the cold, gray buildings, and the green rooms filled with an impersonal system; plastic people running expensive ineffectual programs. He was skeptical that anything good could come out of those drab places. Shelly saw his point, but she felt otherwise. Shelly realized that there was no point trying to convince him. She believed government could make a difference in the lives of people if the programs had meaning.

Childcare could really help families. Education was the way to learn skills. She could not find a better way to do that. She felt now she was making a difference in the education of disadvantaged children and she certainly could do something valuable for many families if the childcare center opened in the building.

Flora left after dinner to meet some friends. The house was quiet.

After Nick left, Shelly looked in on Alison and gently covered her as she bent over to smooth out her hair and kiss her.

Then she went downstairs, put the poker in the fireplace, poured herself a glass of water, and sat on the sofa to study the rather dry, but factual, reports she had brought home. She looked at the proposals and saw how great the needs were. She was not alone.

She got up to put another log on the fire.

She learned a few days before that she had been asked to testify before the U.S. House of Representatives Committee on Education and Labor on the proposed childcare center and how the concept of work-place programs could be added to the legislation.

Shelly wanted the new legislation to include comprehensive childcare benefits for the children of all civil service (federal, state and city) employees. She was determined to move the Committee members so they would really understand the wide-spread dilemma. She wanted to inspire them so they would be even more willing to respond. She knew that childcare could increase the productivity, dependability, and morale of all workers in and out of government service.

Late that night, she fell asleep on the sofa, in front of the crackling fire, with the various documents, reports and papers scattered over her chest, spilling onto the floor. Nick was no longer in her dreams.

Flora covered her with a quilt when she entered the house, then quietly went to her room after she also looked in on Alison.

When Shelly arrived at the office the next day, she learned from a memo that Marvin Felder could not meet with the visiting doctors in for the Head Start conference. Another high priority meeting had come up at the Commissioner's office. Marvin's assistant, Julie Darnell, had hurriedly helped him put together a set of questions he wanted them to present to the medical consultants.

Marvin suggested to Julie, "Focus on exactly what you think can be accomplished." He suggested ways they should proceed. Marvin told Julie quickly, "Look, we've got to get the doc's imprint and approval on the issues of delivery of healthcare or the program will never fly."

Julie asked, "Do you want each of them to give their views or get a consensus?"

Marvin responded, "Get each of them to give their own viewpoint. Let's see if they are in synch or not. Take Shelly with you. Between the two of you, get their agreements. Let's find out where the weaknesses are. Then we have to figure out how to overcome the problems."

Julie made notes and left his office. She went directly to Shelly's office.

"Hi." said Julie as she entered the office. "I just finished talking with Marv. Did you get my message that he can't go with us to meet the Docs? He briefed me."

She continued, "I have a set of questions ready. Do you have anything you want to add to the list?" She handed Shelly a paper to look at.

Shelly nodded her head. "Sure, we could talk for days on this topic alone, but for the moment, let's see how the program could mesh with the plans for a new healthcare delivery."

"Yes, that's Marv's view, too. Let's get ready, Shelly, We can talk along the way."

Shelly had been asked by Marvin Felder to consider a transfer from Health, Education and Welfare (HEW) to the Office of Economic Opportunity (OEO), the Office of the President. He told her that after the first of the year she would be in the position to act upon the plans not only agreed upon at this meeting on healthcare, but to launch, once the bill passed Congress, the new program based on the proposed childcare legislation.

Marvin told her he was planning to leave the Office of Education to become the new Director of Program Development at OEO. Located in the Northwest part of the city, at 19th and M Streets, OEO was the Headquarters for the President's "War on Poverty." The location was ideal; closer to home, easier to get to, and to get home, especially if Alison needed her. She already thought about starting a childcare center at that new building.

Marvin told Shelly that she would be responsible for developing the plans for the new childcare program. She would become the "Director of Childcare Services" for the new program. He told her to think "linkages."

He said, "You will have $2.5 million for the start-up of the Research and Development Program. If you play it smart. You could multiply that link-up with all relevant federal programs. You could extend operating funds to be equivalent to $25 million."

She nodded in agreement. "I understand what you mean."

Shelly was excited at the prospect and promotion especially since it would also help to advance her goals to help all working parents who needed child-care. Of course, getting agencies that agreed to cooperate, or pool resources were another "kettle of fish."

Shelly gathered a pad, her own list of questions, a current report on "Un-met Needs," and the latest fact sheets on Head Start into her briefcase. She found Julie in her office putting the final touches on the list of issues they were to deal with. Julie quickly made some copies so they could share them at the meeting.

"Julie," said Shelly, "You are truly well organized. I hope we can get a real-istic picture from this group for what's possible in the healthcare community. It's a great chance to move ahead."

Julie grabbed her coat. They walked together to the elevator chatting as they went.

Shelly drove her car to work that day so they traveled in her car through Rock Creek Park, hardly noticing the winter landscape, lost in conversation about their questions, many issues, and unmet needs.

Julie told Shelly, "Marv said to get a consensus." Isn't that funny? Did you ever hear of doctor's agreeing on anything? What is he thinking?"

Shelly responded, "Marvin should have known better. Everyone argues about childcare as if it were an elephant that blind men grab onto. They each try to describe it by telling about the part they see. It's always different de-pending on the part you are holding. Men don't get it, do they?"

They laughed. Even though Julie was single, she knew the on-going struggles of her sister and other moms, and she wanted to help.

Shelly headed up the Connecticut Avenue exit and turned right on Cal-vert Street toward the Embassy Restaurant. Shelly felt excited as they drove up to the restaurant, and pulled up to the parking space across from the restaurant. The morning air was crisp and cold as she felt her head to arrange the soft, warm, green, felt hat on her head. She gathered herself to be ready for the next big new step.

Chapter 4

Starting New

The only limit to our realization of tomorrow will be our doubts of today. Let's move forward with strong and active faith. Franklin D. Roosevelt

Doug Fine's morning had been filled with coffee, cigarettes, and chatter; the usual dialogue, understood only by "insiders" who comprehend "Inside-the-Beltway" lingo. He was trying to make sense of the new regulations being discussed that would help "Head Start" continue to thrive.

Back-to-back meetings meant he never saw anything of the "real" Washington except glances at passing history revealed by aging monuments from the windows of the airport bus, or an occasional dinner at a local restaurant just a short distance from the hotel. He had stamina for more. He knew he was missing something, but there was never any time.

The Academy of Pediatrics had offered him a special role as its consultant to Head Start. It was considered "politically correct" to have enthusiastic, sincere, and savvy doctors at work on the many crucial, challenging, and often unlimited social and health problems, all somehow striving for "politically correct" solutions. Doug was more than willing to participate. He wanted to make a difference and he believed in the value of the challenging program.

He knew how desperately low-income children needed regular medical, educational, and pre-school services. His work in the inner city community clinics of San Francisco and Chicago gave him plenty of first-hand experience. He was rare among professionals who graduated from med school. Instead of immediately ringing up high incomes from anxious, middle-class parents, he was willing to take the time to give back to those in need as part of his position in Community Medicine at the University of California Medical School in San Francisco.

He felt he had an opportunity to make a difference. He knew by just being in attendance he could make a tangible contribution. He would listen, learn and contribute as he could to discussions. He was glad he had not gone into the established family practice to continue what his father had already lucratively built. He wanted a major lifestyle change. He was there in Washington DC ready to prove it. Enthusiastically, he joined his colleague Bob in the hotel lobby. Bob had been a social gadfly for years and knew the ropes.

They stood to stretch their legs from the long meeting and caught up on the morning activities. Bob had a chance to tell Doug what he anticipated would come out of the scheduled luncheon meeting.

"Doug, we can turn this thing around if we focus on the cost- effectiveness of health care delivery to kids directly in childcare centers. We will have a hard time convincing Academy members this makes sense, but what else is new?"

Doug laughed as he reminded Bob, "You know better than I how self-centered most of our fellow doctors are. They can't wait to get out from under the hard years of sacrifice, the long hours, and make their futures financially secure, and as quickly as possible."

They were soon joined by Dr. Mary Pechant, a petite, charming woman with a soft Viennese accent who had established, almost single-handedly, a well-recognized training program for pre-school teachers in Chicago. Dr. Maria Pechant had suffered greatly in Europe during World War II, losing her entire family and all her friends. When she finally arrived in America, she wanted to contribute to her new country in all the ways she could. She was feisty, knowledgeable, and committed. She shared the jaundiced views of her long-time friend, Dr. Bob Mendel.

Dr Pechant joined in their discussion, "I think you two are very optimistic. The medical profession has a long way to go before it begins to serve all the children who so desperately need medical attention and education. "

"I've told Bob many times doctors don't do enough. Teachers in early childhood have their hands full trying to educate too many children who are still in need of basic medical examinations and treatment. Teachers can't also be nurses, but many times they are asked to do those services also. "

Mary was frustrated at the enormous ignorance and apparent apathy to children's needs that she found as the political policies and realities of her new, and much loved country. She wanted more for children regardless of their income, race, or religion. She knew that single mothers had a particularly difficult time providing for all the needs of their children. She was concerned for both mothers and children. She felt a lot more could be done, but how?

"Maybe," she continued, "this first meeting will be a new step in the right direction. I am glad to take time out to be involved, Bob, if you think we can do some good."

Bob and Doug nodded their heads in agreement.

At that moment an energetic woman quickly joined them. Dr. Gertrude Howard, a striking, tall, African American pediatrician, headed pediatric services for the National Head Start program. Gert (as friends called her) had many fresh ideas to add to the group's combined concepts, perspectives and years of experience. She was determined to change the lives of all those children she knew were still waiting for basic health-care services. She had worked her way from adversity to success, but had not forgotten those with fewer resources and greater needs. Gert was always amused at the earnestness of white professionals who wanted to solve the problems of the black community; but she knew this "trio" well, and over a long time, and she appreciated and respected their sincere dedication, credibility, and willingness to match her own zeal and determination.

She was, however, very skeptical of Congress, the Governors, and, most of all, the President to enact any measurable changes. But, despite her misgivings, she was more than willing to be part of the planned luncheon discussion to forge a new plan and to lend her ideas to move ahead on a bold, new agenda for poor families.

Besides, she enjoyed the challenge of change. It was her new job after all. Gert was determined to make things better, but she knew she could not do the job alone. She needed lots of other committed friends who were willing to give of their time, and to lend support, and make an intensive effort.

They walked toward the door engaged in animated conversation and out into the cold November morning. They walked quickly down the few blocks along Connecticut Avenue toward the restaurant where Julie and Shelly were just parking.

Doug watched as the two women emerged from the car. He noticed Shelly immediately, catching her glance from under her large-brimmed, soft, green felt hat. She smiled quickly, as her smile radiated across the cold it touched Doug, but then she turned back into the car and reached behind to the back seat to grab her briefcase. Shelly wanted to have everything ready to fill in the facts and to make a good impression on the visiting doctors. Doug was already warmed by her friendly smile and then he looked at her.

Shelly caught her breath as she made eye contact with Doug Fine. She thought about how nice he seemed to be. His friendliness and good looks, she thought, will make this meeting even more pleasant. The other people in the group seemed intense, and she felt they were all ready and in synch to roll up their sleeves and get to work. That was a good start.

The two women greeted the group.

Julie immediately said "Hello everyone! I am Julie Darnell. So sorry Marvin had a policy meeting with the Commissioner to prepare for Congressional hearings and he could not join us this morning. He apologizes, that he is not able to attend, but he gave my colleague Shelly Stern and I a long list of questions, and an even longer agenda."

They all understood and laughed as they shook hands and entered the restaurant.

Doug warmed to Shelly immediately. She seemed so fresh and friendly. They smiled at each other

While they were waiting to be seated, they talked briefly in the lobby about the newly proposed childcare legislation, and about the program of the national Head Start meeting. They were friendly. They each thought how much they wanted to know more about each other, but there was no time.

The maitre d' quickly showed them to their reserved table. The conversation of the group became even more intense as they discussed different approaches and possible problems of the new program.

Doug opened, "I feel doctors will agree to provide direct services to programs, but they will need some concrete incentives. Not me, of course. The university is always looking for "linkages" to the community. This is a perfect way to "link-up!" He smiled and he glanced at Shelly as he said, "Link-up!"

He liked the word, and it's implied double meaning. She looked at him, slightly noticing, but she was so focused on maintaining the "link-ups" and taking notes from the list of items in front of her on the agenda, she could not be easily distracted.

Shelly remembered that Marvin had asked her to find out if their new plan was realistic, if it would hold up under scrutiny, and whether the Academy would approve it. She intended to find out how viable it was and find out as quickly as possible.

Shelly asked, "What incentives do you think health professionals will need?"

They replied in unison, "Money!"

Then they all laughed.

Bob added, "Position!"

Gert added, "Power!"

Mary said, "Prestige!"

Then Doug retorted, "Proposals...and the other incentive, funding of course!"

Then they all laughed again and drank from their glasses.

Doug felt Shelly's energy and enthusiasm as they talked. He liked the directness of her questions and her quick understanding. He liked watching her take notes. She seemed to readily understand the very thin line they each walked. He liked the way she smiled, her voice, her optimism, obvious concern, and empathy to the underlying issues. He knew what they wanted to do was a major upheaval and success, even if legislated, would not be easy.

During the meal, he looked at her often. She didn't notice his glances as she was too busy listening and jotting notes. Shelly was intent, because she wanted to get it all right. She knew Marvin would ask a lot of questions when they returned to the office. She wanted to be accurate and give him a full report.

As they became more involved in the discussion, the merits of the issues, Doug was carefully taking mental notes about Shelly.

Before dessert, Bob interjected that he and Doug had to excuse themselves to return to the hotel to co-chair a panel discussion on "Immunizations" for the afternoon session. They laughed again as a group at the excitement that swept over them for the plans might have far reaching benefits to millions of families.

Doug went around the table to Shelly. They shook hands and exchanged cards. They looked at each other's eyes again as they firmly shook hands.

"Please do not hesitate to get in touch if there is anything else I can do to be helpful," he said as Shelly looked at him directly. He added" I will always be available for any foreseeable 'linkages' that you may need." He smiled again at her, looking deeply into her eyes.

She felt her cheeks get warm.

"Thank you so much, Dr. Fine, for your generous offer, time, and for making so many contributions to the plans." Shelly said.

Then she turned to shake hands with Bob and to thank him for organizing the meeting. She felt Doug's eyes still on her after she shook Bob's hand. As he turned to leave she still felt his warmth. After the two men left she sat down as she had to prepare for the next steps at work. She remained calm and clear.

After coffee, and more talk with Mary and Gert, they soon realized that their common issue was still very much their issue—a woman's issue, a mother's issue, and unmet childcare needs continued to be a huge problem.

They each nodded their head in agreement as Shelly said, "Women get the kids to the doctor, arrange for childcare so they can go to school, or a job interview, or to work. I guess we will just need to work harder together to solve these problems."

"Yes," said Julie, but "who has the time?"

They all laughed together and knew it was true. The women agreed to forge a "network" and stay connected with each other for the "duration."

"It's the least we can do. Maybe by working together we can begin to make a dent to solve these enormous problems." They all agreed with Mary. They were in it for the long haul.

Julie and Shelly gathered their papers. They offered to drive the other two women back to the hotel, but they preferred to walk back, clear their heads, and stretch their legs.

"It's so hard to ever get out of that hotel once the meeting starts." said Gert.

"We are so glad you rescued us and for such a good cause," Mary smiled.

"Good luck on the next steps. You can count on us," said Gert. "These meetings are so much talking and sitting. We're off to catch some quiet time and a good walk," said Gert as they departed. "We need it to clear our heads so we have enough oxygen to keep up with this meeting."

Shelly and Julie crossed the street, got in the car, putting their briefcases in the back seat and drove back to the office. They were very pleased at what had been accomplished in a very short time. They each typed up their notes, and presented their report to Marvin at the scheduled 4:00 p.m. meeting. He was glad to learn that most of the ideas he had suggested had been reviewed, discussed, and were accepted. Julie had to rush to another meeting and left the room.

Marvin faced Shelly. He now felt reinforced, and was more than ready for the move to the new agency, the Office of Economic Opportunity (OEO, as they called it). Marvin saw childcare as an integral part of its mission on the "War on Poverty." He felt he had to continue the work John F. Kennedy started years ago, which inspired him to join the Peace Corps and to work with Sergeant Shriver. Something tangible could be done to make a difference in the lives of families. He was very glad Shelly was interested in making the Agency shift, and she could follow through, and handle the tough issues.

He told her, "Think about how the 'link-up' of 'in-kind' services with pediatricians, and other health personnel, can make a huge difference. Then there are those myriad of possibilities of 'link-ups' with other agencies like HUD for buildings, Agriculture for food programs, Education for content in programs, Labor for parent and staff training, and much more." Shelly smiled to herself every time he mentioned the word "linkup." She thought about Doug and how kind he seemed.

"Shelly, you can begin plan a program with a start-up R&D budget of say, $2.5 million. You will have to pinpoint first the most critical, unmet needs of childcare. Could you make things begin to work with that budget? Can you develop strategic 'link-ups' to other federal programs?" Marvin asked.

Shelly nodded in agreement. It was a start, but getting agencies to do more, and cooperate was another challenge.

Marvin was laying out the plans. She carefully listened. She could not afford to miss a beat. This was her future. She was determined to make everything work out exactly as he expected and do even more.

Marv continued, "You could have it all if you play your cards right. You have to think 'maximize.' Multiply the amount of related services. Think how over time the program can expand into a $25 million program. We will be right in line to launch operations just when the Legislation passes. The bill just has to be passed. There is no 'Welfare Reform' unless childcare is in the equation." As he said that, Marv hit the top of the desk for emphasis.

Shelly nodded her head and jumped at his emphatic response. He has a lot on his mind, Shelly thought. He will be responsible for all the components of new program development at the new agency, and it will be a lot of responsibility. She would have to work out all the details on the childcare segment. She had to make sure that it fit with all the other segments. Putting the whole puzzle together would be a major game they would put into play.

Marv told Shelly, "You will have to keep the federal guidelines in mind, find new ways to build on current childcare services, expand plans, and find the ways to get all the different professional groups to work effectively together. It's a tall order! But you are just the right kind of pushy broad. You can make it happen just like you got the childcare center to happen right here in the building despite all the setbacks. Anyone else would have stopped trying." He smiled as he praised her work.

She knew he appreciated her efforts and respected her. She did not mind his teasing her 'modus operandi' as it was his style, too. New Yorkers instantly understand each other even if they live in Los Angeles. He always treated her with respect and he provided a meaningful challenge.

Shelly liked that Marv recognized her abilities. He was willing to help her to move forward on what they both believed in. She heard all his ideas. He listened to hers. They understood what was needed. He knew she could make it work. It was just a matter of realignment, timing and ingenuity. They agreed on the different aspects needed to make it all turn out to be a cohesive whole.

Shelly admired Marv. He was a "shaker and mover." He got the whole picture fast and was able to delegate responsibility. Unlike most of the men in the hierarchy of the government, he was willing to delegate, share power, and give support to women's concerns. He was rare, and someone she wanted to work for. He treated women as professionals, and not as pawns. She was glad they would finally have the chance to move into a new, and certainly, important and challenging position.

She felt lucky to be going forward on her plan to make childcare a universal service—to be available to all families in need. She knew that with the best childcare women could resume training, find jobs; stay employed, and still visit a doctor. Everyone with children needs some time off to do the important things in their lives. Only poor women did not have the luxury of family support, babysitter, or a nanny, to give them time to pursue the essentials. She and Marvin were certain Congress would share these views and support the new legislation. Then, if the childcare legislation passed, anything could be possible.

Chapter 5

Political Promises

*Unexpected magic happens when you least expect, if you stay
open and willing to experience magic.* (The Author)

Shelly went back to her office, cleared some papers from her desk, put
some into folders, and some into her briefcase. She was motivated by her talk
with Marvin. Maybe she would be able to review the report again that night
to see if everything was clear. Her head was swimming with information,
potential problems, and all the unmet needs moved her. She saw the faces of
the moms she had gotten to know since working at the Office of Education.
She saw their children home, alone, as she had been as a child. Shelly realized
that no matter what else happened... some family problems would have to
get solved.

As she walked down the quiet, dull-green hall toward the elevator, she
decided not go home right away. Since the Head Start Conference occurred
only once a year, and since it moved to different locations for each meeting,
she thought it would be a good idea to stop by the hotel to try to obtain some
more resources. She was uncertain if travel to another location was in the
budget and she wanted to learn more now while it was easily accessible.

Shelly wanted most of all to see the educational exhibits at the Head Start
convention. She gathered her things, adding the notes she had taken earlier
to her briefcase, found her car outside, and drove through Rock Creek Park
directly back to the hotel. She left her briefcase on the back seat.

She entered the hotel and walked straight for the exhibit hall to pick up
materials that might be helpful later. She then walked through the maze of
covered tables. The rows of tables were full of many teaching aids for young
children, alphabet blocks, "how-to" books, and all the latest and best materials for a modern pre-school. She saw blocks, dolls, puppets, tapes, puzzles,
wooden toys, and learning products of all kinds. A few of the vendors were
selling items directly, so Shelly selected a set of soft puppets to bring home

to Alison.

As she left the exhibit hall with a shopping bag full of samples, and the bag with Alison's new animal puppets on top (the bunny and kitty were certain to be a big hit) she started up the escalator when she suddenly saw Doug talking with three other men. They made eye contact as he waved, smiled, and walked over to her. She thought he looked very handsome.

He said, "Hi, Shelly, what a nice surprise! It was really good to meet you at lunch, and to help plan what I hope will launch a new program that will actually happen. Maybe this time things will be different, and if the gods are with us, childcare will finally become a reality."

"Hello, Dr. Fine. It was very nice to meet you, too. I was glad you could be there to lend your expertise and share excellent ideas. We must be optimistic."

"How did your meeting with Marvin go?" he asked, looking for a sign.

"He was quite pleased! I hope we can count on you and your colleagues for the next phase, which will be the really hard part. There's lots of follow-up work to do with the health professionals. No one thinks it's going to be easy."

She spoke matter-of-factly, looking directly into his eyes. She saw the kitty and bunny puppets were sticking out of the bag and switched the shopping bag to her other hand. She was tired, her feet hurt, and it had been a very long day. She wanted to smile, and needed to go home, because she needed rest.

Doug wanted to take the initiative, but despite his outspoken commitment, he was unsure about his magnetic personal charms. He wondered if she would accept a dinner invitation. "Well, what the hell," he thought, "Here goes..."

"Shelly, would you join three friendly physicians for dinner this evening?" Doug asked in as casual a manner as he could muster.

She was tired, her feet cried out to be released from pain, and she was concerned about that magical "quality time" with Alison. So she had to refuse as politely as she could. She smiled at him. But, reality crept into her brain. After all, he should be the first to understand how she felt about not being secure being away from her child all day, regardless of the quality of the arrangements.

When she said, "No, not tonight. I must go home to give my baby sitter some time off." He looked obviously disappointed. But, he would just have to understand. He tried to cover up his disappointment as he introduced her to the group. He did understand "the juggling act," but he wanted to spend more personal time with her. After all, he already had three kids, and they were safely at home with their mom, and why shouldn't he enjoy the short time he had left in Washington?

She shook hands again with Doug, and added, "Sorry, I just can't do it, as much as I would like to!" She warmly looked at his friendly eyes once more. But she left immediately to return home, shopping bag in one hand loaded with samples, the puppets looking back at him as she traveled up the escalator.

Alison was eating her dinner as Shelly walked in the door.

"Mommy, Mommy! Look at me! I ate all my dinner! Mommy, come see!" cried Alison.

Flora said, "Hello, missus." Hoy Alison es muy buena Nina. Ella come toda la comida. Me voy pronto. OK?"

Shelly nodded, set down the bag, and pulled out the puppets. She kicked off the shoes, and then walked to the kitchen with the puppets behind her back.

She told Flora, "No problema. Si vaya. Yo esta en la casa este noche." She knew Flora was tired, as she didn't even try to talk in English. It had been a long day for both of them.

"What a good girl you are, Alison. A clean plate, que bueno, muy bonita—such a sweet, dirty face. She reached over for a napkin to wipe off the food particles that clung like saran wrap to Alison's face.

"Look what mommy has for you! Una sorpresa!" She had the puppets behind her back and as she pulled them in front and gave them to Alison, but the puppets began to talk.

"Hello Alison. Are you ready for dessert?"

Alison squealed. She held the soft animal puppets in her hands trying to figure out what to do with them. She would soon find out as Shelly lifted her out of the high chair. "Go and play. Alison," she said as she gave her a kiss and then set her down to watch what she would do with them. If she waited, she was sure Alison would create some live action between the cat and bunny.

Flora excused herself, and got out of the house as quickly as she could change and go. She was definitely adjusting to the job. She also liked her newfound freedom. Shelly could not imagine how Flora ever managed to cope before as a nun.

Alison wanted her story, some conversation between her new puppet friends, and practice brushing her teeth. Then, she would finally be ready for bed. After tucking her in her little bed, Shelly sang her a favorite lullaby, turned off the light, and quietly went out the door. The puppets had found a new home on the bed.

Finally alone with her thoughts, Shelly mused, why did I cut him off? He seemed so nice. Dinner might have been fun! Why did I rush away?

She went to the phone and called the hotel, attempting to reconnect with Doug. He was not in his room so she left a message. She had plenty to do.

She also did not want to be impolite to a helpful ally. She wanted to remain in contact with each member of the group as she knew that the months ahead and success in her new responsibilities would depend on their continued linking up of information, support, and suggestions.

She cleaned the bathroom, which was always a bit of a mess after Alison's bath. She folded sheets, towels, and straightened the linen closet. She checked her nails, surveyed the house, and peeked in at Alison. The puppets had fallen to the floor. She bent over and placed them back on the bed. She put all the scattered pieces of a construction project together so Alison could rebuild it tomorrow.

The house was quiet. She took a deep breath as she changed into comfortable clothes, socks and soft slippers. Her feet finally stopped hurting.

Shelly went downstairs, picked up a magazine, took off her slippers and stretched out on the sofa near the silent fireplace. She finally succumbed to tiredness and closed her eyes. At 9:30 p.m. the phone rang. She woke startled.

A deep voice said, "Do you want some company?"

She knew it was not Nick. She suddenly realized who it was…Dr. Doug Fine. She could hardly remember what she had done to deserve the surprise call.

Thinking it was too late; she hesitated and replied, "I'm not sure. I don't feel terrific. I'm tired, and I may have a cold coming on. "

He quickly responded, "But, I'm a doctor, I believe in 'major medical miracles.' And I make house calls. Where do you live?"

She smiled and remembered again how nice he was. She replied, "Across the street."

Doug laughed, "Great, I'll be right over."

She laughed again, and said "OK" before she could think of another excuse. Shelly went to the bathroom, washed her face and combed her hair.

She checked her face, in the mirror, not bad for an overworked, unappreciated, and underpaid, single, mother, she thought. Maybe they would have a nice evening after all. She was pleased he was coming. She put on some soft coral lipstick, some cologne, and changed her slippers to a pair of comfortable loafers. She had not felt special anticipation of this kind for a long time.

Within ten minutes, Doug was at her door. She went to the window of the door and looked out to be sure. He smiled through it. She smiled back as she opened the door. He looked at her in a very pleased way. She was fully awake now, and welcomed him.

She was thrilled to learn he was from San Francisco, a place she had only visited as a child, and a place she very much wanted to visit again.

He looked around and immediately enjoyed the warm surroundings,

"Well, how's the patient now?" said Doug as he walked in.

Shelly replied, "Much better. I think it's a case of too much work, and not enough help."

She smiled at him. "May I get you a drink, scotch, brandy, or some tea?"

He quickly responded, "The tea is not for me. You should try it though, and just sit back and relax. I'm here to help."

They both laughed.

"What would you like first? A drink or a fire?" she asked.

"I'll take both. You fix yourself some tea, and I'll play Boy Scout, and get the fire going, to help us both feel better."

Shelly took a deep breath, walked into the kitchen, and relaxed. She poured the tea. With cup in hand she walked over near the now crackling fire and settled onto the couch. She felt comfortable in a white turtleneck sweater and brown slacks.

Doug sat on the other side of the sofa closest to the fireplace. He watched her in the light of the softly burning flames.

She laughed at herself as she realized she was not being a perfect hostess. She turned to him and asked, "I haven't gotten you a drink yet, I'm sorry. What a great fire you made."

"If you have brandy, I'd be delighted to accept."

"It is coming right up. Now, you just relax," she said as she bounced up and went to the cabinet where she stored scotch, and a few bottles of wine, and found a half bottle of good brandy. Deciding to join him, she poured two snifters with just the right amount, and returned to him. She gave him one of the snifters.

He raised the glass to her and said, "Here's to a major medical recovery!"

She smiled, sat down and sipped from the snifter. He reached over, tapped her glass and toasted again.

"Here's to our new friendship." She returned the toast with a smile.

He sat back, enjoying the fire, the sofa, and her face. He was glad she had the ingenuity and interest to call him back. He had been attracted to her from the first glance, catching her eyes beneath the brim of her soft, green felt hat. He liked the professional, yet warm, way she looked at him when he surprised her with a dinner invitation. He believed he understood what it was like for her to be a working mother; he appreciated her efforts, and even her reluctance to go out.

Shelly was glad she had the sense to leave a message for him and to not remain aloof. She liked this "house call." She was already feeling better, and he had only just arrived. She liked how he looked, very friendly, and at the same time very professional in his manner. He was certainly eager to be with her again. She liked that.

"These Washington winters remind me of growing up in Chicago," he said.

"I guess you had it a lot worse than I did growing up with winters in New York. I recall many feet of snow when I was a child. Somehow it is a lot less cold here. Maybe it's just because of all the hot air blowing in from the Hill," Shelly responded.

They both laughed.

"How long have you lived here?" asked Doug?

"Nine years," she answered.

"What pulled you away from New York? I thought no one ever left there." He looked at her quizzically.

"A man, what else?" she retorted. "I wouldn't have otherwise left Greenwich Village in 1960 for the heat, humidity, and all the hot air of D.C., would I?"

They both laughed again. It was easy to talk with him, so she relaxed and took a deep breath. It was good to share a laugh

"I understand. I only come here for business. I know there's got to be more to this place than hotel lobbies, restaurants, and this overly reactionary government."

"Actually, Washington can be very beautiful if you only take the time to look," she offered. "Maybe someday you'll have the time for some discovery of the city before you rush back out to Dulles."

"What do you like to do?" Doug asked her, genuinely interested in her response.

"The theater, movies, museums, being with friends, Quiet dinners, enjoying my daughter, Alison, walking in Rock Creek Park, and the zoo…" her voice trailed off as she thought about all there was to do in Washington, D.C. if one had the time.

He looked at her with renewed interest. She was a professional woman, independent, yet also a mother trying to make a life for herself, and her daughter, on her own. He met women like her infrequently; he knew facing life after a divorce is never easy for anyone.

"How old is your daughter?" Doug asked wanting her to feel comfortable.

"Oh, she's two, and," Shelly added, "really cute. If that is immodest to say, I don't care. Here's a picture of her. You can see for yourself."

"My little girl is five," he replied quietly, "and she's cute, too." They both laughed.

"You're married? I should have known." She was afraid she was unable to hide the disappointment in her voice.

"Well, actually, 'separated'...He paused, realizing he was not telling her the whole truth, but it was too late now. "I have a daughter and two sons." He continued trying to explain or cover his deception, "I was married 13 years. The boys are seven and eleven."

He sounded proud of this accomplishment. He had lied, but she would never know. He just knew that she would not continue to be relaxed and trust him if she knew that he had been only thinking about separating from his unhappy marriage for months, but had not yet taken any action. He felt, for the first time, that there was a new incentive to being free. He made up his mind to do something more about his situation, but he did not want to discuss his actual marital status.

She brightened and breathed a sigh of relief. She felt strongly about dating married men. There were many in Washington who made passes at her hoping to crack her scruples. She made friends, but avoided them as lovers. She learned soon enough there was no way to win anything in that sort of relationship. She could not imagine what it would be like to make love to someone and have him then return to another partner that same night to maintain appearances. She wanted none of that pain and avoided it.

"Do you have any pictures of your kids?" asked Shelly, now taking a deep breath and willing to relax. He retrieved a wallet with photos from inside his jacket. She looked at three shiny faces, complete with a broken tooth, straggly hair, freckles, and impish looks.

She smiled. "They are certainly cute." Three children! She was awed by the thought.

"Must be a handful," she ventured. "Where do they live now?"

"With their mother" He added quickly, "I'll try to get custody, of course," Doug replied, sipping on the cognac. He was planning as he spoke aloud. He wanted to tell her the truth, but he also did not want to spoil the illusion.

"Of course," she agreed, thinking, why not? Fathers are often as good at "mothering." They also make more money and live better than most mothers who are alone with their kids. She thought here was a unique 'new man.' She liked him all the more. He was handsome, sincere, and she thought, a single parent like herself. He seemed genuine, available, and, best of all; he was someone she could easily talk with. They had so much in common. Not a bad combination, she thought.

"Do you live near them?" she asked aloud, sipping some tea.

"Yes." He quickly changed the subject, as he did not know where he was going next with his deception, "Who takes care of Alison while you're working?"

"I am very lucky to have Flora. She had been a nun in a convent in Spain. After leaving, she came to D.C. for a change, without being able to speak a word of English. That took a lot of guts. She loves Alison and has been wonderful. She now enjoys being a 'nanny' instead of 'nunny.'"

They both laughed and turned back to the fire. Then she faced him and asked, "How long have you worked for Head Start?" trying to regain a bit of her professional demeanor.

Doug answered, "Not long enough. I'm still learning at every meeting. This one is more than a meeting, though, it's an event. I met you. How are you feeling?"

He smiled, and examined Shelly, watching for a sign that she was interested in more than his brains, or his medical consultation services delivered to her door.

"I'm definitely feeling a lot better since you walked in," she answered, sensing the question in his eyes.

As they talked, they found even more in common. They both loved music, especially jazz.

Shelly said, "I bet you know the twist, the shag, and all the new dances, but I just love soft jazz and it always puts me in a melancholy mood."

Shelly got up to play something; the house was quiet except for the crackle of the fire. She remembered she had just purchased a new album he might enjoy, Roberta Flack's "First Take." She told him the singer was a favorite of hers, and that she had been a teacher in a local school. Then she told him, "Roberta started singing on the Hill in small clubs, and she has a loyal following," Shelly said as she turned on the stereo and put the album in place.

Just as Roberta Flack began to sing, "The First Time Ever I Saw Your Face," Doug walked toward her, took her in his arms, and kissed her warmly. She felt his passion. She responded.

Then, attempting to regain composure, she moved away, slowly, and poured two more drinks. She was uncertain about how to handle her feelings, even though she was excited.

"Well," she thought, "He's going back to San Francisco. I'm safe. I'll never see him again, or at least not for a year. But, I wonder why I feel so drawn to him?"

Before she could resist, he took her gently and firmly into his arms. She made him feel warm in his chest. He drew in a breath. She seemed to want to be as close as he did. He had broken through the fragile, thin layer of her official "mask."

He found the woman beneath the veneer. He felt triumphant, full of joy. He found someone real, and warm, even in Washington, on a very bitter winter night.

Jubilant, he began to make love to her. Her response made him feel alive. He needed to be as close to her as possible. She opened the door enough, to let him reach deep inside her. There was real warmth, tenderness, softness, and a deep hungry passion. He kissed her face, breasts, and arms. He loved her for hours. He covered her with his body and his passion. She responded, hungry for his taste, his tenderness. She returned his passion.

At dawn, he woke from a few hours of delicious sleep, kissed her again, dressed and rushed out and back across the street to the hotel, where he gathered a few things into his suitcase, checked out, and found a cab to drive directly to the airport to catch an early flight out of Dulles.

Shelly awoke, said goodbye at the door, and returned to bed filled with thoughts of Doug. She thought of the change in their professional relationship, of his passion, and how he had filled her with bliss. She liked his wit, warmth, and intelligence, his energy and dedication. They shared many interests, especially children, music, and their passion for work. Thinking of work, she quickly showered and dressed. Then she looked in on sleeping Alison, noted Flora was home, so she could take off for work.

She felt she had found the man she had waited for during all those long lonely hopeful nights. He somehow 'cured' her. She worked all day and thought of him often.

A long, white shiny box with red ribbon awaited Shelly's arrival home from work that night, filled with long-stemmed red roses and a note.

"Here's to major medical miracles." She felt happy and full of him again. She checked herself in the mirror and thought, "This is absurd! I can't be having an affair with a man 3,000 miles away."

Over the thousands of miles, flying back to San Francisco, Doug thought about Shelly. He was confused, but he knew something special had happened, and his life had changed. Had he fallen in love with a woman who lived 3,000 miles away? He had too much to face and to sort out. He knew he liked her, and she knew how to make him feel like a man when they made love. He smiled as he thought of her breasts, her mouth, and all that they shared together that night.

What happens now? He wondered aloud as he finished the plastic glass of juice and the seat belt signal went on. He would return to life as usual, but he kept tuning into the memories of their time together and smiled.

On Monday morning he received a call at his office. He reached for the phone.

"Hello?" Shelly's voice sounded close. "I was catching a cold. But now it's all gone. You managed a major medical miracle." She smiled at him through her words as she said, "Thank you for the roses!"

He replied, "We West Coast doctors know some things about holistic medicine those East Coast doctors haven't discovered yet. It's fabulous stuff. You need a lot more of it."

She knew she wanted to see him again and soon. He felt the same way. They did not have to say it. He checked his schedule for the month ahead to see how he could arrange a return trip.

He told her, "I'd like to return to Washington in several weeks. Since I have to go to Dallas for a meeting, I might as well continue the rest of the way and check on my new patient." She easily agreed.

Suddenly, he was in her life. She was happier than she had been in a long time because he had touched something deep, strong, and alive in her. She went to bed that night filled with a warm energy flowing softly throughout her body.

Thousands of miles away he closed his eyes thinking of being close to Shelly, of sex, and of all they had in common. He felt himself aroused. He felt the unexpected as he lay next to his wife of thirteen years listening to her breathing, and then he slept.

The moon was full outside, shining through the clouds quietly rising over the hills of San Francisco. Diamond Heights was still, and the darkened night very cold.

Chapter 6

Long Distance

There are voices we hear in solitude, but they grow faint and inaudible as we enter into the world. Ralph Waldo Emerson

Shelly sat poised "at-the-ready" at her gray, steel, desk in the pale-green walled office filled with shelves of files in the federal building that housed the Office of Education. It was very early in the morning, but she was totally prepared to deal with the day's pressures along with the piles of countless papers facing her. She looked forward to the phone call that would come in the middle of the afternoon. The warm voice at the other end would remind her of the other side of her deeper self, her true being.

She was, after all, more than her brain. She was more than the person she had to be to function in the world. She was also a woman, with feelings, passions and yearnings. She wanted more. Beyond working and commitment she was also sensual, sensitive, and she sincerely wanted warmth, affection, a touch of romance, and most of all a permanent loving relationship. She wanted it all. The years following her divorce from Arnold had been filled with child rearing, hard work, and a few casual dates.

The men she met in Washington were mostly overly ambitious, powerful in their own circles, somewhat interesting; but they were also workaholics, usually insensitive to tenderness or physical intimacy, and they knew little of the pleasures of simple playfulness. They were not interested in taking on new responsibility that involved a child, or sharing in "family" time.

Shelly dreamed and looked for more than the stereotypical man-on-the-move, upwardly mobile man. She desired someone with whom she could share herself, and her daughter, completely. She wanted a nurturing life beyond a career and to have someone to enjoy sharing all of life, family as well as intimacy.

With Doug, she suddenly believed she had finally found the man she had been waiting for. He was good looking, but he was much more. He was intelligent and easy to talk to about everything that mattered to her: work, kids, music, and the sharing of personal thoughts. He had style and sensitivity. His philosophy of life excited her. He seemed dedicated to the same higher purposes in life and he cared about children. That was, most of all, hard to find among the ego-driven men in Washington. She felt glad at the coincidence of meeting him as part of their work. She had liked him at their first meeting. That meeting seemed to be fated, as if it were all part of her life's perfect timing.

Exactly at three o'clock, the phone rang. It was Doug. She smiled.

She got up and crossed the room as she thought he could see her wide grin from 3000 miles away. She closed her office door so she could focus privately on their conversation and not reveal it to anyone else passing by.

He said, "I miss you. You are so important to me."

His words opened her heart. His warm tone made her crave his touch. She yearned for a hug, a quiet dinner, playing with Alison, and wonderful pleasure later in bed, and being close and warm. She realized her mind was racing. She had not been able to slow it down since that first night together. She felt happy and excited.

Then Doug said something that made Shelly hold her breath. She had expected him to express affection, or a comment about work, but not what came next.

"I didn't tell you this before, Shelly, because I did not want to alarm you. But, I will now be separating, and plan to get a divorce after thirteen years of marriage."

She found it hard to breathe. The office walls seemed to close in and she felt there was no air. She did not want to be involved in the dissolution. She thought he was already through the anguish of divorce and was free. She did not expect this news.

She asked, in a barely audible voice, "When did this start?"

"I decided back when I was in Washington driving to Dulles that morning."

The news made her feel as if he were somehow using her. Perhaps she was nothing more to him than a springboard for his own leap to freedom. She thought he had told her the truth when they talked that first night. She had no way to know what was really going on in his life. He had told her he was separated, and living alone, but now she realized he was just launching his freedom. She now had doubts. He had not been completely honest with her. She felt he should be free and be complete with his past before they became involved.

He sensed her pulling back. "Since I came back I arrived at reality. I've moved into my own place," he quickly added. "I am close to the children. I had to get out of the situation right away."

She breathed a sigh of relief.

He seemed to be struggling with all the same issues she had to face years before. She wanted to believe this was all part of the larger plan. Perhaps he just could not talk about it when they first met. He took the easy way to overlook the complete truth. She wanted to believe everything he told her. She certainly understood what he was going through, but she also felt uneasy.

He added, "It's been hard to keep my mind on work when so much has been happening at home. How did you handle your divorce?"

She responded, "With great difficulty. I was in shock most of the time. It's not easy on anyone, most of all on children. I hope they are okay." She waited for him to respond.

Doug said, "They're amazing kids: strong and resilient. They know no one is at fault. They can handle it. It's better for everyone. We are finally being honest."

Shelly was glad he was being direct. He was telling her more about what happened in his life. She started to relax and breathe again.

"I know it will be much better for everyone. It just doesn't always feel that way," he added.

Shelly added, "Well at least you are sure of what you needed to do, and I hope no one is hurt by the decision, if you have made the right choice."

She added, wondering if his wife was as willing to just cut the knot like that. It all seemed a bit too pat, but she wanted to trust him. Most of all she wanted to believe what he told her was the truth.

Doug responded, "I really appreciate your understanding, and will accept what I have to do next."

Shelly replied, wanting to be supportive, but also she wanted to keep her distance from his problems, which she did not want to be involved in.

"I hope everything will work out," she added wistfully trying to remain objective.

Doug expressed his appreciation for her understanding and said, "It helps a lot to know you are there."

She wondered what his wife was like, and what the real reasons were for their divorce. She had no more time to talk, nor did he. Finally, she sighed and felt relieved. At least, she thought, he was being honest now.

When she put down the receiver, she sat without moving from her desk. She felt confused. She wanted to be close to him even more, yet she knew she needed to stay apart. She did not want to be involved with him, not if he had years of resolving many issues that are always part of a divorce.

She got up to stretch. She looked at the roses on her desk. They were darkened, dying, but she felt again the surge of pleasure at his romantic gesture. Then she thought… be patient, don't expect too much too soon.

At 4:00 p.m. she received another call.

Mr. Butts, the Assistant to the HEW Assistant Secretary, would see her in half an hour to talk about the proposed childcare center for the children of parents who work at the agency. She gathered her papers into her briefcase, and she was ready. It had taken two years of hard work to organize. Now she had a shot at moving forward with a real place that would be concrete, visible, and make an important impact on many lives. She went to the elevator, pushed the down button, and left the building.

She crossed the street, entered the older HEW building, and walked down the darkened corridor to the last bank of elevators. She rode up quickly. Once in one of the offices of the higher echelon, she was asked to wait. She sat down to open her briefcase and prepare the papers in the beige manila file.

One of the typists, Yvonne, was an active member of the childcare committee. Talk about infiltration! Yvonne gave her a smile and wink, and then she raised her fingers in the sign for victory. They smiled at each other.

Shelly felt more confident. She knew many parents were counting on her to make this meeting work out well for everyone. Finally she was asked to enter. A tall, thin unsmiling bureaucrat met her at the door.

Shelly said, "Good afternoon, Mr. Butts. Thank you for making time to see me," as she sat down and arranged her papers in her lap.

Mr. Butts had a massive desk, curtains on the large window looking out over the mall. His office was very comfortable, considering it was all government-issued furniture. There were not many papers anywhere.

Mr. Butts intoned, "I understand you have been pushing for a childcare center. I want to know why we should have one of those schools for kids in an official building. We don't want a 'fish bowl' atmosphere here with real children."

Quickly, Shelly replied to overcome the first of the arguments on his list of reasons to resist.

"Mr. Butts, there are several hundred parents with children who are having a very hard time getting to work due to the inadequate childcare that now exists in the City of Washington. It's much more than a "school." It makes all the difference to all families to have full day care when moms have to go to work," she continued without taking a breath.

"The women who work here want to stay off welfare and be productive. They have jobs in the agency that is supposed to be the leader for services for children in America. They want to continue to do their jobs, not lose any time from work, and know their kids are safe, and learning at the same time. This could be the first model for what the government, as an employer, could do to help these mothers and the children…" Her voice trailed off as she realized she was at the last barrier, and it was not going to be easy to convince him.

He retorted, "But, not here in our agency, in our own building!"

She responded. "Well, perhaps you can look at this problem from another viewpoint. All of senior management, including the Commissioner himself, has agreed that the childcare center would be a valuable part of our building, and it's mandated in the agency's mission and services. It is perfect timing to show the agency's employees and employers everywhere in the federal government that this agency actually cares about children!"

He shook his head, "I don't want our place to be scrutinized and become a "fish bowl". We are very vulnerable to criticism in this agency. There could be many problems, and we want to avoid problems!"

"Yes, Mr. Butts," Shelly added. "I understand that argument, but there is yet another side. The agency can take the lead for childcare, not only in the federal government, but be a model for what should happen throughout the country, as a valuable service, and it could show support on behalf of all employers, companies and to all families who need it. This is not just for low-income employees; the center could help all those administrators who might otherwise lose their secretaries because they don't have childcare arrangements. They would be able to use the service on an emergency basis and not lose valuable time at work. Even Capitol Hill and the Pentagon need childcare services!" she added.

He looked at her, but did not budge an inch toward accepting the plan. He seemed ready to easily dismiss her along with the plan, along with all the years of hard work, and turn his back on all the workers who were already on the list to enroll their children as soon as the place opened. She took a deep breath and smiled at him. Then she took the initiative, and with great courage she replied firmly.

"Mr. Butts, if you do not approve this center, within the next two weeks we will arrange to have all the parents bring their children here to your office, and you can be the babysitter for all the children. We can also inform The Washington Post. They would love to investigate the full story."

She smiled as she said it, but he knew as he glowered at her impudence and realized that she meant it.

She added brightly as she rose to leave, "The Washington Post, on the other hand, could do a splendid story on how well you care and rise up and take care of your employee's children." She was at the door as she turned and smiled at him.

He said begrudgingly, "You'll get your approval, as long as it's in your building across the street, and not in this one. We need our Executive Dining Room!"

She turned, crossed back across the room and, after shaking his hand and thanking him for his approval, walked out in triumph.

She gave Yvonne the victory sign and a big smile. Yvonne jumped for joy.

Shelly wanted to celebrate her victory, but there was still too much to do. She quickly went back to her office, and typed up a memo to the Commissioner to report on the meeting so that he could go on record and then move forward to make the necessary contacts for the next steps–GSA planning, approval of the budget, and the many stages of architectural and other planning details to establish the actual facility. She now had the right news to present in her testimony to the Congressional Committee holding hearings on the pending Legislation.

Finally, she had met with real success. Shelly thought of her first lunch with Thelma Carter, her secretary, where they talked about the many childcare problems they both shared.

Thelma said, "Gosh, every morning I never know if I can get to work or if the childcare lady will be okay to take care of the kids. I worry all the time, I will lose my job."

Shelly responded, "If we had a place you could bring them here in the building, like over there," pointing to the half-empty Executive Dining Room, "you would not have to worry." The dining room led out to a vast block-long empty space that would make a perfectly safe playground, a delightful outdoor play space. She could envision the children at play there.

"Jeez, you've got to be kiddin'; they don't ever let us employees into that room, let alone would they make it into a childcare center. You are totally dreaming girl."

Shelly responded, "What do we have to lose? Let's go for it. We can try!"

She added, "A childcare center for the children of employees. It's perfect. Just what our government should have for all employees, and everywhere."

Now, finally, after two years, the dream was closer to becoming a reality. Of course, Thelma and Shelly's kids were now too old to use it. They shared a lot of good times and hard work getting to this point. All the employees with kids in the building would soon be celebrating with them; once Shelly knew that her work to create the center for employees was finally a reality.

She turned her attention to the reports from the state education departments. She was responsible for a careful review to find the discrepancies in standards for all schools receiving Title One federal funds. She completed the review of the reports, and she checked through all the information she had gathered on the proposed "Welfare Reform."

She knew it was going to continue to be hectic right through until Christmas. She knew that doing a lot of work was the best thing to avoid getting too sentimental, or needy, the work would keep her mind off feeling lonely. She wanted to be with Doug again before New Year's. But it might not be possible to reconnect again, except through telephone calls and letters. She called him late that night just to hear his voice before she fell asleep.

"Hi," she said as she pulled down the covers and got into bed.

"Hi," he replied, pouring a drink.

"How does it feel to be all alone?" she asked quizzically.

She turned on her pillow, reaching for a cup of tea.

"Well, strange. I miss you very much," he added softly.

"What do you do all day?" she asked. She wanted to tell him all that happened, but it would take too long and take the feeling of romance out of their conversation. She wanted to hold on to the romance as long as she could.

"Meetings are my thing. Day in and day out," he laughed.

"Sounds tedious," she said laughing, too.

He asked quickly, "Will you meet me in my dreams tonight?"

"Yes. Space travel is my specialty. How about around midnight? Let's rendezvous in some romantic little café in North Beach. Is that close enough?"

She smiled as she put the cup down. She thought of how a Café in North Beach might look with the two of them seated sipping cups of espresso, gazing into each other's eyes, totally absorbed. She was totally into her imagination.

"Please kiss me right now," he said whispering in her ear. She felt warm all over.

She pursed up her mouth near the phone, and sent him a kiss across the thousands of miles.

"There, did you get it?" she asked.

She put her hand on her breast, yearning to be touched.

He said, "Got it. Here's a big wet one right on your lips and another for the left nipple."

She looked surprised. He must have sensed her hand was on her breast, or was he being psychic?

He did say he was open to holistic medicine. Maybe this was another talent he had. She felt wet between her legs. She wanted him.

She replied, "You've got my kisses on your lips."

She felt slightly shy, but also free to be herself with him.

They both laughed as they both said, "Good night. Sweet dreams," at the same time. "Mine," he added, "are full of you." She shuddered.

He was romantic, and it had been so long since she had felt "turned on."

He called her again as she arrived at the office. "Good morning. How did you sleep?" he asked brightly.

The three-hour time difference forced them to stop to check the time before dialing. They continued talking back and forth sharing tidbits of news, or tiny titillations. She fell asleep sometimes as he kissed her all over as he talked with her over the phone. He touched every place on her body with verbal caresses. The phone was their link to romance. She yearned to be closer to him.

The letters they wrote were filled with issues at work, children, and family matters. They expressed their feelings and their ideas openly. He wrote to her about the children, and he talked to her about them. She wrote and talked about Alison. Between her work, mothering, and talking with and writing to Doug, she found she had little time left for any other kind of social life.

She carved out time each day to be with Alison, giving her all the attention she could. Her evenings and weekends were filled with mothering. She managed somehow to do her holiday shopping. She stayed up late at night to send cards and notes to her family and friends in Baltimore, Boston, New York, and Washington. She wrote long letters, and read bedtime stories to Alison.

Before she realized, it was New Year's Eve. She went to a friend's New Year's Eve party with Harry, a nice, friendly, slightly balding lawyer she had known for many years. She had dated him briefly long before she met Doug. Afterwards, though, when she resisted their former intimacy, Harry was irritated. He wished her "Happy New Year!" and walked out of her life. She was relieved.

Doug called the next day. She was pleased to talk with him, yet sad because they weren't together.

"Happy New Year… my Shelly! May we soon be together!" he said.

"Thank you for giving me so much of what I needed most," she replied.

She knew this would be an important year for both of them. She played, read stories, and talked with Alison all day. They made Tollhouse cookies. Alison added in the walnuts and chips and ate them at the same time.

Snow began to fall in the early evening. Alison was excited as she watched from the window. Shelly made a fire in the living room, sat silently, listening to music and the crackling logs. She felt both happy and lonely. Alison climbed up and put her head in her lap and fell asleep, as Shelly stroked her shiny, soft, little head.

At the office the following morning, she looked over the year's accomplishments and felt a deep sense of satisfaction. Despite great difficulties, she had managed to organize the employees and everyone else to create a real childcare center for the children of the employees. Although there had been a lot of resistance all along the way, there was also a lot of support from the staff, the union, and fortunately, many of the administrators. Hundreds of women employed in the building had young children who needed childcare. She believed the energy she put toward building more childcare services was of paramount importance. She believed the government must set an example as an employer who cared about children. Certainly she felt it was essential for the very agency advocating educational services throughout the country to provide for the childcare needs of its own employees. The levels of red tape, countless studies, ongoing consultations, and endless reports had been so cumbersome.

She spent months pulling together an organization of employees. The plan they had been optimistic about had be approved by the higher echelon in the agency. Finally, now with the approval of the HEW Secretary, The General Services Administration (GSA), and a few more agency heads, they received the needed approval to develop the plans so the center could materialize. There were yet months of details to work out on the designs, program plans, discussions, and contracts, but it would all be well worth the effort.

The childcare center would finally be opened with most of the program's early opponents taking full credit for their innovative new service. After all, the pilot center would stabilize the workforce, improve morale, and become a national model. They would even get their picture taken with real children. The center would make a big difference in the lives of employees. The Center was something they wanted recognition for even though it was their resistance that made it take twice as long to finally open.

Shelly understood the politics, she saw how things were garbled, or glossed over, and gnarly, and how many great ideas were long gone before they ever started. She was glad that she was willing to stick it out, and to push through the layers of resistance. She knew it was right. Even though Alison would not be eligible to use the center she was still glad that she did what she could to help other parents.

Soon there would be laughing children playing on colorful play equipment in what had been an empty area outside the Executive Dining Room. Soon, real children would be learning, singing, napping, and eating where before only well-financed executives had used the space for only a few hours a day. She felt satisfied. She knew it was only the start.

Within a few days she received a firm offer, to become the Program Director of the Childcare Research and Development Division, in the Program

Development Department at the Office of Economic Opportunity, Marvin had made it real as he promised. The move would make the transfer official, and with it would come as an excellent promotion. This was the opportunity she had dreamed of, to direct the expansion of the national childcare program, to be planned first in the President's Office of Economic Opportunity. The new program was to be part of a whole new approach to Welfare Reform. Mothers would have the childcare services they needed to seek employment and training. The debate was just warming up. She knew this issue was not going to be solved easily. She would be needed for a long time to come. She found her future professionally, and was ready to do all she could.

The planning for national day care services, research, and actual demonstration programs would be set up around the country and be funded and administered by the new Division. This was to be her new challenge. She wanted to be sure to move the program in the right direction, and to help as many families as possible.

Shelly knew this was the chance of a lifetime–to direct the whole program. She knew the only way the program would be effective was to link up with other agencies and organizations, and to build upon the limited resources that had been struggling to somehow manage for years. Together they could make a difference. Everything might work for everyone in new ways.

The decision had been made. Marvin Felder was asked to be the Director of the entire Department of Program Development at the Office of Economic Opportunity. He would have some flexibility in terms of staffing, so he asked Shelly to also move to the new agency. She was pleased he had high regard for her abilities.

Shelly felt her career was essential, regardless of what lay ahead in her relationship with Doug. She wanted to retain her separate identity, a purpose in life, and independence. She was glad for the heavy workload awaiting her each day. There would be a steady increase, endless meetings, reports, phone calls, and, of course, endless correspondence, proposals and processing contracts. The work would keep her really focused and busy, so she would have little time to think much of anything else.

She discussed the job with Doug.

"I am sure it's going to be a great new program once Congress passes the legislation. Things will get better, and the services will improve and move across the country." Shelly shared her thoughts enthusiastically.

Doug agreed, "Yes, it can happen the same way that Head Start launched. It never seemed possible when it started out." He added wistfully remembering the long hard fight for support.

"It will be a great new job," Shelly added brightly.

Doug agreed.

They talked about jobs and their dreams. She knew it was not time to move anywhere else except to the new job, and the promised higher grade level. She knew this was the right career move. Besides, Doug had a lot of his own personal business to handle.

When she got home in the evening, she had dinner with Alison. Then they played together with a small dollhouse. Alison loved moving the small pieces of furniture and the little people around from room to room. She held the puppets trying to fit her hands inside and get them to talk to her little people.

Shelly talked to Flora to find out about Alison's activities that day, as she gave Alison a bath she noticed Alison was growing so fast. They sat talking and reading stories until bedtime then she tucked her in and turned off the light.

Shelly felt very tired as waves of loneliness fell upon her. It seemed that of all her dates with different men in the past, no matter how interesting, were only temporary diversions. She had missed a deeper commitment, the one person she could count on for affection, to cuddle with in bed, and to wake up with, and to share music, coffee, read and discuss the Washington Post. She picked up the newspaper, and lying across her bed she read.

If she and Doug were not talking late at night, she turned on "Johnny Carson" and fell asleep during his monologue. The paper fell to the floor in pieces. She awakened briefly several times throughout the night. Each time her mind swirled around, thinking about Doug. She felt her needs were being met somehow despite the distance. She was full of love and excitement about the deepening relationship.

During the weeks, she kept very busy. She called her sister, Julie, in New York City to wish her a Happy New Year, and to find out how she and her sister's husband, Matt, were. Despite the usual ups and downs found in almost every marriage, their marriage had persisted. Shelly had introduced them to each other while they were in college. Shelly showed an early ability in perfect matchmaking. She made excellent connections for many friends who, over the years, became lasting couples after she introduced them. She was pleased love was working out for everyone else. Now, maybe, it would be her turn and she would find the right partner and it would last over time.

She called her mother, Jeanie, who lived in Queens, not far from Manhattan, but yet it was another whole world. Her mother still resided in the house Shelly had lived in as a child.

"Mom!" "Happy New Year!" said Shelly. "What's new?" she asked.

"Not much. I gained weight over the holidays with too much 'fressing' (eating).

What's new with Alison? Does she eat enough?" asked her mother.

"She's fine, and growing fast. She loves the dollhouse you sent her for Hanukkah. Thanks for thinking of her. She misses her grandma," replied Shelly cheerily.

"When are you coming to New York to visit?" asked her mother.

"Not for awhile. I've got a new job, a transfer with much more responsibility, and an increase in salary," said Shelly.

"Good. It's about time! You work too hard for those 'shnorers (selfish). How about your father? Did you hear from him? Did he send you some Hanukkah gelt (money)?" asked her mother.

"Yes, Mom. He's fine. Thanks. Have you talked to him?" asked Shelly, trying to keep open the doors for her parents to at least be friendly to each other. There was little point to it. They fought constantly when they were together. Peace would not be something they would enjoy before or after their divorce. There was just too much history, anger and frustration between them.

Her mother replied, "No. Why should I? I just get the check each month. It's enough. He's so cheap, and so difficult. So impossible…so…" she responded, starting to wind up.

Shelly cut it off. She needed to handle her own problems and quickly said,

"Mom, we'll talk soon. Please don't start. Be happy. Everything is fine. Just get busy. Find some things you can enjoy."

Shelly added, "Take care, mom, I'll call next week."

"Don't be a stranger!" added her mother just before she hung up.

Shelly felt it was best not to begin talking about Doug, although the news that she was seeing a doctor would fill her mother with pleasure, but the rest of the story would not. Her mother having been a nurse had the utmost respect for doctors, if only her mother had married a doctor. She felt her mother had never had enough respect for her father who had been a fireman in Harlem. He could not find employment as a teacher in the middle of the depression so he did what he could. They managed somehow but her mother was disappointed that he was not using all of his abilities. The tension between them was apparent almost always.

She kept silent. When she went to the bathroom later she had a funny feeling. She thought it was that she had not been to an Ob-Gyn for a while to get a Pap smear. She made a mental note to call for an appointment. But, she felt strange, and she realized that she missed her period. She suddenly got a big knot in the pit of her stomach.

The next day she called and made an appointment. She went to her Ob-

Gyn the following week. She discovered to her astonishment that she was pregnant. She knew immediately what she must do. Yet, there was a great deal of sadness mingled with a clear knowledge that this was definitely not the time for her and Doug to have a baby. There was nothing else she could do. The timing was not right. As much as she wanted another child, for Alison, and for herself, as an expression of deepening love, she knew there was no other choice. She believed that the decision as to what to do with her body was between herself, God, and her Ob-Gyn. But she also knew that she had to share the news with Doug. She told him the news that afternoon.

He said, "I want to hold you close. I am very unhappy that you must go through this."

She felt relieved, yet sad at the news. The decision had to be made, although she loved the idea of having another child, and with Doug. She said, "I really am glad to know how compatible we are, but I think we will have enough to deal with in the future without any additional complications. I will talk with my doctor and make the arrangements."

The sudden crisis brought them closer. She arranged for an afternoon visit the following week to have the D&C. She simply resigned herself to it. Shelly was realistic. She felt Doug and she would be together sometime soon, and they would have more children. There was time enough for more children. Afterwards, she took a few days of sick leave until she felt better.

Shelly took Alison to the National Zoo for a quiet afternoon walk among the birds, monkeys, panda bears, tigers, lions, and elephants.

That evening as she tucked Alison into bed, she felt a strong wave of sadness. It contained all of her feelings and how much she yearned to have a brother or a sister for Alison. She let the thoughts pass and they disappeared as smoke rings into the night air.

Shelly felt a deepening love for Doug and she missed him terribly. Then she got into bed turned off the light, broke down, and sobbed. She felt her tears were mingling with the rain outside her window, as she cried herself to sleep.

Chapter 7

Promises

Character cannot be developed in ease and quite. Only through experiences of trial and suffering can the soul be strengthened, ambition inspired, and success achieved. Helen Keller

The next week Shelly continued working on many different tasks. Not only was she working on all the complicated aspects of a new program, but she was also asked to get involved in planning for the Day Care Forum of the White House Conference on Children. This was a new and exciting addition to an already full schedule.

This event would occur in Washington, D.C., in one year and would bring people together from all over the United States concerned about every aspect and all the issues about children. For a week, experts and community leaders would discuss programs, policies and progress, past and present, and delve into problems and potential solutions. It was a huge undertaking, but it could prove to be essential to shore up the eroding climate of support for many children's services.

Shelly was thrilled to have the opportunity to bring together the people who could make a difference in this fledging proposed national childcare program. The people who would attend were the people who knew the problems and who were committed to deliver services and who knew how to make the changes needed at the state and local levels.

Shelly talked first to Dr. Betty Carter in Little Rock, Arkansas, a long-time professional who had a good view of the whole field and who could provide some of the right guidance in the planning.

"Hello, Betty. I am so glad you are willing to work with us on this event. I know you have a lot to offer as we move ahead on planning the new program."

Betty answered in her soft, southern voice, "Well, considering this is a once in a decade opportunity, I am sure I can find the time from my current research to lend a hand."

Shelly asks, "Who else do you feel should be on the committee?"

Betty named about a half dozen people off the top of her head. "I am sure that each of them knows many more experts across the country," Betty offered.

Then she added, "Look, I think these are well recognized research and university names, but," she cautioned, "it is important to include folks who are more community minded, locally oriented, and who can bring in their own social perspectives. We certainly don't want the same professional people talking only to each other as they already have for many years. That won't get us anywhere."

Shelly agreed. She asked Betty to send her the list of the people she had suggested.

She shared her thoughts with Betty, "I know we can locate the best people to be representatives from across the diverse population. I will be in touch with some of my contacts in some of the national organizations. I know this will be an exciting opportunity to bring people together to make the issue of childcare more widely recognized, to gain more support. It's time the folks in the 'Ivory Towers' began talking with the "real folks" who are on the firing line. Betty, please call me whenever you want to suggest anything. I will be here."

Shelly spent many days talking with the people she knew at many different organizations. She contacted the Day Care Council, Black Child Development Institute, Children's Defense Fund, National Association for the Education of Young Children, Association for Childhood Education International, Child Welfare League, American Nurses Association, American Academy of Pediatrics, National Association of Social Work, American Psychological Association, American Orthopsychiatric Association, National Education Association, Educational Staff Seminars, United Federation of Teachers, American Association of Lady Garment Workers, League of Women Voters, American Association of University Women, National Council of Jewish Women, Defense Advisory Committee of Women in the Military and others.

She knew they all had local members. She also made contact with other federal agencies: Agriculture, Health, HUD, Labor, Office of Child Development, and the Defense Department. She knew the problems of childcare affected military bases, hospitals, schools, community centers and factories, and all of them needed to have a stable workforce, more childcare services, and more help to solve problems.

With each person she spoke, she tried to find out his or her level of involvement, expertise, and interest about childcare. She also asked who in their organization was working on childcare services at the "grass-roots" level. She asked what each Executive Director felt was the area of greatest unmet need.

Some said, "I think it is infant care," others said, "after-school care." Others continued, "We need on-site centers," "family homes," "emergency 24-hour care." It was clear the needs were extensive. She kept notes on what everyone was telling her. Her list of potential participants for the White House Conference grew each day.

She also was working on getting more unanimous bi partisan support for the pending childcare legislation. The bill was wending its way through Congress. Hearings and testimony continued. She prepared her presentation including the plans for the new center

Shelly found everyone wanted to be involved in some way, and everyone made many good suggestions. She also knew they each had their own agenda, their own concerns, and their own constituency. Getting a consensus would not be easy. Getting agreement on the basic need for childcare services was almost unanimous.

Shelly worked on expanding the themes that people suggested. She worked hard to locate people who knew about each specific area of focus. She found people all over the country who were experts in at least one area, either directly involved or doing research. She also searched for geographic, ethnic, and work diversity. The list of those interested, qualified and diversified grew each day.

Some of the issues she noted involved the unmet needs of children, what was known in research, lack of resources, design of program, program development, and costs of building and maintaining the physical facility. She gathered information on the issues focused on educational programs, health care, nutrition, social services, and much more. The issues concerned before- and after-school care, on-site and off-site campus and work place care, military-based, home-based, community-based, center-based, and hospital-based care. Then there were issues involving cross-cultural, social awareness, self-esteem, separation anxiety, single parent, mixed-age care, and sibling care, historical precedents, disadvantaged, disabled, disenfranchised, creativity, toys, equipment, coordination, consultation and parent involvement—the whole gamut. The planning for new childcare services had begun. Shelly continued learning more about the problems other working mothers were facing due to lack of both adequate childcare services and a clear national policy that supported families.

Shelly meanwhile had her own problems to deal with every day. She wondered why it was all difficult as she fell asleep with piles of paper on her chest late into the night—after Alison, Flora, Doug, and everyone else was cared for. As she contacted the specialists throughout the country, Shelly soon found, to her surprise, an increasing mix of both strong political resistance and high enthusiasm. She felt most of all growing enthusiasm as she spoke to people to gain their interest and support. Everyone had many different views as to what a credible, well developed, comprehensive, culturally-based, quality, affordable program would look like.

Shelly did not tell anyone of her special secret. She remembered she was enrolled in a WPA childcare center during World War II so that her parents could work as a nurse and fireman in New York City. Those involved in planning could not know that the inspiration for her work came from her own experiences as a child and the special legacy of Eleanor Roosevelt. When she met Mary Keyserling, the woman who worked directly for Mrs. Roosevelt during the war, the missing "link" of her purpose in her work was finally pieced together.

She was referred to Mary by a program specialist at the United States Labor Department who told her that Mary held a key position in the Women's Bureau for many years, and prior to that she had been a special assistant to Mrs. Roosevelt. Her husband, Leon, worked for President Roosevelt in the "New Deal" Administration as an economist and planner. He had helped forge many of the programs that were enacted for the country's social, economic, and recovery benefit.

Mary had wanted to talk to Shelly since she had heard the new childcare center was underway and would be located at the Office of Education and that the new program for national childcare would be launched at the Office of Economic Opportunity. After Shelly talked with Mary she was inspired even more, especially after hearing her many World War Two stories. She and Mary talked over tea one day.

Shelly asked, "Why did Mrs. Roosevelt start childcare centers?"

Mary responded in a wavering voice as if caught up in both memories and speech delay.

"Mrs. Roosevelt and I went to migrant camps in the Midwest and in the South. We found children sleeping in dusty wooden bins, or directly on the ground, or in the fields, sometimes with little water, and with no covering in the hot sun. It was awful," Mary continued.

"But, one day when four children were found asphyxiated in a hot car with the windows rolled shut, Mrs. Roosevelt became really agitated. She decided to do something immediately. As soon as she got back to Washington she met with congressional leaders to enact what became known as the Lanham Act. That was the legislation that made it possible for new WPA childcare facilities to be built. Without her support, many more migrant children would have continued to die in the fields. The Kaiser shipyards would not have had the care for children while the women helped to build the ships. The hospitals would not have had any nurses…" She paused.

Mary sat and reflected on history with Shelly. She was glad that she was interested in knowing what had happened to launch childcare services in the first place on a wider scale.

Shelly then told Mary something that she had not revealed to anyone else in Washington, including Doug.

"Mary, when I was a little girl, about two years old, my mother worked in a hospital as a nurse. She would not have been able to do that unless she had the services of the WPA day care center to care for me. It was in a housing project located in the shadow of the Queensboro Bridge. My mother took me there every day so she could go to work at the hospital in the Bronx. She had to take me there early in the morning, then travel a long distance by subway and return for me at night. Or my father picked me up on his way home from being a fireman in Harlem. He also traveled a long distance every day by subway. That program and my parents were pioneers."

Mary smiled, "I had some help with my son also at that time, but later on in order to work for Mrs. Roosevelt I had to place him in a day-care center."

They laughed. They both understood the dilemma of other mothers as they continued to talk about what was needed now.

Shelly's childcare problems, and those of the working women she knew, continued to plague her. She wondered why so many millions of working parents had to face these difficult problems, mostly by themselves. There was so much left to be done.

It had taken months for Shelly to find a person who was loving and consistent with Alison. She knew at the time she found Flora that Flora would only be able to help her, if she were lucky, for a year.

Arnold, her former husband, provided a very small amount of support money for Alison. The two hundred dollars a month did not even cover Flora's salary. So Shelly had to work hard to provide the balance of the money that she and Alison needed. After the divorce, despite all her efforts, there was never enough money to cover everything. She had to give up teaching elementary school to make their life financially more stable. The salary of $7,000 as a teacher in the inner city schools of the District of Columbia was not enough to live on alone, much less raise a child.

Having a sitter to take care of Alison was essential for her to maintain any job stability. The strain showed. She worried about Alison being without her all day. She was also concerned about Alison's stimulation, nurturing, play, nutrition and development. Alison also had special needs.

Shelly thought back to when Alison was an infant, Shelly suspected something might be wrong, when she noticed weakness on Alison's left side, her feet were pointing inward, her difficulty with swallowing, and she had a very small weight gain.

Shelly talked to the pediatrician.

"Dr. Spiegel, I think something may be wrong with our baby. She's having problems, and she cries a lot. I just feel something's wrong," Shelly told him.

"You are just worrying for nothing," he replied. "Relax. You are just a nervous mother."

"I'm not nervous. I just feel something's wrong," Shelly insisted.

Finally, when Alison was three months old, after months of almost continuous crying, and endless sleepless nights, she was admitted into Children's Hospital, where almost immediately an alert neo-natal specialist called for some special tests.

Dr. Banks, Chief of Pediatrics, called Shelly and Arnold into his office. They confirmed Shelly's intuition.

There was something, he suspected, when he said, "Your baby may have cerebral palsy, or be brain-damaged, and might never be able to walk."

Shelly and Arnold were stunned. The news hit them with the force of an elephant's foot bearing down on their chests. Arnold recoiled, retreated.

Shelly withstood the news. She responded with positive new determination. She knew intuitively Alison would be all right. She would do everything in her power to help Alison in every way she could.

She worried that Alison might not be able to walk. Every day she intuitively massaged Alison's legs, taught her to swim, and helped her exercise. Doing something physical and stimulating every day was her first priority. Shelly believed her earlier training in special education would help reduce or alleviate any of Alison's problems.

Arnold instead withdrew. He was not available to assist them or to give either of them what they needed most: love and support. He was too busy with his own work and hardly was in touch with their needs. He wanted things to be perfect and they were not.

The way they each responded to the crisis was typical of how they each handled life. Arnold moved more forcefully toward business and money; while Shelly moved toward her work, being a mother, and being of service.

They finally had nothing left to say to each other. Jazz was no longer the music they enjoyed together. There was simply a rift instead of a riff. The blues was more the background music in their lives; they did not hear the wail. They had drifted apart.

Shelly loved Alison just as she was. She wanted to do all she could to help her to gain all the skills she could. Alison showed encouraging response to the physical activity and there was an increase in her ability every day.

Nick gave Shelly just what she needed. He helped Shelly a lot when he spent time with them, playing with Alison, coaxing her to walk and to express herself. He was very playful with her. Shelly was grateful to Nick for his loving attention even if he had difficulty being committed to their own relationship.

Alison was a happy little girl, showing new skills every day and gaining confidence, and was such a joy to Shelly. Shelly played a game with her, "Look What I Can Do!" Everything she did was a miracle.

She and Doug continued to talk over the phone every day, and sometimes twice a day. One night Doug wasn't home when he said he would be. She called several times and then fell asleep.

The next day he told her he had gone out with another woman. He had met a new neighbor at the apartment building where he now lived.

He said, "I do think it is important for me to sometimes meet other people. After all I am just getting free again after many years of marriage."

She reluctantly agreed, "I know. You need time. But, I do really miss you."

She also felt pangs of confusion. She really missed him. She realized he was lonely. She wanted to understand and accept his needs. When she dated, it was only occasionally and with someone "safe," a dinner-only social evening. She thought constantly of Doug.

When she went out with Peter, a friend and college professor, she always felt comfortable. He also was going through a divorce, was certainly not prepared for any real emotional involvement, and was just in the mood for good company. He made no overtures for sex once she established her preference for being "friends-only" sort of company. They just had a good time talking about their work, sharing their ideas and views. She did not want to go to bed with him. She didn't feel free. She was in love. Peter wanted to go further and at first he tried. She did not respond. He finally understood she firmly meant "No!"

Shelly talked to her family in New York as often as she could. She finally confessed to them about the new relationship with Doug.

Her mother was not at all pleased, "How could you get involved with someone who lives in California, even if he is a doctor, and Jewish? It's too far away! California? Phooey. Why did you ever leave New York City and teaching? That's what you should be doing now! What's going on in your head, mishuganah?"

"He is getting a divorce," replied Shelly, cheerfully, overlooking the unwanted career and personal advice.

"Shelly, you listen to me," her mother retorted. "You should remain in Washington. Stick to where you are," she added, "You have good job security, a house, and friends."

Her mother continued, "You are also close enough to New York, and it's an easy reach so we can see Alison. I don't like the idea that he has already made a family of three children. What about the ex-wife? Did you talk to her? Maybe he's no good. No! This is not right for you."

Shelly concluded, "Mom, thank you for your thoughts. I hope you are not right. It feels right to me. You will like him!"

"It's much better you should like him. I don't trust the situation at all. Please be careful." Her mother cajoled, and then she said, "Goodbye! Enough already!"

She thought carefully about what her mother said. She also realized her family would object regardless, so she learned to ignore their judgments about whom she should be with, what she should do, or how she should live her life.

She thought she knew Doug. She thought everything would be perfect one day in the not too distant future. She was patient and she had a lot to keep her very busy. Her parents' own marriage had been very stormy. They never agreed about anything. They fought about money, relatives, how to wash the dishes, what to eat, smoking, and, of course, how to raise the children. Sometimes their fights erupted into violent explosions. The strain had taken its toll on both her and her sister, Elaine.

They could each see the good side of each parent, but living with them was something else. She was glad they were not living nearby. She was able to see how things could be different. She would make a new life for herself. It was not easy to be without any family nearby, but when they did come to visit she realized how much better it was that they had distance between them. It took days and sometimes weeks to recover from the effects of being with them for just two days.

Her mother's large family was in Baltimore. Although only an hour away, they hardly ever called or came over to visit. She felt very alone. The idea of a warm and loving family and their support was just not part of her family inheritance. She thought about this a lot. She wanted a lot more.

Still, both her parents had each made strong and positive contributions. Her mother could be generous, open, sensitive, and warm-hearted. Her father was also very enthusiastic, energetic, outspoken, and in great physical condition.

Shelly knew what didn't work in her parents' marriage, but there was very little if anything that could have changed. She also knew what had not worked in her own first marriage.

Regardless of how much she wanted things to be different, they were not able to fit together for the long haul. People should think carefully before getting married.

She was determined to do something different, given the opportunity in the future.

Shelly wanted to make her relationship with Doug better. She believed he was very different. He must know how to make a commitment to children, to a wife, and to his work. After all, he had three kids, a marriage of thirteen years, and a good job to prove it. He respected her. He liked talking about the things that mattered to her. She wanted a partner. She felt strongly that Alison should have a home with parents who understood, respected, and really loved each other. She wanted it all.

She believed Doug felt the same way. Even if he did date now just to get out, she would not let some stranger trigger feelings of jealousy. That emotion would only get in the way of her deeply loving feelings. She would not succumb to fears, insecurities, or the challenges of the distance. She thought she knew him. His dating appeared not to be serious.

Doug laughed about it. He told Shelly, "Nothing was going on except talk over a pizza."

Shelly wanted to believe him. She wanted to trust the strength of their relationship, and believe they had a future. She held back her fears, tucking them inside.

Shelly tried to not appear nonplused about her fears whenever she spoke to him. But, instead of being outwardly stressed, she found she often smoked, ate, and talked too fast. She realized she had to change and control her own inner stress. She had worked for so long, had so much to juggle, and had so little free time to really relax. It was clear that something had to give, and soon. She knew she could change for the better. She did her best to be aware of stress every day. She tried to remember to breathe. She worked too much, all with a growing passion, with a lot of built-up tension. Shelly had hopes that he wouldn't notice her fears. She did not reveal her fears and stress and did her best to overcome them. Doug came to Washington every chance he could. She tried to relax, but there was hardly time enough to relax. She tried to do it all.

They had glorious days when he visited: Mornings together in bed, followed by long walks in Georgetown, along the B&O canal, or through the paths in Rock Creek Park. They went to parties with friends, or to the theater and dinner. She was always excited to see him. They laughed a lot. The sex was great, and the cigarette they shared afterward was delicious.

Doug took special interest each time he visited to be with Alison. He walked with her, played with her, and read her stories. Doug enjoyed Alison, and he was very happy with him. On the walk in Rock Creek Park they collected leaves. Doug carried along a bag with pieces of bread when they went for a walk. Shelly rested while Doug took Alison over to the creek to feed the ducks. Shelly watched them together and felt complete.

In April, Shelly visited Doug in California. It was an incredibly perfect four days.

She fell in love with San Francisco at first sight. Tears streamed down her cheeks when they drove to the top of the hills at Pacific Heights at Broadway and Divisadero. She just stood there, her eyes taking in the whole scene, viewing the Bay in awe. She felt this could easily be her new home. She enjoyed everything about the city.

They headed out to Ocean Beach. She marveled at the majestic Cliff House. Then they drove down the panoramic Pacific Coast Highway towards Carmel and Monterey. She was thrilled by the sheer beauty of the trees: eucalyptus, pines, redwoods and cypress, and the endless vastness of the ocean. The great ocean came clashing against the rock formations as comical sea otters played in the waves.

As she experienced her first amazing sunset off Big Sur, sitting on the deck at the strikingly constructed Nepenthe, she knew she wanted to live in California. They made love that night in front of the warm fire in their cozy quaint cabin in Deetjan's Big Sur Inn. Shelly was ecstatically happy.

The first trip together was delightful. She was content. She was totally, madly, in love. When she and Doug kissed good-by at the San Francisco International Airport, she promised to do everything she could to make whatever arrangements necessary to return to California as soon as possible, but she had no idea of how or when.

Back in Washington, after nights of restlessness, Shelly decided to apply to graduate school. It was a long shot. She also decided to put in an application for a government employee's fellowship for a year's leave for study toward a doctoral degree.

The fellowship would be very hard to get. There was a lot of competition. Despite her strong eligibility they had never given one to a woman before. Despite her years of service and many special contributions, the bias that was not always seen, was very much part of the system. Getting it would not be easy. There was plenty of time. The process took a long time. She felt that she had to try. She still had plenty to do to keep her occupied. She became even busier at work.

One night when she was staying late at the office to do some paperwork, rather than taking it all home, she was surprised by a visit by the man who held the key to the final evaluation for her next grade, the promotion, the transfer and the salary increase. Red tape is part and parcel of the career maze in the government, and cutting through the tape is not easy.

Jim Hardy, an African American political appointee, who had little interest in the issues of the programs, but much more interest in "power ploys," entered her office.

"How's it going?" he asked as he entered and took a seat.

Jim was a large man, well dressed, and very assertive. He knew how to wield his power, and he never hesitated to take advantage of the situation.

Shelly responded quietly, "Hello, Jim. I'm trying to get caught up on reading through these many proposals before the White House Conference. There's a large stack — as she pointed to the pile — and just too much to do."

She then she said brightly, "We have had some great childcare plans that have been submitted by community groups from all over the country."

He was not interested in discussing the needs of the communities. He had his own needs to think about.

He suddenly said, "How about some dinner together tonight. Then later we can go over those 'plans' at your place?"

Shelly wasn't sure why he wanted to create a problem between them. She tried to be tactful as she responded.

"But, Jim, won't your wife expect you home for dinner soon? We can go over the plans tomorrow, in your office."

"No, I want to see those plans, up close, tonight. Can't you make some time for priorities?" he replied, smiling at her in a teasing way. He was a very large man, an ex-college football player, with strong political connections that had landed him his job.

Shelly felt very uncomfortable. She got up and walked over to the window.

She said, "Jim, you're married! I don't make any of my very limited free time available for any married men after work. Besides, the report I finished on priorities is now on your desk ready for your review."

He stopped smiling, got up, and came closer to her and crisply sputtered, "You want your promotion, don't you? How much of a priority is that? You 'play ball' and you'll get what you want."

He turned away from her. He was angry at her rebuff. No one turned him down.

As he got to the door, he snorted back, "You play ball or else!" and walked out.

Shelly fell in her chair. She lit a cigarette, shaking all over. She felt like screaming. She felt trapped. He was appointed by the Agency Director, Donald Rumsfeld, and his close friend and associate, Dick Cheney. They were not to be toyed with. She knew there was no one to talk to. She could not tell Marvin. It just would cause a lot of problems. What good would it do?

Not even Doug would understand or know what to do in this difficult situation. There was nothing she could do except to avoid hassles with him. He held the upper hand. She had to remain in her position, but she would not succumb to his demands. She prayed she would be accepted for graduate school.

Songs filled her mind and heart - "California Dreaming on a cold and wintry day" and "I left my heart in San Francisco."

Shelly stayed busy with work and tried to avoid Jim. He did not respond to her package on the priorities of the program plans, nor did she get his approval for her raise in grade. Marvin was too busy trying to put out fires. Problems seemed to be erupting on a daily basis.

The Nixon White House was all over the programs in place, dismantling services as fast as possible. They were hard at work trying to stop anything new from emerging. Poor people were not on their political agenda. There was a totem pole for programs that faced out for the public to see, and leaning up against the totem pole was a long ladder of needs. The rung for children was at the bottom of the steps in the hierarchy. She had no way to resolve the problem with Jim. She decided to just focus on the job, and hope that things would get better.

There was plenty to do. She stayed active in planning the Day Care committee for the 1970 White House Conference on Children. Doug was invited to participate on the committee as the "token" pediatrician. He had been involved in Head Start medical services for years. He knew he could make a contribution. He decided to become actively involved on the committee. His work for the Academy of Pediatrics coincided with the Conference, so he was glad to take an active role.

Shelly and Doug talked and met frequently at these meetings. They discussed the work of the committee, the national issues, and their own family activities. They made love verbally as frequently as they could on the phone. As the needs for the program increased their discussions also increased. They talked every day.

Exactly one year later, she found herself with Doug at the Sheraton Park Hotel, the same hotel where he had stayed when they first met. This time they were attending the White House Conference along with 4,000 representatives of children's organizations from across the country. As she and Doug rode up the escalator, she recalled how they had first met, and how they met again just at the top of the same escalator. So much had happened during this year. She was certain she was in love. They smiled at each other knowing each other's thoughts and feelings.

Numerous issues were presented at the White House Conference. Every important problem concerning children was discussed. Still, when it came to choosing priorities, the delegates selected, almost as one, the lack of adequate childcare as the top national priority.

One of the debates centered on what to call the program. There was a consensus to change the term to describe the program from "day care" and to "childcare" to refer to the services needed by millions of mothers. They selected, as their most important goal, the creation of a national childcare program. The legislation to provide childcare had been introduced in the Senate, under the direction of Minnesota Senator Walter Mondale and in the House of Representatives the legislation was introduced by Indiana Congressman John Brademas.

In December Shelly was called to testify before a House Committee about "The need for childcare for the children of parents who were also employees of the government." She spoke poignantly.

"I am asking for support of all workers, many are barely off welfare. They struggle to arrive at work every day. They are trying to find almost invisible credentialed childcare workers, and cope with undependable sitters. There are so many problems that must be looked at in this legislation. Many problems continue for all those families that lack consistent quality childcare.

"I speak for all parents at all levels. Children must have care when they go to work. We are doing something about it at HEW, with the plans now underway to create a childcare center right in the building." She continued to present the issues, and expected results.

The members of the committee listened with great interest. Congresswoman Patsy Mink responded when she was finished presenting her paper supporting her position that it was a great idea–an idea whose time had come!

"I agree with you!" Mrs. Mink said emphatically. "We need a childcare center on Capitol Hill to take care of our own staff's children. I just lost my secretary because she lost her sitter. We need childcare legislation, finally after all these years of hard work and countless reams of testimony and support."

Finally the first comprehensive childcare legislation in Congress passed with a resounding "Yes!" and with almost full bipartisan support.

Then the bill was sent to President Richard M. Nixon. He had promised when he spoke at the White House Conference to care about children. He knew that childcare was voted on by the delegates as the number one priority. He knew the bill was passed by bipartisan support.

Despite all the pressures from the Democrats and support among Republicans, President Richard M. Nixon vetoed the comprehensive childcare legislation. He did not understand or care about the great need or the obvious solution. Instead of "Yes" and signing the bill, he said, "Childcare would 'Sovietize' America's children." But, he never explained how anyone could possibly get off welfare, get training, or improve their living standards if they did not have good childcare.

Women had to work in America, as they do in the Soviet Union, in Canada or anywhere else. They also needed childcare when they volunteered for services to their community. His "Welfare Reform," like so many other programs he promised, instead was halted and fell completely flat. Shelly saw all her work to gain recognition for childcare services suddenly go down in heart wrenching defeat.

When she heard the disappointing news, she thought about finding a voodoo doll, but instead went directly to Marvin's office and angrily expressed her deep frustrations,

"Marv, how could Nixon do this…after all our work, all the support from so many groups, and the obvious need? How could he do this?"

He laughed, "Why not? He never has to think about hiring a baby sitter. Pat does it all!"

Shelly didn't think it was funny. She was feeling deeply depressed, and very upset about the veto.

"Marv, he just killed our program! All the work we have put in all these years. All of the meetings, and the huge number of proposals, asking for assistance that came in from everywhere. Childcare was the number one priority at the White House Conference. There are so many families that need childcare. This is the Office of the President yet he killed the program. That man should be impeached!"

Shelly retorted and hit the table for further emphasis.

Marvin totally agreed. He said "You should think seriously about graduate school. I think you would get the fellowship, if I put in a good letter of support."

He added, "There is very little else we can do now. Congress will not overturn the veto. They do things that are most expedient for them. Even what they do is just "window dressing." Meanwhile, if you get your degree, who knows, perhaps things will change for the better later. Then you can return and resume where you left off."

He said smiling, "Who said transforming and improving the social conditions in America would be easy?"

Shelly replied, "Thank you for everything you have done to be of help. I am in shock. Maybe the best thing I can do is to get away from all this, get some perspective, and get that doctorate. We can work together again, later on, hopefully…" She said wistfully trailing off.

She felt dismayed as she left his office.

The impact of the veto would have an effect on all parents, all over the country, especially those who had to work. What surprised her most was the lack of strong objections from all of the women and children's organizations, or the complete failure of a Congressional override, or even a loud public outcry. Childcare was merely expedient to politicians.

Children again were the victims of the apathy of adults. What would it take to shake them up? Neglect of children did not seem to get anyone to change things. Years before when children died in the fields someone did respond. When children were left alone in empty apartments or died in fires someone did respond, but, there was little change in policies at the national level that responded to the needs that for so long only grew more intense.

Her hopes that the government would act to improve childcare services came to a sudden halt. A job with no program, monies, or support held no interest or future for her.

Shelly considered her choices. It was time to leave the "security" of the job, and everything else she had previously held important in Washington. She had to find another way to approach a solution to the problem. She was convinced that her professional life would work better if she got her Ph.D. She could return to government when politics changed. It was a matter of time. She knew she needed the credentials. Crying would not solve any problem.

Marv wrote an enthusiastic letter of support. Shelly submitted everything and then got the good news that her application to graduate school was accepted. She would be able to study in California. She would enter the National University Graduate School. She would be able to develop an innovative research program on childcare in California.

She suddenly felt that a whole new chapter of her life was starting. She was ready to turn the page. Shelly was happy when she got the news. She could hardly wait to tell Doug.

He shared her happiness,

"Congratulations, Doctor to be. I am proud of you. Screw Nixon. He'll get his. Believe me. He will get his comeuppance."

Shelly laughed at his use of comeuppance as she thought of both karma and comeuppance as the potential fate of payback for Nixon ignoring the needs of children.

"I just don't understand," said Shelly, "that a man, who could become a president, and was the governor of California, could also be so out of contact with families and reality. How could he make the excuse that the services would 'Sovietize' America's children? Europe is far ahead of the USA in support of children! What's wrong with that?"

Doug replied, "It happens all the time, unfortunately. You should know by now the way politics works. It's not about people. It's about power and manipulation. Anyway, you will be here. That's what's important now. Just try to let go of what happened. I am waiting for you. I am horny for you. I want you!"

Shelly lay back on her bed and touched her heart and her belly, as Doug talked her to sleep. She did not turn on the TV that night.

The next week he called to tell her that his divorce was final, and he was able to gain custody of his three children, and had moved back to his home.

He was free, and so was she.

She could hardly believe it was all true.

She finally was able to put the whole program together—school, funds, focus, and the most of all the approved leave. She would be able to continue to make the contributions she was determined to make, especially after she took the needed educational detour. What else? She was not sure. She decided to put all the plans together. The destination of her dreams, the program, and her love life was to finally be in San Francisco.

The final piece was the lab for the research, that came together also through her connections with the right people who supported her efforts. So finally, Shelly was able to stitch together the quilt containing the pieces of her future. She worked on all of the details. Each piece of the quilt came together slowly as she planned what was needed: to find an apartment close to Doug, the relocation move, and all the rest. She wanted to move slowly so everyone would get to know each other. She would work on the school program, study, and the other details. Slowly she was remaking the quilt of her life, the past, the present, and the unknown future. Her thoughts raced ahead as she flew to join Doug. He welcomed her with open arms. Her body and her heart were wide open.

Alison was content to be at home with Flora.

Within two days she found a cozy, completely furnished apartment just a short distance from Doug's house. It was convenient, at the end of a little quiet street, Rosemont Street, just off 14th St., near Dolores Avenue. It was close to the Mission Dolores and the miles of palm trees. It was all perfect. They would be near everything, and the rent was reasonable. The apartment had two bedrooms, a yard, and plenty of space for Alison.

She told the landlord, "I will be back within the month."

She signed a lease, and left a deposit on the first month's rent.

Shelly, Doug, and his three very noisy and active children, spent a few days together touring San Francisco. She and Doug had very little time together, but Shelly was filled with happiness. She felt confident, as she felt his children's excitement, and was glad they were so enthusiastic.

Then Shelly returned to Washington to make all the final arrangements, She would rent the house, finalize her work, and say good-by to her many friends. The Apollo moon shot had landed. Shelly was also about to make her big move, "one small step for womankind." She would miss everyone, especially her dearest girlfriend, Rhonda.

They had grown up near each other in Queens, New York. Shelly had connected Rhonda and Richard Hartfield with their very first date when they were sixteen. They were perfect together from that first evening. She saw how perfect their marriage was. Rhonda and Richard stayed close together; Shelly wanted an enduring relationship, too. Now, she finally had Doug. They would love each other in ways they had never experienced before, love their children, love their families, and grow old together. She met Rhonda for lunch at DuPont Circle one day.

"Shelly, I know you will be happy. You deserve it," said Rhonda.

"I don't know for sure what is going to happen in the future, but he sure is wonderful. I love him very much," replied Shelly.

"Great. It's time for you to have someone special, too. Richard and I are so happy for you. I don't want us to lose touch even though you'll be 3000 miles from here." Rhonda reached out to hold her old friend's hand. She wanted to reassure her.

Shelly responded, "No way. I would never forget my dearest and oldest friend. Besides who knows me as well as you do?"

They laughed. Then they talked about their children, their families, and the future for Shelly and Alison in California. Shelly was very happy that Rhonda liked the idea of her plans even if her own mother and sister did not. The month passed quickly.

Her former husband, Arnold, had no objections to Alison leaving Washington.

He was only seeing Alison infrequently. It did not matter and he was actually relieved.

Arnold called her after he got her message, "I am glad for you, Shelly. I hope that you find a lot of happiness. I am glad for Alison. She will love California."

Shelly asked him, "Will you stay in contact? Come out and visit sometime?"

"Sure. Why not? I could get to like California, too." He seemed pleased to learn Shelly was having a relationship with Doug. Perhaps his own guilt about abandoning her and his child at an early age was lessened now by Shelly's new relationship.

Shelly handled all her business, the house, and she got things ready for herself and Alison. She gave Flora specific instructions on everything she needed, and how to keep in touch with her while she was in California. She promised to call every day. Meanwhile she made sure Flora had a new family to live with after they left Washington, DC

She and Doug talked every day. They discussed the plans, school, and their new life together in California. She reviewed all the activities she was expected to do for the doctoral residency program.

Shelly and Alison talked about California.

"Alison, I am so glad that you are happy about going to California. Mommy found a great place for us to live...an apartment. You will stay here with Flora for one more month. I have to go to California to go school. Then I will come back and get you. Then you and I will go back together to San Francisco. Then we can ride together on the cable cars and have lots of fun."

Alison clapped her hands and got into bed. Shelly sang her favorite song: the one that she had written for her when she was a baby:

"Go to sleep now pretty little one,
Go to sleep now, dear.
Close your eyes and dream a little dream,
When you awake I'll be here.
Sunflowers tall on the mountainside,
Blue bells ring from afar,
Clouds go rolling over your head,
You can reach for a star.
Mommy loves you in all that you do.
Daddy cares just the same.
There will be a place for you in the sun,
And in the wind and the rain."
When the song was finished Alison was asleep.

Shelly hugged and kissed Alison good-by the next day. Alison wasn't exactly sure of what was happening, but she waved good-by and blew kisses from the front door as Shelly left for the airport.

As the cab drove across the Memorial Bridge in Virginia, Shelly looked back at Washington, her home for the past ten years. She wondered how life could suddenly be condensed into one speeding reel. Memories brushed her mind's projector as the cab sped to the airport.

Shelly saw herself ten years earlier, a hopeful bride leaving New York City to be with Arnold. She recalled the house getting remodeled, the dog-training classes, the birds and the baby birds, and dinner parties. She knew how much she had wanted it all –love, marriage, and success in her own right – she tried. She saw Alison's smiling face. She remembered the different jobs she held during the ten years in Washington. She thought about how much she had tried to work things out with Arnold. She was ready for a new life.

Moving towards love and the future, she boarded the plane and headed west in the direction her mind and hopeful heart were headed.

Chapter 8

California Dreaming

We are such stuff as dreams are made of. William Shakespeare

A new beginning! Graduate school for a doctoral degree! Shelly held tight to the dream for ten years. The graduate school program would allow her to study and to develop a special project. She decided to focus on parents' problems finding the right childcare for their families' needs. She would create a solid but flexible program. She would need all the flexibility she could gather to manage everything. Shelly knew she could make a valuable contribution in her field. She made a plan for a study that, in the future, could improve planning for childcare services.

One of the requirements for the program at the New School for Innovation at the National University was to spend a month in residence. The first residency program was to be held near the small historic town of Sonoma, forty miles north of San Francisco.

The plane ride to San Francisco, which normally takes five hours from Washington, D.C., was the shortest trip. Her mind was so full of thoughts that five hours passed without noticing. She felt her life was moving in an exciting and new direction, and she thought about how finally work and family would all be in balance along with a committed personal relationship that was dedicated to the same purpose of serving and full of sharing, caring and loving.

Shelly's dreams finally were all coming true. She was gathering the kindling to create a fire under a new life with Alison in a new place full of new adventures, people and challenges. But, Shelly felt ready to handle whatever was in store—she had known fire and ice before, but now she was ready for warmth and comfort.

Doug was eagerly waiting for her at the gate.

He waved and greeted her with a warm smile, then embraced her tightly.

Doug said," I'm so glad you are finally here. The plans are all set: you will stay over at the house tonight, and. early in the morning we will take off to Sonoma with the kids."

"Are they excited? She asked

"Yes, they could not wait to pack the sleeping bags and get their gear together. They love to go camping," he added.

Shelly nodded, thinking how much fun that would be, and added, "I would love to do that with Alison, too, sometime. I went camping when I was a Girl Scout," she told him.

They both laughed.

Doug described the state park where he was going to take the children. The park was a short distance from the ranch in Sonoma where the month-long seminar would be.

He said, "The Park has campsites and good accommodations. The kids love to gather wood and sit around the fire making 'smores.'" Shelly smiled, because she could almost taste the ones she enjoyed as a Girl Scout.

He added, "It's safe and they can handle things at the camp when I come over to keep you warm." She smiled at him and thought of the good times they would all have together.

"It's wonderful that they can fend for themselves and be responsible."

"Yes," he replied. "I feel they are able to manage without me for a few hours. They read, play, and stay close to the campsite. It's all safe and there is nothing to worry about."

She relaxed, because he had it all figured out, and she convinced herself that everything was going to work out."

As they drove in from the airport, she felt a special pang as she caught sight of "The City." She was excited to see the water, the hills, and the magnificent sunset.

Doug said, "Everything is ready!"

She smiled at him and said, "I am so happy to finally be with you on your side of the country for more than just a few days."

As they arrived at Doug's house, nestled on Twin Peaks, she looked at the sparkling lights of the city. Excitement permeated her whole body.

Doug grabbed her suitcase from the trunk of the car and they walked to the door. The children weren't home yet. They were visiting their mother, but they would be arriving shortly. Suddenly, Shelly felt uneasy. She suddenly saw clearly the new challenges of their future together. Thoughts rushed in her head, as she imagined the problems, the adjustments for herself, Doug, and for each of the children.

All of the thoughts about the possible problems suddenly flashed in her head: It might be difficult for them accept her. They would be jealous of any attention she or he gave Alison. Alison has special needs. She did have to focus on her adjustments. Could she be fair and treat each one as an individual? What about their mother? Was she angry about the divorce? Would she be taking out her feelings on the children? Would they dislike her for being in their father's life? Was she moving too fast? Was she the fish in the pan or the fire?

She quickly dismissed her growing fears. Reality was setting in. She tried to get a handle on the flood and find a few mental sandbags to defray the flood of thoughts rushing her brain.

She drew some deep breaths. Shelly felt confident in her ability to get along with the children. She would solve each problem as it arose. She could handle the challenges. They would work things out. It would only take time and patience, balance and a solid sense of humor. Yes, she really needed to locate her funny bone. Things had not felt funny for a long time—not at work, nor home, nor dealing with the strain of starting a new life a long distance from everything she knew.

Shelly thought about her years of training and experience working with children. She was confident that her past had prepared her for whatever might happen. She remembered all of the children she had taught over the years. She knew children, and she could manage whatever challenges they might each have. She knew they would come to accept and love Alison like a sister, and Alison would be happy to have a sister and two brothers. They would all get along and be one big happy family. Then she realized she was the fish flying out of the pan of comfort into the fire of the unknown.

She turned to Doug, "Have you told the children I would be coming?"

"No, not really," he said. "I wanted them to get to know you again themselves. I thought it best for them to form their own opinions without a big buildup from me. The last time they seemed to like you."

She nodded in agreement. She took a deep breath to reassure herself.

Doug poured two glasses of wine and they took their first sip and toasted to the future as the children burst in, all of them chattering at once.

Shelly felt overwhelmed by their noise, yet comfortable with them. She saw they were as active, bright, and as talkative as they were on the last visit. They asked her a cacophony of questions.

"What do you do in Washington?" I work for the federal government.

"What are you doing in California?" I will be going to graduate school.

"What do you like about San Francisco?" Everything!

"Do you like the 49ers?" They are a great team.

"How old is your daughter?" She is five years old.

"Where is she?" in Washington DC

"Is she alone now?" No she is with her sitter. "

"Do you like Hamburger Helper? It's handy for a quick meal"

She managed to answer every question. The bombardment of questions and answers flowed in a steady verbal stream of staccato interrogation.

Andy was eleven, the biggest and loudest. He was heavy in appearance and in his behavior. His voice matched the sound of a bass drum. He had a constant barrage of wisecracks that punctuated each statement he made. He also picked on his brother all of the time, and teased him constantly. He was not quiet for long, and he was quick in banter and had all the makings of a shrewd lawyer.

Ross was the middle child, nine years old, and seemed to be very nervous. He constantly moved when he talked, and never stopped twitching. He tried to shield himself as he received the onslaught of verbal and physical blows and constant teasing from his older brother. He was nevertheless enthusiastic and smiled, despite the attacks. He was curious and asked a lot of good questions. He was slim with a very nice face that showed sincerity.

Molly was the only one she felt was ready, and open to meeting and accepting her. She thought she could be a great influence on Alison and maybe soon would even grow to like each other. She was seven, curious, relaxed, talked very fast, and laughed a lot. She also asked a lot of questions. Molly seemed to like Shelly. Shelly liked her. Molly had a head full of dark curls and a ready smile.

Shelly thought, "Well, at least it's a start."

She asked them about themselves.

"Where do you go to school?"

"What do you like to do in school, and after school?"

"Do you go to the 49ers' games?"

"Where have you traveled to?"

They answered all of her questions easily and then added more of their own. She felt they would accept her when they knew she had no intention of interfering with their own relationship with their father or mother. She hoped they would continue to be open to knowing her and Alison. Their noisy preparation for bed finally dissolved into quiet slumber, as one by one they fell off to sleep.

Finally Shelly and Doug were alone in front of the fireplace in the living room talking. The crackling fire warmed them from the evening chill. She was content and glad she had jumped all the hurdles to come the three thousand miles to be with him.

When he kissed her, she felt alive again. The 'work' person dropped away easily, as she felt herself opening her whole self as a new woman for the first time ready to begin a new chapter of her life in California.

They went to his bedroom, undressed, and soon were in each other's arms. The walls were paper-thin, she constrained herself to not make sounds as she climaxed for fear of waking the children. They made love quietly and very slowly that night, before they fell asleep.

The next morning, after breakfast, they quickly filled up the car to head for Sonoma.

Shelly was pleased they were getting an early start. Finally, the car was packed. The suitcases, sleeping bags, supplies, and all of Shelly's stuff filled every crevice of the station wagon. Everyone piled in.

Then Molly had to go to the bathroom. Andy forgot his toothbrush. Ross just sat and rocked back and forth listening to the pocket radio in his hand. This was going to be a real adventure. It already was, and they hadn't even pulled out of the driveway.

Along the way the children continued to ask more questions of Shelly.

"How long are you going to school?" This is the start – a month.

"Why are you going to school?" I want to learn more about helping people.

"Why is your daughter at home?" She has to finish school, too.

"Why didn't she come with you?" She cannot attend school with me.

"Who's taking care of her?" She has a great sitter named Flora.

"Do you like Star Trek?" Sure.

"Do you like camping?" I Love to be out of doors in nature.

"How did you meet Dad?" We met at a business meeting.

And on, and on, and on, it went until finally they joined together and all sang choruses of

"Row, Row, Row Your Boat," and "Frere Jacques," and the "Woman Who Swallowed a Fly."

They crossed the Golden Gate Bridge, traveling along Highway 101 past green and yellow rolling hills, cows, horses, sheep, goats, and many beautiful trees. The vistas changed to long stretches of wine groves and vines full of green grapes. The landscape was so different in California. Shelly drank in the changes with her eyes and felt elated. She was drunk on scenery. They finally arrived at the beautiful old Watermark estate, Shelly's school for the next month. The estate in Sonoma sprawled over hundreds of acres. Nestled among the trees were a Mexican hacienda style building, many small cottages, sprawling pathways, and a huge swimming pool. The green acres were filled with plenty of sheltering trees and wonderful fields of wild flowers. Graceful peacocks strutted about and roamed among the flowers in the fields. It was the perfect setting for peace, recapturing one's inner strength, a place to retreat and study. The Watermark Ranch has just opened for the first time to the students in the graduate school she was enrolled in, The New School for Innovation at the National University.

The cottage she was to stay in for the month was a lovely, old, pale yellow house, with a small kitchen, bedroom, and a deck. Behind the cottage, Shelly looked out onto rolling brown, yellow, and green hills. She felt very glad to be there. The Yellow House was to be a nest for her to write her thoughts, experiences and firm up her plans.

She sat on the deck for a moment, weak with pleasure. Then the children joined Doug and Shelly for a noisy swim.

They walked around the place, looking at the peacocks and wild flowers, until it was time for Doug and the children to leave for the nearby campsite in the state park. They were going to have dinner around the campfire. Doug was looking happy about having time away with the children. They drove off down the road as Shelly stood in front of the gates and waved goodbye.

After dinner, Shelly and the other students assembled with the school's coordinator, Dr. Roy Fairfield. He was quick, enthusiastic, clear minded and positive coach for each student as he helped to guide each on their own pathway of deeper study in their areas of specialty. Roy discussed the plans that lay ahead for the month's program. The students asked many questions:

"Will you want to see our journals at the end of each week?"

"When do we start working on our projects?"

"How much time will we have to read each day?"

"What do you need us to show you as we get ready for independent study?"

"How much free time do we have each day?"

They were each feeling their way slowly in a new situation. Some were ready and some were not quite ready, but they were all moving ahead one way or another.

There was socializing among the students afterwards. They sat around the Spanish tiled pool in intense pods of conversations. Shelly found each one of the students interesting. Each had a different path that had brought them here and a plan that was formulating for their individual program. She was among a stimulating group of people from whom she would learn a great deal. The diversity of the students' interests, geographic origins, and personalities was impressive. She knew she had made the right choice.

During the month of study, there would be guest presentations by outstanding people that she had only heard of or read about before. The visitors would include Carl Rogers, a renowned psychologist and author, John Vasconcellos, a humanistically-oriented California State legislator, Anna Halprin, an extraordinary dance and movement performer and teacher, and many others.

Best of all she would grow to know Roy Fairfield, the Director of the entire program, who envisioned this new school without walls. He would talk with her about her plans and inspire her to keep track of everything in a journal. She never had a chance to do that before. She was able to take stock of her years working in the government and all the changes that had transpired. She was ready to reflect, and to write, and live out the challenges that were hers to face. Roy was there to provide guidance, support and coaching as she needed it.

The daily interactions among the students were a source of inspiration, interest, and personal challenge. They discussed their personal goals with each other and shared their fears and fantasies for the future. They all had plans, only some of them were more clearly spelled out. They shared their experiences of the past. They struggled with defining what they wanted to achieve. They explored.

The students learned from each other in each encounter session, which gave them time to discover their own needs for personal growth. There was a lot of laughter, listening, sharing, and often tears, as old defenses crumbled and melted away.

They were to each clarify and develop their own specific programs for their studies. This was the more intense and challenging part. The structure was theirs to create. The process and the outcomes were theirs to shape. They received guidance, but they had to work on the details until the plans were approved.

During the first two weeks, Doug came to the ranch once a day, sometimes with the children, but often alone. During those few precious hours, Shelly and Doug caught up and talked about their own plans, and learned more about each other. They did not sleep together during the entire month. They did not feel comfortable leaving the children at the campsite for more than a few hours, but the children were happily occupied reading the books they had brought with them, playing games, and doing quiet things around their campsite.

Washington slipped farther and farther away. Shelly missed Alison very much. She called her to talk every day even though it was not easy to make phone calls from the one phone booth that seemed to be always occupied. She also called Rhonda, her old friend, to let her know everything was going well.

She realized what an incredible opportunity attending this innovative graduate school was. She began to write in a journal, and felt free for the first time to write exactly what she wanted, and let it flow from her thoughts through her fingers. A trail of her own consciousness was forming.

Journal writing was an amazing process: before, she hardly had time to capture her feelings within herself, let alone take the time to describe them. Now she was laughing a lot at what she was feeling and writing in words. This would be a very interesting and worthwhile experiment.

In her free time, Shelly loved walking in the sprawling woods and up the hill, where gnarled trees shaded her from the sun while she sat reading and writing. Quietly she contemplated her future. As the days slipped by, she realized it would soon be time to return to Washington.

While the month she had spent in residence was stimulating on a professional level, it was even more satisfying personally. She liked the networking, the personal exchange the program provided, and the opportunity for students to talk, share, and grow. Though informal in nature, it was designed to be a new form of structure to "support the capable, thoughtful, and independent graduate student."

During the month she got to know Penny Watermark, the tall, robust, energetic woman who owned the ranch; Dwight, her impressive and friendly husband, and their three outgoing children. The Watermarks liked the idea of having students studying at the ranch. They were warm, and hospitable to each of the students.

Shelly felt a friendship with Penny would develop. She was the only student that would remain in the Bay Area and she hoped to see Penny again. They enjoyed chatting together over breakfast, remaining over coffee long after it got cold. Penny had a unique view about life and she was open about sharing her views. Her easy laughter was infectious.

She asked Shelly, as they shared the warmth of the coffee and sunshine, "How on earth could you stand working in a cold office in Washington, D.C., when there is so much more to do outside in the world?"

Shelly nodded her head, "You are right. I needed to get far away to get a new perspective on what I have been doing to just survive."

She looked around at her new perspective and liked what she saw. It was time for a big change.

Then there was Roy Fairfield, the remarkable person who initiated the new innovative graduate school program. He was the most supportive person she had ever met, and cared deeply about his students and gave them ample opportunities to delve into themselves. He warmly supported Shelly's ideas by encouraging her to write in her journal, and helping her think about writing articles, and work out her focus on what was needed to fulfill the goals of the program. She had not seen herself as a writer before. She was inspired by Roy to open herself to creative expression, and to try spreading her wings. He asked her thoughtful questions that challenged her. He was short, wiry and curious about everything, but most of all a dedicated teacher.

She felt connected to her inner self again because Roy encouraged and gave her permission to experience what she needed most to feel–authenticity. It was a new feeling. She had pushed herself so hard for so many years to achieve in school, marriage, work, in one job after another, teaching, earning her master's degree, and then working in federal service, that she barely recognized the woman behind the façade.

In the past she had written many papers for the government, plenty of professional articles and speeches, and prepared strategic books for others. Now, it was her chance to write personal observations and thoughts in a journal. She experimented by writing poetry. She made lists, and thought about all the articles she wanted to write. She jotted down memories of dreams. She made short notes and comments. She made a few sketches to help her to remember thoughts that felt profound at the time. While she made plans for the childcare study, she continued writing daily in her journal:

"The place we are living in is beautiful. I feel closer to nature than ever before. Part is the sun, the water, and beauty of this place. It is a perfect natural setting. I am returning to my inner spring. I want to drink of that water until I am no longer thirsty. I may finally quench five years of fear by drinking from the well of myself…"

One day at poolside she met Herb Stone, a Rabbi, who originally lived in New Jersey. Now he planned to travel to different parts of the country pursuing his studies. He and his wife, Marsha, had come to the Sonoma class to plan to deepen his studies of Judaism. He wanted to study important integrating rituals such as the Sabbath, and he shared many interests in music and family. Herb talked about the importance of the Sabbath to bring the whole family together. He said it was not only a special time each week to rest; it was a time for the family and community to rekindle the lights of self-renewal. It was a time for everyone to celebrate. They decided to prepare a Sabbath together for the other students. As they made preparations, Shelly shared with Herb her love for Doug.

"When we met it was like a door opening. I had to enter to find out what was on the other side." Shelly told Herb. "Look how that step brought me here," she added. "It's all mystical to me."

Herb replied, "We never know the path God has created for us, but we take a single step at a time and it all works out just as it's supposed to."

Shelly asked "Did he open the door for me or did I choose it?"

Herb explained "We always choose!"

Herb met Doug when he arrived later that afternoon.

Shelly excused herself to get drinks from the kitchen. Herb and Doug nodded hello, walking towards the lounge area near the pool they shook hands.

Doug said, "Shelly tells me you are new to California. How do you like the change?"

"We haven't had much to go on since my wife and I arrived a few days before this program started. The heat feels like summer in Michigan."

"I'm from Chicago. I still remember those sweltering days. Shelly says you're doing a Sabbath tonight. I would like to help out and do one of the blessings," Doug offered.

"Sure. I can use all the help I can get. How is the camping going with the kids?" asked Herb.

"It's fun. So far, there have been no bears or mountain lions, just lots of noisy kids in the wild. It's good for them to tear loose. Sometimes, I'm not sure if they need a dad or an animal trainer…maybe a little of both. Shelly will have her hands full using child psychology on this group!"

They laughed.

Shelly heard them laughing as she returned with several cans of soda, and passed them around.

"How are you fellows getting along?" she said.

"We are talking of your using psychology on little wild animals with two legs," smiled Doug.

"Actually, we also started talking about the Sabbath tonight. Doug has offered to help. Maybe he's a regular 'born-again Rabbi' and not really a doctor." Herb laughed and looked at Doug.

Then he added, "Actually, Shelly, I was going to ask you to light the candles. Do you know the prayer?" asked Herb.

"Yes," Shelly answered quickly. "I'll be happy to do it. After all, it's a woman's place to light the candles on Friday night, isn't it?"

"I'm glad she knows her place," said Doug. "Of course lighting the candles is only a beginning."

"I enjoy lighting your fire, too, Rabbi Douglas," she said, playfully reaching for him.

"It's nice to be an inspiration for you. Maybe it's time to get this relationship into focus and make it more solid than only flames, unless of course, you just want to continue to float together indefinitely," Herb said.

Shelly and Doug looked at each other and laughed.

"If you are referring to marriage, all I can say is who has time to get married?" Doug said.

"We're too busy and having too much fun!" They both said in unison.

"Actually," said Doug, "it's not the right time. We have been on the phone, traveling, and never in the same place long enough to make it 'official.' But it sure feels right to me."

Shelly quickly added, "Me too!"

With that, they finished their drinks, watched the swimmers in the pool, and laughed.

They each had their own picture of what, when, and where the wedding might take place.

Shelly jumped in the water. As she swam back and forth she dreamed.

Shelly visualized her wedding in the synagogue, dressed in a long cream colored gown, with attendants dressed in pastel lavender bridesmaids' dresses, and lively Klezmer music. This time there would be everything she had missed the first time around with Arnold. She wanted to experience some of the great traditions and take time to have it all.

Doug sat at poolside watching Shelly swimming. He imagined Shelly and him at City Hall rushing in with four children in tow, saying, "Quick, we're all on our lunch break. We have to get right back to work and get the kids back to school." He laughed as he pictured it.

Herb watched the peacocks strutting by and imagined Shelly and Doug around the traditional Chuppah (tent) with their parents, children, and friends around. He saw Doug break the glass as he pronounced them man and wife.

Everyone then shouted "Mazel Tov!" "Good luck!"

Herb said he had to return to his cabin to get ready for the Sabbath. He walked away next to the Eucalyptus, not a native California tree, but still a very prolific tree. It was sunset. Sabbath was coming soon.

Chapter 9

Hill Top

To be a Jew is a destiny. Vicki Baum

Friday evening, The Sabbath, Shelly and Herb gathered the other students around the table, near the pool, on the patio of the Hacienda at the Ranch, to celebrate. Doug brought the children. Their sleeping bags were secured on the deck behind the Yellow House.

Shelly looked at Doug, and at the children, with smiles of great love. She was happy to share a special experience, of peace, joy, and a time for rest, with her new friends, fellow students, faculty, ranch staff, and all of the Watermarks. Shelly felt a connection with each one, and she was at peace within.

The sun was setting over the green hills and the air was still.

Lighting the Sabbath candles, Shelly closed her eyes, raised her outstretched arms, covered her eyes with her hands, fanned her face, turned her hands toward the light of the candle flame, and then spoke softly, from a deep place within her heart,

"Blessed art Thou,
O Lord our God,
King of the Universe,
who has sanctified us
to light the Sabbath candles.
It is kindled in our hearts.
Love and light.
Blessings to all around this circle,
who have the opportunity to study,
to learn, to share, and grow together.
Blessed art Thou, O Lord, Our God
who has brought us all together. Amen!"

Shelly gave Doug a long loaf of sourdough bread.

He held the bread and easily recited the traditional blessing for the harvest providing the bread.

Shelly gazed at him, filled with happiness. She felt she had met her match: they were unified in love, the history of their historic past, and were reunited finally after being so long apart. The prayers melted away the centuries, the history, the blessings, the distance, the pain, the ritual, all fused into the light of the candles. Memories melted with the candles and the sanctity of the Sabbath.

Doug passed the loaf of bread to others in the circle as they each selected small pieces of the symbolic bread to eat.

Herb raised his glass as he blessed the delicious Sonoma Valley wine. Doug joined him in the blessing. Ross and Andy were moved to see the two men joined in familiar prayers. They were studying Hebrew (in preparation for their Bar Mitzvahs) and had heard the prayers many times, but this was the first time they celebrated the Sabbath as a family and with strangers. It made them feel proud.

Molly smiled and looked happy. She was glad her dad had found Shelly, and they were all together. She felt better about her parent's divorce, adjusting to Shelly, and whatever was going to happen next. She felt secure and ready. She paid attention to the prayer for the candles and thought it was time to learn it.

Shelly missed Alison. She felt an emptiness that she was not there at that moment to share the joy of the Sabbath. She wanted her daughter to know she would soon be with them and have a happy, safe, and fun new home. Shelly knew there was a lot to look forward to. Right now she just wanted the Sabbath moment of peacefulness to sink in.

They passed a few bottles of the Sonoma vintage around the group and poured glasses of the robust local wine. After the last piece of bread was eaten they raised their glasses and in unison said, "L'Chaim."

They walked, all together, laughing and talking, to the dining room where they continued congeniality, songs, a delicious meal, and a wonderful evening. Everyone felt happy to be part of their first Sabbath celebration. Herb happily answered many questions while Shelly and Doug were content just to look at each other. The children ate and then went directly to their sleeping bags. They crawled inside their bags without much effort and quickly fell asleep behind The Yellow Cabin.

Very quietly, as the moon shone in through the window, she and Doug finally made love. They did not want to waken anyone. She silently experienced the ecstasy of feeling complete.

The next day, Saturday, was sunny and beautiful. The kids grabbed buckets, and went berry picking with two of the Watermark children. Happily they ate berries wherever they found them.

Herb, Doug, and Shelly walked up into the hills behind the cabin. Talking of love, of the long journey, how precious their relationships were, and how much fun they had sharing the Sabbath.

At the top of the hill, Shelly looked at Doug and said, "I love you."

"I love you." Doug replied.

They clasped hands and embraced.

"You can be married at this moment on this hill under the sky." Herb suggested, "You only need your pledge to each other and to God. I am here only as a witness."

Doug looked into Shelly's eyes. "Will you marry me?"

Shelly smiled and quickly answered, "Of course I will."

They smiled at each other, touched hands and kissed.

Herb created "an instant ceremony."

He blessed their commitment, love, and with raised arms said aloud:

"I now pronounce you husband and wife."

They kissed again and held each other.

Herb looked at them and witnessed their love and commitment to each other.

They all laughed.

Shelly felt so ecstatic, so she climbed an Oak tree and sat in the branches.

Doug reached up. "I love you so much."

She looked at him. "Can you feel my heart?"

She slipped down into his arms and they kissed.

Shelly opened up her pack, removed an apple, some bread, cheese, and a jug of water. With the water they made a toast. She cut the apple, cheese and bread into pieces they could share. Then they sprawled out under the shade of the trees for an instant "Wedding Celebration Picnic."

That afternoon when they came down the hill, everyone was curious. It was clear something special had happened. Doug and Shelly hugged the children. At last, the years of waiting were past. Shelly's heart was full.

Later on when she had some time alone Shelly wrote in her journal:

"What I want is more time to share these precious moments.

Knowing you understand.

I learned you unfolding before me.

We come together, not afraid to stand bare as the hills.

We explore the hidden valleys of ourselves,

Learn to trust one another.

Sunlight passes gently over our heads.
We have been alone too long.
Lengths of times flow when I am with you, even in thought,
I am closer to the shadow crevices of myself.
I am not yet able to cast light into all the dark places.
They grow smaller with love.
Time is all.
We have so much to share.
The time is now."

That night after the children were asleep, Shelly and Doug embraced again, more happily than ever. They were finally connected. Shelly felt they were 'soul mates,' ready for whatever the future would bring. Secure in their union, they slept easily after making love again very quietly, so no one would hear them.

During the month of study Shelly was continuously grateful for the opportunity to be in the innovative graduate program. She learned from the other students; they had many discussions and gained many new perspectives. Each day they spent discussing their own process and plans.

As the days passed Shelly became more confident about what she would attempt to accomplish. But it soon became a much larger, more detailed, and more complicated project than she first imagined, but she felt confident she could do anything.

During the last week together, after much discussion and thinking,

Shelly hugged Roy and said, "Roy, I am finally certain about what I want to do next."

"Roy, when I return to California in the fall you will receive my entire plan in written form. I will work out everything from this outline and indicate clear markers that will define each of the goals. I understand what I must do to get everything ready for the approval of the committee."

She continued, "I know I have to bring my full committee together. That will be a challenge as they are spread across the country, but I am sure we can exchange and get all of the details worked out. They support my efforts."

Roy agreed and then he suggested, "Write in your journal every day. Try to be more patient with yourself. You have taken on a lot to handle all at once. Take time to also be alone. As much as you are a nurturing mother, taking care of others, also care for yourself."

She thought about his sensitive suggestions. Only once before did she know a teacher at Queens College, her professor of Education, Dr. Deborah Partridge Wolfe, who considered her well-being as a whole person. This was a great realization. This program was indeed an innovative experience. He would not only read and respond to everything she wrote. He also provided careful, thoughtful, and astute guidance on both professional and personal goals.

Shelly laughed at the suggestion he made about being "alone." She hardly knew what being alone was. She was never alone. Things were changing rapidly. She barely had time to think and write. Time passed quickly.

At the final gathering of students, everyone was sad to say good-by. She knew she might never see some of them again. They would scatter back to the places they had come from. Despite common goals they would not all cross the finish line. She had come to know each of them very well during the month. Those she had deeply connected with she would miss.

She knew she would continue to be friends with Peter, Herb, his pregnant wife, Marsha, and some of the other students. She liked Dean and Sol. She would definitely want to see them whenever she got back to New York City. Betty was hard to talk to, and remained aloof and distant. Reggie was enthusiastic about his work and what the future held for him. Tom knew exactly what he had to do in health services and was determined to complete the program. They had each made new friends, some for life. They each would follow their own path. They wished each other a successful journey.

Shelly felt happy and excited about the future. She felt deeply connected to Doug. The time together for the launch of their new life was perfect in all ways, for mind, and for heart.

The last night at the ranch, they slept together under the stars, not far from where they had spoken aloud their vows. They were filled with the lights of the starry night. They drank to love with a glass of wine and celebrated their very brief honeymoon. The children were asleep in sleeping bags behind The Yellow House dreaming of wild berries.

In the car the next morning on the way back home, Shelly and the kids enthusiastically sang camp songs. When she and Doug sang some of their favorite songs from the '40s, the kids quickly pretended to fall asleep after making a few funny faces.

Back in San Francisco, Shelly went by to check on the apartment. Everything was in order.

Then she met Doug for dinner.

Everything seemed perfect. She was really happy. They had one day left to be together before she had to return to Washington.

The last day she spent a few hours with the children driving around to some of their special places in Golden Gate Park. They showed her the Carousel, Stowe Lake, and the Japanese Teahouse. Then they drove out to Playland

and the Cliff House to run on the beach, watch seagulls and enjoy the Ocean.

That evening Shelly and Doug went out for a romantic dinner on Nob Hill at Julius' Castle and looked out at the bright and sparkling city. Then they drove across town towards Doug's house at the top of Twin Peaks.

Looking down again she felt elated to capture in her mind countless lights like millions of fireflies. The night was bursting like the sparklers on the Fourth of July. She loved her new city: the diamond hills, twinkling lights, clanging cable car bells, and comfortable coziness of the city. Everything blended together and made the city shine and sparkle like a gigantic jewel.

She saw many parts of the city from many views; the large multi- layered Bay, the stately Victorians, Pacific Heights mansions, the hippy stragglers, retro stores of the Haight, the diverse landscape of Golden Gate Park, the fishing boats and the hustle of the piers of Fisherman's Wharf, the bustling neighborhoods of the Mission, SOMA, Chinatown, Bernal Heights, Japantown, Sunset, Richmond, the Castro, Portrero Hill, and North Beach. She appreciated the majesty of City Hall, The Opera, and the Ocean--and everything was beautiful.

Her new favorite walk was around Stow Lake and taking time to share some bread with the ducks. It was a perfect crown jewel. San Francisco was a city of magic, a crystal ball spinning the future.

The happiest thought of all was knowing Doug would be her partner. She would make a new life for herself and Alison. They would all be as one, a new blended family. In one month she would return with her child, her possessions, her past behind her, and totally ready to start a new life.

This time, when Doug took her to the airport, there was no sadness. She knew she would be coming back very soon. They warmly kissed good-by.

As Shelly boarded the aircraft, Doug waved again and blew her kisses.

As she buckled her seatbelt Shelly felt content.

As the plane taxied down the runway she closed her eyes and remembered the last time she and Doug had made love. She was full of the events of the past month, safe in the knowledge of the new life, now just really beginning. The time passed quickly and finally landing at Dulles Airport

Alison was standing at the gate wildly waving her arms. Flora assured Shelly everything had gone well in her absence.

Arnold, her former husband, had made time to be with Alison once a week, stopping by the house on his way home from work.

As she lifted her, Shelly noticed Alison seemed to have grown. A new family would be great for Alison. Doug's children would come to appreciate, understand, and accept Alison.

Flora filled her in on all of the news. They chatted in English and Spanish all the way through the airport and continued as they picked up the suitcases, found a cab, and went back to the house.

Later that night, after Alison was asleep and Flora went out for the evening, Shelly called Doug.

"Hi. Guess where I am?"

"Wish you were still here in my arms," he said.

"I am. Just use your imagination."

"I miss you!"

"Are we really married?" she asked.

"Only God knows for sure. Do you feel married?" Doug asked.

"Yes, I do," Shelly replied.

"Well, that settles it, doesn't it?" laughed Doug.

"Doug, we're not legal," cautioned Shelly.

"Legal schmegal! Herb said, It 'is what's in our hearts. I feel more married to you in these last few weeks than I did being married for the past thirteen years," replied Doug.

"I guess so! But, one day I really think we need to make it really legal. It wouldn't change anything. Things couldn't be much better."

Shelly realized she wanted reassurance.

"Hurry up and get back here before I get horny. I love you."

"I love you, too. Meanwhile, play tennis, and take a few cold showers," she advised laughing.

Doug laughed. "Talk with you tomorrow. Goodnight, my darling, kiss Alison for me."

"Goodnight." Shelly kissed him over the phone.

Then she fell asleep.

Meanwhile, things were not going so easily for Doug at his job. He had plenty to cope with: Meetings every day on some urgent problem or another new crisis to solve. The latest was the growing discontent of the nurses. They wanted more benefits.

Janet Grover was a sharp-tongued, attractive, and experienced nurse. She knew her way around the system at the hospital. She had graduated from the UC system years before and knew how to handle the doctors, and supervise the nurses. She was a "tough cookie," but with a little encouragement could laugh and have a great time when she let her hair down.

She decided to let Doug know exactly how she felt. "It's about time you doctors took the side of the nurses instead of siding with administration. It's too bad you are so selfish by only looking out for your own interests and not seeing ours," she said to Doug in his office the next morning.

She stood her ground. She knew what she was saying from experience.

She saw that the nurses were not treated fairly by the doctors or the administration. They both took advantage of them most of the time. Nurses worked long hours for inadequate salaries, and enjoyed few of the doctor's benefits.

If they had young children, they also had childcare problems. Many of the nurses were also single mothers. Although Janet did not have children, she did feel sympathetic to those who were not able to come in because their sitters were sick, or when they lost their arrangements. She knew the hospital should have a childcare center, but that was far down the ladder on the list of priorities. Right now all they hoped to get was at least some semblance of a living wage, and some additional retirement benefits.

Doug responded as politely as he could. "I am sympathetic with your situation, Ms. Grover, and that of all the nurses. I am aware of how hard you work. You should have what you want. But, the city has cut the budget for the hospital much more than we expected. We are caught in the squeeze..." He tried to reason with her.

"Well, Dr. Fine, what have you had to give up in order to meet the budget crunch? I wonder..." She continued, "You may understand, but I don't see you taking any cuts in salary? Or did I miss something? You even get a place to park!"

"No," he replied. "I understand your feelings, but what good would a strike do–everyone would suffer, especially the patients."

"Why don't you take care of the patients more than you do? All I see is that you go to a lot of meetings," said Janet frustrated with the broken system.

"I don't want dissension between us," said Doug.

She looked at him, as if seeing him for the first time, and noticed he really appeared concerned in trying to work things out.

"Well," she huffed, "maybe you are different. I'd like to talk away from the office sometime. Should we have a bite to eat and see how much the same or differently we feel?"

He was surprised at her response and was hesitant.

Then he suggested, "Well, perhaps we could have a drink sometime at the Rite Spot and try to work things out between us."

She smiled. "Yes, dissension only keeps people apart. Maybe we could find some ways to work things out in the best interests of everyone concerned. I'm available whenever you are. Let me know when you're free, won't you?"

She smiled again, gathered up her clipboard, and walked out of his office.

Doug took a deep breath and sat down. He reached for the phone to call

Shelly. He lit up a cigarette and took a deep drag.

"She's not home. Darn! Probably went to do errands. She's so efficient! It's scary. I'm going to get into trouble if I get involved with Janet Grover, but what a fun time we could have in the sack. I probably could easily get her distracted away from organizing the strike." He smiled at the thought. He felt horny and curious at the same time.

He made some doodles on the pad, took time to sit back, and contemplated his fantasy. Smiling he sat and thought how much fun he could have to create a "score" instead of a "strike." He could make working on resolving conflicts into a fun evening.

He had not been entirely honest with Shelly. A few "quickies," he thought, wouldn't hurt anything, or anyone, especially if she didn't know about it.

As he got up to leave his office, the door opened. Jake Carter, his resident, walked in glancing back over his shoulder at Janet.

Jake said, closing the door, "Wow, you must be a master of negotiations. It's the first time I think I've ever seen that woman smile." Doug kept quiet about the reason, and quickly changed the subject to medical matters.

Chapter 10

Real Life

No pessimist ever discovered the secret of the stars, or sailed to an uncharted land, or opened a new heaven to the human spirit. Helen Keller

When Shelly returned to work, she tried to complete all of the projects she had been working on for the past year. It especially pleased her to bring to fruition some of the special childcare projects.

She was proud to have won the fight to get approval for the funding to open the first federal childcare center, which opened a Pandora's Box of interest in all agencies. She published the first study of national issues by the National Committee for Working Women, "Views on Childcare." Everything was very hard to get approved.

The Agency was now run by people who were not concerned at all about how to solve the War on Poverty, but rather on dismantling the entire operation. Somehow, despite the obstacles, the program was able to make some small, but important inroads, such as the survey on national licensing to study the standards and regulations in every state. Other studies were allowed on policy issues, curriculum, training, health facilities, and operational costs, but resistance was met at every step and stopped on any actual services.

The Administration knew services were essential to break the cycle of poverty, but solutions were not of interest to the Nixon White House, or to Donald Rumsfeld or Dick Cheney, who were running the Office of Economic Opportunity, The Office of the President.

The work Shelly faced was endless. She needed much more help to make the programs effective, but little help was forthcoming. She found real people everywhere who shared her concerns, burning to make a difference in their own community, but were helpless with no funds and no support.

There was much more to do, but that would have to wait for the right President, a more committed Congress, and a big shift in America's national priorities.

She felt she was doing the right thing to leave her dead-end job (although she was tenured and it was possible to find another non-childcare related one) now for graduate school. What else could she do?

The President, instead of supporting childcare services as he said he would, changed the course of her life by his veto of the first childcare legislation passed by a bi-partisan Congress. He stopped the potential of the program that had been passed by Congress, which did not act to overturn his decision. She had to move on. It was time to complete her studies and return one day with more clout or so she thought.

Shelly had countless preparations to make. She finally found two women to lease the house. She packed, cleaned, and prepared what she needed for herself and Alison. While she worked on everything, she also realized the enormity of the transitions taking place in her life. She felt anxious about all that was needed, but was reassured every time she thought of Doug.

As she walked slowly through her house late one night, her thoughts shifted to the past. She remembered her discovery of the house, eight years before, as she slowly packed personal objects into boxes.

She remembered how she found the house by coincidence. She had a meeting at the hotel and as she parked her car, right in the front yard, there was a "For Sale" sign. She looked at the house and knew right away, even without going inside, it was perfect. She called the number from a phone at the hotel and found out the real estate agent lived next door and had just put up the sign.

Shelly looked at the house that afternoon. She couldn't wait to show it to Arnold. He would agree, she was sure, and with a little imagination and some hard work, it would make a nice home, and be a great investment. Despite his initial objections, he thought it was a good investment and agreed finally to buy it. He wanted to be like all the old friends he grew up with in Washington and live in the suburbs and commute to the city every day.

She finally convinced him to do something different. Shelly could not remove the "New Yorker" from her blood. She opted for life in the city. Woodley Park had all the in-town community feeling she had hoped for. She liked the area even more than Georgetown. It was convenient, accessible and the house was larger at much less money. As far as she was concerned, she wanted to be as close to Rock Creek Park, culture, and her new life, as possible.

The house inside was old, drab, run-down, and needed a lot of work. But she immediately saw its potential. Arnold finally agreed. He was, after all, in the field of designing commercial spaces and furnishing them. The house was a large remodeling project and would be a real challenge for Arnold's expanding creativity.

During the remodeling project Arnold changed. He became more and more belligerent, dominating, and difficult, just as the physical work on the house began. One day he loudly erupted, shouting at her in front of the workers.

"But why, Arnold, can't we have central air-conditioning? All we have to do is install the ductwork now while the house is torn up anyway. It makes sense. "

"We don't need to add expenses now," said Arnold

"But think of the added value. Next year when we can manage, all we'll have to do is add the machinery, the ducts will be finished."

"Stop making things more complicated. Look, all we have to do is break through the brick wall and install an air conditioner there," responded Arnold

"But, our next door neighbors did the duct work. It's quiet and works perfectly all over the house. It would be so ugly to break the brick and shove an air conditioner under the window. With ducts you don't see the units."

She suffered terribly from allergies. Her condition grew worse in the hot, muggy, pollen-infested Washington spring and summer. But to Arnold, her opinions or needs didn't count. He sharply refused to listen to her suggestions even if they were practical.

Suddenly, and in front of the workers, he shouted, "This is my house! We'll do it my way!"

Shelly felt hurt, humiliated, frustrated, cried, and wondered about "mutual" in their relationship. After all, it was her money, time, and energy, too. Why was he treating her so badly? The feelings she had that night returned many times over the next few years.

She felt tense remembering the incidents. Shelly folded some of the table cloths as she tried to think about happier times, dinner parties, and she placed the cloths away. She remembered how noisy the window air conditioning units were, and how much she felt things changed.

She announced happily she was pregnant a year after the remodeling project was completed. Finally, the house was livable, they had some money saved, and everything should be perfect. When it seemed they were ready to start a family, their relationship unraveled. He was not happy she was pregnant. He did not want to attend childbirth classes, and became increasingly hostile.

Shelly did her best to stay happy, calm, and tried to be optimistic. She deeply wanted to be a mother. She felt Arnold would change in time. But, suddenly, in the third month of her pregnancy, after some unexpected bleeding, the doctor insisted she spend most of the day in bed. The doctor went on to prescribe a new drug that was supposed to be helpful, named Stilbestrol. He prescribed it to "help to avoid a miscarriage." When the danger was past,

Shelly felt content, but could see that Arnold clearly wasn't.

The charming house, successful work, comfortable lifestyle, and child did not bring them any closer. She collected all the kitchen gadgets, read and cooked from all the popular cookbooks, and tried to be as attentive and loving to Arnold in every way she knew. She entertained his boss, his clients, his business associates, and their friends and neighbors. Shelly was an excellent cook, a charming hostess, and was a loving wife who tried her best to please. She finally realized he wasn't interested in her cooking, her ability to entertain, or in her mind, spirit, or body. She felt he was no longer interested in their future. But, by then, it was too late.

She wondered why she did not see the changes coming. She saw how he treated his mother who doted on him in every way possible. She remembered how he angrily threw his shirts down the cellar steps in his mother's home. She had them washed and pressed and back in his closet the next day. All this and she worked full time, too, in the family's grocery store. She was from the old country and believed her first born son was king. She expected Shelly would treat her 'sonny boy' exactly the same way she did, and Shelly tried, but the crown got heavy.

The child was growing inside her, so she made the best of it. She wanted to have a serene pregnancy, and thought maybe Arnold would change after the baby was born. But sadly he didn't.

As Shelly walked through the rooms of the house that night gathering treasured things to pack away, she remembered her marriage promises with Arnold when she was twenty.

She had left New York and a tiny, but charming, Greenwich Village apartment she enjoyed so much.

She recalled their listening to jazz and their early passion. She recalled how unaffectionate he was otherwise. She recalled how mutual interests lessened, their personal desires and temperaments grew and they drifted apart.

Shelly, lost in her memories, walked back into the patio, sat on the brick wall under the bamboo trees, and wept for the shattered dreams of the past. The jazz of her life with Arnold had turned into discord. She sat among the plants and looked at her little bamboo garden.

She thought back to the days in the Village. She saw how she and Arnold met at the Jazz Festival in Atlantic City on the boardwalk while waiting in line for tickets. That summer in 1960, the world glowed. The Atlantic City Jazz Festival was the first to feature Count Basie and his Orchestra with Joe Williams, Sara Vaughan, Julian "Cannonball" Adderly, Dave Brubeck, Art Blakey, Dinah Washington, Oscar Peterson, Dakota Stanton, Ray Charles and His Orchestra,

Gloria Lynn, plus the one and only, "Symphony Sid," as Emcee.

The music was hot. In between sets they were hot together leaning together toward the moon strategically just above their heads and it seemed just a short distance over the boardwalk.

After that weekend, a wonderfully romantic musical weekend of making out and enjoying each other, Arnold wrote her a love letter that touched her heart:

"I want to say so much, to hold you in my arms,
To kiss your lips, to look into your happy eyes, and
To tell you how great my love is. My darling, you are my life;
Without my life I cannot exist. Life is now so beautiful and wondrous
That the trees appear greener, the people seem happier,
And my love grows deeper as each minute passes.
I can see your face before me, smiling, flowing,
Telling everyone with your smile,
The search has ended and our life is beginning.
We will grow and mature together like the two strong elm trees,
Standing side by side in all kinds of weather.
How deep you are, like a beautiful ocean."

She dreamed of these words of passion being expressed to her. He visited her in the Village where they spent romantic days and nights that hot August between the damp sheets. Hot and sticky, the heat fueled their passionate feelings.

She laughed out loud as she thought of those hot nights.

When he asked her to marry him, they stood in the moonlight under the Washington Square Arch and celebrated later with champagne at the Village Gate. They danced home and climbed the stairway. Their passion that night was steamy.

A month later it all came together when he proposed. She made up her mind she would join him in Washington, D.C. and she would teach. They would share a cozy apartment. They would make a new life together, share life and be happy forever.

Shelly still ached for love that lasted, expanded, and was nurtured over time.

The past with Arnold seemed so far away. She slowly watered the plants in the yard and went back inside. Memories faded. She resumed the rush to get ready to leave, again. But this time it would all be different.

Doug and she would make it, no matter what.

Shelly called each of her parents and told them her plans. She patiently listened again to her mother Jeanie's objections,

"Why don't you listen to me?"

"Do you think it will be better this time?"

"You are going to a foreign country. California! It's not New York!"

"You are thousands of miles from your family and friends."

"What if he is not serious about getting married? Then what will you do?"

Her mother dampened her dreams with doubts, and Shelly respectfully did not argue, but she wanted to not hear any negatives. She was certain she was on the right pathway to happiness.

But, her father Nat's happiness for her was expressed differently as he said,

"Yes, you are going in the right direction. Follow your heart and things will work out.

Be patient with him, not like your mother was with me. A man needs patience and understanding. He will not be perfect. Who is? But if you feel he is the right person then make your choice. Be happy!"

She agreed with her father, of course.

She then called her sister, Elaine, who immediately called for her husband, Matt, to get on their extension phone.

"You can't be serious," said her sister. "California! It's so far away. So different from all you are used to. Californians are 'free thinkers.' I don't think you will be able to manage."

Shelly insisted things would be great. She already felt free from the bindings of Washington—the strangle hold was releasing and she was preparing for transformation and freedom.

"I've found a darling furnished apartment not far from Doug. There will be school, studies, and lots to do. Who knows, I might even find new thoughts, especially if they are given away for free." Shelly laughed at the notion of "free" thoughts.

"You don't know anyone there, but Doug," she said.

"It's okay," replied Shelly, "I'll make new friends. So will Alison."

"Shelly, what you should do is stay in your job. Things will get better. You'll see. Nixon will not last. He is bound to screw up even more. After he leaves office you'll get the support you want for childcare programs. You should just be patient."

Shelly laughed. She said, "Meanwhile, while we are waiting for I'll get further along with my education. Then, when things are different politically, I'll be in a better position to get involved again."

Matt, who had joined in on the extension phone, so he wouldn't miss the details, interjected, "There won't be many chances for you to get back to visit, in New York or Washington. Everyone will miss seeing you and Alison."

"Thanks," said Shelly, "I'll miss both of you also. Now don't worry. Everything will work out! It always does. You can come to visit us anytime you want."

Shelly took some time to have lunch and dinner with several of the men she had casually dated, and still valued as friends.

During the three years after her divorce from Arnold, she had dated a lawyer, a professor, and a few other interesting men but they were not able to handle a young child or just had different interests from Shelly.

But, Nick, the theater director, was special to her. They were loving to each other and had spent a great deal of time together, but things had changed. She wanted to remain friends. She wanted to tell Nick what was happening. They had dinner at The American Café, a favorite restaurant on the Hill. They talked about the theater, her work, Alison, and his new play.

Shelly said, "Nick, do you remember my mentioning a doctor I met who lives in San Francisco?"

"The one who's divorced, has kids, and the whole enchilada?" Nick's view was as wry as ever.

"Yes, but he is also working to help poor kids, he's smart, and he's very sensitive." She was determined to impress Nick with Doug's virtues, especially the ones Nick himself didn't possess.

"But how is he in bed? That's the really important thing. Who cares about smarts between the sheets?"

Shelly blushed. Nick was so direct. He knew the answer without a word. Her face showed the truth.

"I will miss you, and Alison," said Nick looking at her determination.

He then looked at her a bit sadly, sighed, and said, "I hope he'll make you happy, and that his brats behave like your books say they should. I hope they treat Alison well."

He looked up at her as he kissed her hand.

She squeezed his hand, smiled, and thanked him. She would miss him.

After dessert they walked out into the warm night air and strolled on the Hill awhile before he took her home. They hugged; she kissed him once, and then quickly got out of the car.

Inside her house, Shelly realized Nick was very dominating, and in his own way, possessive. She learned a lot from Nick, and she experienced for the first time the unknown pains of jealousy and rejection. Yet he remained a caring friend.

She felt now so deeply connected with Doug. She felt only the pleasure of love.

She did not want the pain or those other terrible feelings to recur. The five lonely years of raising Alison by herself had happily come to an end.

There had been no one to share her deepest feelings of love. Nick was great, but she felt he never really loved her for all of herself. She was a good opportunity for him to polish his directorial craft, and he did a good job. She did change. She found courage.

She was heading for California. She wanted to be with the man with whom she could share all of herself. The one she talked with every day for two years. The man she really wanted to marry, to have a child of their own, and to make a whole new blended family together. The man she wanted to share life with in all of its incredible, unknown manifestations. They would nurture each other and their children. She felt as if she had won first prize in "The Love Contest." She finally had a home where she could safely place her love.

Doug's sister, Lucy, arrived from Chicago during the last week Shelly was preparing to leave. She came to visit and do some business in Washington. During the short time they had to talk, Shelly got to know her.

They found they had much in common. Shelly also gained some new insights into Doug by listening to the experiences his sister shared about him. A new friendship began with Lucy. She was sure they would remain friends despite the distance between the families.

Shelly felt they would all get along. Lucy told her about Doug's parents, Lorraine and Philip Fine. She shared some family background. It was clear Doug had been given the position of the highest placement on the pedestal of his family. Lucy loved her brother Doug, despite their mother's unrealistic adoration. Another King Shelly thought although she had not noticed the invisible crown he was wearing placed by his parents.

Lucy revealed to Shelly, "My feelings and accomplishments always took second place compared to Doug. He could never do anything wrong. My mother worships the ground Doug walks on. She placed him on a very high pedestal and that is where he has always remained. It seems impossible, but it's true." Shelly laughed at Lucy's stories. They agreed winning over Doug's mother would be a challenge as no woman was good enough for her son as Lucy revealed about his first wife.

After Lucy left, Shelly pondered what Lucy shared but thought it was just sisterly envy. She went ahead with plans and made arrangements for two students to drive her car to San Francisco. A van filled with clothes, household items and books was to be sent ahead. Alison's school and medical records were forwarded by mail.

Shelly said good-by to her close neighbors and friends.

As she packed, she thought of the community association in Woodley Park that she had started; the newsletter, "The Acorn;" and about the organizing work in their precinct for the first election held in the District of Columbia; of the many new friends she had made; walking her beloved collie, Friday, in Rock Creek Park; dog training classes; the neighbor's gourmet dinner parties where everyone enjoyed the dishes they each had worked hard to prepare; activities she had been involved with all passed in a slideshow of wonderful memories of the past ten years. As the memories rushed past, she readied papers and things for storage or travel.

Finally she was ready to leave. The house was rented, furnished, by two highly recommended women who signed a two-year lease. Her list of "items to handle" were almost all checked off.

She had found a good home for Friday with close friends who had another collie with whom Friday had "play-dates" and she knew Friday would be happy there.

The birds also found a new home with a family who often visited and liked the bird's "love nest" which Shelly sent with them.

The hardest part was ahead, saying good-by to Flora. Shelly had found her another excellent job nearby, but the separation was wrenching for everyone. They had grown attached to each other. Flora wished "the señora, Buena suerte, good luck, buen viaje–good journey"–and begged Alison, "esta una buena nina–to be a good girl."

Alison asked, "Por favor Flora can you come with us?"

They all cried and laughed as they separated.

Shelly and Alison entered the cab, waved goodbye and they went to Dulles Airport. As they boarded the plane, Shelly said a mental good-by to the ten years in Washington, her eyes were open and totally focused on the future.

From the air, Washington looked quite white and almost pure. She remembered the pain of losing JFK and all that he stood for, the riots and despair after Martin Luther King's assassination when she was teaching, the hypocrisy of Jim Hardy, Nixon's veto of childcare, and the pain of the past---It was finally time to let it all go. She sighed and took a deep breath trying to banish the bad memories. Then she laughed out loud. Alison laughed, too. She was glad her mother was happy. The plane gained altitude, leveled off, and headed west across the country, for California, slowly leaving the graying memories of Washington, D.C., far behind.

En-route to San Francisco, Shelly and Alison talked about the adventures awaiting them. They ate a dry, drab airline lunch that filled almost one hour of flying time. Shelly watched the film, "The French Connection," while Alison napped. The rest of the flight she played with Alison, read magazines, made lavatory trips, and listened to scratchy music on the headset while watching the country's topography pass by below.

Sleep was impossible. She was too excited. She had too many memories; the ups and downs of life in Washington; Nixon, pompous politicians (full of their bloated uncaring attitudes to the growing serious social problems) who were against anyone in need of education, childcare, health care, medical care, welfare, job training, or any benefit of a civilized, socially sensitive society. They did not think much, if at all, about the disenfranchised.

She remembered the frantic days of fixing the house, and sadly, of the many struggles with Arnold. She smiled as she thought of the improvisation and acting classes at Arena Stage that expanded her experiences and ability, and taking those new abilities into the inner-city classrooms with Nick Gavin, and Bob Alexander, who created the program.

There were some exciting days and nights during that time of her life. She was grateful to Nick for everything he contributed to her and to Alison. He cared and influenced her a lot. He came through for both of them in many ways. She would not forget him. He was also a challenge, but they planned to remain good friends. Time would tell. She was very glad they had met. Her life took a different path. It was a time for a real lasting change in California.

She remembered the stuffed-shirted, single, straight men that had little else but "one-nighters" on their mind. They were easily forgotten. She remembered the over-teased, under-sexed, airhead, females who were only interested in name-dropping, clothes shopping, and compiling the right guest list. She hardly wasted her time thinking about these things.

She thought of the winding, brick-lined streets of Georgetown, the stately monuments, the expansive museums; so much began to fade along with all the memories, as the plane moved farther away from what had been for a long time the center of her life on earth.

Thoughts crammed Shelly's head while she flew far away from everything she had known that was familiar in Washington. She faced an unknown future. She only knew Doug. She trusted him.

Fears crept into her mind and she thought for a few dark moments that maybe her mother's predictions were right. She dismissed them.

Instead she reminisced about their courtship, Doug's quick trips to Washington, their trips to Big Sur, Carmel, and Sonoma, and the long, frustrating horny phone calls. She remembered the old songs they sang, the dances they danced, and the intimate, magical moments they shared.

As the plane descended, her mind was put on hold. She gathered her courage around her and held her little girl's hand. She would be strong. She would find a new life. They were landing in a bright new world.

Chapter 11

Starting Again

The future is so bright it hurts my eyes. Oprah Winfrey

The plane landed at San Francisco International Airport and taxied to the gate. As soon as they could release their seat belts Shelly gathered their overhead bags and took Alison's hand as they deplaned. Doug and the kids were waiting at the gate. Everyone talked at once.

"Hi, Alison."

"Hi, Shelly." "How was the trip?" asked Doug.

"What did they feed you?" asked Andy.

"What movie was on the plane?" Andy wanted to know.

"Do you like pizza?" Andy asked Alison as he always thought about food first.

"Do you watch Sesame Street?" queried Molly. "We can watch it together if you want." She wanted to be a big sister right away and Shelly was relieved at how she responded.

Alison was overwhelmed. She was very excited by all the attention she was getting. Shelly noticed the boys made snide comments about Alison immediately between themselves. They were making fun of her, the way she spoke and acted, but she tried not to show she noticed. Shelly just watched. She wanted to be patient and wait to see how the chemistry among the children unfolded. They walked together, busily chatting, toward the luggage area and waited for the baggage belt to start.

Doug got their luggage. They moved outside toward the car. Everyone was excited, eager to make a good impression. The two girls chatted away. The two boys continued their side comments and jokes gesturing with their hands and faces. It was hard not to notice or respond, but Shelly turned her attention instead to the girl's animated conversation. She wanted everything to go smoothly.

They found the car, loaded the bags, and got in the car as everyone was talking at once. The noise level did not subside once during the trip back to the house. Shelly thought, aha, this is what a BIG family feels like. She smiled at Doug and turned back to watch the kids chattering. Shortly, they pulled up in front of the house. Everyone grabbed something to bring in except Andy, he grabbed his house key, ran for the door, and the bathroom. Everyone else helped to bring the bags inside and set them on the landing.

After they entered the house, Doug held Shelly for a long time in a deep embrace. But, as Shelly looked around Doug's house, she saw it as if for the first time. It now seemed rather empty. There were no plants, pillows, or pictures. Nothing warm or decorative! Only some dark, well-worn furniture some faded beige carpeting, and bare walls.

Apparently, when his ex-wife, Kristie, finally moved out, she took most of the furnishings. A lot of work would be needed to redecorate, and to make it homey and comfortable.

Shelly was willing to make the place a real home, when the time was right. Shelly felt she had so much to contribute to their lives. Doug did not know all of her skills yet. It was not yet the right time. She imagined that life was like an onion, the layers would slowly unpeel.

Her common sense, but also feelings of caution, as well as propriety, caused her to be firm in her decision to live apart from Doug. Her own apartment with Alison would make their transition into their new life in San Francisco a lot easier for everyone. Some space between them was needed for everyone to make their own personal adjustments. We must not rush into being a family, Shelly thought. The apartment would not be far away. They had plenty of time.

Doug's home was near the top of Upper Market Street, in Diamond Heights, in an area also called Twin Peaks. Set back on a winding tree-lined street, the house had been built in the 1950s by the Eichler Company. It had a weathered gray fence in front of the house, giving some semblance of privacy. The door opened onto a small patio, the garage was located to the right. The entire street was similar with slight variations. A sliding glass door opened into a hallway that led to the bedrooms upstairs, and down into a living room and kitchen. Upstairs, there were four functional bedrooms. The master bedroom was now stark, with no decorations on the walls, or any-where else.

Molly's room was simple, comfortable, and located in the front of the house. She had plenty of dolls and soft animals spread out everywhere.

The boys each had their own rooms. Andy's was in front next to the master bedroom. The room overflowed with planes, rockets, and space replicas hanging from the ceiling and pieces of games, die-cast cars, and electronic parts were scattered over most of the floor.

Andy's was in the rear beyond the children's bathroom. He had a prominent stereo system that blasted music, and all of his things were spread out all across the entire room. There was one bathroom for all of the children.

Shelly imagined the mad early morning scramble among the three kids getting ready for school. Then she tried to imagine Alison fitting into the melee.

Downstairs, the kitchen and family room combined into a large room where the television dominated the activity. The counters were built very low. It seemed dark, crowded, and not well equipped. Shelly knew she could brighten things up later. The living room and dining room looked quite drab. The backyard, open, spacious, and private, looked out to the Glen Park Canyon. Shelly enjoyed the backyard; it was like being far away from the city, quiet and peaceful.

The fog and clouds, Doug told her, filled many of the days with grayness on the top of the hill. Shelly thought when she first saw the fog that all of San Francisco was like that. Later, she discovered, down the hill in the Mission and South of Market the best and brightest sunny weather in the city was to be found. Cloud banks rolled in from the Pacific Ocean to cap Twin Peaks, covering the entire area with a quiet mantle of clouds. The cloud bank rested on top of the city most of the time, but it sometimes permeated the entire seven miles with its gentle, gray wetness.

Shelly realistically wondered if she would ever be able to work on her writing, studies, or have any peace in a house with no extra space. Close proximity would be a real challenge for everyone, she thought. She laughed, recalling how much space she had for Alison and herself before.

Shelly basically liked the house. She would later learn more about Eichler's designs and construction. The style was classic modern, and very functional. She liked it, yet she had an uneasy feeling about the house, knowing it was the place of Doug's past, of his marriage, and where the children grew up. She felt uncertain about moving into the house because he had shared it with his former wife, Kristie. Maybe someday they would find a new place to live, or they would remodel and expand some of the existing space so they could have something new together, but for now it would work, and there was plenty of time.

Shelly set aside any disturbing thoughts to begin making dinner from what she found in the refrigerator, basic hamburger, some celery, and a few onions. She found several cans of red kidney beans in the pantry. She promptly began chopping and preparing a large pot of instant chili and she ignored the box of Hamburger Helper .

As Shelly fixed the meal, the girls played with each other's things. Alison played with Molly's dolls, and made some pictures. Molly looked at the books Alison brought along and read them all quickly. The boys were fixated in front of the TV rocking, biting their nails, or hitting each other.

Oblivious to the din, Doug kept Shelly company while she cooked and enjoyed watching her efforts while he drank some wine, and nibbled on sourdough bread. He poured her a glass of wine as they smiled at each other. She cooked proficiently and he was impressed.

Later, they ate all the chili, right down to the last bean, and finished every piece of bread, devoured with a gallon of milk, and a few glasses of wine, and some cookies. After dinner, and after the children had gone to bed, Doug and Shelly held their own special reunion.

Her car was being driven cross the country by a student and it had not arrived yet so the next day after breakfast Doug drove Shelly and Alison down Market Street. They went past Castro, turned right on 14th Street toward Dolores Street. Shelly noticed the long stretch of tall palm trees all the way down Dolores Street. They reminded her of Miami Beach. They turned left off 14th Street onto Rosemont Street. At the end of the street, they stopped at the small apartment building and parked. Shelly was pleased she had easily found the apartment. Everything was ready to move in. The moving van and her car would be arriving in a few days. When they entered the apartment, she was shocked.

All the furniture, which had been there when Shelly rented the apartment, was gone. There was no bed and the stove and refrigerator were missing. There was no note of explanation.

When she called the landlord, she found an answering machine saying, "I'm out of town for the next few days. Leave a message." There was no other way to reach him, and nothing else to do.

The only solution was to return to Doug's house. When they arrived back at the house, Doug explained to the children what had happened. They thought it was very funny. Shelly took that as a sign that they were willing to stay open about her relationship with their father, and would also be willing to accept Alison. The girls were close in age, Alison, five, and Molly, seven; the boys, Ross and Andy, were nine and eleven. Together they seemed like a full-blown squadron. The girls agreed to share Molly's room. There was an extra bed across from Molly's. They found a sleeping bag in the garage. Alison thought it was fun, her first away-from-home sleeping experience.

"Mommy, this is fun. I'm sleeping like a turtle tonight," she said gamely as she peeked out from the sleeping bag.

Molly showed her how to open and close the zipper.

"That's in case you have to get out. Here, I can show you."

Molly jumped in the bag to demonstrate. Alison laughed when Molly tucked her head in like a turtle. Shelly felt Molly was being very nice to share her room so graciously. The girls got ready for bed.

Shelly kissed them both good night.

Doug came in and read a story, and then he closed the door.

The boys, however, were fighting.

Andy accused Ross of taking something from his room. They were yelling.

Andy stood outside Ross's locked door, banging and demanding, "Give it back or I will break you in half, you squirt!"

Ross was yelling from the other side, "I don't have anything! You leave me alone, you big ape!"

Doug called up the stairs, "Andy, leave him alone! You'll disturb the girls. They're trying to go to sleep now."

Andy ignored him and screamed, "It's my business! Leave me alone! I want my rocket back! Ross took it! Make him give it back!"

Doug quietly told him, "Do it in the morning. Go to bed!"

Andy continued banging on the door with his foot. "You better give it back, Andy, or else! It's mine, mine, all mine!" he bellowed.

Shelly heard the commotion. She thought it best not to get involved. She was exhausted. It did not seem the right time to try to settle their conflicts.

She went into Doug's bedroom and washed her face. The sounds of the boys' thumping and yelling easily permeated the walls, shook the silence, entered under the door, and filled her with dread.

As she looked in the mirror, she wondered if the spirit of Doug's first wife, Kristie, was still contained inside the bedroom. She thought she could sense her presence. Perhaps it was just nerves, but she felt uneasy. She put her feelings aside while she brushed her hair.

She tried to hum her theme song, "You have to accentuate the positive, eliminate the negative, latch on to the affirmative, and don't mess with Mr. In-between!"

The comforting words to the song helped to keep the noise down inside her head and to drown out the screams flooding in like a torrent from next door.

Doug finally came in and quiet reined. They made love quietly. The walls were very thin as she remembered.

The next morning, Shelly made scrambled eggs for everyone while she tried to talk with each of the children. This was not easy.

Andy, already very large for his age, was overweight and always dominated the conversation with his loud, booming voice, often bordering on hostility.

The other boy, Ross, thin, handsome, curious, and friendly, was also very hyperactive. He seemed easily nervous, upset and frustrated. He was receptive to Shelly and Alison, but was dominated by his older brother and played along with his tendency towards negative reactions to everything.

Molly with her quick mind, and positive attitude was ready to talk. She smiled often and was genuinely the happiest of the three. She was definitely the easiest for Shelly and Alison to get along with. She was willing to share her things with Alison and seemed to be confident about herself.

Alison seemed excited and enthusiastic about being with the children in all of their different forms. She laughed at their jokes and their snide comments. She was overjoyed to have other kids to listen to, and hoped they would play and talk with her. She craved their attention.

They each wanted to show her their rooms, toys, music, and collections: Ross had several airplanes, rockets and space models. Andy collected '49er football memorabilia and miniature Hot Wheels and Matchbox cars. Molly's wide variety of stuffed animals and dolls stuck around her room provided soft comfort from her brother's rough surliness.

As Shelly unpacked her suitcase, she was certain the living arrangement would only be temporary. The next few days would be an interesting "trial-run" at residing with Doug and the children. She would return to the apartment and visit sparsely at first by getting to know them slowly, or so she thought.

They spent the weekend together sightseeing. They went walking in North Beach, eating in Chinatown, exploring in Golden Gate Park, driving up, down, and all around hills, winding slowly down Lombard Street, "The Crookedest Street in the World," and climbing to the top of Twin Peaks. They wanted to show Alison the amazing view. It was all great fun for Alison. They showed off San Francisco while they all talked almost all at once, all of the time. Shelly soon realized as the din did not subside that the entire day with four children was a huge undertaking.

Shelly wondered if her teacher training and years of experience was sufficient. She began to question if she would be equal to the task, the challenge of a large second family. A second family! It all seemed so simple when she and Doug first talked of blending them a year ago from a distance.

The "them" now seemed a lot more "bulky" than she had imagined before. "Them" seemed to grow as rapidly as protoplasm, eating, moving, expanding, talking all at once, and getting bigger and bigger as the days passed.

Being a large blended family would take time for many adjustments. She still wanted to learn more about Doug now being up closer. She wanted him to know her. Shelly knew that getting to know each other would take more time. Shelly was patient and eager to learn and to handle the challenges that lay ahead.

Shelly felt what it might be like to be a pioneer woman, although this time her travels were not in a covered wagon, but in a jet plane. She knew the distance was great from point to point, and a lot of adventures lay in store. Was she capable of coping with all of the new challenges?

Chapter 12

Sudden Changes

Women must be the pioneer in this turning inward for strength. In this sense she has always been the pioneer. Ann Morrow Lindbergh

When Monday arrived, Shelly left Alison at home with a sitter, Bobbi Clark, who had been favorably referred by a neighbor. Shelly was hopeful that things would work out fine, and Alison would have a good experience. After they met and went over all the necessary details Shelly felt more confident. She was reassured that the woman would be able to keep Alison happily engaged for the day.

Shelly kissed Alison goodbye and went to the car. She drove along upper Market Street, made a right at South Van Ness Avenue, and then across the Bay Bridge. She looked at the view from time to time and pinched herself. She was really in California. It was all too good to be true, and sometimes she had trouble believing it.

She crossed the bridge, and turned right on Powell St. in the center of Emeryville. She turned right again and easily pulled into a small parking lot. She gathered her papers and bag and went to the door. Once inside the Educational Research Lab building, a red brick structure not far from Interstate 80, she called the landlord to find out what had happened to the furniture and appliances in her new apartment. He hurriedly apologized.

He explained, "I had forgotten that you told me you were arriving on Friday. I had to leave town. My niece, who was living there before, decided to take all the furniture and appliances for her new apartment in Vallejo."

Shelly replied. "Right, it was a shock not to have a note or anything."

"Well," he replied, "I'm sorry I asked her to leave a note, but I had to let her take what was there with her. I could not find your phone number. Can you find some new furnishings for the apartment? I will cover the costs."

Shelly said, "Thank you. I appreciate your response. I will do what I can as fast as I can. I did not expect to have to do this right now." Shelly realized shopping for all these things would now take more time and effort.

She then called Doug. They decided to go to the Sears store on Geary Avenue that evening to replace the necessities as quickly as possible.

After the calls, Shelly went to the Lab office to find her mentor, Dr. Gary Newheart. He was on the phone, and motioned for her to come in and sit down. She looked around the room and saw a table with a pile of reports, several stacks of publications, and a scattering of colorful wooden toys. She picked one up to examine it. After completing his conversation, he turned to her over a desk also littered with toys, books, and papers. Files were piled high on shelves; books and toys filled the room in tall stacks from the floor up.

Gary stood up and reached for her hand. She put down the toy she was playing with and made a mental note to continue examining the toys as soon as she could. She had so many aspects of the Lab's program to learn about – toys, reports, and studies were all part of the program.

"Welcome to the Lab, Shelly. Glad to have you here. Whatever you need, just let me know," he said.

Shelly replied, "I am really happy to be here, finally. I want to find out all about your program, like this report, and this new toy. I have not seen anything like this one before"

She motioned to the toy she had been playing with and Gary nodded in agreement. "Yes, he said, we have been working on the prototype"

She responded, "I am most interested in learning more about the design and concept." He nodded.

She added, "I will review the plans for my research with you when it is convenient. "I know how busy you are."

She motioned to the publication she had been looking at while Gary nodded in agreement. "And also I want to review the plans for my research with you when it is convenient," she said.

Gary handed her a copy of the same publication she had glanced at, a report on the program, and added, "I will be available whenever you want to review your plans. Don't try to do too much this first week. Just get to know the people on staff, and find out what they are working on. They'll be help-ful. We have a very interesting group here involved in the pre-school program, Head Start, and in teacher training. They all appreciate toys and are playful and dedicated. I am sure you'll enjoy meeting everyone and working with them"

Shelly nodded her head and said, "I've heard so much about the reputa-tion of the Lab. I'm very pleased to be associated here. I'm open to any of your suggestions. Thank you for letting me study here. I share your dedication to play and toys, of course, and love the new program that involves creating parent toy-lending libraries. They belong in every community."

Dr. Newheart, a short, pleasant, scholarly man with thick glasses and a warm smile, said, "I'm glad you made the choice to come to the Lab. We have a lot to offer you. You certainly will benefit from our program. We have training going on with teachers in schools throughout the East Bay, in a few communities in the City, and across the country, in Atlanta in the inner city, on a Navajo Indian reservation in New Mexico, in Bakersfield for migrant worker's children, and in rural Appalachia among very poor families. If the preliminary services get significant results, we will be considered later for larger grants. Now we are testing the concepts of the toy-lending program, and doing research to see if the parent and teacher training and our methods have validity."

He pointed to the many toys on his desk. Shelly looked over the toys and books and picked up a few of the toys as he spoke.

He added brightly, "I hope you will be interested in the toys we have developed, and work with us on the Parent-Child Toy-Lending Library. You could make a big contribution in that program." She nodded agreement.

Outside, Shelly stopped at Dr. Newheart's secretary's desk. She asked Gail if she could get a list of the staff so she could learn what activities they were working on.

"I suggest you talk with Pat Robinson. She's been here for three years. She knows everybody, as well as all the projects. She shares your interest in childcare, which we've talked about already. It's an issue we are all interested in."

They gave each other a knowing glance, both fully understanding the problems.

"By the way, Dr. Newheart has assigned you a workspace. Let's go see it, and I'll help you get settled in."

They walked downstairs to the back of the building. There was an open room with a series of partitions, and within each partition a desk, chairs, and file cabinet. Gail opened the window next to one of the empty desks.

"This is it. It'll be your place in the Lab. Do you need any supplies?" she asked.

"For now a few notepads and pens would be great, a bunch of file folders, then I'll just get started," replied Shelly looking around the cubicle. She wanted to add a plant to the desk.

Gail pointed to the desk drawer and said, "I already anticipated the supplies. They are all in there."

Shelly smiled, said "Thank you!" and sat down.

She looked more closely at her new office. It was efficient, sparsely decorated, but at least a warm and friendly cream color, not like the dull green walls of the government building she endured for so long. Luckily, she had too much to do and think about than to think about re-decorating, except for adding a plant.

She quickly remembered all the work needed in Doug's house, the apartment, and turned to focus on the workload in front of her. Shelly made a list of tasks she needed on one of the yellow legal pads.

She asked Gail to help her locate Pat. They found Pat taking a break in the staff kitchen. Gail introduced them, pointed to the coffee pot, and returned to her desk.

Shelly said, "Hi Pat, Dr. Newheart wanted us to meet."

"Yes. He told me you would be here today. I'm glad to meet you, Shelly." Pat greeted her warmly. As a tall, strikingly attractive African American woman, Pat was vivacious, cautious, and yet forthright. Pat shook her hand firmly, and motioned Shelly to follow. They moved down the hall as Pat shared some information.

"Shelly, are you aware of the political problems and programmatic issues of Head Start in California?"

"Yes, to some degree. I have to get acquainted with the specific childcare problems, the aspects of coordination, and the range of issues such as how politics affects the program services."

Pat brightened. "Glad to hear that! The Lab really needs to be doing some research in childcare as it's been sorely neglected. There's plenty to look at. I can tell you some of what I already know, but you're going to have to dig deep to get the facts," Pat told her. "I've always been interested, but no one here really has the time to delve into what's really going on. There is some heavy resistance on the part of politicians and agencies to help poor families with kids. Most are single moms struggling to make ends meet."

"Well, that's what I'm here for," said Shelly. "I'm ready to follow-up on any of the leads you give me."

Pat continued, "Okay, good. The problems are not enough money, too many kids, long waiting lists, and other barriers you wouldn't believe. I've been to some of the centers located in the Mission, Tenderloin, Hunter's Point, and in Oakland, and it's rough, desperate, sparse, and honestly, below standards. Believe me."

Shelly replied, "What's different than everywhere else?"

Pat responded, "Plenty! There's a lot of parental pride, strong community organization, and lots of cultural connections and strong emotions; also there's the usual problems, but I think there is a lot of potential that can help solve some of the issues. I think the problems and potential resolutions are the same whether it's in Chinatown, Western Addition, Hunter's Point, or South of Market. You'll have your work cut out for you."

Pat looked at her quizzically, wondering if Shelly was up to it. She was after all, white. Would she face resistance as she tried to ferret out the answers to many questions?

Shelly felt right away that she and Pat would get along. She realized she had a lot to learn from Pat, and from others working at the Lab, about each community's specific problems, the parent's needs, and the political issues that were unique to each area. She wanted to find out about the people at the Lab, the work they were doing, and the future of the programs. She had to cram in a lot of information fast. It made her a little dizzy just thinking about all the work and the challenges that lay ahead.

Shelly responded in rapid fire, "Well, it looks like there's community action and service agencies in each community to contact, teachers and parents to talk to, evaluations to develop, centers to visit, administrator's to talk to, city agencies to visit, and…"

"Whoa! Take it easy girl. Remember, this is California," said Pat with a laugh and continued. "Nothing gets done the first day. Relax. Slow down!" Shelly smiled. She was still going at her East Coast "let's-get-it-done-now" pace, and she needed reminders to change speed.

Shelly did slow down, took a deep breath, and shared her feelings with Pat.

"It's ironic. As I sit here, talking about all this, I'm thinking about my own little girl with her new sitter—whom I never even saw before today. She's taking care of my daughter, Alison, today for the first time. Can you believe it? As we study, we also experience the same problems at the same time."

They laughed together wryly at this common reality they shared. It is part of the pressures and strong realities that face working mothers.

Pat remarked, "Well, I go through the same hassles all the time with my two kids. It's tough to get ahead as a professional when you have to deal with childcare, or rather the lack of it. You would think the government would wake up already!"

Shelly responded, "I worked so hard on this in Washington. But, the current mentality of those 'men in power' doesn't go much beyond their wives staying home and taking care of their kids, or they have live-in nannies, so they only have to arrange their busy social lives. Most of their secretaries are single girls, and they are not even thinking of kids yet. That's why few of them even get interested in childcare issues. They don't diaper their kids. They don't have to cope with the kid's problems, schedules or needs. Besides, kids don't vote for them, do they?"

They laughed together.

Pat added, "I have a neighbor who stays home. She looks after my kids. But, you never know when that will suddenly change, so I'm always on "pins and needles". So I know exactly what you mean."

They talked more about childcare, the Lab, and the people working there. Then they arranged to meet the next day for coffee, and for more talk and introductions.

Shelly went back to her office cubicle. After asking Gail for reading materials about the Lab's current research, she busied herself reviewing those papers for a few hours. She learned the Lab staff traveled a lot; so to talk to each person would not be easy. She also decided to slow down, to breathe, and to try to relax and try to be more on 'California time.'

Her main focus would be to proceed with her own childcare study. She made notes, lists, and read more about the Lab's research studies. She saw many ways that her study would benefit the Lab's program. She was adding to the depth of their activities and probing into an area they all agreed was important, but no one had time to explore.

When she remembered to look at her watch, it was already 3:30, time to start home before the Bay Bridge traffic back to the City became heavy. A long drive lay ahead of her on the freeway.

She drove first to the apartment to change clothes, hang some things in the closet, make a list of what she needed, and then she went to Doug's house.

She found Alison quietly watching "Mr. Rogers." The sitter, Bobbi, was relaxing reading a magazine nearby. Shelly took a deep breath. "See, you worry for nothing," she hissed at her conscious.

She asked Bobbi how things went and was reassured. She thanked Bobbi for her time, paid her, made arrangements for the rest of the week and sent her home. Alison continued to watch TV. Shelly bent over to give Alison a kiss, as she asked her, "How did things go for you today?"

Alison replied, "Oh, fun, Mom. We go walk in park. Nice kids. We played, a lot of play. We ate 'sammiches' lunch. I like it here," she added.

Shelly said, "I'm so glad, Alison. I really want you to be happy in San Francisco. I think Bobbi is very nice, too. Do the kids you played with live nearby?"

Alison nodded and turned back to the TV. "Mr. Rogers" was putting on his sweater and slippers. Alison loved "Mr. Rogers." She felt safe and happy in his nice, playful and serene, "Neighborhood." She was glad to know his neighborhood traveled to where she was now living.

Then Shelly started supper. She wanted to save time, so when Doug returned they could go right to Sears to get the appliances and furniture for the apartment. She found some ingredients for spaghetti. Let's make it simple, fast and easy, she reasoned.

As she began to cook, Alison came across the room and said, "Mommy, big fun today. Bobbi's a nice sitter. The park is fun. Nice Mommy." She hugged Shelly around the legs. "I'm going to talk to 'Mr. Rogers.'" She returned to the TV.

Molly came downstairs. "Shelly, what are you making? I hope you make something to eat real soon. I'm soooo hungry."

Shelly smiled at her and replied, "Spaghetti!"

Molly replied, "Great. Anyway you make it is fine with me!"

Molly could be a perfect big sister for Alison. She was enthusiastic, sweet, smart, patient, and seemed ready to accept the new situation. Shelly liked her. She had a happy, bubbly personality and was being very kind and attentive to Alison.

At least Shelly hoped they would not be in conflict the way traditional siblings usually were. Shelly decided the best thing to do so there would be no conflicts was to always listen to both of them, be fair, and give them equal treatment. Shelly wanted to be objective about Alison even though she was concerned about how she would manage in the midst of three children and in such close quarters.

"I've got homework to do. Let me know when dinner's ready and I will set the table," said Molly quickly and returned upstairs.

Ross came in a few minutes later and was very excited and rushed over to see what was on the stove. "Hi! Wow! It smells good! What are you cooking?"

"Spaghetti," said Shelly.

"Great. My favorite! Just don't put any sauce on it. I only like it plain with butter. Okay?" he asked.

Shelly made a mental note of it.

He left and walked over to where Alison was sitting. He popped her gently on the back of the head. She turned to push him away. He then plopped down on the seat next to her to watch TV. He rocked back and forth. Alison looked at him and rocked too. She thought it was fun.

The door banged again. Andy rushed in. He went right to the refrigerator without saying hello, opened it, grabbed a jar of peanut butter, a gallon of milk, and a loaf of bread. As he spread the peanut butter, he loudly said, "Ross, why did you let dad get this weird smooth peanut butter? I told you to get crunchy! Why don't you ever listen?"

Ross did not answer. He had come in quietly and was watching "Mr.

Rogers" with Alison. They were both rocking and did not hear Andy.

Shelly smiled. Hopefully, some problems as simple as the style of peanut butter would take care of themselves.

She asked Andy, "Hi! Do you like spaghetti?"

"Sure," he replied, drinking the milk right from the container, "as long as it doesn't have butter on it, or cheese, or tomato sauce. I only like pesto." Then he smeared peanut butter on a slice of bread and took a bite.

"Pesto? What's that?" Shelly asked.

He didn't answer, he snorted, "Look it up in a cookbook. I don't like smooth peanut butter, either. Remember that when you go shopping," Andy emphasized as he drank more milk and swallowed the bread. Shelly decided not to say anything about the milk.

"I'll try to remember," said Shelly. Somehow she didn't think she would soon forget this little lesson.

Then Doug walked in. "Hi! It smells good." He looked quickly at the pots as he walked to the stove. "I love spaghetti. You picked my favorite food. What kind of sauce?"

He walked to over Shelly, who was tossing salad at the sink, and kissed her.

Andy gave him a look of disgust. "Smooching is for sissies," he snarled taking a bite of peanut butter coated bread

Shelly tossed to Doug his choices, "Yes, we are having spaghetti, plain, or with tomato sauce, or butter, or pesto. Is there any other way?"

Doug said, "Olive oil!"

They laughed.

Andy ate the peanut butter sandwich in three gulps, grabbed the container of milk, drank from it again, and then put it back in the refrigerator. Then he went to the TV and without asking the other kids changed the channel to "Star Trek." Ross stayed to watch, too. Alison got up, gave them a look, turned away and gathered some napkins and placed them around the table,

Shelly felt squeamish about Andy's gulping the milk from the container and wondered who was teaching them consideration for others. She wondered why he did not pour it from the bottle into a glass, but she kept quiet. She did not want to be critical. She was a guest, and it was not her place to say anything about his behavior.

Doug went to the desk to look at his mail and seemed to be preoccupied in his own thoughts. Shelly wondered about his former wife. Why was she willing to leave the kids with Doug? How was their marriage? Did they always expect her to always make spaghetti four or five different ways?

Alison placed the napkins around the table as well as she could and then had to go to the bathroom. Molly was in her room. Andy was watching TV with Ross.

Molly rushed downstairs to kiss her father, glanced at the TV, then the table, and decided to finish the place settings by gathering some forks, quickly placing each on a napkin, and then putting all the plates down.

Then Alison came out of the bathroom, and over to Shelly, and asked for help getting her zipper closed. Molly looked over at Shelly when the task of setting the table was done, but she did not get any response as Shelly was fixing the zipper on Alison's pants and did not notice Molly seeking attention for getting her task completed. Molly stood watching.

Doug said, "Let's eat now! We've got to go out after supper, kids, to do some fast shopping. You've got homework to do while we're gone. Molly, I'd like you to help Alison while Shelly and I are gone."

Molly nodded her head and said, "Sure, no problem. I can read her a story and we can play. I don't have any more homework to do tonight. I got it all done," she beamed, again looking for approval.

Doug did not respond.

Shelly made a note that each child needed to have more encouragement. She also kept her thoughts to herself, as she just wanted to observe how things were going and not interfere. She noticed the places were all set and assumed that Molly did it all. She said,

"Oh Molly, thanks for setting the table!" Molly beamed.

Alison interjects, "Mommy I put napkins on table!"

"Good for doing that Alison!" Shelly gave her a hug. She made a note that Molly was a good influence on Alison.

Andy made another peanut butter sandwich, and returned to the TV. Doug said nothing.

Shelly said, "Molly…, thanks for helping with Alison."

Then she asked, "Andy, do you want more spaghetti?" He said, "No, I'll eat later."

Molly and Alison each had a bowl of spaghetti with sauce, a lot of it on their faces. Then they went over to sit with the boys. Shelly put out two bowls for Doug and herself both with olive oil and parmesan cheese. They ate, and Shelly put their bowls in the sink, and filled them with water. Shortly afterwards, Shelly and Doug left for Sears, leaving Andy in charge of the kids.

This was their first shopping trip together. Shelly smiled at Doug. She thought about the many changes occurring so fast. They made selections in the appliance and furniture departments and arranged for a Saturday delivery. She laughed as she told Doug about buying appliances for her home. She said, "The sales clerk tried to convince me to buy turquoise colored appliances. But, I cringed at the thought."

"Kristie chose white too," said Doug, "But, the kids would have probably loved the turquoise."

When they arrived back home Shelly was even more aware of how much still had to be done. The house was a mess: there were books, jackets, and toys scattered everywhere; all the dishes were still dirty, piled up high in the sink, napkins rolled up on the counter, some on the floor; utensils and glasses left strewn all over the counter. The knife covered with peanut butter was left on the counter. The pot of left over spaghetti was cold and sticky. The salad bowl had not been touched, and nothing had been put away. The place was a disaster. Everything needed full time attention!

The girls were in their room playing. The boys were still watching TV. Doug did not ask them if they did their homework or check their homework. He did not ask them to clean up. Shelly wondered how he could be so laid back about what they were not doing.

Everything consumed Shelly at the moment. She later wrote in her journal,

"Doug has a tendency to be very easygoing about everything. The boys need a firm hand, and a lot more structure. Discipline is not apparent. The boys are very loud, rough, and belligerent in their manners. Ross is very nervous. Andy is very bossy. Molly is very good natured and happy. The boy's behavior is often erratic. I am sure they will be fine eventually, but when, is what I'm not sure about. Meanwhile after a long day (of driving, orientation work, shopping, preparing dinner and much more) it's still good old mom that cleans up""

Shelly was relieved to be able to share some private thoughts in her journal, her mental sanctuary.

She wanted to spend as much time as she could with the children. She saw the need for more focus and some new activities directing them away from endless TV viewing. There was so much more possible in their lives. They definitely needed more consistency.

She thought about the boys and how they might benefit from music lessons since they both liked music so much. She thought Ross would be a good drummer because he was always in motion. Andy might calm down and be more patient if he learned to play a guitar. She made a note in her mind to revisit these thoughts later on.

Coming from the outside, she thought she saw their problems and issues much more clearly than Doug. Or perhaps he just did not want to handle their challenges. He was preoccupied with his own issues at work.

She felt Ross' pain. Ross seemed (more than the other children) to be hurting from his parents' divorce. He showed his displeasure at the slightest provocation. Shelly hoped she could help him express his feelings, and to help him gain more confidence. She was sure that learning a new skill like playing drums would help to give him confidence or more of whatever it was he needed.

She wanted things to be good for everyone, and was willing to do whatever it would take to make the situation work out by listening, and showing each child she cared about them individually.

Shelly watched Alison to see her reactions. The balance between each of them needed gentle handling. She had to go slowly.

Doug invited them to stay at the house as long as she wanted, and until everything was delivered and set up. Since there were no beds to sleep on at the apartment it made sense for them to stay longer. It would give her more time with the children, and Doug, plus it would cut down on one more challenge—commuting. She would then only go to the apartment to study, or if she felt the need to get away.

Doug said, "The only way we will find out if we can all make it together as a family is to give all of us the 'test of time' – day-by-day."

Shelly agreed it made sense, but she had concerns, too. Alison was told she would be staying at the house. She seemed happy. Shelly realized the new combined family arrangement might not be easy for her, but she felt hopeful. She would have new support and stimulation that could benefit her. Somehow, they would find ways to solve what she saw at the moment were not impossible problems, and find a way to create a strong blended new family.

When Doug came home from the hospital the next night, he looked pleased to see Shelly preparing dinner. They looked at each other. The waiting was over. They were finally together for the children, and for each other.

As they sat around the table before dinner was served, the two boys started to fight over a remark Andy made. Doug ordered Andy to his room, which left the other three children at the table. Shelly felt very uncomfortable.

She asked Doug if it were possible to have Andy come back to the table. He appreciated her concern and called Andy back.

But, Andy stood sulking in the doorway and responded, "I am not interested in joining you!"

Shelly said, "Andy, I thought it would be more fun if we could all be together. It would be much nicer to have you join us. It's important to be together at dinner."

Andy looked at her with surprise. Then he suddenly sat down and quickly grabbed a hamburger and a bun from the plate.

The rest of the dinner was uneventful except for the high volume of continuous noise, rocking in the seats, pushing, and lots of teasing back and forth.

At these times, she wondered about "togetherness." A quiet dinner alone with Doug faded into the categories of "romantic" and "probably impossible." They were, after all, parents first, lovers second.

After the children had gone to bed, she and Doug talked seriously about all the changes they were experiencing.

Shelly said, "Doug, has it always been like this with the boys?"

He said, "Always. They enjoy fighting with each other."

She replied, "Can't you ask them not to fight over everything?"

"I think they will outgrow the battles," he replied.

"But can we?" Shelly laughed.

"Boys will be boys!" Doug said. "Don't worry about them!"

Shelly responded, "I'm not worried. I'm worn out. There's a lot of tension between them. It spills over and it makes me feel nervous. The girls have to listen to the loud fighting, too."

"Relax…Just let them be boys." Doug reassured her. He added, "It will take time and plenty of patience. We can solve any problem as long as we are together. Am I right?" And with that hopeful comment he reached over and turned off the light.

Chapter 13

Juggling Everything

*Planning the future is tenuous at best as unexpected events do happen
and what hatches may not be at all what was planned.* (Author)

Shelly began each morning with the sounds of several alarm clocks going
off. She could hear the children rushing to or from their bedrooms, fighting
in front of the bathroom or in and out of the bedrooms.

"Hurry up!" "I gotta go now!"

"Stop wasting time!"

"Whew, it stinks!"

"You took my socks give them back!"

'Hey, take your stuff! They smell!"

Shelly stretched out and moaned softly.

There was only one bathroom for the four children to share. The rush for
showers, dressing, and eating was like a very fast Max Sennett comedy: One
big jumble of sound, fury, and scrambling that continued for a full hour every morning starting promptly at 6:30 a.m. She was not quite sure how they
would all be able to manage, but they did, somehow.

As soon as Shelly heard the first alarm going off she climbed out of bed
and headed for the kitchen to prepare breakfast — cutting oranges, making
toast, putting out bowls of cereal, and a pitcher of milk, and glasses. She put
on a pot of coffee. Then she intently listened, as the stampede grew closer.

Every day, the three children dashed down the stairs, mouths and feet
moving in unison like the herd, roaring by her, rushing around the kitchen
grabbing and stuffing pieces of toast in their mouths as they grabbed books
and then jackets, and headed like panicked steer at roundup, out of the door
at precisely 7:30 a.m., just in time to catch the bus to school. Shelly took a
deep breath. The herd was gone. The house was silent for a moment.

Her time with Doug in the morning was spent over a cup of coffee, scan-
ning the Chronicle, and a quick kiss at the door. Doug was disciplined, and

he never ever changed his routine. She soon put aside thoughts of lazy mornings in bed after the children had left to make love and relax.

Then she had all she could do to get ready herself, to help Alison finish dressing, have some cereal, and get the kitchen tidied up before racing for the door. Then Shelly and Alison drove across town toward Pacific Heights School.

The Pacific Heights School, transformed from a sprawling family mansion into a busy, creative, yet comfortable, school, was surrounded by large trees. It had well-equipped rooms, pleasant surroundings, and a warm and friendly staff.

Shelly felt pleased she had found one of the few places that had arrangements for before- and after-school care. Alison could play early in the morning, have a snack later, play outside, and then rest until Shelly was able to pick her up at the end of the day. She felt it was a good place because Alison looked forward to school every morning. It was an exciting place for her because she was practicing new skills, meeting new children, learning to read by typing, and that was helping her learn words and gain confidence.

When they arrived at the school, Hilda, the early morning staff person, welcomed them. She was also Alison's teacher so that helped make Alison even more comfortable.

Alison kissed Shelly, waved good-by, ran happily up the steps to greet an embracing Hilda, and entered the school. She drove away content she had found the right place for Alison as she headed across town.

She turned East and went through the Broadway tunnel, on the other side was bustling Chinatown to the South and colorful, quaint North Beach on the North. She eventually reached the Embarcadero Freeway, which easily led to the Bay Bridge. She thought about what had happened in only a few short months. Her whole life had turned around, again.

In Washington, she had the challenge of raising one child alone, a pressure-cooker job, and a lot of personal issues to cope with. Now, she was managing a full load of school, with so many more new responsibilities at home multiplied by four kids. Whew! She took a deep breath. She could barely do the arithmetic in her head, but was still undaunted.

Her mother would not believe the arrangements, so she thought it best to keep the situation under wraps for a while, and just cope with everything as well as she could. She had Alison, Doug's children, her relationship with Doug, commuting, cooking, plus preparation for her study and research to worry about. Life had become really full, challenging and very different.

In a very short order she began to sense that traffic was not quite as noisy, nor as congested, and drivers seemed more courteous. She felt more relaxed everywhere, except at home. There was a lot to handle each and every day. But, Shelly was sure things would change. She felt everything would soon get easier, when the children were past the first steps of adjustment. She hoped it would not take too long for them to settle in, to step up and accept the new arrangements.

She found shopping for food amazingly different. She marveled at the new world of foods, the wide array of colorful and delicious fruits and vegetables, some of which she had never seen before. She examined the displays at the grocery store of jicama , very large green avocados, even larger artichokes, mangoes, kiwi, bok choy and squashes (of many colors, sizes and styles), and many different fresh herbs, cilantro, Italian parsley, and her new favorite, bouquets of basil. She loved all the new tastes and the amazing new sensations. The smells and the sights of San Francisco resonated in a sensational syncopation of sensual delight. Shelly felt satiated, challenged, and deeply happy.

The weather pleased her the most. It was cool, clear, and sunny much of the time. She finally felt able to breathe easier as the east coast allergies subsided.

She was swept up, in tune and in love with the City. It felt inviting, delicious, and exciting.

Doug took her to the Rose and Thistle, his favorite jazz club, on Sunday afternoons after the children returned from Sunday school. They were busy playing around the house and she and Doug took off for a few hours. The Rose and Thistle, located on California Street near Polk, looked like an English-styled pub. On Sunday it featured music played by a doctor friend of Doug's, Benny Kalman on clarinet, Bert Bales on piano, plus a mix of other fine Dixieland musicians. They went there to relax and enjoy the music. Shelly felt enriched by their discoveries of common interests while the children were happily busy at home. They managed to carve out some special alone time for themselves.

One afternoon when Shelly happened to be home alone, the phone rang. Shelly found herself talking with Kristie Fine, Doug's ex-wife. Kristie wanted to arrange a time to see the children and to shift the usual visit to the following weekend. Shelly knew it was best to be flexible, positive, and to keep things peaceful. She had not talked to Kristie before, so this was a good way to get acquainted, without Doug or the children.

Shelly and Kristie continued to talk after the specific arrangements were cleared up. Kristie still sounded angry, as she tried to express her feelings. Shelly was curious and sympathetic. After all, she understood marital problems, from being with Arnold. It was usually frustrating to talk to him any time.

Kristie said, "Well, I hate to tell you this, but Doug was hardly ever home. All he ever cared about was his job. His job always came first. When he was home he never wanted to discipline the kids..." Her voice trailed off hesitantly, as if she was not sure she should be talking about him to his current girlfriend.

Shelly said, "I understand. I know how important work is to Doug. You can speak honestly with me. I promise it will be private between us."

Kristie retorted, "Yes. I guess you know, but I never really mattered to him. I was a full-time nurse before I met him. I wanted to keep on working." Her voice dropped off as if she was thinking about all the things she had missed.

Shelly said, "I am trying to understand."

Kristie said, "Well, how can you manage working on your degree and handling four kids? It's a 'no-win' situation. He will never appreciate you, or anything you do for him."

Shelly listened thinking she sounded a lot like her own mother and responded. "I care about making a family. I was alone before raising a child."

Kristie snorted, "I was alone raising three..." then her voice trailed off again.

Shelly responded, "Well, I am sure it wasn't easy. The kids are a handful, I must admit." She wanted Kristie to know she was sympathetic, and understood her feelings.

Kristie continued, "I wish things had turned out differently. Maybe they will for you. But, then again, you never know. Maybe you will find out how much of a 'Jekyll and Hyde' he really is."

Shelly responded quickly, "That's not fair. I don't think he is split on his commitment to the children or his work."

Kristie sighed, "I wish I could believe that. But it's too late now to think about that. He always does what he wants first. He rarely, if ever, thinks about anyone else. He is totally self-absorbed. So there you have it."

Shelly responded as cheerfully as she could. She did appreciate the warning, and replied with as much resolve as she could, "Well, it's not too late for us to get to know each other. We can try to be friends."

Then she added quickly, "I am not to blame for your separation. I stayed away from Doug. I do not feel any anger; so please don't be angry with me. I am not to blame for what happened in the past." Shelly tried to reassure her.

Kristie said, "Doug always criticized me about the children. He told me to leave them alone. He has a kind of persistent personality; he always knows best and he is never sorry about anything. His mother made him second only to God and he believes it."

Shelly said, "I know he is forthright in his views, but maybe he can also learn to be more flexible."

She wanted there to be a better understanding between Kristie and herself so she listened closely.

Kristie shared her feelings, "The boys are impossible. They always were, and they always will be. No matter what you do for them, it's never enough. He lets them get away with anything they want. But, that's the way Doug is, too. No matter what you do, it will never be enough." She said, again her anger rising.

Shelly took another breath, a sip of coffee, and listened.

Shelly added, "I understand how you feel, Kristie. I know you must be in a lot of pain. I do want us to be friendly. The kids are not to blame for what went wrong. That was long ago. Let's try to stay in touch for the kid's sake, anyway." Shelly wanted Kristie to know she understood.

Kristie said, "Okay, there's not much point to staying mad anyway. What good would it do? Nothing will ever change." Her voice dropped.

Shelly added, "I do appreciate your telling me more about the kids. It will help me a lot to understand them better." Shelly wanted to reassure her. She said, "Whenever you want to arrange for a visit, just let me know."

They said good-by and hung up.

Shelly got up, walked to the sink, and put the cup under the running water. Then she hit her head with the edge of her hand and said out loud, "What did I get myself into?"

When Shelly's mother called the next day, Shelly tried to sound natural, upbeat and like everything was perfect.

"Hi, mom, how are you? Everything is fine. I've been so busy. I'm sorry I haven't written very much. Time just slips away."

"It's all right. I don't expect you to write to me when there are so many other important things to do," said her mother, hiding her irritation, but with little success.

Shelly continued, trying not to notice, "Mom, you can't believe how nice it is out here. The weather is perfect, the food and the people are great. I have not gotten lost yet driving, and my work at the Lab is going great, too," Shelly tried to sound bright and very cheerful.

"So what else is new? You always sound like things are perfect. I suppose the mess you are in with all those kids is perfect, too. I suppose that wonderful man with all those kids to support is wonderful, too. I'm sure he is also great in how he much he appreciates you. You will find appreciation only in the dictionary. Look it up!" added her mother sardonically.

"Now, mom, please don't start. Doug is happy to have us here. He has been just wonderful. So have the kids." Shelly implored her mother.

"Sure, he's wonderful, but he's not for you." Her mother continued without a breath. "All he wants is a housekeeper. He will never appreciate what you do for them. He will take, and take, and take, and use you up, and then spit you out. Then you will be alone again and have to look for yet another 'mishooganah' (crazy person) who doesn't know any better." She took a breath finally and continued, "At least in Washington you had your own place. You had help. You had security. What do you have now? I know…a lot of aggravation, very little rest, and a lot of headaches — somebody else's headaches. Why don't you ever take my word for it?" her mother lamented.

Shelly's mother had been saying the same thing, but in slightly different ways for years. She always took the negative, foreboding side to life. She looked at the glass half empty instead of half full. Maybe she was being practical, realistic, or trying to protect her, but Shelly always felt she dumped the negative on her and hardly paid attention to anything that was going well. Shelly knew things were not easy and gave her plenty of new challenges. Shelly had never taken her mother's "word" verbatim, and often lived to regret it later, because in the end her mother was usually right. But, now she was very sure her mother was just exaggerating, and making things seem more difficult, after all, she was fully prepared to make all the necessary adjustments.

Beside the musings of her mother, and the tale of woe that Kristie shared with her, she learned there were hidden dangers, but the warnings did not ring true in her ears or match her view of perfection, so she ignored them. Shelly believed all things would work out. She trusted that only the best things would happen for all of them. Life was challenging, and also exciting, and she was certain they would work out all of the details somehow, together.

Her mother got more upset when Shelly forgot and told her about the apartment mix-up, and that she had moved in temporarily with Doug.

She warned her, "You are making a big mistake. He will never marry you. You give it all to him for free. Why should he? Take your time. Don't rush. What's the rush anyway?" her mother reminded her. "I worry about Alison and her adjusting to all the changes. Is she ok?"

"She's fine. She is doing great. It's going to be okay, mom, believe me." Shelly tried to reassure her.

"I will tell you those 'no-neck monsters' will eat you up and spit you out. Believe me. You will only have heartache. I wish you would learn before it's too late," her mother added advice embedded with years of her own frustration, foreboding and fear.

Shelly shook her head when she hung up the phone. The phone rang again.

Then, she had to start the whole process of reassurance all over again, with Doug's parents. They both talked at once on the extension phone from their apartment overlooking Lake Michigan in Chicago.

"Shelly, isn't our Doug wonderful?" they said almost as one.

"Yes, he certainly is," she replied while nodding her head.

"So how are the children? We could never talk to Kristie about them. She never appreciated Doug or all his wonderful qualities. He finally found someone worthy of him," Doug's mother Lorraine exclaimed.

"He is so smart, so kind. So perfect!" added his father, Phil, quickly.

"Yes," said Shelly, again nodding her head to somehow reinforce what they were telling her and to confirm her own feelings.

"Well, how do you like San Francisco? They asked and continued in the same breath without waiting for her answer. "Doug shouldn't have left Chicago. It would be better for him here; with all his abilities he could go very far. He could still go into the practice with me," his father emphasized, reflecting on what might have been, imploring Shelly to speak to Doug about making a change.

"Well, I am sure that was a hard decision for him to make years ago," said Shelly sidestepping the thought of moving to Chicago.

"So, everything is going well for you and your daughter, Alison, isn't it?" asked Lorraine.

"Yes, she is great. Everything is just fine. Thank you for asking." She repeated as she reassured herself simultaneously.

Shelly felt close to them as she spoke with them. They seem very "haimesh," (familiar/comfortable).

"So what else is new? You are going to school? How can you do that? Do you have enough time to be with your child?" asked Lorraine in a motherly way.

"Yes, there seems to be time for everything. She is having a terrific time at her new school. I hope we will meet sometime soon," Shelly added cheerfully.

"So, when are you getting married?" they asked in unison.

"Well, we really don't have time to get married right now," Shelly added. She laughed at the thought.

She sensed they were not happy about the freestyle living arrangements, but she changed the subject back to the children. Finally the conversation ended with, "We hope we can come to visit by spring."

Shelly could hardly contain herself to share the news with Doug that night, and to tell him the details of all of the conversations. Then she thought about it. She realized she would have to modify some of the discussions and not tell him exactly what each one of them said, her mother, his parents, or his ex-wife. She also realized she needed help or she would not survive. She would ask Doug to agree to hire a sitter that they could count on to move in and help with the chores. She could not juggle it all herself. She was practical and she wanted to be able to manage all the new responsibilities.

In her heart she wished the uncertainty were over. She dreamed they were really married and all settled. Life was perhaps approaching a normal, regular routine. But, she knew that many of her dreams were impossible. The mountain of work she had created and had yet to climb over still loomed ahead. So she simply tried very hard to stay focused and take one day at a time.

Preparing her childcare study absorbed most of her day. She designed a good format for the parents' questionnaires. She planned how she would conduct the study. She designed the procedures she would need for data analysis. She planned to interview the parents in childcare centers, childcare homes, or in their own homes. She knew this was the best way to collect the data she needed, but she also knew it was not going to be easy to gather.

She decided to focus all her attention on the childcare issues in San Francisco. The communities in the study included: The Mission, Hunter's Point, Western Addition, South of Market, Chinatown, and Pacific Heights. She selected the diverse populations that each had their own cultural and social differences: Hispanics, African-Americans, Filipinos, Chinese-Americans, and Caucasians that represented the diversity of the population of San Francisco.

She arranged for translations of the basic questionnaire into each of the parent's languages. She also arranged for translators to be included in follow-up interviews. She wanted the parents to speak freely in their own language. She made many queries and visits to different childcare facilities in the city.

She investigated to learn which programs were public, which ones were private. The public programs were operated by a variety of different systems, social services, the school system, or the Catholic Archdiocese. Some private programs also existed. Shelly arranged to visit all of them.

She took time to talk with administrators and teachers. They all had plenty to say about their programs. She took a lot of notes, learned a lot about the problems and made many observations.

Shelly focused on the typical available childcare services in each community. She decided the only way to get the best information was directly from parents. The introduction to the study was translated into Cantonese, Tagalog, and Spanish so the parents in each community could read about the study plans and better understand its purpose and could feel more comfortable in responding to the questions.

She made arrangements for translators to go with her to the follow up parent interviews. Her interview questions focused on issues parents had to deal with when they tried to locate childcare in their own community. She was trying to find out if and to what degree the parents were satisfied with the childcare arrangements they made, what else they needed to assist them, and what was wrong with the services they found, if anything.

The staff of the early childhood program of the Educational Research Lab was involved in many different professional aspects — training teachers, curriculum for children, bilingual learning approaches for young children, training for parents to learn about their child's development, learning how to use toys to teach basic development to parents and other concepts, and developing skills for directors and teachers to understand how to more effectively cooperate with one another.

Studies and projects were under way to produce a curriculum for Chinese-speaking children, a new method for training teachers for the Head Start program, a project on self-image of African-American children, and another study on how feelings and self-esteem of a child affect how a child learns. The papers and potential for studies were endless.

Shelly was delighted to be at the Lab. The different people involved there and their different kinds of projects fascinated her. They were doing great things on many levels. This was change in action, not only theories or philosophy, but also direct testing to find out what was making a difference in the lives of young children. She was happy and challenged.

Shelly was glad the program she had designed fit the goals of the Lab. The staff liked the area she carved out. They recognized childcare was a large and unmet need in every community they knew about. They each shared different insights and useful information on services in San Francisco as they knew them as they had time.

She always made time to talk with Pat. They often had coffee breaks or lunch in the café across the street and chatted about people, their plans, and their families.

Pat told her, "It has not been easy for me. I left the inner city of Detroit. I thought I would never go back. Now, when I return I will try to make a difference with our Head Start model. It's ironic, isn't it? We can actually change things if we only have a little help."

Shelly nodded her head and added, "Yes! It also helps to have a grant to cover expenses. If only we could have enough money to do the job that's really needed."

"That's the truth! Yes, indeed, honey," laughed Pat teasing her new friend.

"What do you most want to do, Pat?" asked Shelly.

"Make a real difference somewhere. Know the kids will be helped before it's too late." She smiled thinking about what they could do if only given a chance.

"I want to make a difference too. I can start with myself, my kids, the community, and then see what happens next," said Shelly.

"Listen, girl, if you can do that, then you are better than most of us. We still are whistling old tunes in the dark, or trying to shoot at windmills with paper; lots of the time, all the paper falls flat. No one reads the papers, or the melodies are out of tune." Pat sighed,

"Well, we have to keep on singing and marching; that's for sure," Shelly added.

They finished lunch, still talking as they headed back to the office.

Pat updated Shelly on other people's work as she spent time with her. Pat and Shelly spent many enjoyable days talking, sharing, and laughing. They talked of work and families, their goals and frustrations. They shared about their past. They laughed at how much they had in common. They spent stimulating time in discussions with other staff members learning more about each other's goals, projects, interests and problems.

At the Lab, she stopped as often as she could to talk with her mentor, Glen Newheart. Shelly saw him as totally perfect in his philosophy, personality, and style of work. He was accessible and forthright. He was almost always available to discuss questions on strategy, study design, or needed resources. He frequently asked her how things were going. He encouraged her to spend time with each of the staff people so that they could each explain their work. He was a gem to work with and she felt lucky to be there as part of his team.

Dr. Newheart said, "I am pleased that I encouraged you to join our facility. You are making a solid contribution. Shelly I want you to feel free to ask me any questions about anything involved. I want to clear up anything before my hectic travel schedule kicks in. Let me know if you need anything or want any of the toys to see how they play."

Then he returned to his meeting. Shelly respected him greatly and appreciated his interest, insights, and support of her work. She became increasingly involved in Lab issues and discussions. She learned more about the design of the toys and how they would each help to teach a child new skills.

When Shelly was not at the Lab, she visited different childcare programs in San Francisco. She obtained agreements to conduct the study at each childcare center. She had dozens of books to read, her daily journal to maintain, papers to write, and faculty members and peers to communicate with.

Shelly also knew if she didn't get across the Bay Bridge by 4 o'clock each afternoon, she could forget about picking up Alison on time. So when she left early to get Alison at school, she made up an extra hour or two of work later at night, after Doug and the children were asleep, slipping downstairs to continue reading books or writing reports.

Late at night when the house was quiet, she set out four cereal bowls, spoons, and glasses for the children's breakfast. She made their sandwiches and added an orange or apple and put them in bags with their names before she went upstairs for a few hours of well-earned, but never enough sleep.

Finally, after a lot of searching, calling and carefully arranged interviews, she found Nora Jones, a capable young woman who had references, and a two-year-old daughter Ginny who was temporarily living in foster care. Nora needed employment as part of the arrangements for her to regain custody of her child. Shelly thought it was a good tradeoff for both of them and agreed to hire Nora. She would help her learn more parenting skills and she could have lots of hands-on practice. The boys reluctantly agreed to share one bedroom and noisily adjusted to the move. When Nora moved in, they met Ginny, Nora's two-year-old daughter. Somehow, eventually, everyone would get what they needed.

In November, Shelly learned she was pregnant. She knew she would have to once again have to undergo an abortion. With the demands of school for at least two or three more years, and the many pressures of her new life, she knew it was not the time to even think about having a baby. She tried not to show her real feelings of disappointment to anyone, not even to Doug. Shelly was upset about having another abortion.

She felt so much love for Doug. She knew somehow one day they would have a child of their own. Then it would be really "yours, mine, and ours." The kids would accept each other completely. Things would become a lot easier. She was awakened from her daydream by the nurse at the doctor's office.

"Shelly, would you like to schedule an appointment for the surgery now? The doctor will be going on vacation in ten days," she said.

Shelly shook her head and said, "I will call you back and let you know when I can go in."

Shelly had tears in her eyes as she left Dr. Bensen's office. She hurt. When she picked up Alison at school, she tried to be cheerful. Why take it out on her daughter?

She parked the car. Alison got out, kissed her good-by, and went to a friend nearby to play. Shelly went inside the house, to the kitchen, poured herself a glass of white wine and thought to herself, I guess it won't make any difference if I drink this now anyway. She knew she would feel very differently if she learned she were pregnant and able to carry to a full term. She tried to put the thought out of her mind.

The kids came home. They were busy with their homework, then TV. The noise increased with every commercial. She cringed. Her head was hurting and so was her heart.

Shelly prepared a simple tuna and noodle casserole. Nora fixed some vegetables and dessert. After Shelly put the casserole in the oven, she went to the bathroom to fix her face before Doug arrived. She did not want to show her sadness. What good would it do? She tried to hide her disappointment. She already knew what his response would be so what was the point? Later in the bedroom, she told Doug what the doctor said.

"I guess we are more fertile than I suspected." He tried to laugh.

"I want to be fertile in my mind only. I was so surprised. I never thought it would happen again. I think the diaphragm must have a hole in it, but I couldn't find a hole even though I looked." Shelly laughed at her weak humor and tried to be cheerful.

"When do you want to have the D&C?" asked Doug.

"There are not many choices. Doctor Bensen is going on vacation, so it has to be this weekend," She responded emphatically.

"Well, who knows, honey, maybe there will be another chance sometime in the future. Of course, four kids are plenty. There is not enough space here for more!" He added as he got up ready to leave the bedroom to get a snack downstairs.

Shelly nodded her head as he went past her. "Yes, but I still want one of ours. School, work and everything else must come first, I guess."

He nodded.

She added so softly, that he did not really catch her comment, "We certainly don't have any time to get married." as he went out past her to the door.

She had to talk to someone about her feelings. She turned to Melanie Schwin, a consultant at the Lab. She was working on her Ph.D. at Stanford University, and had plenty of her own challenges with part-time teaching, classes, work at the Lab, plus the long commute to Palo Alto three times a week. Shelly and she met at a meeting, began talking, and found they had lots of mutual interests. In addition, she lived only ten blocks from Doug's house. Melanie had discovered a special place and told Shelly about it. Soon it became a weekly ritual.

Every Tuesday, Shelly brought Alison directly home after school and left her in Nora's care. When Molly came home from school she had homework to do. Then she played with Alison or they both watched TV. Shelly was then free for a few precious hours.

Then she drove over to pick up Melanie, and headed down the hill from Diamond Heights, to Market Street, and into the parking lot of O'Reilly's Funeral Parlor near Noe Street. There was a special place next door, a place that gave them a special respite from work and stress. They dashed into Finnila's Finnish Baths.

After going there for a while, Shelly discovered there was a special room just right for small groups. Shelly's circle of friends expanded and she decided to invite several other women friends to join them in the steam baths each Tuesday afternoon. The time together to steam and talk helped each of them cope better and feel more relaxed.

Finnila's was a funky, 75-year-old place, with very thick gray concrete walls. It had originally been created by the current owner's father after he left Finland and settled in San Francisco. He brought the idea with him of the traditional sauna and created a unique, much-needed hideaway, a steamy oasis. From a tiny lobby, the hall split into two parts. At the counter you could purchase bottles of juice or water, towels, a cup of salt, and make extra arrangements for a massage.

At one end there was a women's public bath; at the other, a public bath for men. The public baths had shelves, hooks, and lockers for dressing, a large shower room, and then the very hot steam room. In individual rooms off the hall, one or two people could share a private sauna and shower, and a private dressing room. All of the seats in the saunas were tiled in white. The place was kept spotless and was a delightful secret Shelly treasured.

Shelly preferred Room 21, the reserved group room, because there she could feel free to be with friends to talk, gossip, and relax in a larger and more comfortable space. There were three rooms connected — shower and steam, resting room, and dressing room. The time spent away relaxing in this unique place helped Shelly cope with all the challenges, especially when she was able to arrange for special extra times for a massage.

Melanie soon felt like Shelly's new best friend. She had grown up in Modesto, an agricultural town two hours east of San Francisco. Melanie was bright, energetic, and going through the final stages of a painful divorce, she had been in an unhappy marriage for a long time. She was perky, pretty, and playful when she got to the sauna, although the strains of the divorce were taking a toll on her energy and depleting her playful nature.

Melanie expressed her frustration as she grabbed for her towel, "I've had it with lawyers. They should be banned from the practice of the legal voodoo they call law. What manipulators they are. I would strangle mine. If I only knew how to get lawyers banned, like a bad book or a terrible movie."

"What happened now?" asked Shelly scrubbing her leg with a brush

"Well, mine is just a cold, ineffectual shark only interested in his retainer. He doesn't get anything resolved. The battle has been dragging on for months. We're not any closer to a settlement or to anything." Melanie told her as she applied salt to her body.

"Could you make your ex do anything fast?" asked Shelly, smiling. Adding, "Mine did nothing fast!" "The only thing he did fast was sex. One, two, three; bam, bam, bam and thank you Ma'am! That's about it. I want to get free of John already. It's enough torture for one lifetime," Melanie pleaded as she headed for the steam.

"Do you have any energy for a date?" asked Shelly, hoping to change the subject and cheer up her friend. "I was thinking of introducing you to a sexy young intern who is hot, smart, and fun. Are you ready?" They closed the door and breathed in the hot steam.

"Me...energy for sex? You've got to be kidding. I barely can get class papers marked up and ready for the next day. I hardly have the energy to get to school. I am ready to take a vacation, though, and get away from everything. I don't know how you handle what you are doing."

They talked as they sat on their towels in the very hot and steamy room

"Well, there will be time enough for a vacation when things get resolved and you are a free woman again," said Shelly cheerfully trying to convince her friend of the potential of a new man in her life. She stretched out. She could forget for awhile all of the challenges she had.

"Sure," replied Melanie, trying to laugh, "When I get finished with this divorce, the only vacation I will be able to afford is to go home to my mother for a weekend in Modesto."

Shelly picked up her towel, and headed for the shower with her soap and razor. Melanie wrapped the towel around her head, picked up her shampoo bottle, and followed her friend to the shower in the next room.

Other friends joined them. Sara, one of the other friends who came by, worked downtown in a public relations office. Each of them, Betty, a sex therapist, Susan, an author, and Brittany, a elementary school teacher, and Sara, were glad to have this healthy break once a week, to relax, and to talk and be with women friends they could easily relate to. They were all in the steam room.

Melanie complained, "I could never have a totally loving home with

John. He was so cold and distant. My heart hurts."

They all listened with their eyes closed breathing in the steam. I wish I had someone to come home to," sighed Sara. "Working all day typing press releases with no one to snuggle up with at night is dismal, and I hate singles bars." She scrubbed her body with salt.

Melanie continued, "The commute is killing me. It's destroyed my sex life. I'm too tired. You should try driving to Palo Alto twice a day. It's murder, even though I'm going against traffic. Traffic is really appalling."

Brittany said," I am so glad to be here after a long day in the classroom. Teaching is murder on my feet!"

Sara interjected, "There's just no payoff being alone. Shelly, you just don't know how lucky you are!"

Melanie applied salt to her back.

Betty interjected, "Keep applying salt, brush your body, keep the water flowing, breathe, and be thankful... Just relax and cut the BS!"

Shelly laughed and looked over at her friends and added, "We're all lucky. We're alive, living in San Francisco and enjoying this amazing steam room. I am thankful! Now I will shut up!"

They all laughed and looked at her in amazement.

They saw Shelly's new-to-the-city captivation, but they each knew better. Things that look so rosy from the outside do not always remain sweet and perfect. No, they each knew how badly a love affair could feel when it went sour. They knew that from their own hard knocks of reality. The steam passed away and things could get very cold very fast. It was not all "sugar and spice and everything nice." Despite reality, they each held onto their dreams.

The city was shining, but there were plenty of rusty places just below the surface that were not shiny at all. When you live inside a jewel case, life seems like a gem.

Chapter 14

Earth Mother

We must be willing to give up the life we had planned, so as to have the life that is waiting for us. Joseph Campbell.

On Tuesday night, after she returned home from Finnila's, Shelly felt more relaxed, refreshed, and better able to deal with whatever challenges or conflicts were going on.

Nora gave her the day's messages, and then reported on new problems with either her social worker or some misunderstandings with Ross or Andy.

Despite her inexperience, Nora did her best to help with the children and keep up with the details. She could always count on Alison to have stories from school, or some new conflict with Molly or Ross. Ross and Andy were certain to be fussing with each other: something was either missing in their room, damaged, or one of them was "bothering" the other. The level of belligerence varied with what TV show was on.

Shelly tried to handle each crisis. Then, it dawned on her, that the children might benefit if they had a chance to talk, express themselves and their grievances openly, calmly, and on a regular basis. Some of their conflicts might even be ironed out or reduced through discussion if actually learned to listen to each other.

She felt this was an important next step toward improving family communications. She would try to create a time to have regular family meetings to clear the air. It would just be one more item on an already crowded weekly agenda. She asked the children to join her in the living room. Doug would not be home for at least an hour. It seemed clear he was leaving "family problems" and other matters to her. They had already eaten dinner so she thought the timing might work as they were not hungry. She was going to wait until later to eat with Doug; she was willing to try something new.

"Look," Shelly began, "you kids seem to be having a lot of difficulty talking with each other. It sometimes sounds like feeding time at the zoo." They laughed, but they listened.

Shelly continued, "What I'd like to do is find time for an experiment. Let's give each of us a chance to talk. We will each listen. We can solve a lot of problems in our family circle meeting.

Andy jumped up. "The only person who could solve these problems as far as I am concerned is a cop!"

Shelly said, "We are a "blendship", and it will take each of us to make this family work. It's like a cake being made from scratch with no box with directions on the back like a cake mix. Each member of the family is an ingredient in the cake, and if one ingredient is left out then the cake is bad or least not as good. We have to try to make a good cake, listen to everyone's problems and iron out difficulties."

Then the boys immediately started bickering. The explosion of arguing sent shivers up Shelly's spine. She had hoped the proposed "Family Circle" time could end the continuously noisy squabbles. She was overly optimistic.

They sat around looking at each other. It was very clear Andy wanted to continually dominate. He hardly gave anyone else a chance to talk. When anyone did speak up, he mocked them.

"There's not enough time in the bathroom in the morning and it smells terrible," Molly complained. "It bothers me that Alison still wets her pants. It smells up our room."

The boys joined in, teasing Alison about wetting her pants, as she hid her face in a pillow. She was embarrassed, but that did not stop their teasing.

In the midst of the erupting "family council" meeting, Doug got home, saw what was happening.

He had no interest in joining the discussion. He had been listening to hospital problems all day.

"I'm okay, just too tired, and I need to relax." he said as he walked past them, loosening his tie as he went upstairs, and quietly closed the bedroom door.

Shelly looked up the stairs, at the children, and then told the kids she would get together with them later.

Andy smirked and said, "I'm tired too of all of this jabber," and he walked over to the TV and turned it on as the other kids joined him and sat around the TV.

Shelly went to the kitchen to prepare dinner. Doug returned downstairs to eat. As Shelly and Doug sat at the dining room trying to talk, they were interrupted every few minutes by one of the four kids grabbing attention: they wanted help with homework, permission to buy something, a way to resolve a conflict, or mostly wanted to complain.

When he was finished with dinner, Doug went to bed and watched television. He was usually tired on those nights when he did not have late community meetings at the hospital. Shelly said good night to the children and opened the door to the bedroom.

"I don't think a 'family circle' will work." Doug said.

Shelly replied, "Maybe we should wait until you are home to join us next time! Then it might work!"

He looked at her, shook his head and turned off the light. She knew it was a lot to handle. It was only the first time. She would be patient.

Friday night was Shelly's special time. She felt like a Queen on the Sabbath evening. When Shelly got home on Friday, she began making matzo balls, rolling them in her hand, shaping them into small balls and dropping them into boiling water. After the pot was covered, she put the finishing touches on chicken soup, vegetables, noodles and the rest of the meal that she had started preparing late on Thursday evening.

She wanted help to set the table, but by then Nora wanted to take off for the weekend, so she could be with her daughter, and the kids were outside playing with friends. Shelly continued to complete the arrangements. It all looked just right, and it was the end of another challenging week. She took a deep breath. No one said being a pioneer woman was going to be easy.

Almost always, friends appeared to join them on Friday evenings for supper. They always arrived on Friday afternoon. Friends enjoyed being with their noisy family, especially those without kids, who thought four kids were a great novelty. Everyone enjoyed the madcap scene, besides the meal was great and it gave them a touch of traditions, home and a glimpse of what was missing without having four wild kids. They were grateful.

After a short game of "Jewish Geography," (who knew whom, what they did, where they went to school, or where they worked) everyone soon discovered everyone knew everyone, whether or not they were there that evening. Such was the vortex. There was always a connection, only two degrees of separation.

Shelly had always found it easy to meet people. In a short time, their Friday night gatherings became well known to many who enjoyed their home and hospitality.

The circle of friends, invited each week, was exiles from strange places, but were strangers no more after a bowl of Shelly's grandma's "secret" chicken soup. You could taste the secret, but you were not sure exactly what ingredients made it taste so good. Shelly did not ever reveal the secret. She just smiled.

As the children rushed in to do their respective last minute activities, Shelly would be cleaning the kitchen, and putting the final touches on the meal. She was happiest on Friday nights. It seemed the best time, and the culmination of everything she wanted in life. She felt she was home, and her home was a magnet for joy, friendships and the gatherings of family and friends.

She knew Rabbi Herb was right about the importance of the Sabbath. There was a special magnetism that brought everyone together to celebrate the end of the week, a time for gathering, and of rest. It felt like a very special time and problems and stress diminished.

When Doug came in the door about 6:30 everything was ready. He relaxed a short while, and went upstairs to change his clothes, and waved as he went by. When he came down he went over to Shelly to say hello and took out a bottle of wine, as he happily surveyed the kitchen. They had survived another week.

Shelly watched over the stove, the kids, and made sure the guests were entertained. When everyone was ready and seated at the table, Shelly blessed everyone around the table and lit the first candle.

She said, "Blessed are Thou, O Lord our God, King of the Universe, who sanctified us to light the Sabbath candles. This candle warms the heart of each of us around the table. The light gives us energy to do our work or go to school. Now is the time to rest from all our work and join together as a family. The energy of the light is within each of us now. May we rest so we can be healthy and strong for the week that lies ahead. Amen."

She turned to Doug, who raised his wine glass to bless everyone.

The blessing over the "fruit of the vine" came forth. He enjoyed sharing the prayers and the wine. As he poured the glasses, Doug was content. He felt that although it was a challenge to bring the families together, it was worthwhile. Shelly had jumped right in, and did a lot his kids had not been exposed to before. Kristie was not Jewish, nor did she try any of the traditional family rituals. Now it was different. He could see the children enjoyed the new experiences. They were more interested in going to Sunday school classes.

It would be another year before Andy reached his Bar Mitzvah, but he was already learning the prayers. He knew the blessings over the bread, and he said it as he raised a piece of Challah, the traditional twisted loaf of egg bread.

Their Friday nights became a special family celebration. Alison looked in awe at the other three children. She learned from each of them. She smiled, and was happy being with them. They ate, made music and song, and had a joyous celebration. Everyone enjoyed the food, asked for more soup, and of course, the recipe.

Shelly was content. She felt like a bountiful "Jewish Earth Mother," but she would not divulge the "secret" ingredients for the soup — (keep this to yourself: plenty of fresh chopped garlic, fresh chopped parsley and a pinch of pepper and salt all added just at the end when you add in the matzoth balls).

Shelly created a new treat that everyone seemed to like a lot. She called it "Earth Mother Mix" — she combined in a large bowl, nuts without salt including walnuts, pumpkin seeds, almonds, cashews, soy nuts and added raisins. She put handfuls into plastic bags and gave them to the kids for snacks. They were excellent munchies at the lab also. She did feel like an Earth Mother on most days.

One by one the children went to bed, and quickly dropped off to sleep. The guests left. The dishes got washed. Shelly and Doug were left in the living room, holding each other in front of the fire. This was the best night of all to make love. She was deeply thrilled to finally be alone with him. He was smart and funny, and he cared about her but she knew he was not perfect.

She had no desire to return to the apartment she maintained, but hardly ever used. From the very first night they were seldom apart. Doug held her close. She surrendered to his embrace. They were happy together through the weekend.

Saturday and Sunday more than made up for the pressures of the week. Saturday morning, after outdoor athletics, Ross and Andy went to hang out with friends or made arrangements to visit their mother. Kristie didn't drive a car, so Doug took the children over to her apartment. Doug's children were usually gone by noon.

Alison spent the day with her mother, or played with friends in the neighborhood. Sometimes Alison stayed with one of her friends on Saturday evening. When she did, Shelly and Doug went out. If they were entertaining at home, Alison stayed in her room to play, or invited a friend to spend the night.

It was Sunday morning Shelly most relished. Doug got up early, and took the children to Sunday school at Temple Sherith Israel across town on California Street. It was the oldest (1851) Reformed Congregation, with many families, and an impressive historic sanctuary. The Rabbi Martin Weiner and Cantor Martin Feldman were friendly and understanding of their situation. They had children and understood the challenges of a new blended family. When Doug left to drive the kids or to pick up the kids at Kristie's apartment, he took Alison along. They drove across the city to the Temple.

Shelly would finally have three hours of quiet in the house: She read the paper, or lay in the sun in the backyard. She was almost always entertained by small blue or yellow butterflies flying freely outside in the yard. Glen Park was next to the back of their house. This was the home of many butterflies; in particular, the Mission Blue butterfly, which she soon learned was listed on the endangered species list. They were small, fragile and needed Lupin to survive. Shelly wanted to plant more flowers in the yard to attract more butterflies. She made a note to get more plants as soon as she could.

Doug went to play tennis during the time while he was waiting for the kids to finish Sunday school. He enjoyed staying fit, and except for smoking, was in good shape.

Months passed quickly. Each of the parents called almost every Sunday. They wanted to find out how Alison and the other children were doing, how Shelly's work was progressing, what Doug was up to; and they each always asked, "When are you getting married?"

It was a question her mother asked in every conversation, especially after her mother found out that the separate addresses were not happening in reality. They were not living apart. The apartment seemed like a good idea, but things changed. They were working out the arrangements.

She told Shelly, "It's not proper for you to be living together without being married. What can I tell the family? It isn't right! No one will understand. Why don't you ever follow my advice?"

"Mom," Shelly asked, "why do you have to tell anyone in the family anything? I thought you were a liberated woman?" She tried to tease her away from the continuous reprimands. Her mother was adamant.

"If you are living together then you will never get married. It's not right."

Doug's mother and father, the Fines, felt the same. Just like his son, Phillip Fine was "old fashioned," middle-class doctor with a certain position he felt he had to maintain. Besides, the family in Chicago was always asking him what was going on with Doug. Although they did not approve of his divorce, they were glad their son was finally involved in a new relationship with what seemed to them to be the "right" woman. She was Jewish, and knew how to manage the children. She seemed to be making their "sonny boy" happy. They felt Shelly was turning the situation into something more manageable.

They said, "It is time for you both to announce your plans. What are you doing? When are you going to make things final?" They asked.

Doug's ex-wife, Kristie went back to work as a nurse at the hospital. She resumed her career after it had totally stopped during their thirteen-year marriage. She continued to talk with Shelly about the children; the faults as she saw them in her marriage with Doug — and she always blamed Doug for what went wrong. Shelly called it "chemistry" and tried to shrug off her comments. She felt Kristie was judgmental and did not want to see Doug's side. But she listened to her, to learn more about what went wrong and it was clearly lopsided.

On some Sundays, Shelly had a chance to meet their neighbors. Some of the neighbors were very friendly, others were reserved.

She particularly liked the neighbors who lived only three doors away. They were a committed couple in a long-term relationship. They had remodeled their home in a "designer-perfect" way, and were charming, and were very hospitable to her.

Shelly enjoyed herself so much that she visited her neighbors, Peter and Charles, as often as she could. She loved their exquisite taste in furniture and food. She could hide away for a little time in their quiet, elegant oasis.

She laughed at their quips that flew back and forth between them about their relationship, about other gay men, and about the pros and cons of relating as a couple. They were always "dissing" each other playfully. They loved to give her advice about everything, and they did especially about the kids and decorating. Over cocktails one evening, she laughed with them about their own relationship.

"It took years before Charles was ready to settle down," complained Peter. "He was always into one night stands, or cruising on the Castro, trying to score as many conquests as possible. I always wanted closeness, the intimacy of one relationship, so I waited patiently."

"Oh, you queer! You were just afraid of being out in the action. You're just a homebody after all; admit it, a real Queen. You wanted a throne, and now you have one," responded Charles.

"Hell, what's wrong with that?" Peter replied.

"Nothing, except you missed out on all the fun. Moving, as I did, from a small town in Ohio, coming here was like entering the city of 'Baghdad.' I wouldn't put aside all those experiences I had for the entire world, and I am the better for it." Charles snorted.

"I could never come out of the closet until I hit San Francisco," Charles added "I think you're still in it. You never went out. You never did the 'scene' like I did."

"I was willing to make a commitment right after I met you," said Peter, verging on tears. "There was no one else for me until you were willing to make a commitment."

Charles, trying to calm him down, asked, "What are you complaining about? I have been with you ever since we met, haven't I? Besides, I always come home to sleep."

At that point, Shelly tried to change the conversation to a more mundane topic, like omelet recipes, so she announced, "The 'secret of life' is, a 'yolk.' Or is it an omelet? I forget."

I'd love to do an "Omelet party" where everyone brings their own pans and fixings," Charles replied. "We could make omelets, drink lots of champagne, crack yolks and just laugh our heads off. Why don't we plan it?"

"I only have a poor facsimile of an omelet pan," Shelly said, thinking this would be a great excuse to buy an authentic one.

She hugged Charles and Peter and returned home.

The kids were getting ready for bed. Doug was listening to music, oblivious to all the noise, rock music, both water taps running, the dog barking, and the kids shouting.

Shelly helped the girls get ready for bed, kissed Doug good night, and returned to the dining room table to read.

Shelly was trying to find time to read, conduct the study, travel, and manage the house and children. She could not manage at all at this point without Nora. Despite the help she was tired by the end of the week and could barely keep her eyes open. However, she knew she had to keep up with the large amount she had to read, and she forced herself to stay up and learn new information.

She decided to get more involved in the community. She heard about the local chapter of the National Association for the Education of Young Children, an international group of teachers dedicated to preschool children. She had been a member in Washington, D.C. She made contact with the local chapter and started to attend meetings. When she had the opportunity, she described the work she was doing. Some of the members were very helpful in connecting her with new people she needed to meet in the childcare community.

Clearly they all shared that the need existed in the City for more, consistent, and improved childcare programs. There was some talk at the meeting of organizing a demonstration around the threatened federal cuts in existing childcare programs. The people she met in all the programs whether staff or parents deeply cared about children, and they wanted to improve the programs and services. There were just not enough resources available, but plenty of dedication.

When she left Washington, she knew what little childcare remained was endangered. Shelly managed to stay as involved as she could. She expressed her ideas to the group.

She suggested ways that might work to help raise broader public awareness. She suggested that an organized demonstration for more childcare at City Hall and also in front of the Federal Building might indeed help to get public and media attention. It might also provoke some local and state action. The group was interested and discussed the details and decided to move ahead.

Sometimes along the way, she had a few moments to be alone. Her thoughts dominated her mind, sometimes taking her away from her studies. She had to stay focused. She learned to compartmentalize her thoughts, and to focus on what she had to do at the moment. She had to keep in touch with her committee, her faculty advisor, and several other student peers with whom she was involved. The students in this program supported each other and exchanged insights and information. She also had to write in her journal every day. She had to talk with so many different people at the Lab, in the community, and friends. How could she find time to juggle everything?

But, on the way to and from Emeryville, in the quiet hours of the morning, when she was supposed to be working on something serious, her mind often drifted to romantic thoughts of Doug. She usually felt happiness when she was near him. The future was uncertain. But, as long as they were together she was determined to make a go of their growing relationship. She felt secure that he loved her. She knew she had to love him or she would not have taken it all on.

One of the couples with whom they made friends was Paul and Eileen Sandway. Paul was an attorney involved in legal matters concerning children and teens. He specialized in being a legal advocate. Eileen had been staying at home, not working for a number of years, raising their two children. She was a wonderful cook and liked to create delightful dinner parties.

Whenever they spent time together, they found their children related well with each other: their daughter, Kate, played happily with the two girls, and their son, Adam, got along with the two boys. Somehow the pressure was off each of the families when they were together. The six children could easily become a group of ten or twelve children, depending on which house they were visiting. As the group swelled, the activity and noise level increased, but the fighting decreased. Shelly made a note of this, and thought it was an encouraging sign.

Shelly occasionally received phone calls from Arnold, her ex-husband, when he called from Washington to talk to Alison. Shelly sent him pictures Alison made at school. As the months passed, Shelly thought about Washington from time to time. She called Rhonda as often as she could and wrote letters, but it was hard to find enough time. Bits of news from Washington were sometimes in the local papers. She missed Washington's daily dynamic of politics and intrigue found in Art Buchwald and The Washington Post, but she turned now to Herb Caen and The Chronicle for the latest local news and insights.

She focused on the new intrigue, the dynamics of her new family, and the new and different kind of energy among the new friends she found in California. Shelly felt it had been right to leave Washington, and to establish a new life, whatever the cost, or loss. She was ready for change and the next adventure.

Shelly tried every day to remember to take vitamins. Juggling all the pins of the family circus was a constant challenge. If one pin fell, everything tumbled; so Shelly tossed all the pins as fast as she could, to keep things balanced.

Chapter 15

Challenges

The holiest of all holidays are those kept by ourselves in silence and apart, the secret anniversaries of the heart. Henry Wadsworth Longfellow.

As fall merged into the Thanksgiving season, the lives of Shelly and Doug became increasingly more complicated.

Shelly made the rounds of childcare centers, made arrangements to interview parents, teachers, and administrators of programs, wrote up her observations, arranged for photographs to be taken at each place, and observed children in the programs.

Periodically, she visited Alison at school to see how she was doing. Alison was making adjustments, slowly. She was fascinated with the typewriter that her astute teacher, Hilda introduced her to. She spent a lot of time typing new words. She was learning to read more easily and to express herself. Shelly thought she might also write and draw in a journal, but there was hardly enough time.

While driving back and forth to Emeryville every day, Shelly tried to maintain a semblance of quiet, to think. It was a conflict to drive, and to think too much. She tried to remember all the items on her "to-do" list. Shelly's mind often raced ahead of the car as she headed for the freeway.

Then on Tuesday she had a few precious hours at Finnila's sauna to look forward to — a refreshing respite. Her friends listened and laughed as she shared what was happening. They knew with certainty they would not want to trade places. What Shelly was doing was to them a major personal challenge. They thought that the kids were a royal pain especially since each of the women had visited for dinner and dropped by to visit.

"Shelly," her friend Terry asked, "How can you do everything you do for Doug and the kids? They are taking advantage of you."

Before Shelly could reply, Betty chimed in, "I can't understand why you would ever want the position of the under-appreciated Five-Star-General-of-the-Army-of-the (ever needy, always hungry, demanding, unruly, emotionally exhausting)-Battalion-of-Unruly-Children-at-Home."

Shelly laughed at herself and the image of her being a general.

Then she replied, "I am only trying to figure out why Andy won't stop being angry? He does not give me a break. Every night he finds fault with something. If it's not me, it's Alison, Molly, or Ross. He never picks on Doug. Strange! The rest of us are his constant points of attack. It's really hard to deal with. Wonder what Dr. Spock would say if he had to live with them? No, he would not want to subjugate himself to being tortured. He plays it safe from a distance doling out advice freely, word by word, but first you must buy his book!"

They all laughed again. Then as they relaxed in the sauna, Shelly's mind drifted to other issues. She asked out loud,

"Do you know about that childcare center in the Mission? Can you believe that the Archdiocese is charging the Latino Community Group more for rent than anyone else in the city is paying? Why don't they donate the space? They should make a contribution to families?"

The group agreed and said, "Yes, they should."

Then Shelly asked her girlfriends, wondering why life was not exactly as she pictured it would be,

"Why is Doug so preoccupied with the hospital? He never has time to relax, any morning or even on weekends. He's like a mechanical man, moving up, down, in, and out. I wonder if it will always be like this, or is it because, he has so much on his mind? If he doesn't work hard, he will never get all he wants to accomplish to change the health-care delivery system, to solve the endless political problems at the hospital, and make the changes needed in the city public health-care system. He is doing the best that he can all the time!"

Her friends all nodded in unison, as they knew things were not easy nor would they ever be easy in her complex situation.

Then Shelly said, "Alison is upset. Although she is making her adjustments, I wonder if she misses her father. She hardly says anything. It's so hard to find out what she really wants or is feeling."

They all agreed again for they sensed that Alison had to be struggling to keep up with the other kids at home and in school.

Shelly then had another brighter thought and said, "Melanie, you are having tough time. How about coming over for dinner next week? Let us introduce you to Jake, that nice resident at the hospital. I am sure you will hit it off. Are you interested?"

Melanie jumped up with a towel wrapped around her shoulders and said emphatically, "Yes! Would love it! It's time for me to meet someone new and intelligent. I'll be there and bring a salad, if that's ok? I don't mind the noise and confusion with the kids."

Shelly nodded her head agreeing to the plan and said aloud to her friends now that she was content about her matchmaking:

"What's so ironic is I thought everything would be somehow much easier here. I have more to do than ever before, with a lot less help. Oh, for those simpler days, the government bureaucracy, the days of Flora with a nice hot meal all ready when I got home, and time to play. Now I hardly have any time or energy left to play!"

Shelly's mind raced as she sighed and she said, "There was nothing else to do, but keep on moving ahead. We all just need to stay on track, and try not to get lost along the way. Each of us has plenty of challenges every day."

She relaxed for the rest of the time at the sauna — her thoughts floating on top of the steam.

She decided that she was given exactly what she could handle, and she could manage it all somehow. They showered, dried off and dressed. She said goodnight to her friends and headed back up the hill. It was another evening of chaos, but again she felt she could handle it, and she did. Even if it felt like a four ring circus, she was the ringmaster of her fate, so she thought.

The next morning after dropping Alison at school, she again drove to the Lab. Shelly pulled into the parking lot as her mind was thinking about Washington, the past, her home life in the present and the future, and then all she had to do for that day.

She caught herself and said finally to herself — "What did Ram Das say? "Be here now!" Right she sat back, took a deep breath, and fixed her face in the rear-view mirror. She erased the memories and she got busy with her work and managed to get a lot done.

Pat was on a trip, so she couldn't talk things over with her friend. She held the concerns inside her head. But, when she had a few moments they were written down in her journal along with observations, experiences, and jottings and notes about Doug and the kids. Then she headed back to the city to pick up Alison.

Alison came running out of the play yard and jumped into the car.

"Hi, Mommy!"

Hi, Munchkin. I'm happy to see my big girl!"

They buckled up and headed home for the usual evening "free-for-all."

The days passed quickly. Time would take care of life, and everything would work out. Over the next few weeks, Shelly found herself involved in discussing, with many childcare teachers and parents, the plans that were growing for a large community-wide demonstration to take place at City Hall and at the Federal Building.

She began writing about the conditions she found in childcare centers everywhere. She was shocked at what she saw. She had expected California to have better programs than anywhere else in the country. She had anticipated accessible, quality services, good facilities, and easy enrollment for all children. She had visited many programs across the country and was usually not impressed. She had not had the special chance to spend extended time, make close observations of programs, or be as close to issues as she was able to do now in California she thought programs would be perfect, or at least fairly good.

But, as she got deeper into the Bay Area community, she discovered many obvious and not so apparent problems, especially in Hunter's Point, Chinatown, the Mission, and in South of Market. Each ethnic group was supposed to have programs that reflected its children's background and upbringing, but the real situation was quite different.

Teachers were often poorly prepared. The educational program of the ethnic childcare programs left much to be desired. Food, language, and play products did not reflect the needs of the diversity of children.

Shelly grew increasingly concerned about what she was seeing, even in the highly touted programs of the school system. The children needed more nurturing; the staff needed more support and more training and cultural sensitivity to the children, especially when it concerned food, bi-lingual products for learning and play. They did not speak the same language nor understand each other. They were all in need.

Nixon's veto of childcare services the year before in Washington pressed down to dry up the limited resources of the sparse state and local resources that were left. Not much money was available now to meet local needs.

The plans for the demonstration for childcare would bring everyone together. But, Shelly now doubted any good would come of it. Nothing would change until the "power-brokers" in Congress recognized the importance of childcare, and that day might never come despite the urgent needs, protests, or reports. Shelly realized she was not alone in her deep concerns, but she also felt helpless. She wanted to focus on what she could do best.

Each morning when she picked up the local paper from the steps outside their home, she read of the problems growing in Washington, and the unrest in government. Nixon was believed to have part in a scandal called "Watergate." The Viet Nam War had taken its toll. With all the complex problems in the White House, the focus was still not on childcare.

In the "Style" section she could see the women pictured on Rodeo Drive in Hollywood wearing the new "hot pants" and boots that came up to their knees. She smiled thinking of the New York winters, and she knew girls on Fifth Avenue would too be also wearing this silly style. Thank goodness she wasn't into having to keep up with the latest fads and she dressed to fit her lifestyle, simple and functional.

She and Melanie greeted each other at the sauna on Tuesday.

"Hi. Have you started your book yet, 'Divorce ala Flame,' or is it 'Burn the Lawyer?'" asked Shelly, hoping to get her friend to laugh at her situation.

"I'm about to throw the whole book at him, if he doesn't do something soon," replied Melanie, getting some bottled water from the clerk at the counter. "Do you want some water, Shelly?"

"Yes, thanks a lot. I'm always thirsty these days. I must be moving faster than ever. I get a good workout keeping up with the kids, that's for sure." She laughed, took hold of the bottle and her bag, as they headed for their dressing room.

As they undressed, they talked about the divorce Melanie was going through. Melanie said, "We are finally making some progress. My lawyer actually woke up and now seems to be doing something. Maybe it will all get settled before the end of the year. Pray for me, Shelly, please."

"You are in my prayers," Shelly said as she grabbed the soap and got ready to go into the shower. Melanie joined her. As they washed their hair, they sang:

"What a day this has been what a rare mood I'm in, why it's almost like being in love. I've a smile on my face…"

The other women had joined them. They were all laughing and throwing water around at each other. Then they went into the sauna and got quiet. They stretched out on their sheets and relaxed. They breathed deeply, enjoying the heat…chanting — Ohmmmmm!

Shelly scrubbed her back and her skin all over. She scrubbed Melanie's back. They applied salt liberally to their skin and rubbed it in. They breathed deeply, and smelled the Eucalyptus leaves, which opened their nostrils to allow deeper breathing. Then they were silent, stretched on the sheets, breathing in the moist steam, the heat, and the smell of the eucalyptus branches. Time melted away. Tensions melted. Time in the sauna brought healing. Each of them enjoyed the camaraderie in that special oasis of relaxation. Sometimes they did not talk at all.

Every day Shelly tried to write something in her journal. She described her feelings, about the relationship between herself and Doug, between herself and the children, between her work and what was emerging — observations of the city, childcare centers, Lab, and new ideas, dreams, creative thoughts, complaints, and even a little poetry.

She was thankful Roy Fairfield encouraged her to write. Writing opened up a deep reservoir of repressed feelings, and gave her a way to safely channel her self-expression, feelings, thoughts, observations, fears and frustrations. Okay! Complaints were safer written in the journal than expressed out loud. They allowed her to say what she needed to, no one took it personally, and she got no negative reaction to the complaint. That helped, at least, to offer her an escape valve when she felt the pressure building, not unlike a pressure cooker.

When they were meeting in the living room, Shelly taped the "family council" sessions. She wanted to give the children a chance to hear themselves more clearly after the session was over. She thought it would be fun to document. But afterward, none of them ever seemed to have time to listen nor cared to. She kept the tapes and listened herself, and was amazed at what she learned hearing their issues all again.

It would have been great, she thought, to have a hidden video camera for a glimpse into the reality of raising children. Now she thought that would make for an amazingly reality TV program that would be something completely different, revealing the reality and drama of a real family over time, warts and all. She laughed at the idea. No one would believe what she saw and heard.

The "Family Council" was a circle that took place with the four kids and Shelly. Seldom was Doug a part of it because his new responsibilities took more time and he did not get home until after the kids were asleep. Shelly felt the time for the "Family Council" was very important. Shelly asked them "to come to order," and asked for the topics on the agenda. At first, they all talked at once:

"Alison's bothering me and my clothes."

"Molly won't take turns. She leaves me to do all the work."

"Ross is going into my room and taking my stuff."

"Andy is always hitting me."

"Ross won't let me watch what I want to on TV."

And Alison would sit quietly and take it all in.

Shelly had her own list:

"The chores are not getting done."

"Who forgot to feed the cat?"

"Can you pick up your clothes, hang up your towel, and put dirty laundry in the hamper? Please!"

Slowly each time they convened they began to listen to each other, to pay attention and to take turns. But, most of the time there was just a "free-for-all." They were all talking and complaining at the same time. Shelly tried to stay as calm as she could. The process would take time. Who said anything would be easy?

Doug said one night, "I think you are nuts for trying to do this ""Family Council" or whatever it is. I have a better solution! Take away privileges! Send them to their room! No allowance!"

Shelly disagreed. She said, "Those things will not help them in the long run. They need to find better ways to relate to each other, express their feelings in a safe way, and not to fight. Is it too much to ask them to learn to listen to each other, and talk together?"

Doug shook his head, and turned off the light.

Shelly thought herself to sleep. Some nights she was too tired to think. She wanted to go straight to sleep, but her mind raced as she knew they could not escape issues they had to face. It was a day-to-day struggle to get the children's attention, gain their interest, or get their willingness to work things out together.

Meanwhile, at the hospital, Doug was having his own problems. He was in charge of new community health programs. He was facing political issues almost daily from many directions–the hospital, the city, the mayor, the supervisors, the public health department, and community leaders. He spent his days going back and forth between the University, San Francisco General Hospital, and the new community health center in South of Market.

A threat of a strike among the nurses was looming. Services would be seriously affected by a strike. Administrators were trying to do everything they could to avert the strike.

Doug was deeply involved in negotiations with the nurses. He had to work with Janet Grover again. She was still miffed at him for his avoiding her and not making out with her months before. She fought with him, yet she still found him desirable. She saw he was occupied. But, she persisted again as she thought she had a chance to gain his attention.

"Dr. Fine, it is time doctors took the side of the nurses instead of siding with the administration."

She thought he was still being selfish, looking out for his own interests, and not seeing the problems of the nurses. She knew from experience nurses were not being treated fairly by the doctors or the administration. They both took advantage of them most of the time. They worked long hours, had difficult working conditions, received inadequate salaries, and had few of the benefits that the doctors enjoyed. Then, too, they also had childcare problems to deal with, if they had young children. Many of the nurses were also single mothers.

Although Janet did not have children, she was sympathetic to those who were not able to come in because their own sitters were sick, or they lost their arrangements. She knew the hospital should have a childcare center, but that was far down the list of administration priorities. For now, they mostly hoped to get a living wage, and some additional needed benefits like overtime pay.

Doug responded, "I told you before several times what the problem is, and the reality of the situation. The City has cut its budget for the hospital. We are caught in the squeeze." He tried to reason with her.

"Well, Dr. Fine, when are things going to change? We have to pay our bills, too," she said looking directly at him. He looked past her pushiness and was firm.

He replied, "I understand your feelings, but what good would a strike do? Everyone would suffer, especially the patients."

Janet was frustrated at the slowness of improvements. She felt nurses deserved better treatment. She wanted better treatment from him, and at least dinner and a night of relaxation, but instead he acted indifferently to her personally, and he stood adamant on the strike issue. She would not be pushed aside so easily and had another plan. She gathered her clipboard, got up, turned toward the door, and walked out of his office. She did not plan to depend on him for anything. Janet had other ideas.

Doug took a deep breath and sat down. He reached for the phone to call Shelly. He lit up a cigarette and took a deep drag. She's not home. Darn! Probably went to the store or to shop again. She's so efficient! Kristie could not manage all that Shelly does, but then again I don't think anyone could.

There was a knock on the door. Doug said, "It's Open!"

Jake Carter walked in.

Jake, a former student of Doug's, had worked his way up the ranks through his residency. He came by to talk with Doug about a special problem he was having in developing a change in the OB/GYN service. Jake was rotating through different programs. While his main interest lay in pediatrics, he found himself doing a variety of other necessary tasks at University Hospital. Jake was asked to organize student doctors into special interest groups. He realized community medicine was the one area that intrigued him the most.

Doug and Jake talked. They shared some of their problems. Jake confided to Doug about the recent breakup with a woman he had been dating for a year.

"She never understood me. She didn't understand the long hours, my exhaustion when I got home, or the fact I wasn't interested in getting laid every night. She was the horniest woman I've ever met."

Doug laughed. "Stop complaining. A horny woman these days is not hard to find, it's the quality that counts."

"Hey," Doug said, "how about coming over Friday night and having dinner with us? I'd like you to get to know Shelly better."

Jake, eager to have a home cooked meal said, "Great! What time should I be there?"

"Why not right after work? We seem to have an earlier dinner because of the kids. But, it's always a special celebration for the Sabbath. Hope you like wine and chicken soup."

Jake smiled and nodded his head. "That sounds perfect to me. I am already hungry. What can I bring along?

They talked together about wine when Doug suddenly remembered another meeting and dashed for the door.

"See you Friday, Jake. Keep up the good work. Bring that bottle of Merlot you like." Doug was gone.

Shelly decided to go back to the house before picking up Alison because she needed to run some errands in Diamond Heights.

As she began to walk toward the house, she heard Andy and Ross fighting in the backyard. She could hear their loud voices before she even got inside the gate. She heard the phone ring, but she went directly to the backyard instead.

Then she found Andy sitting on top of Ross, hitting him hard with his fists.

Shelly ran over and pulled Andy off, and holding him saying, "Leave him alone! You're bigger than your brother. You must stop beating him, verbally, and physically. You're too much, Andy."

He pushed her aside and ran off. Ross cried. "He is always on top and he's too big! Then, he rushed past her to his room, and slammed the door.

Nora came out shaking her head. "I don't know. They always seem to be at each other's throats. But I've got my own problems. I may lose my daughter, Ginny, because the social worker doesn't think I can handle her."

Shelly asked, "What do you mean?"

Nora replied, "Well, I haven't proven I can handle her to their satisfaction. I don't know what to do. I need to have a place for her if she's going to live with me. If I don't get her with me now, I'll lose custody of her permanently. She's been in a foster home for the last six months."

Shelly thought to herself, all I need is another child in the midst of everything.

Nora asked, "Would you consider letting her come to live here? The kids are wild enough already. I don't think one more kid would hurt or add to the confusion. Besides, I'd do everything. She can stay in my room.

I wouldn't have to go off every weekend. I could stay around and help you take care of things."

Shelly replied, "You have a point. Ginny is cute, and might be just what the other children need. Let me think about it and talk to Doug."

Shelly felt she had a point. Nora did have a good heart. She deserved a break. The Department of Social Services didn't always consider all the circumstances of the people involved when they made decisions.

Shelly decided it would be right to try to give Nora some help. But, it would be up to Doug to make the final decision, of course.

The kids were already doubled up in the two bedrooms. Nora could have Ginny with her in the back bedroom that she slept in now. She could move her work things into a cabinet in the living room for a while as she uses the dining room table at night anyway, and it's quiet.

Shelly thought about five kids, a teenage mother, and Spot, Nora's pregnant Dalmatian, and Rainbow, the yellow-striped cat, and it seemed impossible they were all together and under the same roof. It all seemed almost too much to even think about, much less handle. Life was a full bushel basket with no more room left for one more apple.

It reminded Shelly of the Sholom Aleichem' (she heard from her grandfather) story about a poor man who complained to the Rabbi about not having enough space for his growing family.

The Rabbi told him, "Each time you complain, you must increase the occupancy in your house by adding your chickens, then the cow, the mule, and then your ducks."

Finally, the man could stand it no more. He begged for relief. When the animals were finally taken out one by one, the man said happily, "I feel like we now have a lot of space."

When Doug got home that night, and after he had dinner, Shelly sat down across from him.

"Doug, the boys got into a serious fight today. Andy exploded at Ross and was beating on him. When I came home. I rushed back to stop it, and I don't know what damage could have happened, if I had not been there."

Doug was not surprised, but a little preoccupied with his own issues, and expanding conflicts at the hospital.

He said, "Shelly, you should let them fight it out themselves. If you were not here, they would have to work it out somehow. You can't protect them from their own issues."

"Okay, fine, if that's how you want it. I just don't think Andy has to work out his aggression and physically hurt his brother so much.

Doug nodded his head.

"I have something else to talk with you about," She continued.

"Nora is in need of our help right now. Her daughter, Ginny, is two years old, and she has been in a foster home for the last six months. Nora wants to get her back, and the only way she can do that is to have a home to bring her to."

"Are you thinking what I think you are thinking?" asked Doug, stopping her in mid-sentence with his mouth open and his wine glass in mid-air.

"Let me finish. Nora is great with the kids. We've met Ginny. She's a very cute little girl. I think she would fit in here fine. They would be part of our family for a while. It would help us out even more since Nora would spend more time with Ginny on the weekends. We could get away by ourselves. I feel a "fifth child" may somehow balance things out all the way around."

"But, we already have a fifth child with Nora. She's barely able to take care of herself. We have a dog that is expecting puppies soon. Why do we want more aggravation?"

"Doug, it will work out, believe me. Let's give it a try. Please. We already have a full house. One more little girl can't make that much of a difference."

Doug shook his head reluctantly. It was a situation he never dreamed of, but there was little choice.

Shelly went around the table and hugged him.

Spot, the deaf Dalmatian dog, came over to Doug, and put her head in his lap.

Doug petted Spot, and then said, "Okay, if you feel it will work out. I guess it can be helpful to everyone, one way or another."

Then he went upstairs and quickly fell asleep.

Shelly told Nora, "Go ahead and make arrangements. Things will work out."

Nora was happy. She said, "Now I can go to bed and for the first time in many months have a good night's sleep."

Shelly went back to reading her professional books and did not sleep much that night.

The next day Nora arranged with the social worker to have Ginny move into the house the next week, just in time to be there for the birth of the five puppies.

It became wilder as each day passed. Dinner at their house was mostly a circus. Friends often dropped by just to watch the fray. With all the kids they had, it was a rare sight to behold, especially for the single friends who barely could think of managing one child. They laughed a lot. The fussing over the puppies, the kids, and the general pandemonium was a din that did not easily subside, even if royalty had been visiting,

Shelly had little time left, but tried to visit the neighbors. They helped her to laugh a lot and that helped Shelly relieve some of her the tension.

Charles said, "Your house is like The Castro on Saturday night, but you don't score and there is hardly any room to spare."

Shelly laughed with them and appreciated their point of view.

The next week, Shelly noticed Alison was having a hard time. She was wetting her pants more frequently, not sleeping well, and being edgy. She tried to find out what the problems were.

"Alison, what's happening with you lately? Are you unhappy about something?" Shelly asked Alison on the way home from school as they were driving in the car.

"Mommy, Ginny gets all the attention. Nobody plays with me."

"But, honey, Ginny needs you to be a big sister to her, too. Maybe you can help her to learn a lot of things like you have. Maybe you could read to her, and play teacher with her, too," encouraged Shelly.

"But mommy, I want to play with the puppies."

"I know. Aren't they cute? But they are too small yet for anyone to play with except their mommy, Spot."

"I want a puppy for me, too," Alison answered.

"When they get a little bigger you can have a puppy for your very own."

Shelly tried to cheer her up. Alison smiled and looked happier. Shelly drove home singing the rest of the way.

"Zip-a-dee-doo-dah,zip-a-dee-ay
 my, oh my, what a wonderful day
 Plenty of sunshine headin' my way…."
 and her other favorite song
"When the Red, Red, Robin comes bob, bob, bobbin' along…"

Ginny was living with them. Molly was the only one who was very enthusiastic, and mostly helpful. Later, both girls welcomed the changes. Alison saw that Shelly did not change toward her, even with all the extra kids around. She was happy to share her mother with the other children. She began to treat Ginny like a younger sister and looked out for her as much as she could.

But, the boys acted like they were put out of their space, crowded in their bedroom and in the bathroom. Every day they pouted and complained loudly.

At least once a week, via phone calls from the Fines in Chicago, the Stockers in New York, Shelly's sister, or Doug's sister, there was a constant barrage of similar questions, mainly, "When are you getting married?"

Doug and Shelly wondered what their future was going to be like. Whatever time they had to be alone together, they seized it, and took a few hours off and went out. Trying to find time to just be a couple and find out what they felt like instead of being in the family barracks, or military encampment, or a bivouac.

They went to dinners in restaurants, spent time with friends, and found themselves singing in the car when going to or from events. They discovered, enjoyed, and shared a whole repertoire of songs from the '20s, '30s, and '40s — show tunes, pop, and jazz. They liked to sing together, and that seemed to ease the tension they were often feeling. They enjoyed talking about each other's interests, about the children, and about their feelings. Shelly was happy to be with Doug. Any problem seemed to disappear when he was being warm and affectionate.

When it was finally late at night and they were being sexy, they were aware that the walls in their bedroom were paper-thin. All sounds seemed to penetrate. She could easily hear the children talking in their rooms. As a result, Shelly found herself holding back the natural sounds she wanted to make when she and Doug made love. She repressed some of the passion she felt. She didn't want to do anything to make the children any more uncomfortable.

Andy and Ross directed constant comments at her or at Alison. Most often they uttered critical "put-downs" and sarcasms about her food, or the preparation, or Alison's way of speaking, or something Alison had done that they found reprehensible, like wetting her pants.

It was difficult to get them to help out, either doing the dishes, or cleaning up after a meal, or taking out the garbage. She felt under constant pressure to try to keep the house together, look after what was needed to be done, get the food, have enough energy for her own work, and also be sexy for Doug. Still, she didn't want to be anywhere else. There was some reason she was sure that she was given this opportunity and she tried to make the best of it.

Nora helped as much as she could, but she was mostly unreliable. She said she would be helpful, but she was a scatterbrain, and she forgot to follow up on details like cleaning the stove, sweeping the floor, or watering the plants. She did somehow manage Ginny, and the puppies, and that was an improvement.

Shelly juggled it all.

It was the only way she knew to have completion in her life, to have a family, a man, and a career. It would all come together somehow, and she would also try to remember the plants needed to get enough water.

On Friday night for the Sabbath, Doug had invited Jake to come for dinner. Shelly had already invited Melissa. Melissa and Jake would be meeting for the first time. Shelly was sure they would like each other, and they did.

They spent the evening talking and getting to know each other. Shelly always had good luck making matches for her friends.

Shelly invited Melissa and Jake to join them for Thanksgiving dinner. Nora and Ginny were going to be away with her mother in Sacramento. They decided to include the couple to celebrate their first Thanksgiving together. It would be a traditional dinner, hectic, full of good cheer, with lots of delicious food among good company.

As Shelly prepared Thanksgiving dinner, she felt thankful for the relationship and love she had with Doug. Her mother would be coming for a visit the first part of December. She would be glad to see them together as a family.

Thanksgiving was all it promised to be, hectic, lots of delicious food, and plenty of company. Shelly was exhausted by the time the last dish was put away. But, she felt an intense sense of accomplishment. She actually got the whole dinner together, and it all turned out very well. Now, if everything else could come together like dinner, she would really be pleased. She might even win the larger piece of the "wish bone."

Her mother's visit in December was very short. Jeanie surmised the situation rather quickly. She thought Shelly was "out of her mind" to put so much energy into the relationship and the "no-neck monsters," as she referred to the boys. She didn't hide her displeasure from her daughter.

The first night of her visit, after Doug went to bed, she chastised her daughter, "You should have your head examined. You have your hands too full. Things are spilling out. I don't see how you can do everything. You've got to stop trying to be all things to everyone. You hardly have time to do what you need for yourself, such as school, let alone take care of all these children. Why don't you move back to Washington now before it's too late?"

Shelly defended her actions.

She said, "Mom, everyone pitches in. It makes things easier," she lied.

She was trying to cover up and to defend herself. Doug was pleasant to her mother. He reassured her "So many good things are happening for Alison. She has two sisters to play with and school is working out."

But, her mother was convinced Shelly should never have left Washington. She insisted she would be better off back living in her house, working for the government, and living with Alison in a quiet and uncomplicated home.

Shelly tried to reassure her mother, but her mother was determined and convinced she was right. Shelly felt sad when she said good-by to her mother. She never thought Jeanie would ever agree with her decisions, no matter what.

When Hanukkah arrived, they exchanged presents. There were a lot of good feelings, happiness, and latkes (potato pancakes) applesauce and sour cream, a sense that they had all survived through a tough year.

As they lit each Hanukkah candle, the glow made them each feel a little warmer. Shelly was sure the worst had passed, and now things would only get better. She settled into her feelings of being domesticated, and felt a growing "togetherness." She passed around the sour cream and applesauce for the latkes, and smiled. The pancakes were delicious.

Alison and Molly had received new dolls for Hanukkah. "Chatty Cathy" talked when you pulled her string, and Shelly thought that another "mouth" was all that was needed in the nosy chaos of their home. The "Barbie" dolls were teachers, astronauts, and doctors. She smiled glad to see "Barbie" was encouraging girls to have careers. She wondered if "Barbie" would ever have children and if she did, would there be adequate childcare centers for them. Mattel was a leader in the toy industry and perhaps in new ideas…if Mattel invented a childcare center for Barbie's children…oh well it was a thought."

She was certain all the necessary adjustments would be made. Love works, she thought. Later they would marry, but when wasn't so important. Their love, commitment, children, friends, and the desire to make each other happy and to work on everything were now the important things. They would survive, she was sure. The sun was shining, and weather was perfect.

It was almost New Year. Who knew what lay ahead?

Life offers many opportunities, but the challenge is making the right choice.

Chapter  16

Turning Point

What we call the secret of happiness is no more a secret
than our willingness to choose life. Leo Buscaglia

The New Year began with a fullness Shelly had never quite before known. She felt complete in her love for Doug, in their relationship, and with the children. The challenges were great; yet, somehow, she managed day by day to cope with everything she had to do. Doug seemed to understand her, and gave her as much attention as was possible for him. Shelly was grateful for everything he did for Alison.

She realized he was very preoccupied with work and was doing his best for her and for the children. She wanted everything to work out. She wanted to prove she had made the right decision, to move, to take on three children, to help Alison adjust to a new family, to live with a man she was getting to know over time but at a long distance, to include Nora, Ginny and Spot in their family, and to complete her degree.

She felt like "Wonder Woman." She needed the bracelets to get through the challenges and the rope to pull her through the maze, but she struggled on without the props. She thought she knew how to roll with punches and go with the flow. She felt confident, resilient, and mostly found solutions where there did not appear to be any. The best thing was that she was in love. Doug was the perfect partner for her; despite the reality of his workload and realistic shortcomings, she was confident in her choices.

Her head, in between the right side of the brain that focused on issues and daily challenges, and the left side full of plans, was the middle segment stuffed with hope, rose petals, lace and a repertoire of tunes that burst with romance that overshadowed the daily struggles.

With Nora's help with the children and the house, she managed to keep things together. The family was fed, family councils were held, fights and other conflicts continued, and the house began to look and feel more lived in, colorful, and far more comfortable.

The work load mounted. She coped with daily trips to Alison's school, then to Emeryville, visits to childcare centers, and the myriad of other family related errands she had to do. She experienced how traffic increased, parking space decreased, and how the little bit of time to manage everything became even more precious. She handled as efficiently as she could the details of her study, doing the research, plus all the reading, writing and talking she had to do for everything she agreed to do to meet the criteria of the program.

Despite the frenzy, Shelly was inwardly content. The boys had started music lessons. They enjoyed practicing guitar and drums (fortunately, the full set was not installed and the well insulated drum pad worked wonders so that the constant rat-a-tats were barely audible throughout the house). The boys were enthusiastic about music and stopped beating up on each other verbally and physically.

Outside Shelly saw positive efforts emerging in the childcare community. Plans were being firmed up for the first demonstration at City Hall and at the Federal Building. The demonstration was finally scheduled for the first Thursday in February. The plan was as many parents and teachers as possible would go to City Hall armed with banners and signs; they would meet the press, then they would cross over the square to the Federal Building and continue to loudly protest the badly timed budget cuts. They would openly express their objections to the drastic cuts being made to the services in childcare programs; instead of more funds being allocated, there was much less provided, which meant more mothers returning to welfare instead of working, or being productive and able to plan for the future.

Mothers wanted a chance to make it for themselves and their children. The help they sorely needed was being cut and they could not sit idly by and do nothing. Parents were encouraged to bring along their children to the demonstration.

Shelly adjusted her schedule to prepare for this event. She helped make calls and share ideas with the other organizers. The number of groups and individuals that wanted to attend grew. With the pressure growing, on the Monday just before the event, she spontaneously decided to do something unusual and get away by herself for a while.

Shelly drove Alison to school and then proceeded down Broadway and when she got to Columbus turned left to Fisherman's Wharf and soon found a parking spot. Happily, she walked to Ghirardelli Square to do some spontaneous shopping. She bought some things she thought would be fun: a huge orange butterfly kite for the ceiling in the girls' room. She bought a large loaf of still warm French bread at the Boudin Bakery that would go perfectly with the simple meat loaf and mashed potatoes dinner she had planned. Then she found just the right omelet pan in the kitchen store, complete with a few non-fail recipes plus a handy spatula. She wanted to be ready for her neighbors' party.

As she watched the mime, musicians, and the jugglers who entertained in the courtyard, she sipped a coffee on the bench, watching people pass by. She was fully enjoying the few moments of private relaxation.

Then Shelly looked across the courtyard and noticed at the Ghirardelli Cinema that a new film was being shown in previews. She had not heard about, "Made For Each Other."

She thought, "Why not? I haven't been to a movie in ages. It will be fun to sneak off alone and just do something for fun."

She bought a ticket and went into the dark theatre. She watched the love story unfold. As she relaxed, ate some popcorn, and drank a diet Coke, she greatly enjoyed the story.

She felt somewhat naughty at evading her responsibilities as a student, organizer, and mother. However, she loved the idea of going off alone to see a movie during the day. It was a first. Her pangs of guilt lasted only a short while, as she settled back to enjoy the film.

She loved the two character's problems, but they seemed tame by comparison to her situation. Although she laughed a lot at the story, she realized there was a huge difference. It was fun to see the couple meet at an encounter group and talk and then to finally decide to meet each other's families. Where the couple in the movie only had themselves to consider, and their respective families to think about, they were not challenged in the same way she was.

Shelly had five children, an immature teenager, a cat, a deaf Dalmatian with needy puppies, a Ph.D. to complete, a much too busy life, and on top of all that, she was in love with a very busy doctor who had no time to think about planning a wedding.

She wondered, "How come life has gotten so complicated?"

As she left the movie theatre, she heard others talking about their relationships. She caught snatches of their conversations:

"Do you think they got married?"

"Why bother getting married?"

"Marriage ruins a great relationship."

"Only fools fall in love!"

"Yeah, 'fall' is more like it, and I am no fool!"

"Love lasts as long as a love story lasts. Then it's all over, except for the shrink and legal bills."

"Every marriage I know is more like a horror movie."

"I'm still paying alimony. I don't have any money or energy left for love."

"Love has nothing to do with money, but it sure helps."

"Who can afford to get hurt? Someone always gets hurt."

"I like freedom. I play it safe and take it a day at a time."

Shelly stood for a minute and then suddenly noticed a sign in a promotion display in front of the movie's poster. It said in bold letters, "FREE WEDDING CONTEST!" and in a box next to the poster were entry forms.

She picked up an entry blank, thinking, and "Wouldn't that be the perfect answer? We have no time to spend a weekend away on a honeymoon much less plan a wedding." She quickly put the entry blank into her pocket.

She found her car, luckily without a ticket placed on her windshield by the ever-vigilant meter maids, and started to drive toward home. "The Contest" entry blank fell out of her pocket and onto the seat, and almost blew out the window. She caught it just in time and put it into her bag

She then drove to pick up Alison who was happy to report on all that she had learned that day. Then Shelly drove up to Twin Peaks wanting to savor a wee bit longer the few hours of well-earned freedom.

Looking down at the City, she reminisced with Alison about their first visit. They looked out. She thought of all the time that had passed since then, the meetings, phone calls, letters, frenzied travel, visits back and forth, and snatches of time they spent together. She smiled as she realized the children were finally coming closer together. A whole lot of activity had already happened since their arrival and life had changed

They looked out at the deepening orange sunset wrapping itself over the city as the light lit the Golden Gate Bridge even brighter She smiled again as she thought about the first time she and Doug looked down at the twinkling gem of a city from Twin Peaks that first magical, sparkling night. She sighed. Gave Alison a kiss and got back in the car.

Then recovering from her daydreams, she resumed driving down the winding hills on the drive home. As she approached the house, she saw Peter, her next-door neighbor. She got out of the car and walked towards him. Alison made a bee line for the door and raced to the bathroom.

Peter exclaimed, "Shelly, I'm so glad to see you. I had such an over the top experience today. I thought about everything I have gone through with Charles. It was so complete! So total! Remember the 'Create an Omelet' party we were going to have? We're going to do it for sure, tonight. Bring your pan and come over at about 7:00 PM!"

Shelly said, "What fun! I just knew you were going to do this so I bought a real omelet pan, the Cuisinart one you suggested. This will be my first time using it. Now I can learn how to do a perfect omelet from an expert. We'll be there with lots of 'yolks.' and a bottle of wine."

They both laughed.

Then they turned and went to their doors.

Shelly entered the house with her arms full of packages. She placed the bread and the pan on the kitchen counter, and moved to carry the butterfly kite over near the stairs, picking up clothes that were dropped and scattered as she went along.

Exploding sounds filled the place and came crashing down on her ears.

The TV set was turned on full volume. Spot, the Dalmatian, with her yelping puppies, were lying in one corner. The girls were jumping up and down, absolutely fascinated with the puppies. Ross was practicing drums. Andy was yelling at Nora. Nora was yelling back at Andy. The girls were taking turns screaming and chattering. Between them was Ginny, Nora's daughter, crying because her diaper needed changing. The cat was sitting next to her dirty kitty litter meowing for attention. The pot on the stove was boiling over, and the teakettle blasted away at full steam.

Shelly couldn't believe the deep, drastic, and rapid compression change from the quiet of the movie theater, the top of Twin Peaks, and the quiet inside her car. She felt like she was suddenly submerged in a very real, animated, and volatile "Yellow Submarine."

She tried to cope with each combat challenge in turn: She placed the chopped meat and other ingredients in a bowl. She took out instant mashed potatoes to make dinner a bit easier for her to complete. She asked Nora to complete the meat loaf and potatoes.

Finally, she decided to move out of the middle of the "battlefield." She withdrew from the combustion and went quickly upstairs. She needed more time for quiet. She took along the butterfly kite and put it in the girls' room and put the dirty clothes in the hamper near the washing machine. Then she went to the bedroom.

She found a message from Doug saying he would be late. The strike action pending at the hospital had started. They were embroiled in negotiations.

When Shelly called, Doug's secretary, Gert, told her, "Dr. Fine is very busy!"

Shelly replied, "I would like to talk to him, please, as soon as possible."

After she hung up the phone, for a few moments, she sat trying to meditate in the dark. Then the phone rang... It was Doug.

He said, "I'm sorry; all hell is breaking loose here right now."

She wanted very much to talk to him about everything she had been through that day – the movie, her feelings, and her dreams.

As she listened and heard him tell her of his problems about the pending nurses' strike, she slowly pulled out "The Contest" entry blank from her bag, and put it down casually on the bedside table. She took a deep breath.

Then she calmly asked him, "When are we getting married?"

Doug said, "You've got to be crazy! We don't have time to get married. I'm in the middle of a strike. You're in the middle of your studies, plans for a protest for more childcare, and the kids – your little – 'family councils'– and their homework; the puppies and all the rest. With the kids, we hardly have any time to spend together. I have to be here a few more hours working to try to settle the strike. How can you even think about getting married? I don't even have time to think!"

"There's a dinner party tonight at Peter and Charles'," Shelly said, quickly changing the subject.

Doug replied, "I don't even have time to eat dinner. I can't come home, but maybe after we solve a few things I can get there. Can we discuss marriage after that? Please?" He implored her to understand and to be patient.

Shelly sat quietly in the bedroom trying to regain her composure. She put "The Contest" entry blank back into her bag. She did not want Doug to find it until she had a chance to tell him more.

Suddenly, Alison knocked on the door. She walked in and as she approached her mother she asked,

"Mommy, why wasn't Spot's husband here when the puppies were born? Where do puppies come from? When is their daddy coming to visit?"

Then Ross barged in without knocking and screaming, "I have a splinter from that 'blankity-blank' broken drum stick. I need you to take it out. Now! It hurts! When can I have a new set of drums?" he cried as he stuck his finger in Shelly's face.

Shelly promptly cauterized a needle and fixed the splinter.

She wished Doug had been home instead for the "surgery" as Ross did not take a deep breath or stop complaining for one minute about the drumstick and his desire for a full set.

Her head was aching from the noise, from him, and the background bombardment of voices, screams, TV, and yelping puppies. Shelly went into the bathroom. She has to remain calm and quiet her fears. She showered and dressed for the party

She then went down to get the new omelet pan, and gathered some ingredients from the "fridge" and put them all into a paper bag, and she put a few glasses and dishes into the sink. The house was quieter as the kids were eating, rocking, and watching TV. The puppies were nursing again. It was the calm before the storm.

She kissed each of the children goodnight, grabbed a piece of bread, the bag with the omelet pan, plus the dozen eggs, Swiss cheese, some parsley, and a handful of mushrooms and headed to the door.

"See you later!" she said to Nora, who was preoccupied with moving Ginny, who was pulling a hungry puppy away from Spot's teat.

"But mommy, the puppy is eating too fast!" squealed Ginny.

When she entered Peter and Charles' house, she hugged each of them, and took a few deep breaths. At the same moment, she noticed how serene it was in their sanctuary. She sighed. She had a wonderful evening learning to make omelets, talking with everyone, swapping gossip, tips, recipes, and relaxing.

Peter asked, "Where's Doug?"

She replied, "It's just another crisis at the hospital. This time a nurses' strike. I feel like a widow, and I'm not even a bride. Maybe he'll get here later."

Peter asked, "When are you getting married?"

"Now you sound like my mother!"

Then Shelly revealed, "You won't believe this. I discovered 'A Contest' for a wedding today at Ghirardelli. I would have to write an essay on why we are 'Made for Each Other' to promote the new movie. But, listen, if I win 'The Contest,' we get a free wedding, on a yacht, with everything included, plus a big, free honeymoon!"

She added, "Doug told me we don't have time to get married. But, how could he turn down the first prize? We wouldn't have to do anything at all!"

"Look at Charles and me," Peter said. "We don't need to be married. We've been together 15 years. Marriage is just a formality. Legal, schmeegle, how bourgeois?"

"I hear nothing but horror stories from friends," Sandy added. "Insane bits of jealousy. The fastest way to ruin a good relationship is to get married."

"Oh, don't be ridiculous!" Peter said. "That's what commitment is all about. You can't be committed without marriage and making it legal. Gays want to be married, too!"

"If you get married, you should be committed," yelled Charles from his selected position at the stove among all the hot omelet pans. "We are 'domestic partners,' don't you know. Can you ask for more, sweetie? Do you want a wedding? You can wear white! Bah humbug!"

Marta, a chic fashion designer from Pacific Heights, careened into the room. Not being fully aware of what was going on, but hearing the word "wedding" stimulated her to blurt out, "Everyone I know has been married, and divorced, at least twice."

She tried to pour wine into her wayward glass, not knowing quite what to do about the cigarette ash heading directly for her pale pink silk blouse at the same moment.

Ben snorted back at them, "I've been married and divorced three times, and that's enough for me. I wouldn't go through it again for any 'cunt,' sorry to be so bold, or for any price." He took a sip of wine and sneered. "They should pay me to marry them! Yes, from now on I want plenty of palimony!"

They all laughed, but he was serious, and he took another sip of wine to swallow his words.

Doug never made it to the party.

Shelly enjoyed her mushroom and cheese omelet, drank some wine, chatted, listened to the fun conversations about life in San Francisco and their varied perspectives on marriage, and then went home alone.

Nora gave her a full report about the kids and puppies as soon as she stepped inside. She was drooping with battle fatigue. As usual, Andy had acted up. Nora suggested to Shelly that Andy clearly didn't like the idea of Doug and Shelly being together.

Shelly wondered aloud, "Would it make any difference if we told the children we are getting married?"

Nora said, "You've got to be crazy! Why would anyone want to get married in this situation? Four kids are just too much for anybody."

"Four kids," said Shelly, "there are five kids plus you! And now puppies! Yikes!"

She told Nora about "The Contest." "Can you imagine, Nora, someone else does it all without us having to think about it?"

Nora said, "Yeah, but then you're stuck with the whole mess to clean up afterwards. Remember, if you can't stand the heat, get out of the kitchen, or in this case the battlefield. These kids are just too much! Forget about marriage! Escape before the battle, think about it now, and save yourself a lot of aggravation later."

"Now you sound like my mother!" teased Shelly as she went into the bedroom to undress.

She sat on the bed trying to read one of the many books on childcare, child psychology, and child development that had piled up in a stack alongside the bed. She was trying to keep up with all that she had to review. Reading was a luxury she had to postpone until late at night and precisely when her eyes most needed sleep.

Alison knocked on the door.

She came asking aloud at the same time, "Mommy, how do babies come?" She crossed the room and sat down next to her mother.

Shelly proceeded to tell her daughter as briefly and simply as possible about the process.

Then Alison asked about her father. "Where is my daddy now?" And then she added, "Is Doug going to be my daddy now?"

Shelly realized how complicated it all was for Alison to understand. She tried to explain as simply as she could, "Alison, your daddy loves you, but he and I are divorced now, and he lives in Washington DC. Doug loves you, too. He wants you to be a member of his family just as his children are part of ours."

Alison seemed content. Shelly took her back across the hall to her room, tucked her in, and kissed her goodnight. She covered her, she then covered Molly. She put the butterfly kite up on a hook on the ceiling and closed the door. The kite spun around in the dark. Shelly went back to bed to read.

Doug came home shortly after midnight. He brought a couple of glasses of wine with him into the bedroom. As he opened the door, he said, "Hope you want some wine. I just want to relax."

Shelly put the book down, took off her glasses as she took a glass from Doug, and sipped the wine.

Shelly asked, "How is the situation going with the nurses?"

He replied, "Everything is still on hold and building each day. It is gaining momentum and is very stressful for the operations of the hospital."

Then Shelly said, "Doug, I've been thinking. There is something I did today that was very unusual for me. I took off by myself and went to a movie. As I left the movie I picked up an entry blank for a free wedding contest."

He was listening as he got undressed.

Shelly opened her bag and pulled out "The Contest" entry form and placed it on the bedside table for him to examine.

She continued, "The time I took off today felt great. I went shopping and then saw the new movie, 'Made for Each Other.' It made me even more certain we need to make a decision about getting married. I want us to think about entering 'The Contest.' We need to simply write an essay about why we are 'Made for Each Other.' Maybe we'd win. That means everyone can get what they want without any great efforts." She then reassured him with, "And, we don't have to do anything!"

Doug looked at her and without a word went into the bathroom, washed his face and was perplexed. He could not believe what he was hearing. He was tired, and this was the last thing he wanted to hear tonight. Then as he dried his face he said,

"Shelly, we can't possibly get married now. You are busy with school, and the childcare protest. I have my hands full with the pending strike, and all the work is piled up, it goes on and on." His voice trailed off. He replaced the towel on the rack.

Finally he asked, as he walked over towards the bed, "How can you possibly think about a wedding now?"

"Why can't you understand how I feel? We have been together for more than two years. I moved from Washington. I am with you as much as I know how to be. Everything seems so perfect. It's not easy, but I know we can handle the challenges," replied Shelly.

"Sure, but who needs to get married? I'm not interested right now in changing anything," said Doug, taking a long sip of wine, then he lit a cigarette.

"Listen," said Shelly, raising her voice slightly and feeling like he was not understanding the situation, "whenever your parents and my parents call, they want to know 'when are we getting married?' If you don't want to make all this legal, I can go back to the apartment with Alison, and we can just live apart. Okay?"

He paused and looked at her. He realized the impact of what she just said would have on his life, and he quickly responded,

"Now wait a minute. Calm down. No one wants you to leave. It's been fantastic. I never could have made it all these months without you. It's been even more wonderful with you here. Despite the problems, there is a lot of joy, lots of changes, and all for the better. I know that, I'm not a fool. I can see the differences, in the kids, in the house, in my life," Doug responded. He stopped and sat down next to her on the bed taking a sip of wine and a deep breath.

He looked at Shelly trying to figure out what to do. Then he jumped up and headed for the shower. He needed to think about what he felt and said to Shelly, "I've got to calm down and clear my head."

She sat staring at "The Contest" entry blank. She started writing some notes down on the paper. She sipped some more wine.

She walked out of the bedroom and went to check on the kids. They were asleep and all was well. She returned to the bedroom and closed the door quietly and waited patiently for Doug to emerge from the shower.

When he did, he walked over to her while he was all wet and said, "You want to get wet with me? Are you sure you want to take the plunge? Jump in and have a real wedding? Can we sleep on it?"

Shelly hugged him. Then she grabbed a towel and dried his back and dried herself.

They both laughed.

She nodded and said, "Yes, I do want to get 'all wet' with you and 'take the plunge!' Let's have a real wedding! It was a symbolic wedding for us at the ranch. It felt great making a commitment. Now, I want the real thing. I hope you do. Yes! Let's sleep on it. Let's see how we feel in the morning."

They fell asleep in each other's arms.

Their dreams were reflections of how each of them was feeling.

Shelly dreamed of being driven in a long white limousine to the door of the temple. She got out of the limo dressed all in white with a lace veil with the girls throwing pale rose petals in front of her as she slowly climbed the stairs. Then she saw Doug wearing his "whites" from the hospital, opening the door. The boys were standing next to the girls. They took their arms and led them inside. The boys were followed by Spot, who was wagging her tail and leading a line of puppies. They met Nora and Ginny standing inside the door with baskets of rice. Behind them, sitting in rows inside the temple were all their friends and family. Everyone was smiling and saying, "Mazel Tov!" as they went down the aisle, they saw their parents standing together saying,

"We told you so!"

"It's about time!"

The Rabbi was smiling. They stood under a chupah (canopy) and said their vows.

Then the Rabbi pronounced Shelly and Doug husband and wife.

Doug stomped hard on the cloth-covered glass on the floor, breaking the glass into little pieces. Birds flew out from under the canopy. Klezmer music started. Everyone started clapping. Then Shelly and Doug melted together into a waltz as the children danced together and everyone else joined them. Shelly dreamed on. She was content in her picture perfect wedding.

Doug dreamed a different dream.

He was playing tennis. He was in a white t-shirt and white tennis shorts. Suddenly the woman he was playing with was Shelly.

She said, "Love!"

He said, "Love, Forty. No, I mean, Yes! I do!"

And she said, "Let's play!"

The kids ran after the balls back and forth across the court as Doug and Shelly hit balls around the court. Spot was running after the kids. Nora was running after Spot. Ginny was running after her mother. The puppies were following Ginny.

Doug saw Kristie, Janet Grover and the other nurses at the hospital laughing on the side of the court thinking the whole scene was terribly funny. He was sweating and wiped his brow with his hand.

On the other side of the court, he saw all of their parents. They were asking:

"What kind of game is this?"

"When are you going to stop fooling around?"

"When are you going to settle down in 'home' court?"

He saw his friends in the grandstand shouting,

"Play the game!"

"Stop fooling around."

"Play the game, already!"

He then saw Shelly in a white tennis dress, a veil tucked into her white headband saying, "Why can't you play with me?"

He was sweating profusely.

He wiped his forehead again. He was panting now. He needed water and searched for a jug.

But, the balls kept flying around. "30 love!"

He was getting hotter.

"Love! love! love! 20! 30! 40! That's the game!"

Doug looked around confused. He was sweating, hot, tired, and he could not find water. The Rabbi was standing as the referee waiting for his signal. He was asking Doug

"So when will the wedding start?"

Doug felt helpless. He was thirsty. He wanted relief.

When they woke up in the morning, the sheets were totally wet, and they were both drenched in sweat. The dreams they each had during the night were very real.

Then they got up, dried off, and went downstairs to get something to drink just as the San Francisco Chronicle arrived.

Over her morning coffee, Shelly saw "The Contest" announced in a small paragraph in the Entertainment Section.

"Couples 21 years of age and older who would like to marry can be married at 20th Century Fox's expense. They are invited to write 200 words or less on the subject of, why they are 'Made for Each Other.' Entries must be delivered to or mailed to Ghirardelli Cinema by noon today. Winners will be married aboard the boat Victoriana at the Saint Francis Yacht Club with a champagne reception and flown via PSA to San Diego for a honeymoon stay at the Evergreen Hotel with a Hertz car at their disposal. Tickets will be provided to the bride and groom and guests for the new film 'Made for Each Other.'"

She looked at "The Contest" entry blank she had picked up at Ghirardelli the day before and wondered, "Should we do it?"

She asked Doug, quietly, "What is your opinion about a wedding this morning?"

He crisply responded, recalling the tension of the tennis match, "Enter it! Let's play" and then he added, smiling, "But maybe you should think about marrying the man who wins! I really don't have time to get married!"

He laughed, kissed her, turned to go, and added, concerned,

"Besides, how can a man in my position get married as part of a promotional stunt? You've got to be kidding!"

He was out the door before she could say anything else.

The children left for school. Alison had been given a ride to school that morning with another parent who lived nearby.

Shelly tried to arrange carpooling as often as possible. She also didn't have to go to the Lab that day. She had made arrangements to stay home to read, visit several childcare centers, and complete some paperwork. She had phone calls to make for Thursday's childcare demonstration. The list of items to do was always growing.

But, she couldn't get her mind off "The Contest." She didn't have time to arrange a wedding. The idea of someone else doing everything appealed to her very much. She thought time off for a honeymoon with Doug would be great. She had many thoughts going on inside her head, but she decided to take some more time to think out the plans.

On an impulse, she decided to drive to Golden Gate Park, take a walk around Stowe Lake, visit the Japanese Tea Garden, and continue to think about what she really wanted.

The time away would help her make the final decision.

As she drove there, she noticed couples sitting on benches, walking or running together. She thought how little time she and Doug had to relax in the Park, one of her favorite places, despite the months they had been together. She loved the Park and walked around Stowe Lake every chance she got. It was hard to find the time these days for anything else.

At the same time, Doug was working on the strike at the hospital. He was also trying to deal with his own concerns. He sat alone in his office thinking back over the last 15 years, before he had married Kristie, single life, and what his marriage had been like.

He recalled what he had felt with Kristie; there was not much sex, plenty of poor communication, and also lack of mutual interests. He was glad about the children, of course, but he realized they all had lives of their own, and they would soon grow apart and be on their own.

He thought about Shelly and smiled. She was so full of life, energy, and love for him. She made him feel alive, vigorous, and happy. He thought of Alison and how she looked up to him. He was not in opposition to the idea of getting married. He just realized how little time either of them had to arrange anything, how far away their parents were, and how little extra money they had. It would be expensive to do it "the right way."

They didn't have the extra money they would need for a special event like a wedding. "A Contest?" No one he knew ever did that before. It would be a first, and he was not sure he wanted to be a pioneer.

He was deep in thought.

Someone was at the door, calling into his office. The voice brought him back to the real work problems at hand.

While Doug was alone in his thoughts, Shelly finally arrived at the Japanese Garden. She sat down to rest, looking out over a pond full of Koi fish.

She thought back on her life with Arnold, the promises, and the pains. She remembered how little they had in common. He showed so little interest in any of her activities or appreciation for what she did to try to make him happy. She did try to make things work. She thought back about the time they were remodeling, his indifference to her ideas, his rudeness. She felt sad. She remembered his lack of touching, tenderness, and most of all his lack of interest in being a father, attending childbirth classes and his indifference later. He had a definite disinterest.

She remembered Alison's birth, and then the problems she had afterwards. Then she recalled the pain of their divorce. Those thoughts came into her mind as she thought about taking a risk on marriage again. Alison's and her own well being were at risk. Thinking again about Doug and their situation, she realized they had not gone all the way to making the full commitment.

Were they ready? Were the children?

A real wedding was a major, and very big, next step.

Taking the step toward marriage is not taken lightly.

Chapter  17

The Contest

When so many hours have been spent in convincing myself that I am right, is there not some reason to fear that I may be wrong? Jane Austen

All of Shelly's dreams were coming true. She was living with the man she loved, a doctor, committed to the same issues she felt deeply. They shared a family together. She was settling in as a pioneer woman, transplanted from everyone and everything she was familiar with, ready to explore a dynamic and amazing new city, new friends, and challenging new work.

She wanted it all to be perfect. But, the difficult times Shelly had experienced with Arnold still haunted her. She could hear her mother's admonitions. The voice inside her head got louder when Shelly was alone.

She was reminded of the litany of all the good, albeit negative, motherly advice whenever they spoke on the phone:

"You never listen to me!"

"You have to know somebody for a long time before marrying him. Why rush into things?"

"Why don't you learn from my mistakes? Take my advice?"

"You give, and give, and get nothing back, but tsorres (problems)."

"Take the next plane back and get your old job back. You will have peace and quiet, a chance to have security. Why do you need the aggravation?"

Shelly carefully and calmly, if somewhat annoyed, responded, "First, you tell me to be good, and not live with him before marriage. Now you say don't get married. Can't you just be happy?"

Her mother spoke about her anxious feelings about Doug.

"I know he's a lovely man. I don't know if he's a good father or a good husband. Maybe he'll be good for you, maybe he won't. But, mark my word; his children will never appreciate you. Sooner or later he will show you what he is really made of, and you will be sorry you made that schlep, the leap of faith, and you will regret it."

After the talk she sadly recalled her honeymoon with Arnold. She recalled his lack of warmth or sensitivity on their first night of marriage. In his rush, he didn't use lubrication during lovemaking. The force and friction resulted in pain, bleeding, discomfort, and disappointment. Later, even more intense pain came from the unexpected urinary tract infection and left her unable to have sex for several weeks. The hurt stayed with her as a painful memory. Where was the gentle yet rollicking romance Arnold had demonstrated before they married? The music, the beat of love like a bad riff went kaput, only faded memories were left.

She had yearned for real romance, a real fireplace, real warmth. Arnold instead arranged an ersatz honeymoon in a room with a fake cardboard fireplace. He had not checked the details when making the reservation...so much for warmth. The room they slept in on that first night was cold, foretelling what was to come.

Much later, she recalled Arnold's adamant negativity. He was against her going to graduate school despite her winning a full scholarship.

He empathically told her, "You don't need more education! You should be content to be a wife. What else do you need?"

"Now you sound just like my mother," Shelly retorted. "There's not enough for me. I'm not just your wife; you want me to be your 'mother,' too!"

Arnold hardly noticed all the efforts she made cooking "Julia Child's" gourmet dinners, or keeping their busy calendar straight of the many social events, especially those related to his work and advancement. She wanted to help him succeed with his goals. But, he did not share hers, and finally the distance between them grew too great. Their divorce was very painful.

She was haunted by some of the things that Arnold did to accomplish his goals and those things could never be anticipated. So much for faded memories, she faced them and tried to wipe them finally out of her mind. There was no time now to think about the past. She was facing major new crossroads. Life was constantly, precariously changing as so many smaller pieces needed to be constantly juggled.

When she met Doug she was ready for a real relationship that would work. She believed she would be loved. He cared about Alison. She felt his attention was consistent and loving. She wanted more than anything else to trust Doug. She wanted to be loved, to love, and to have a loving family. She wanted love to last and grow. Her dreams seemed to be tangible and within reach.

Shelly thought of her favorite romantic love song,

"When I fall in love, it will be completely,

Or I'll never fall in love...

And the moment I feel that,
You feel that way, too,
Is when I'll fall in love with you,"
She sighed.

Despite all of the other men she had met in Washington, Doug, at the distance of the continent, became the most important man in her life. She thought about how they met, and how quickly he came to see her after she had called him at the hotel. She tingled remembering their first kiss and their first night together.

She realized how important Doug had become to her over the years, despite being separated thousands of miles, and many lonely nights. Their long-distance relationship had become a reality. She wanted it to be permanent. She did not want anyone else.

Shelly most of all desired to be married to Doug, to make theirs a happy marriage, and to work together on their family and all of the other issues in their lives—childcare, health care, and community services. She opened her eyes wide and saw reality staring her in the face.

She remembered without hesitation all that was involved in raising Alison alone. The thought about the five years she struggled to balance work, Alison's needs, and time for herself. She looked down at her notepad.

She began to write the entry letter for "The Contest".

"Dear Twentieth Century Fox:

'We're Made for Each Other' all right! For the past two years, at a distance of 3,000 miles, Doug here in San Francisco and me in Washington, D.C., we kept our love alive and growing through phone calls every morning and evening, trips whenever we could arrange them, and just caring about our relationship. It got better even without marriage, living together, and just loving each other. We now have five kids and five puppies, on top of everything. Three kids are his from his past marriage, one is mine, plus we have a housekeeper who is a teenager with a two-year-old little girl."

"Our parents, friends, and the kids ask, 'When are you getting married?' We just smile and say, 'Someday!' The girls want to be flower girls. We have, all of us, been living together for the past six months. It is wild and wonderful. We have grown as a family, and are definitely 'Made for Each Other.' I loved seeing the movie 'Made for Each Other.' The way it ends makes me feel that there is a whole new beginning waiting ahead for us. I feel that marriage should be when you don't need it, when you're really together, and making it real every day. We hardly have time to create our own wedding, so if we win, it will be because we finally want to make our family and our love complete."

As Shelly was writing the essay, she didn't notice that a photographer was taking her picture. Suddenly, when she looked up she saw him. She saw his camera pointed at her, and she was surprised that anyone would take her photograph without asking first. She looked at him, not sure how to respond. The stranger with a camera was good-looking, and he was very focused on her.

He said, "Sorry if I startled you. I often come here to take pictures. Hope you don't mind."

She shook her head.

He asked, "Are you free for a coffee?"

She was definitely not interested in pursuing a flirtation.

She said, "Why don't you give me your card just in case we ever need a photographer. You never know when we might need to document an important event."

Shelly looked at his card: Alan Rowan, Photographer.

He said, "Yes, please call me whenever you'd like. I'd like to do some photos for you, or just talk sometime."

She said, "It's a really busy time right now, but thanks for your offer"

She thought, "What a funny thing to say. Who has time to talk or to have a drink? Little does he know by seeing me merely sitting calmly in the sun of my crazy hectic lifestyle."

Her days of flirting were over.

She finished the paper she was writing, put it away in her bag, looked at her watch, and got up.

Shelly went directly to her car, drove out of the park and through Haight-Ashbury to pick up Melanie, who had been visiting at Jake's house on Cole Street. Melanie's car was in the garage to get the brakes repaired. Brakes needed to be carefully and frequently checked driving the streets of San Francisco, but there were no brakes on her conviction, she made the right decision to enter The Contest.

She stopped in front of Jake's house to pick her up. Melanie was waiting, she waved and came down the steps and jumped in the car. They went directly to the sauna. As they drove down the Street, Shelly told Melanie about "The Contest." Melanie was somehow not surprised, but she did laugh at the thought of her friend actually winning "The Contest."

She said, "Gosh, if you win, how will you find a baby sitter to go on a honeymoon?"

They both laughed.

They continued talking as they parked and entered the building. They got their towels, salt and water, and found their way to Room 21. Melanie happily told Shelly about the growing relationship she was having with Jake.

They also talked about the plans for the childcare demonstration on Thursday.

When they got into the room they quickly undressed, placed their clothes in the locker, went to the shower room and washed their hair, and then before going into the steam room spread salt over their bodies. As they went in and out of the steam room, they continued talking.

Shelly told Melanie, "I just completed writing the requested essay for The Contest. It has been very emotional just writing it."

Melanie laughed, and said, "I can't believe that you really want to do this."

"But," Melanie added, wanting to help her friend, not discourage her or point out the big chance she was risking, and knowing, after all, it was a long shot like the lottery, "Why not enter it? Marriage is 'The Contest,' after all, any way you play it. It's all a game, right? You never know if you will win, but being in the game and playing is what is important."

Shelly reminded her, "Hey, Jake is long shot too, but I am sure everything is going to turn out perfectly. Just keep the faith."

They smiled and gave each other an encouraging hug.

Then Shelly drove Melanie home and said goodbye.

Shelly returned home.

She went in to handle a lot of details. She quickly finished the book she had to read, made some notes, and then went quickly around the house to tidy up the continuous mess of things laying helter-skelter where the kids had dropped them.

She made arrangements with Nora for sitting that night so she and Doug could go to the 25th wedding anniversary party of their friends, Dr. Stan and Martha Jankofsky. She then went upstairs to the bedroom to change taking along dirty clothes to put into the washing machine.

When Doug entered the house to pick her up, Shelly had just finished dressing so showed him what she had written for "The Contest."

He sat down to read the paper and then he looked up and laughed. "I can't take this seriously!"

Shelly said firmly, "I hope you like it. We need to drop off 'The Contest' entry form at The Ghirardelli Theatre before we cross the Golden Gate Bridge to go to the Jankofsky's party."

Finally, he resigned himself, he did not want to lose her, and said, "Why not? Let's take a chance. This whole thing is like 'Truth or Consequences' anyway."

They went downstairs, kissed the kids good-by, gave Nora the phone number at the party, petted Spot, and the puppies, and walked out the door.

As they drove toward Marin County and cross the Golden Gate Bridge to go to the Jankofsky's, they stopped briefly in the yellow zone near The Ghirardelli Theatre.

Doug sat in the car the motor running as Shelly ran up the stairs to leave off "The Contest" entry form. She placed it in an envelope, and slipped it in the slot of the box in the lobby of the theatre. She felt happy and excited. She said to herself, if you don't enter, there is no chance of winning; so you must play. It was a lark, a real long shot. She felt she also had already learned a lot just from thinking about her reasons for going through with a wedding. She realized the depth of her commitment to Doug and the children. She had already taken the leap of faith

They sang their favorite love song duet imitating Jeanette McDonald and Nelson Eddy as they continued across the bridge.

"Only make believe, that you love me!
Only make believe, that I love you!
Others find peace of mind in pretending,
Couldn't you, couldn't I, couldn't we?
Only make believe, our lips are blending,
In a phantom kiss, or two, or three.
Might as well make believe I love you,
For to tell the truth, I do!"

It was a good party. Many marriage jokes were bandied about. Some of the stories surprised Shelly as she realized some couples were more liberal in their marriage vows than she ever wanted to be. They both drank a lot of champagne.

Shelly and Doug were caught up in the idea that a successful marriage was possible despite all the challenges, potential shortcomings and the many struggles.

They appeared to be the classic "perfect" couple. But they knew the Jankofskys were not entirely happy. Despite their separate interests, separate vacations, separate lovers, they stayed together through sheer perseverance.

Many of their friends behaved in much the same way in their so-called "Open Marriages." This was a new trend, it was the early '70s and it seemed, among a group of likeminded people that the "Summer of Love" continued ad infinitum. Shelly had not heard before of the things these couples were doing. In her cloistered "Wide Washington World," "wild" was not part of the equation.

She considered what these couples did far from her core values, but she understood the complexity of relationships, the range of people's preferences, and respected their alternative choices. Others could choose their own life-styles as they saw fit. She would happily hold on to her precious views of monogamy, even if her views were considered old-hat, monotonous, or even square. It was for her the best way she believed to trust and love. She was not about to succumb to the pressure put on her from others to fundamentally change who she was.

However, she was tolerant and even a little curious at times. She wondered how people could remain in their relationship after having sex with another partner. It seemed to her to break the sacred vows that were central to the core values in the first place. Shelly wanted to remain in a healthy and committed relationship. She assumed that was what Doug wanted also.

Shelly and Doug left the party with an extra piece of cake "for the road." As they drove back to the city, they started to sing again. Then, Shelly feeling spontaneous and a little drunk from the champagne, decided to give Doug a thrill.

She unzipped his pants. As they drove along on 101 through the tunnel she played with him, aroused him with her mouth, and with the icing of the cake.

He grinned and said, "I'm having my cake and you are eating it, too!"

When they reached the tollbooth, he was still grinning. Shelly smiled, too. She had icing all over her mouth. She pretended she was asleep and remained face down and in place so the toll attendant would not see her face covered with icing. They both laughed.

On Wednesday, Doug and Shelly had a very full day.

He was coping with many problems and the growing strike issue at the hospital. She had last minute arrangements for phone calls to make to assist in the childcare demonstration. Many activities were being readied like creating placards to take along to carry to the park across from City Hall.

She also had a planned visit to one of the childcare centers, in her study, to do an observation.

She noticed several children in role-playing games acting out their feelings about "Mommy" and "Daddy." They were playing "Divorce!"

Each child had a soft doll in its hands. Each of them was pulling one arm and one leg. The children were pulling at the same time in opposite directions and loudly fighting over the "baby."

"Give it to me!" said one child pulling the doll in her direction.

"No. Give it to me! Squealed the other child, pulling in the opposite direction."

As they resumed their pulling match, Shelly wondered, children act out their feelings about real life through play. It reveals what's really going on within and is not often observable unless the child expresses inner feelings through play. These essential clues are often missed by adults.

Shelly talked with teachers to find out about some of their problems running the childcare program. They shared their thoughts as they were rarely asked about their experiences. She talked also to a few parents who also had a lot to share

She told everyone about the childcare demonstration plans. Both teachers and parents agreed to be there and to make some signs to bring along.

When Shelly arrived back home, she discovered Nora was upset because Andy was missing. It seemed that he had not gone to school that day. Nora said he overheard the conversation between Shelly and Doug about getting married.

His backpack was missing from his room. Ross said, "He probably hiked over to that Twin Peaks cave he likes to visit."

Shelly jumped into the car. She drove over to where the boys had once shown her their "secret cave" between some boulders on Twin Peaks.

At the top, half hidden behind the rocks, she found Andy. He was sitting on the hill looking out at the view. She got out of the car and went over to him. Andy jumped up and turned angrily toward her.

He yelled at her, "How did you find me?"

Shelly calmly responded, "I thought you might not be too far away. Can we talk?"

He yelled at her, again full of angry feelings. "I don't want to be in this family. I am angry about you being with my dad. I don't want to share him. It's not fair!"

Shelly stayed calm. She looked at him with understanding.

She told him, "I hope we can be friends and work out our relationship. It will take time. I will never want to take the part of your mother. I don't ever want to come between you and your parents. I just want us to have a happy new family. We can all help each other. Your mom and I have talked a lot"

He looked at her, and saw she was trying. He finally stopped being angry.

He calmed down and said, "I guess you really do care about me. I will give you a second chance. But please, get Ross off my back."

She smiled, as he was the one who was always on top of Ross, but then she realized he had a lot of confusion going on.

When she agreed, he got back into the car. They returned home together.

When they arrived at the house, Nora told Shelly a Mrs. Polly Best called, a public relations woman with Twentieth Century Fox.

Shelly dialed Mrs. Best with trembling hands.

"Hello," Polly Best exclaimed enthusiastically you have won 'The Contest'! Would you like to be married this Friday? We will make all the arrangements, if you can be ready," continued Mrs. Best. "I promise it will all be in good taste. It will take place on a beautiful yacht, with flowers and complete with cake and champagne. Just so you know it will be in perfect taste I did a wedding before, for ten couples, and at one the weddings Bob Hope was the best man. I know this one will be wonderful!"

Shelly sat down and began to laugh out loud.

"I can hardly believe it, Nora. I won "The Contest." Mrs. Best just said the wedding must be scheduled for this Friday."

"What did you say?" asked Nora with her mouth dropped wide open.

Shelly shook her head in disbelief, "I can't make this decision alone. I have to wait until I can reach Doug. She's going to call back later this evening."

Shelly tried to reach Doug at the hospital. He was unavailable. She left a message with his secretary. "Please ask him to call home, its urgent."

When he finally called, Shelly said, "I can't talk about this over the phone. Just come home, please."

Doug walked in the door within the hour. Shelly had a glass of wine waiting for him. She asked him to come into the living room. As they sat on the sofa, her hands were trembling.

She said, "Doug, guess what? Polly Best from Twentieth Century Fox called today. It seems we won 'The Contest'!"

He looked surprised, laughed, and then said, "But, you and I don't have time to get married."

She said, "Be serious please. They want us to get married this Friday. They'll make all the arrangements. The wedding will be on a beautiful yacht at the St. Francis Yacht Club. They'll give us a honeymoon in Carmel, if we drive down. They can't fly us all to San Diego. The problem is Nora can't take care of the children this weekend. We'd have to take all the children with us on the honeymoon."

He said, "Oh, great! That is just the way I always wanted to start our married life, with four children tagging along with us on our honeymoon!"

"Mrs. Best said she could give us the hotel and meals at several restaurants in Carmel and Monterey. She could fix us up at the hotel with a separate room for the children. She said she would make all the arrangements for the wedding. All we have to do tomorrow is get the blood test, get the license, arrange for the Rabbi, and invite guests."

Doug said, "How can we do this in the middle of everything? I've got the strike to deal with. You've got the childcare demonstration tomorrow. It's all too much!"

Shelly neglected to tell him about Andy running away, not wanting to add to his pressure. She knew it was an unusual and delicate opportunity. This was a unique moment and required both of their focus.

He looked at her, and realized she was serious.

He said, "How do you feel about it?"

"Well, I've gone through all of my misgivings, the questions I had, the doubts, and especially, my fears. I think we've waited a long time. It feels right. We are living together. Everyone wants to know when we're getting married. We don't have the time or money to do it for ourselves. So why not?" replied Shelly.

"Let's have dinner. Let me think about it. I'm very concerned about having a publicity stunt as our wedding. A man in my position can't possibly be so public about his personal life."

He said thinking at the same moment of the imaginary headlines: "Doctor wins wife in contest! Four kids to go with bride and groom on their honeymoon!"

Shelly replied, "Mrs. Best promised it would be done with great discretion." She told him Mrs. Best had arranged a multiple couple-wedding event, and that Bob Hope was the best man.

He laughed. That did not reassure him at all.

She was already thinking about the guests and thought about inviting Peter, Charles, Melanie, Jake, Paul and Eileen, The Jankofskys, Pat, Sara, Hal Slate, and of course their friend, Steve Hanan. He would love to sing.

Steve and Hal were Shelly's old friends from Washington, D.C., who followed her out to San Francisco. Steve sang every chance he got, as his voice was wonderful and operatic. He was trying to find his way to become professional, so while he waited for his big Broadway break, he sang in front of the crowds waiting for the Sausalito ferry. He made plenty of money to live on while he sang, played the concertina and stayed in shape. Hal lived and worked in the Castro. They both enjoyed the zigs and zags and were flexible.

All of their closest friends could be part of the celebration. Neither Doug nor Shelly had family nearby or could they get they arrive on such short notice, but the friends were close to being like family. These friends were their new family. She knew it was next to impossible to get Doug's parents, or her parents, to San Francisco in time. But, they had to invite them.

Doug said at dinner, "Well, let's call one of those 'family council' conferences."

They called the children in to discuss the news. When the four children came in, Doug told them about "The Contest" and about their winning.

The kids jumped up and down and said, "Great!" 'It'll be fun!' 'Yeah, a trip to Carmel!' 'Hotel and Room Service' 'A wedding!' 'Oh boy!' "Yes!'"

Andy seemed to change. He saw the other children were in favor. His voice in the final "yes!" was his agreement.

The children's response relieved Doug and Shelly of their fears.

Nora stood by listening and she shook her head. She still had doubts, because of her own experience, she felt somewhat cynical about love. She had weekend plans, but she and Ginny would not miss the wedding.

"What can I do to help?" she finally succumbed and asked.

It was 7:00 p.m. They had just finished dessert. Doug put down his spoon, and looked at Shelly and the children.

He announced, "Yes!"

They looked at each other and smiled. "Yes!" was on everyone's face.

They decided they would call Mrs. Best again to ask her to review all of the arrangements, if she did not call them back soon.

But, first they called their parents. As expected, it was impossible for any of them to fly out.

Doug's mother Lorraine said, "It's about time! I am very happy for you, but I could never get my hair done in time to make the trip! But we are very pleased. Mazel tov!"

Shelly's mother Jeanie said bluntly and firmly, "You're crazy! I know it will never work out. Doug will never fully appreciate you. He will find a way to break your heart. The children will take you for granted. If you are determined to go ahead with it, you have my blessing, but mostly you have my prayers. Mishuganah!"

Shelly thanked her, took a deep breath, and kept her composure. She would not be able to come out, but that she gave prayers and blessings was something.

Doug then said he wanted to call Mrs. Best again. He wanted to be reassured about the amount of promotion she planned, and to hear all the details.

Mrs. Best did her best to reassure him.

"Everything will be done in the best of 'good taste.' Other than a few promotional shots, there will not be much time for anything else. And, you can take the children with you on your honeymoon. It's so unusual that there are four children involved. It's such a perfect idea. They will have a separate room, of course! We can arrange meals at local restaurants. It will all be just perfect."

Doug laughed when he asked Mrs. Best, "Are you sure you can't arrange Disneyland? The kids would like that even more."

She laughed and said, "Sorry, not this time!"

She told them they needed to be at the St. Francis Yacht Club at noon on Friday.

"Leave the rest to me," she said.

When Doug completed the call with Mrs. Best, he said, "OK, it felt all right. I think she is sincere and not much is going to happen publicly, so I am safe."

They hugged and kissed.

Then they called the other friends they wanted to attend to give them as much notice as possible. Their comments made them laugh.

Peter said, "Carmel? I'm sure it will be foggy!"

Charles added, "With this kind of Mickey Mouse deal you should be going to Disneyland!"

Doug laughed and said he already asked.

Jake asked, "Are you sure you can't be married on the Johnny Carson Show?"

Melanie added, "Taking the kids with you on your honeymoon? You've got to be crazy! What a way to start off."

Steve asked them what they wanted him to sing.

They said, "Surprise us!"

Shelly and Doug made a list of all the things they had to do. They made plans around all the other crises.

They figured out a strategy. If they moved really fast on Thursday, they might get everything done.

The next morning they started off early by calling the Rabbi to do the honors.

The Rabbi exclaimed, "What? Get married on a boat? Oh no I'll get seasick before I can even perform the ceremony. Oy Vey!"

He finally agreed to be at dockside at noon and to also take some Dramamine before the wedding. He had never been to the St Francis Yacht Club and it would be an interesting first time he was sure.

The next stop was to go to the health clinic to get blood tests. They begged for a rush so they could get the results back after lunch.

Then they shopped for some colorful "second wedding" clothes.

In a little jewelry store on Polk Street they found the only matching pair of gold bands in the store. They were a perfect fit. Synchronicity was working in their favor.

They laughed as they picked up sandwiches and drinks, and dashed back to the car.

After lunch, they picked up their blood test results.

Then they went directly to City Hall.

Just as they turned the corner, the childcare demonstration was just start-ing to be formed at the steps of City Hall. Shelly was in conflict. She could not be part of it. She realized at that moment her personal life had to take first priority. This was the day before the most important day of her life. She had given so much of herself for children, and to the childcare programs she cared about, and to all of the people involved, everyone, but herself. Now, she finally had to take time for herself to put her own life in order. She asked Doug to wait for a minute. She ran over to the organizers, Patty and Margaret and told them what happened and about the unexpected event.

They smiled and waved as she and Doug dashed up the steps past the demonstrators, shouting and holding signs:

"We need more childcare now!"

"No Cuts for Children!"

"It will be a great day when the Navy has to hold a bake sale to buy a ship and childcare gets all the money it needs!"

"Make More Time and Money for Kids!"

Once inside City Hall they had to find the right office. They finally found it. They had to register first at the City Clerk's desk. They were breathless. Their minds filled as they waited their turn. As they waited in line to fill out the ap-plications and show evidence of their blood tests, they composed a statement they wanted to say to each other, and to the children, during the ceremony.

Moving again past the demonstrators, who were now on their way past the City Hall to cross the civic park towards the Federal Building, they rushed back to their car.

They went to Macy's on Union Square to get some special dress-up cloth-ing for the children. Then they drove home with everything.

In a mad scramble that followed, the children tried on the new clothes. They were very excited. They each had to pack a bag to take along.

Shelly and Doug retreated to the bedroom to pack their suitcases.

Between the phone calls to friends, packing, and making final arrange-ments, the rest of the afternoon was frenetic and totally wild, Everyone was busy getting ready and all at once.

Mrs. Best had arranged for everyone to go to Capp's Restaurant in North Beach that night for a big family pre-wedding dinner, where they sat around eating, drinking, and celebrating the beginning of a new life.

Mrs. Best chatted about this being such a unique situation.

"I am so glad you are making it official. There are four kids that will be so much happier now." She exclaimed.

Doug toasted his bride-to-be.

Shelly was filled with happiness. She knew she was making the right decision, even if her mother did not.

She thanked Mrs. Best for all her efforts. She felt joy, energy, and resolved to do everything in her power to make things work.

She looked at the children and at Doug. They were "Made for Each Other." They were "winning" each other. "The Contest" was winning the new game of love, commitment, and working together for their future. What could be better?

Doug frequently had called the hospital all day long to stay in contact with the staff handling the crisis. He was relieved that progress was being made. He finally realized he could stay away for at least two days. A crisis may come and go, but a wedding day is a day to hold fast.

This was the first day of the rest of their lives!

Chapter 18

Wedding Day

How but in custom and ceremony, are innocence and beauty born. W.B. Yeats

As Shelly opened her eyes on Friday, the day of the wedding, she saw the sun shining through the window, a rare occurrence on Twin Peaks.

"A significant sign!" she said smiling as she stretched. She turned to Doug and kissed him. He mumbled and reached out to her. She sat up in bed, inspired by the moment, grabbed her pen and notebook on the bedside table, and quickly wrote a poem:

"He truly loves me,
Everyone can see.
I know it well,
Clear as a bell.
His voice rings love crystal blue,
In so many ways he shows me love so true.
Whenever he looks, it's direct and deep,
I feel his touch softly when I sleep.
For so long, my whole life,
I waited for him to call me, wife.
This man takes all of me with his kiss,
Today together, we share our wedded bliss.
Without him, nothing,
With him…everything."

She closed the notebook, put the pen and notebook down, and got up quietly to get some water as she said softly not sure that Doug could hear, "Well," "at least I am doing what Roy told me to do, putting my feelings, hopes, and dreams on paper, even if it's not Elizabeth or Edna. I have to express myself, even if it's corny, and even if no one ever reads it."

Doug did not hear her, as he was deep in his own thoughts. He wondered if the whole dream of the wedding day was just that. No! He stayed put holding back, not wanting to start moving.

As she brushed her teeth and washed her face, she looked at herself in the mirror and wondered, "Is this all really true? Is today really the 'big' day?"

She put on a robe and left the bedroom to let Doug get himself adjusted. She went downstairs and found the children in the middle of breakfast. The puppies were happily sucking mother Spot's teats. Shelly went to each of the children to kiss and hug them. They seemed happy. They were content watching the puppies, television, and each other munching on cereal.

"Don't worry. We will be ready fast."

"Sure, we are whiz kids!"

"Yes, mommy, don't worry, we are super kids!"

"Right! Super-sized and super-fast!" added Andy.

They said almost at the same time "Don't worry we are all ready!" reassuring her that they were actually ready to cooperate on this, the big day. They would pack and be ready to go. She wondered if everything would go smoothly, but she decided not to worry too much.

She went over to a shelf and took down the map she had located at AAA and laid out a map of the California coast to show them the location of Carmel and Monterey. She showed them the route they would travel from San Francisco. As they studied the map the children talked about the trip:

"There is a beach there."

"There's a boardwalk with fishing boats."

"We're going to have room-service.

"We can order anything we want."

"You better not push me off the boat when they get married or you will be in big trouble."

"No, squirt. You will be in trouble when I push you in because you can't swim."

"I can, too, swim, fatso!" exclaimed Ross.

Nora and Ginny entered the room and Shelly added two more bowls of cereal. As she prepared the cereal Shelly talked to Nora. Ginny took her bowl over to the TV and joined the other kids. While they watched Ginny eat cereal Shelly tried to give Nora some advice about some of the problems she was having with Ginny. She was a two-year-old with a hefty temper and was still getting used to being with her mother again.

"Be patient with her!" Shelly cautioned as they watched Ginny eating and watching the puppies. Then Ginny got off the chair, put her bowl of cereal on the table and went over to pet them. She watched them suckling Spot and was fascinated.

Shelly asked if everybody could ready so they could leave at 11:30. It was just 9:00 a.m. They all nodded their heads.

Nora threw up her hands and said, "It will be split-second timing in the bathroom as usual." Then she gathered the bowls and put the cereal and milk away.

Then the phone started ringing.

The first call was from Arnold. Shelly's mother had called him. He wished her well. She was glad that he thought to call her and to take a moment to speak to Alison. It was a rare kindness and she was grateful. She knew he was probably relieved that she was remarrying and finally to have a little peace of mind. She did not mind. He had already remarried and found the perfect type for him, a stewardess who knew how to serve him with the right attitude and no questions asked. She turned the phone over to Alison.

Alison said, "Hi Daddy, we are going on a boat today. Mommy is getting married. I am the flower girl. Can you come to the wedding daddy?"

They talked for a few minutes. Then Alison said "Goodbye!" and went back to watching TV with the other children.

Doug had decided to call Kristie to let her know they were to be married. He felt it best she learn it directly from him rather than from the children. Kristie reacted coldly and just said,

"Good luck. I hope you have better fortune this time."

Shelly went back upstairs with a cup of coffee and proceeded to tidy up the bedroom. She looked at her dress. Then she started to pack some things. She felt moved to write in her journal again. She wrote,

"I want children, dogs, cats,
With laughter filling the crevices
of every day.
Surprises,
lots of them,
talk and friends at dinner parties,
walks in spring,
picnics in summer,
biking in fall,
snowballs in winter,
music filling the rooms,
sharing songs, symphonies, and
Scheherazade,
Tom Lehrer, and
a jazz tune or two.
Sharing ourselves is
more than we are alone."

Doug came out of the shower. He put his arms around her. They kissed. Then he looked at her and smiled.

He said, "Well, I never would have believed we'd be doing it. Now it all feels right. No, it's perfect! After waiting so long, we're finally going to make it! You really surprised me. I never thought you would win 'The Contest' and decide to marry me after all that we have been through. We have Naches (good luck) after all."

The phone started to ring again. People called to say they were coming, or they needed directions, or wanted to wish them "Mazel Tov!" (Congratulations).

Mrs. Best called promptly at 10:00 a.m. They both listened to her.

"I want to be sure you are all ready." She continued, "I will meet you at the Yacht at noon; remember you cannot be late. Everything is all set onboard and with the reception. I have prepared everything with the hotel. Don't worry about a thing. The kids will be in the room right next door in two double beds."

They looked at each other and smiled. Then they started to dress.

Shelly wore a soft brocade, colorful, paisley print, velvet, lame dress. She had found a florist in Diamond Heights who created a wreath of simple flowers for her hair. Doug wore a hand-made shirt in the same colors as her dress. They looked at each other and felt they were perfectly dressed for a second wedding.

The girls put on their long, colorful dresses and gathered their flower bouquets and two baskets of rose petals. The boys put on their new shirts and pants. They did not fight too much. Soon they were ready.

Nora and Ginny dressed also. Ginny reached for a small basket of rose petals, and threw some petals at the puppies.

"Happy Wedding, Puppies!" she said as Nora grabbed her basket and hand. Then they followed Doug and Shelly to the car.

The children's faces were shining. Nora had a skeptical look on her face, but she felt happy for Shelly. She knew Shelly wanted to be married to Doug, but she still was skeptical. Ginny was in a better mood and stayed that way on the slow trip across town. Doug wanted to go slowly for many reasons. The car was overloaded. He was still anxious about the event that was soon to change everything again, officially, and in every way possible, but he was in the driver's seat of the future. They drove across town toward the Saint Francis Yacht Club.

As Doug drove through Golden Gate Park, Shelly's mind drifted to another poem she wrote in her journal:

"Dressing for my wedding day

Happiness fills me.
Can I say, 'I take this man,
and still be me?'
Soon we will be one,
our life together has begun.
We have traveled so many miles,
our children wait with gentle smiles,
they carry flower petals to bless father and mother,
joy is what we see inside each other.
We share as partners all of our days.
Our communion is celebrated in so many ways.
As we make our way to the harbor I know,
each day we will work to make love grow.

She looked at Doug and the children, Nora and Ginny. She began to sing,

"Only make believe, that I love you,
only make believe you love me,
let's find peace of mind in pretending,
Couldn't I? couldn't you? Couldn't we?
Make believe our lips are blending, in a phantom kiss, or two, or three,
Might was well make believe, I love you, for to tell the truth I do."

Doug joined with her in a duet.

The children giggled.

They continued singing as they drove across the Park to the Yacht club. Shelly felt happy.

When they arrived they saw their friends already standing near the gangplank of the boat. The Rabbi had just pulled up. He looked at all of them.

"I can hardly believe it," he muttered. "To think of Jewish people being married on a boat, at the Saint Francis Yacht Club, to promote a movie, no less!"

He was being good-natured, they thought, and enjoyed teasing them. He wasn't teasing, but had decided to make the best of it. He was concerned about his stomach. Since it was a calm day, he felt the boat would not yaw. He would probably not become seasick since he already had taken the Dramamine.

They all went carefully up the gangplank.

Doug and Shelly let the others go ahead and stayed on the dock to talk for a few moments before joining them. They walked together to the side of the boat.

Alan, the photographer she had met in the park, was called the night before. He was there, waiting with camera in hand. He wished her well.

"Let's be friends," he said, photographing them. "You make a beautiful bride! Thanks for inviting me to be here to witness this event!"

Mrs. Best was on board the boat and greeted everyone with great enthusiasm.

She exclaimed, "Everything is ready! We have flowers, champagne, and a delicious cake. The Rabbi is here, and also the bride and groom. Oh, I always wanted to be a 'Jewish mother.' I am so thrilled!"

"All the arrangements have been made just as I promised. Everything is perfect!" She gave Doug the envelopes with all the details. He put them away in his pocket and thanked her.

Shelly and Doug nodded in agreement. They thanked Mrs. Best for everything she had done.

Shelly added, "You are a real Jewish mother! Our own Jewish mothers are nowhere in sight. You are a perfect substitute."

Doug then said, "Let's get on with the celebration!"

Shelly and Doug walked to the edge of the boat. They looked out over the water at Sausalito, Tiburon, Alcatraz, Fisherman's Wharf, and the City rising majestically against the bay. She looked at Doug. He turned and went down below. When the time was right, she would join him. Soon!

The Song of Solomon began the ceremony.

"I am my beloved, my beloved is mine.

Until the daybreak and shadows flee away.

How much better is thy love than wine?

How fair and pleasant art thou?

Thy voice is sweet, thy countenance comely,

O thou who my soul loveth.

For much water cannot quench our love,

Neither can floods drown it.

Lo, my beloved, the winter has passed,

the rain is over and gone,

the flowers appear on the earth,

the time for singing is now.

My fair one arise and come away.

My beloved come to the fields,

get up early to the vineyards.

At our door are all manner of precious fruit,

which I have laid up before thee.

My beloved, come to me.

Set me as a seal upon thy heart."

The Rabbi blessed them. Then they read the statement they had written the day before at City Hall.

"On this day of ceremony, we pledge to each other again,
and to our children, to love with all we can give
and with all we can accept.
To share our love with our children, family, friends,
and all the other people we touch in our lives.
To help each other to grow to our fullest capacity
while at the same time respecting our different paths
and accepting our imperfections with patience and love.

To always take responsibility for our own words and actions while not taking responsibility away from each other.

To strive to live each day in a way that heightens our job and lessens our burdens.

To communicate in honesty and openness in all our contacts in ways that deepens our understanding of one another.

To create a Jewish home that honors God and
respects our traditions and cherishes the sanctity of our new family."

As they said "family," they looked at each other, at the children, and at their friends. Shelly's eyes filled with tears.

As the Rabbi pronounced them "husband and wife," he raised his hands to make the blessing. He did not feel seasick. He actually enjoyed his first wedding ceremony on a boat. He would have a good story to tell for many weeks.

They embraced, kissed, and sipped some wine.

Then the Rabbi put the glass down at Doug's feet. As Doug stomped on the glass, their friends cried out,

"Mazel Tov!"

Steve began to sing an Italian aria, "Amore." and played his concertina. Everyone stopped to listen to his beautiful voice. Love spread out to everyone and filled the boat with joy.

The boys then quickly moved to where the food table was and started grabbing handfuls.

The girls smiled as they held their bouquets, threw rose petals around, and were too excited to eat. They were being very sweet to each other. They talked to each of the guests.

After they ate, Ross and Andy seemed happy. They began singing with the organist and with Steve.

All the friends were talking, eating, and drinking. Everyone smiled. It was a beautiful love filled day!

Alison held up her bouquet to give to her mother.

Shelly said, "Hold onto it, sweetie. It's for you to keep."

Alison grinned, and moved over to the cake gripping the flowers.

Then, Shelly turned, and threw her bouquet. Her friend Melanie caught it. Jake looked at her.

He said, "Well, maybe we'll be next."

Melanie rolled her eyes and blushed.

Doug and Shelly moved to the cake. Mrs. Best had selected a beautiful one from The Victoria, the best Italian bakery in North Beach. They cut the first piece together. Shelly fed a piece of cake to Doug. He fed her a piece of cake. They kissed and drank champagne. They talked with their friends. They thanked the Rabbi. After he left they all had more champagne and went out on the deck to view the city. .

Steve sang again, even more robustly.

Others joined in.

"I'll be loving you, always.

With a love that's true, always…

Not for just an hour,

Not for just a day,

Not for just a year, but always."

Finally, it was time to leave.

Shelly, Doug, and the children changed their clothes on board the boat. When they were all in their traveling clothes, their friends followed them out to their car. Shelly gave Nora all of their wedding clothes to take home. Jake and Melanie were going to take Nora and Ginny back to the house. They were taking care of things at the house and with the animals so Nora and Ginny could visit Nora's mother as they had not been together for a long time. Love was spreading and infusing hearts.

The wedding was over.

The honeymoon in Carmel lay ahead.

The friends stood waiting to wave good-by. Shelly was filled with joy. The future loomed bright. The sun fell down on them lightly. It was a perfect, brilliant, and beautiful day.

Shelly hugged Mrs. Best and thanked her again for what she had done to put it all together. "You are really good "Jewish Mother, We are so grateful that you chose us to win "The Contest"

Mrs. Best said, "I'm glad you're finally 'legitimate,' although I must say, your group of six people all together on a honeymoon is pretty unusual."

It turned out Mrs. Best was so busy making the wedding preparations that she totally forgot to promote the movie. When Doug heard that he laughed. His fears of inappropriate publicity completely disappeared.

"See," Shelly said, "I told you everything would work out."

The friends threw rose petals, rice, along with their best wishes at them as they drove away laughing.

The newly married family drove directly down the coast along Highway One. The children were very good on the drive and slept most of the way.

The wedding was over.

The honeymoon in Carmel lay ahead.

The children were very excited about the room-service menu, the big color TV, and the two big king sized beds. The four of them, who fought about sharing their rooms, were now happily sharing one room and two big beds. They bounced on the beds with the TV going full blast.

Mrs. Best had arranged for them to eat dinner at The Cannery Restaurant. They had dinner and were mostly well behaved. There were a few spills and a few near misses in tempers, but basically they were on their best behavior.

Then they toured Monterey and the Pier. Later on they went to Carmel. They walked along the beach.

As the children ran and chased each other, Doug and Shelly held hands, watched the kids frolicking in the sand, and laughed. They were complete as a family, and they were full of love.

Doug admitted to Shelly, "I had my doubts," he added, "I was pleasantly surprised that the whole ordeal was almost painless. I am glad the Rabbi didn't upchuck. That was a blessing right there."

The next phase of life was just beginning. Being really married felt very different. It was official, now complete, and Shelly was content. She showed Doug how much she believed that later that night.

The next day, they went to Pacific Grove to visit the Monarch Butterfly Grove. There were millions of butterflies nestled in the trees. Shelly was in awe at the sight. She felt drawn to butterflies. She wanted to write about the Monarchs, and learn more about their long and perilous flight from Canada to Mexico and about the transformation of the caterpillar into a chrysalis, and to later emerge as a beautiful multi-colored, gold, white, orange, and black-winged masterpiece of nature.

The butterflies touched her with their courage, strength, and beauty. Butterflies also touched the place of transformation within her. She realized she was completing her own metamorphosis. The change from one coast to another, and all the other changes they had gone through. The time ahead as a couple, and as a stepfamily, would make for even more changes.

Shelly was ready to spread her wings and fly regardless of what lay ahead.

Chapter 19

High Low

Everything has its wonders, even darkness and silence, and I have learned whatever state I'm in, therein to be content. Helen Keller

When the brief honeymoon interlude was over, they returned quickly to reality. The daily pressures were back on the hot burner of their life, cooking fiercely as usual.

Nora soon announced that it was time to move on and to find a new place to live for herself and Ginny. She decided to return to Daly City, to be near her own mother, so she could get help with babysitting, while she tried to find a job.

Shelly frantically searched for Nora's replacement for childcare so she could continue her own graduate schoolwork on (What else?) the issues of childcare. She was midway into the process and found the challenge not only daunting, but also ironic considering her own work was impossible unless she was able to find a reliable person. She needed to find someone in a hurry, someone who could come in, get used to the children, and handle everything at home before their scheduled trip back east in April. This was a major hurdle at anytime, even with one or two children, and no pending travel. Where was Mary Poppins when you needed her most?

After interviews with a long procession of many different widely varying types of applicants, from weird to very weird, from loose to very uptight, from unhealthy to potentially unreliable, Shelly realized she could do another dissertation just on the process of finding the right childcare arrangement. There were endless phone calls, frantic searches on bulletin boards, seeking referrals from friends, searching newspapers ads, and then the interviews. This was all her responsibility and it was challenging and frustrating and sometimes futile.

She finally found Frankie, a tough young woman who wore black leather, had an interesting smattering of tattoos; a few well placed metal rings and rode a motorcycle. Frankie it appeared would not put up with any nonsense from the children, particularly the boys, who usually loved to go out of their way to harass sitters, and in other ways wear them down until they ran out the door screaming.

Frankie rolled up her determination and was ready and willing to work. She wore her leather jacket proudly on her strong, weight-lifter, work-out-daily arms. She said, "Don't worry, the children will be fine! No problem for me. I know how to handle them!" She looked like she could handle being a bouncer at a SOMA club. Shelly sensed she would easily handle any outbursts without throwing the kids out of the house or more importantly being thrown out by them.

Shelly sighed.

But, true to her persona the kids responded immediately to Frankie's friendly firm toughness in a surprisingly positive way. They started out by being more helpful, and maybe things were not going to last, but at least it was a peaceful, fanciful interlude. Frankie took charge while the kids fell into step.

But, Andy continued to create some daily problems. It was difficult for him to get along, to respond to reasonable requests, or to share, a foreign word in his vocabulary. He argued about everything–cleaning, taking out the garbage, showering, or taking care of his half of the room. He picked fights with Ross whenever he could. That was one of the many different ways he delighted in bullying his younger brother or Alison.

Frankie tried dealing with him, but she often found herself frustrated. She kept working out her body routines with weights in the back yard with more determination. She lifted weights and did push- ups. Andy was a challenge and no push over for anyone, but Frankie was fierce in handling him, the other kids, and she mastered all the routines.

Shelly continued her research on childcare services. For Shelly, her days at the Lab were interesting, but the time in the field was much more fascinating. She wrote as much as she could about her experiences in her journal. She compiled her observations into a full draft. She kept contact with her advisors, who were located across the country, and sent them updates on her progress sharing the pages of the draft report.

When she found time she also wrote letters to family and friends in New York, Baltimore and Washington. She missed everyone, but she knew it was her time to focus on the new chapter she created as she struggled on starting a new life married to Doug.

Soon it was the end of March. Shelly made the needed arrangements to return to Washington in April on business. Doug was to meet her in New York to visit her parents. Then they would go on to Chicago to visit his family. The children and Frankie were filled in on the details. Everyone thought everything would work out. Shelly took off and Doug left a few days later to meet her.

Shelly first met with her doctoral committee in Washington. They were pleased with her results. They each gave her specific directions as to what she had to do between April and the end of the year to complete her work. Her committee was pleased to hear she and Doug married. She held off telling the wedding details and decided to write them later when she had time. First she had to concentrate on getting through the protocol of the process and it all went well.

Then she checked on the house, which seemed to be okay. She called a few of her best friends as there was no time to visit, but they were all glad to hear the good news.

Then she headed back to the airport to fly to New York City and to meet Doug. They had opportunities to tell the story of "The Contest" again. No one could believe it. It was hard to imagine they were actually married and harder to believe the way they were married. The story of "The Contest" tickled everyone. Doug and Shelly each told their own versions of the story along with their favorite anecdotes

Shelly's parents held a party for family and friends to meet Doug and everyone enjoyed the details of the wedding. They showed photos of the ceremony and of the four children. Everyone laughed.

The story of their wedding contest grew more outrageous with each telling of the events that had occurred. Everyone especially laughed at "taking the kids on the honeymoon."

"That's a riot!"

"Unbelievable."

"At least they didn't ask to watch!"

They had dinner with Elaine and Matt, Shelly's sister and brother-in-law, and talked about the children, Shelly's study, and about Doug's work, and their life. It was a good visit, but Elaine had the same doubts Shelly's mother had about how things would turn out, but she did not want to spoil the celebration and kept her thoughts private.

In Chicago, Doug's parents also had a party for them and to introduce them as a married couple to their family and friends. They saw his sister, Lucy, brother-in-law, Dave, many uncles and aunts, lots of cousins, and many friends. Everyone asked them about the wedding. Fortunately, they were able to show the photographs. As the family studied the photographs, it sank in; Doug and Shelly were officially married.

Everyone laughed about "The Contest" and the rush of the wedding, the four children, and the fact that they had actually gone through with it. Most of all they laughed at the idea of taking children on their honeymoon. It became funnier with each explanation as more details unfolded.

They called San Francisco as often as they could check in with Frankie and talk with the children. Everything was going well. They were no longer concerned that Frankie could handle the situation.

When they returned home after two weeks, everyone seemed fine. Each of the children and Frankie received a special gift. Even Andy had made an effort to be helpful and expressed appreciation for his gift. They were surprised that things appeared so calm. They had anticipated instead a dramatic report and felt reassured.

The following week, Shelly met Melanie in the sauna. She found out she and Jake had been spending a great deal of time together. They had decided to begin living together. Melanie reassured Shelly that she was being careful. She felt Jake was perfect for her, but getting married was out of the question. Neither of them wanted to make a commitment. Besides, living day by day was their philosophy.

Things continued at a hectic pace throughout the spring.

In July, the whole family went away for a week to a camp in the Sierras provided for the faculty at the University of California. Camp Gold had activities for children and adults, both separately and together. Comfortable cabins were provided for families. Meals were served in a large dining room.

The children were busy with all the many activities available, and the many new kids their ages they were meeting which left Shelly and Doug some alone time to play tennis, swim, and relax.

One day they decided to explore the area and drove to Pinecrest Lake, a nearby resort. They set up their spot, enjoyed an afternoon picnic, and savored the warm day outdoors. As they sat on the beach, with the children swimming in the lake, Doug decided to join them. Shelly began talking with Carol, a woman sitting nearby.

The woman's husband, Randy, joined them just about the time Doug returned. The four chatted about the area. The couple invited them back to their cabin located nearby in Mi-Wuk village. The Mi-Wuks were the original Native Americans that lived throughout the area.

They were fascinated, thought it was a great idea, and decided to go. They piled in their car and carefully "followed-the-leader" through the unfamiliar roads so they wouldn't get lost.

They soon found Mi-Wuk Village, a pleasant community of cabins, from very simple to more elaborate, nestled among the pine trees, a short distance from Pinecrest Lake.

The cabin Randy and Carol owned was set back, up and away from the road. A high A-frame with a big fireplace, it was quite cozy with one large bedroom, and a large sleeping loft.

Randy said, "Hey we want to give you the opportunity to come up here anytime. You will like it now, in the fall and later for skiing at Dodge Ridge. Just let us know and we can work it out."

Shelly said, "We would definitely like to take you up on it."

Doug added, "It's probably the right time and the right place to get the children started on skiing. I used to love to ski on Dodge Ridge when I first started to ski."

Since Shelly had not skied in California before, she just listened and agreed with Doug about returning to the area again sometime in the future. Then they returned to Camp Gold and enjoyed the rest of the weekend.

When they got back to the city, Shelly found out there were problems with the tenants in Washington, who were planning to leave. It was necessary for her to return to Washington DC again deal with the tenants, which she did. Unfortunately, she continued to have tenant problems. Being an absentee landlord was not a very good arrangement even with the best recommendations. Shelly was unwilling to completely let go of her ties with Washington.

She felt somehow that she and Doug would find a way to go back there for some work in the future. Things might yet change and programs for children might once again matter to a President and to Congress. She knew that in the current administration there was no chance. Maybe in the future there would be a huge shift and, as always, she remained hopeful.

She wanted to hold onto the house, but it had cost her all of her life savings. She handled the crisis with the tenants.

While she was in Washington she had time to visit friends, happily telling them about her newly married life. She and Rhonda met for lunch and had a great chat about everything as they always did. She and her husband Robert were happy together and their two children were doing well. Shelly had introduced them to each other when they were teenagers and they had been together ever since they made her believe that dreams could come true. Shelly was happy to provide a new and happy ending to her old friend.

She called Nick to let him know her news, but she did not see him. He was happy for her and Doug and the children. She felt good about completing the past as she returned to San Francisco to continue the future.

In July, Shelly had to make a decision. She knew she could not return to her job in Washington. She tried to get reassigned to work in the federal office in San Francisco, but there were no openings. She had no other alternative, but to resign her position. She hoped she would be able to find a good position later in the regional office in the same agency when she finally finished her Ph.D. She was just halfway into her studies. She knew it would be at least another year or more before she was ready to begin to write her dissertation. It would all be worth the commitment, if she stay focused, things would get better. It would be worthwhile, she thought, over time. Shelly continued doing the work she had to do to finish her study, and she spent as much time as possible with Alison and Molly. The boys always had other things to do with music lessons, sports, and friends and had little time for Doug or Shelly.

The summer passed by quickly with many barbecues, visits to the beach, and other outings.

One special time for the entire family was a trip to the Renaissance Faire during the first week of August. Shelly had learned about the Renaissance Faire from many friends who told her how much fun it was. They suggested they go in costume.

Shelly stopped by at a special sale at Bill Mandel's old costume shop on Mission Street (before it went out of business) and decided to splurge and buy everyone some things she could make up into Renaissance-style costumes. Her earlier experiences working at Arena Stage in Washington gave her the inspiration to try improvising outfits for the whole family.

So she brought home an assortment of large floppy soft hats, plumes, capes, dresses, fabrics, and faux leather that could be used for belts. She laid out the assorted items for costumes in the living room. The kids rushed in and got very excited. They quickly claimed the things they liked for their own. They were having a great time acting out the characters they might become once they donned the costume: a milkmaid, a knight, Robin Hood, a nobleman, or a princess.

Then Doug came home. He looked quizzically at the array of costumes and the kids preening about acting out their roles. He asked what was happening.

Shelly blurted out, "We are planning a trip to the Renaissance Faire this opening weekend. Would you please select something to wear?"

He thought about it and said instantly, "Okay! Sir Walter Raleigh, it shall be!"

He pulled out a hat and made a courteous, bowing gesture. The kids howled. He looked at Shelly and said,

"I hope I don't meet anyone from the hospital out there at the Faire. I'd feel silly if they saw me in this kind of get-up."

Shelly happily replied, "Who knows, maybe they will also be in costume, too. Isn't everyone in San Francisco always in costume?"

On Saturday they left for the Faire. They were each dressed in their fantasy costume and were laughing a lot along the way.

When they got to the Faire, they made a point to find a spot where they could find each other, if they got lost at the information desk where a spirited wench was sharing the news of the day in full regalia.

Then they started up the main path, which meandered under the trees, full of people, amazing costumes, handmade goods, assorted animals, varied colorful booths, a great deal of entertainment, period music and plentiful food including huge turkey legs. Laughter and natural good spirits were flowing everywhere. Most people were in costumes and very much involved in their own interpretation of their character. The atmosphere felt like Merry Ol' England, even though they were ensconced in Merry Ol' Novato, in a great field full of beautiful old live oaks.

Shelly and Doug strolled through the Faire with the girls. The boys ran off to explore. They stopped at places along the way to sample food, looked at the handmade objects for sale, and watched many talented performers complete with costumes and dialects to match.

They walked down the path to where the Renaissance games were being played.

Suddenly Shelly saw Andy and Ross perched high up on a log. They each had a bag of feathers in one hand and the other hand was planted behind their backs.

The referee said, "Time!"

They began hitting each other with the "Boff Bags" to see who would be able to knock the other off.

Ross, being leaner, was able to move more swiftly than his bulky brother, Andy. He won again and again, much to his delight, and to the growing anger of Andy. When Andy was pushed off for the last time, he saw the girls and his father laughing, and he raced away from the game.

They called out to him, but he disappeared into the crowd. They met him again only at the end of the day at their prearranged meeting spot. He continued to scowl on the way home and for the rest of the evening. Everyone else had a great time.

Shelly really enjoyed the Renaissance Faire. She felt it was yet another reason to love California, where everyone was in costume with their own individual unique style. There were few cookie cutter types, but everyone had fun, or so it seemed.

Ross was feeling really good about himself. It was rare that he could win over Andy in anything. He liked "boffing!" He wanted to hurl the bag one more time at his brother to make up for all of the times Andy got the better of him.

The next time the boys fought, Shelly thought of the boffing and grabbed two large paper bags, puffed them up, and closed the opening so they could "boff" each other in the backyard, where Shelly had placed a board stretched across two benches. Ross continued to win because he was more agile. Andy continued, determined but frustrated, and always won the war of loud words, expressed even more loudly when he lost.

In mid-August, Shelly decided to create a surprise birthday party for Doug at the end of September. She called his mother in Chicago to find out if she could come. She happily agreed because there was enough time to get her hair done and make arrangements. She was to keep this a secret from Doug and she giggled at the thought of surprising her son.

Shelly checked with his nurse-secretary, Gert, with Jake and other doctors, to find out the names and addresses of Doug's associates and his other special hospital and professional friends. She knew she wanted to hold the party at his favorite jazz club, The Rose and Thistle Club on Broadway. They had gone there many Sundays to hear Dixieland jazz. Jake helped Shelly with the party. He made lots of invitation suggestions from the hospital and university staff.

September came. Shelly was very excited about the prospect of surprising Doug. She found photos of him from childhood, college, medical school, and carrying a peace sign at a rally saying, "War is not healthy for children and other living things." Shelly learned that this poster was designed by Lorraine Schneider to protest the escalating Viet Nam War. Shelly had each of the photos blown up in large sizes and pasted on poster board. It was a montage of this life.

When Doug walked into the club on the pretext of hearing some new music, his mouth dropped open as he saw all his friends gathered.

The Dixieland band struck up chords of "Chicago, Chicago." His mother suddenly appeared. She hugged and kissed him. He was flabbergasted. He turned to Shelly and put his arms around her.

They danced and had a wonderful afternoon and evening. His friends wrote inscriptions in a guest book as a tribute to the friendship they all felt for him. Shelly felt pleased she could create such a special event for him on his fortieth birthday. She knew it was a turning point in his life. She was so glad to be with him and to have so much to celebrate together.

A few weeks later, Randy called.

"The cabin in Mi-Wuk is available for a visit." He added, "Would you consider purchasing it, since Carol and I are going through a divorce?"

Doug was surprised and told Shelly about it.

Then he added, "Perhaps Paul and Eileen would consider sharing and buying it with us."

Shelly nodded. They arranged to have both families drive up and look it over. Paul and Eileen were as excited as Doug and Shelly about the cabin and the area. They decided to purchase it together. Doing this together would make the most sense. They told Randy of their decision to purchase the cabin. He agreed.

It would take a few weekends to fix up the place with painting and other repairs. They decided that the families could do their share on alternate weekends. They would each do their part, painting, fixing, and changing the place until it was comfortable and cozy for both families. The loft would be perfect for the kids, with mattresses and sleeping bags. The one bedroom downstairs was reserved for parents.

The place had a comfortable floor plan so there was plenty of room on the main floor. The fireplace was large and inviting, but due to the distracted owners going through a divorce, the once sparkling cabin needed a lot of attention. Everything needed cleaning and sprucing up.

They gathered kindling wood and made arrangements for a cord to be delivered. The town of Twain Harte was delightful to visit. They soon made friends with the local storeowners and the librarian.

The cabin became very special to Shelly. She felt as one with her spirit and mind and experienced a new peacefulness and contentment. This place was now for her a special sanctuary.

It was a simple retreat place for her and for them as a family. It also was a place for rest when they needed peace and quiet. Shelly knew she would be able to work on her dissertation there away from the daily pressure, the stress of all the strings she juggled, the phones ringing, and she could write when it was quiet with only the sounds of blue jays for company. The tall pines all around provided a safe haven and she finally felt she had a special place that she could enjoy with Doug for the rest of their lives.

Both families threw themselves into the work that needed to be done to fix up the place.

By November the cabin was sparkling and ready. That first weekend at the cabin as a family, Shelly made the Friday night Sabbath as special as she could. She brought special food to prepare. Her blessing expressed her deep feeling about this special place they could now come to as a family, and enjoy the mountains, the lake, and being together.

She loved watching the blue jays that congregated outside among the pine trees. She now felt a sense of belonging. Shelly's father Morris came to spend Thanksgiving. After having been a healthy, vigorous man most of his life, he was now greatly debilitated by Parkinson's disease. His gait had slowed down; his hands were shaking more; and he was unable to be as active as he once was. Nonetheless, he took great pride in his new "family." He insisted on playing tennis with the children, going swimming at the local Y, and walking in Golden Gate Park with Shelly and Doug. Throughout his life, these had been his favorite pastimes.

One night after dinner, Morris took Shelly aside. He told her that instead of giving her the money he had saved for her after he passed away; he wanted to give her some funds for the future in the form of "Blue-Chip" stocks. He was so pleased about the four children, the house they lived in, and the new cabin. He made her promise she would never touch the money, but she should let it build up over time. She promised and kissed him. She was given, for the first time, a gift of a little future security.

Finally she had it all–a husband she loved, four children, some "nest egg" money, a house, a wonderful cozy cabin in the mountains, and a loving extended family. All that was left was to finish her dissertation and she would realize all of her dreams. She was very grateful that all of her dreams were coming true. She looked forward to having a child with Doug. She couldn't believe life could be so perfect! She felt complete and she was happy, but that was not to last. Her problems with Andy sadly seemed to intensify.

Then Shelly learned she was pregnant again. She was tormented by the idea of having yet another abortion. She wanted more than anything to have a child with Doug, and to know the joy of sharing a new baby with the man she loved. She believed the children would easily be able to handle a new sibling. They would, she felt, come closer together around a new baby. But, she also saw how determined Doug had become in not wanting any more children. Her feelings and desires were not as important as his determination to not add anymore children to the family.

He carefully and very slowly told her, "I am resigned. I'm sorry, but I am adamant in wanting it this way. I do not want five children."

She heard him say, "If you don't like it, it's too bad. You have to deal with your feelings. I have to deal with mine. If you don't like it, it's your problem."

This would be her third abortion of children belonging to Doug. How could he let her go through this? A child would be the perfect expression of their love, and they were married now.

There were five children in the home. What difference would one more, small child make?

She soon realized he was determined to make the rules, and that there were no other choices. He usually got his own way regardless of what anyone else wanted. She had to accept what was not to be. She suffered silently. The realized now that her dream of having a child with Doug was over. Three strikes and out goes a dream! How many more dreams would he shatter with his selfishness?

A pain she could not explain gnawed at her. She yearned for more affection, tenderness, and for his spontaneous expressions of physical love. Instead, she got perfunctory kisses, and only occasional sex. Then it was late at night so as to not disturb his schedule, and it lasted only briefly. She wondered about his fortieth birthday, and if his hormones had shifted the way they do in women.

Something had changed. She could sense it. If she tried to say what she needed, or express her need out loud, she was told, "Stop trying to tell me what to do, or what to say. I do things my way."

She was surprised, as she thought she could share what she needed to with him, or so it was before they were married. She was feeling strange. She knew that old feeling of being "cut off," or "not heard," and "disregarded." She could not believe she would again feel those old feelings. It seemed so simple in her mind. If she could only say what was on her mind, and have her feelings heard, it would make everything else a lot easier.

She was not asking for a lot. She wanted physical intimacy from the man she loved, a warm hug, a kiss, a few words, and spontaneous sex once in awhile. He seemed to not need now what she needed at all. He just kept going every day through his own work routine like a robot. It became harder for him to just relax. She felt her sexual tension mounting.

To respond to this internal tension, Shelly became even busier. Late at night when everyone was asleep, she got more involved in writing articles about childcare, book proposals, letters, and poetry, or got into whatever else she could do to help ease the inner heartache. She would keep going because she felt things would change. They would once again resume as they were early in their relationship, when he was cozy, warm, talkative, sexy, and affectionate. She was patient. She loved him. She knew he loved her. They would work it all out over time. Things would change for the better she convinced herself.

They had several parties to attend during the holidays. They spent time with Melanie and Jake and other friends. They spent weekends at the cabin.

They also visited with Peter and Charles.

Shelly wrote in her journal, "Life is full and continues to be a great adventure. I am happier than I ever knew I could be," but she really was not telling the whole truth, even to herself.

In February, Margaret Elke, a good friend of theirs, a talented massage teacher and specialist, confided in Shelly after she had given her a much needed massage about a special program. She told her she has just finished a new training method called Enlightenment Series Training, or EST. Marge enthusiastically raved about her experience with this brand new program. She made Shelly promise to attend a "guest seminar" with her that week. She agreed to go, as she felt good about anything Margaret suggested and it always turned out as she said it would.

Doug reluctantly went along. He felt it was an overblown sales pitch, a conglomeration of Zen, gestalt therapy, and a very pushy pep talk. Shelly felt there was something valuable or Margaret would not have insisted, but they were initially unimpressed.

The man presenting it, Werner Erhard, was all too slick and glib, so it seemed. She questioned whether his approach was on the level and if he was really sincere. She was not sure.

A few days later, Shelly accidentally met one of the presenters at the guest seminar while she was shopping on Union Street.

Shelly said, "Now, it's just the two of us. Tell me the truth. Did you really have all those great things happen to you that you described the other night?"

The woman replied, "Everything in my life just got better. EST is fantastic!"

Shelly knew that the woman had nothing to gain, whether Shelly did or did not register for the course. So she began to wonder if it might not be a good idea to attend. Certainly her graduate school gave her ample opportunity and encouragement to be involved in any personal growth program she selected. She found out more about this new method and decided to experience the EST training for herself. She felt that perhaps it would also help Doug deal with the growing tensions he was having and help to bring him back his former state of affection, warmth and more spontaneity. He reluctantly agreed to enroll with her.

The training was 40 hours over two weekends. Shelly found it provocative, and Werner Erhard was quite mesmerizing. She had never known she could sit so long in one place, or hold her bladder for so long. She had never heard anyone talk so intensely, continuously. They both survived the training. They kept their "soles" in the room and survived.

Doug, who had waited until last minute to join her, and was at the end agreeing with her that they had experienced something not only very worthwhile, but life altering.

Shelly submitted the training program for approval for credit by her graduate school. Her paper was sent to Roy Fairfield who approved the course as part of her qualifications in the personal growth segment. She became the first graduate of EST to receive credit for taking the EST training.

She then sent the paper she wrote for graduate school entitled, "A Natural High," to Werner himself with a short note of appreciation. He called and invited her to lunch. She went to his second story office on Broadway on top of Vanessi's. She saw it was a very small, busy, and efficient office. She met several of Werner's staff, Laurel, Stuart, and Randy. They were all enthusiastic. Learning of her qualifications and work in Washington, D.C., Werner offered her the opportunity to be his first consultant in education. She accepted.

Shelly and Doug got even more involved. They continued the different trainings. The seminars focused on sex, money, and relationships.

Werner asked Doug for his opinion while they were having dinner with him one evening about how the training could be used in the field of medicine. Doug said he was not sure, and would need to think about it.

Shelly offered the idea to both of them of creating an "Advisory Committee." She felt it would be advantageous to bring in graduates who were leaders in their specialties and who were doctors, psychologists, educators, lawyers, and others, to review how the training could reach out to others in their respective fields. Doug agreed with her and so did Werner.

Shelly was pleased she could make a substantive recommendation as Werner's consultant. The Committee and other work-related activities began to absorb most of their free time.

They decided to enroll the children in the first EST training created for children. The children were not too sure about going to a new type of class, but they were curious, and finally went along and actually enjoyed the time away from their parents and being with other kids. They had plenty to say afterward. Everyone talked at once.

"I was tired of sitting, but it was fun."

"I had to pee, but I could wait a long time."

"I was hungry, but I didn't eat."

"Werner talks funny, but it was good to listen."

Shelly understood the principles presented by the training, and agreed with much of it.

But the one thing she held onto was her feeling that, although each of us is ultimately responsible for ourselves, we do also have interdependency, a mutual responsibility to make an effort to make things work out with each other, and in a larger social context, a responsibility to be sensitive and responsible to the needs of others. She was not ready to give up her feeling of connectedness, mutual responsibility, and holding on to commitments like vows that should not be broken, no matter what. She remembered a saying she once heard, "there is a destiny that makes us brothers. No one goes his way alone. Everything we send into the lives of others…comes back into our own."

Doug felt differently.

He agreed totally with Werner that everyone was responsible only for themselves, and that whatever happened, they were to take their own responsibility, and do ultimately what is good to do for themselves, first and foremost, and if the other person did not like it, "Tough!"

Shelly continued to manage her responsibilities, although she had to depend on Frankie, and then on her replacement, Terry, and the kids to help out. It was not an easy transition to find another sitter, but the kids were able to pitch in more and were better able to handle things.

Finally, she had to rely on her own ability to remain awake late at night to keep on writing. She summarized her findings at the childcare centers at a series of meetings. The other reports and journal jottings she had to work on needed to be completed in order to finish her degree. When she finished her dissertation, and all of the other products she was to have ready, she had everything reviewed by her committee.

The "Project of Excellence" was enthusiastically accepted.

Shelly was very happy this huge part of her professional work was over. She was encouraged by Dr. Newheart to publish her dissertation at the Lab. He felt it made a good contribution to their larger goals.

Shelly retreated to the cabin to finish the final editing of the manuscript. Doug and the kids managed for the weeks she was there and visited her on weekends.

Shelly also put the finishing touches on her "Journal." She recognized many changes in her personal growth along with the many changes in her life. She could see the application of the EST training she had in everything she did.

She thought of ways to get teachers involved in sharing their experiences in the classroom. She believed education could benefit from exploring greater consciousness among students, teachers, principals, and parents. She felt that adults needed to listen to the children more and make an effort to respect their points of view. She felt that children also had to recognize and respect the experiences of adults, and to allow themselves plenty of room to learn all they could.

From the time they got involved in the EST training, their professional lives expanded, but they were also pulled apart. They became more involved. The entire experience was exciting and worthwhile, but they were both changing in different ways.

Shelly felt deep changes in Doug, but she could not put her finger on exactly what it was. Doug continued to be as busy as ever; but he also seemed to be even more self-absorbed, less romantic, less attached, and much more introverted, as if he were becoming more like Narcissus filled with his own self importance. It was an unexpected awareness that she felt he was turning into a selfish prig.

Shelly brushed off Doug's behavior as due to more personal and professional stresses, changes at the hospital, work pressures, his age, and his need to be constantly occupied. She felt understanding him was necessary, and she wanted to be flexible and supportive. A year after their wedding, they were certainly more conscious and more aware of each other, for better and for worse.

After the children had gotten involved in the weekend training developed especially for kids, Shelly hoped that somehow Andy might be positively transformed from the experience.

She felt she had to give him plenty of space and opportunity to express whatever it was he felt. She hoped he would love both his mother and accept Shelly as his stepmother. Being a stepmother was after all was said and done a very difficult and thankless role. She hated to admit her mother might have been right so she dismissed her feelings. Sometimes she felt she was getting through and other times she was ignored. She wanted at least acceptance.

As he sat in the kitchen looking at her after the training weekend, she asked him, "Well, what did you get from the training, Andy?"

He replied, "I get that I don't have to love you!"

Andy grew in his antagonism toward Shelly and he took it out on Alison, who was an easy target, every chance he could.

Shortly after the training, Andy was home alone one night with the girls. Shelly had gone to the cabin to get some important writing done in just a few days. Doug was at the hospital. The sitter was away doing some shopping. The girls had been playing in the backyard. Andy called Alison into his room, and locked the door.

He proceeded to take off her clothes and tell her he was going to "play doctor."

He made her promise not to say a word to anyone, and told her he would hurt her "bad" if she said one word. He covered her head with a pillowcase.

He then pulled down his pants. He touched her. She was frightened and started to cry. She was scared of him and did not know what to do. After he had finished, he pulled up his pants. He told her he would kill her if she said one word. He told her to wait and keep the pillowcase on her head. He called some of his friends, and told them that he had a great idea. They could have some fun with Alison. He brought them into his room, where she still had the pillowcase over her head. He made her sit down on the bed. He told the boys they could each have a turn putting their privates next to her and have a good time. They followed his directions. She cried, and was very frightened. When they finished, they took the pillowcase off her head and pushed her face down on the pillow.

They said, "If you say anything, you will get hurt really bad. We will kill you!"

Alison passed out.

When she awoke she was on top of her bed. She never told Shelly or anyone. She was too frightened. She also was never the same again. She began wetting the bed and her pants more frequently. She had more trouble in school. She became shy around friends. She babbled and acted strangely. Shelly couldn't understand why Alison was acting as she was, nor did she ever dream in a million years what had happened. She could not understand why Alison had changed so much in only the few days of her being away. Alison refused to say anything. She told her mother nothing about what was bothering her. Neither did the sitter, nor Molly, know any reason as to what had happened, nor could they give any explanation. Alison was from that day a changed person.

Shelly was frightened. Maybe she had made a big mistake. Could her mother have been right after all?

Chapter 20

Family Struggles

Beware the barrenness of a busy life. Socrates

Shelly was juggling more balls than she could handle; sometimes one dropped before she could catch it and things just slipped; but she was juggling as fast and as well as she could.

She continued her busy schedule. Time alone with Alison and Molly, time for herself, writing in her journal, articles, poetry, correspondence with mother, mother-in-law, friends, sister, sister-in-law, dealing with the house in Washington, working at the Lab, childcare meetings, shopping, clothing repairing, cleaning, taking the boys to music lessons, Hebrew School, Sunday School, preparing meals, arranging appointments for the doctor, dentist, and other appointments for everyone, hair washing, hair cutting, teeth brushing, sewing buttons, listening, refereeing, dealing with the house, picking things up, dropping things off, writing in the journal, taking EST seminars, planning social events, solving problems, helping with homework, talking to mom and mother in law, and so much more. Shelly was in constant orbit.

She continued, as much as she was able, her connections with the people at the Lab. She needed more time each and every day, but it was hard to squeeze in any more activities. She also wanted to meet some of the people Doug worked with at the hospital. She invited people over for dinner as she could.

There was barely enough time in her schedule to stretch, meditate, or even to take a walk. She hardly had time to write in her journal or a poem, but at odd moments she tried anyway. It somehow relaxed her to find a few moments to just let words flow. Life was like Haiku: short and very much to the point. She loved to hum melodies and make up tunes while she was driving around doing errands. It somehow helped to try to find an inner moment to relax and to find a musical interlude.

Doug left most everything in her hands to manage, and she did it all, as she was able. He only seemed to notice when a sock was missing, a button was not on his shirt or something was amiss. Otherwise he went along taking her activities all in stride. Things were done as he liked them and he did not have cause to complain.

Shelly found that the role of 'Home Manager' combined almost all the time bits of being wife, mother, helpmate, friend, student, referee, cabdriver, scheduler, cook, and nurse, was exhausting, but also somehow exhilarating. She felt like a CEO (Central Equalizing Organizer). Shelly felt she could handle everything. She did not know exactly how this character would look in her comic book, but she imagined "Super Woman," in a red, white, and blue apron, over pants, with pockets that held all these items — a wooden spoon, thermometer, Band-Aids, work gloves, pens and pencils, screwdriver, scotch tape, stapler and a spatula.

After all, her role models since childhood had always been Wonder Woman, Sheena-Queen of the Jungle, Nancy Drew, Esther Williams, Doris Day, and, of course, Eleanor Roosevelt. She knew they would have each have been mightily challenged to try to solve her daily issues.

Beneath her "get-the-job-done" exterior, she tried to be sensitive to everyone's needs. She was dependable, helpful to her friends, a gracious hostess, and the creator of frequent parties and events. She liked to connect people with each other. She felt she could handle the everyday struggles, and solve them one by one.

She persisted in her larger goal, striving to bring new ideas about the importance of supporting dependable, quality childcare in the community. It was a struggle to find ways to get the decision-makers and politicians to listen. There was a definite lack of childcare, and particularly before and after school. If the girls wanted to be Girl Scouts, or do creative activities after school, it was hard to find available groups.

The boys had their sports, music lessons, and friends, and moved in and out much more easily, but they always needed transportation, as busses were not scheduled easily for their needs.

Far from being a professional with objectivity in relating to children, the issues confronted her, 24/7, smack in her face, right in front of her at home. She felt frustrated. Not only for herself, but she also felt the frustration and challenges for all families facing the same problems, and with very little help; their needs were the same. It did not matter what color skin, what economic or education level, or whatever the reasons, parents were struggling to make ends meet and to find a balance. Children were why she did her work outside, but she experienced the issues every day as she walked in their door.

Doug called her "Earth Mother." Shelly felt depleted.

She struggled to handle things as good naturedly as she could be, graciously and with good humor, and without suffering, or being overwhelmed about all the responsibilities she had been so fully willing to undertake. She felt her struggles ebb and flow as each new situation presented new problems to solve. Some were easier than others. She rocked and she rolled.

Andy fought with Shelly on a daily basis. He picked on Shelly's way of treating Alison. He often loudly complained,

"You baby her too much."

"Why don't you leave her alone?"

"Let her do it for herself."

He was very mean to Alison. She cowered around him.

Shelly thought he would be protective, but instead he was overbearing and manipulative. Alison had special needs and problems that Shelly explained to him. Andy did not want to understand or be tolerant. Shelly thought she knew all too well the problems Alison was facing. Her outward tension and anxiety manifested itself in wet pants, halted speech, and a shy uncertainty. She became more obviously dyslexic, and almost withdrawn. It grew harder for her to respond to the other children, or as quickly as they or her teachers expected. Trying to protect Alison from the other children's onslaught, Shelly felt a gnawing pain. At home, at least, she hoped the children would turn away from their negative behavior towards her and become more constructive.

Time passed. Shelly did the best she could to meet the challenges she faced every day. Despite all the odds, Shelly finally came to the point where she actually completed all the requirements to earn the Ph.D.

Her friends from Sonoma arrived for the final meeting, as did Herb, her Rabbi friend, who had "married" them that sunny day three years before on the hill in Sonoma. Because he wanted to arrive on time, he got on the bus in Denver and rode 36 hours to arrive at their home early on Friday morning.

Shelly greeted him warmly. She made tea. Before they could talk, he fell asleep. When he awoke, Herb smiled, wished her "Mazel Tov!" blessed her work, the house, Doug, their union, the children, the sanctity of their home, and said, now that she had completed her goals, "I am very proud of your accomplishments."

He added, "I still do not know how you did it. I only have one baby and I can't complete all that I must do."

She smiled at him. She remembered being with Doug and Herb in The Yellow House in Sonoma, on the ranch where their first wedding took place, and she thought about the celebration later with their friends. Herb's presence brought all those warm feelings back to her. She was pleased to hear about the birth of his son. Sitting together that afternoon in the backyard, looking out over the canyon, they talked and caught up on the news, themselves, their lives, and the lives of the other students they knew. That Friday night she felt very full.

Shelly ladled out bowls of chicken soup with matzo balls to Doug, Herb, the children, and their guests. They danced and sang. They rejoiced. She had gone through all the steps needed to complete her life's work, the doctoral degree she had sought for so long.

She has prepared her final dissertation about the needs for childcare services that were based on the interviews she conducted with hundreds of mothers. The mother's comments were translated from Chinese, Spanish, and Tagalog. She interviewed representative parents from these and other groups to get a cross-section of families in the sample.

She obtained personal stories from struggling mothers, mothers in each community, rich and poor, from all over the City of San Francisco, Hunter's Point to the Mission, and SOMA to Pacific Heights. She discovered how great their issues were, and how many of the issues were the same among them, and she learned a great deal more. Each mother described how difficult it was to obtain good childcare. It was the major economic stumbling block for all women with children.

"It's almost impossible to find a vacancy."

"The staff it don't explain nada, nothing."

"There are no tortillas, or beans and rice for my child and that is what he likes best. They just give him peanut butter."

"There are no toys for the children to play with."

"I am never sure if she is happy all day."

"His pants are always wet when I get there."

"They don't let me stay to help out. I want to help."

"There is never enough money left for the program, or for us."

"I can never find or afford a sitter on the weekends."

These and many more personal comments were recorded.

As she had tried to be "Super Woman," so were all the other women, struggling to get off welfare, and trying to be fully responsible for themselves, their families, and their children. Many were single parents who could not even locate the fathers of their children. Some had been lucky to find a friend in a gay or straight man who agreed to serve as a surrogate father, or there was a husband willing to include an extra child in activities with his family. Most mothers struggled nights and weekends taking care of their children without any kind of support. It was lonely and difficult being a single parent.

Depending on neighbors, childcare centers, and other arrangements, mothers were desperately trying to resolve their problems. The government had ignored their pleas. Shelly remembered her days in Washington, D.C. She often felt helpless about the needs. She was angry at the lack of response to the growing needs of children. This was the future, the future of our country, yet it was so bleak.

She presented her dissertation to her committee, which had gathered from far and wide. She showed them her journal of life with Doug and the children. She spoke to her committee about the most important aspects of the research and the rest of her activities. They asked her questions. She responded.

Finally, they were pleased with all the work she had performed and saw the excellent results. She had successfully completed the program. She qualified for the Ph.D. degree.

Doug was very pleased. Herb beamed like an older brother taking pride in his "sister's" accomplishments. Her committee congratulated her for completing so much good work. They encouraged her to write more. The dissertation, she told them, would be published by the Lab, because Gary thought it was done so well, that it made a real contribution, was unique to the Lab, yet it fit its goals. They suggested she write more articles based on her findings and observations. She thanked all of them for their guidance and support.

Roy Fairfield complimented her through a poem in reaction to reading her personal journal. He said her journal was "a measure of such a journey."

"No teaspoon small enough
No ocean large enough
to catch the tears
of joy
or love
or fears
or see it through the kaleidoscope of daily sensing
the hurts the parts
the visions of what might be
mixed with strawberry milkshakes
television operas
murky clouds
and nightmares
who won't stop running for garbage
to be ground down kitchen sinks
to be washed
for fights to be stopped

edges of ambiguity
or weave it in a fabric more variegated
and as gossamer as that which old Ulysses' wife wove every day
'twould be torn out that night
while she waited
and waited
and waited
warp and woof
woof and warp
threads solid
threads as thin as the finest spider web
tying life
into knots that disappear
in a cup of tea with a night kiss"

Roy compared her journal to a "Ulysses of a Family," a Finnegan's Wake. She felt proud and happy that he understood what she had tried to do. He recognized her struggles. She thanked him profusely for his generous support over all the years. She felt very grateful to him for his understanding and encouragement. He was one constant source of encouragement, and always expressed the words she needed to hear to motivate her to push through when she felt it was impossible.

That evening they celebrated with a great dinner. Shelly thanked each member of her committee. She acknowledged Doug in front of everyone for everything he did to help while she completed her work. He smiled and took credit.

That night, as the three of them sat in front of a fire at home, Herb reminded them of that day high on the hill in Sonoma. Shelly looked at Doug and returned to that moment, sitting in the tree on the hill, looking down on him. She loved him more than ever. She told Herb about "The Contest," the wedding, and the honeymoon. They all laughed together.

Life continued on with the same number of beats, but sometimes just going faster and in staccato. Each day the complicated balance of children, people, and work continued.

Shelly planned to develop, more fully, the concepts she had been working on. She decided to try to create a place for parents to get support and parenting resources. She felt parents needed all the help they could get. She wanted to create a place they could get books, resources, toys, counseling, and assistance, ease their burden and reduce the isolation so many parents felt. The place would reinforce their natural wisdom, provide guidance and help them find answers they were seeking.

She decided to also work on a book to show how to create quality child-care. She contacted the top people in the field of childcare in many places to share experiences. For the next year, she worked on all these projects and they expanded as she began the project.

She prepared a book to help parents find childcare. It was a unique process, coming out of her own experiences, when she had tried to find the best arrangements herself and continued as she listened to so many parents. She explained how to locate good services, how to interview sitters, carefully. The Lab agreed to help publish it. Each project took time. She wanted to continue to do what she could now to make a difference for children in her sparkling city by the bay. It was far from perfect but most of the time it looked just perfect to her.

As a family, they continued to retreat to their cabin in the pine trees on alternate weekends. Shelly kept in touch with Paul and Eileen to make sure everything was in good shape at the cabin in between their visits. Often they got together for family dinners, going to their home, or their family coming to their home. The children were at their best when they had other children around. Often, Shelly thought how wonderful it might be to live communally with other families, being better able to share the responsibilities, pressures, and pleasure of their children. It all seemed easier when other families were around. Everyone was more involved. She also felt less pressure, generally happier, and more relaxed.

One day when she felt the push for the Ph.D. pressure was finally off her shoulders, she decided to quit smoking. It was time! She decided to stop smoking, so she would have more energy and be healthier. That was a big step to take and she hoped Doug would follow, but some things were harder than others to accomplish.

On Friday night during the Sabbath celebration, she lit candles, but she stopped lighting a cigarette. She relaxed and began to breathe deeply when she again felt the urge to light up. She knew she needed added assistance. She tried eating apples, carrot and celery sticks, and walking, and when she could some meditating. It all helped. She did not smoke again.

Doug did not stop, but continued to light up a cigarette whenever he got into the car, or he went in the bedroom, or got up after breakfast or dinner. Shelly was feeling inwardly angry at his not trying to stop, or trying to remember to be smoking away from her.

One day, the pressure was just too much and she just blew up.

"Why are you so inconsiderate of me and the children? Why aren't you taking better care of yourself? Why do we have to smell the cigarettes?" she implored him.

Doug calmly replied, dragging from his cigarette, "If you want to stop, that's your business. I like the taste and it is relaxing. I want you to stop complaining. Leave me alone about my bad habits. I will change when I want to."

She walked out the door, and walked and jogged around the track at the nearby school. She realized there was nothing else to do but to take care of herself, to not say anything critical, and to hold in her feelings about his smoking. She learned a lesson and she had to remind herself of that often.

One of their friends, David Wilner, a therapist, was moving from his home in Santa Cruz to San Francisco. He said, "How about if I give you my hot tub? It's in perfect condition and I don't have any space for it."

Shelly was thrilled. She had always wanted to have one in their backyard, the perfect symbol of what California was all about, "human mellowness." The gift could not have come at a better time. She needed all the mellowness she could find. Doug agreed.

They installed the hot tub on the deck in the back of the house. The first night they used it, Shelly melted into Doug's arms. She felt content and relaxed even though she was painfully aware of his "smoker's breath" whenever she kissed him. She felt she had to tolerate it and accept him as he was. He would make a change only when he was ready. She wanted to be patient.

Within a week or two, her friend Margaret invited them to take a massage workshop. She and Doug enrolled and learned to give sensual massages that helped to ease each other's tensions, tight places, and soreness. They enjoyed giving massages to each other. Shelly thought maybe Doug would also stop smoking, but he didn't. He did try to be more sensual and that helped.

On the other hand, Shelly had other challenges to deal with and being relaxed helped a lot. She felt Andy was planted to directly cast a shadow on the pleasure they were experiencing.

It was as if Doug's ex-wife Kristie created a volatile extension of herself in Andy to represent her side, to make sure Shelly would never fully enjoy what she had with Doug, and to be the thorn inside the house to turn the children toward being negative. Kristie said or did nothing to him to suggest that he behave differently, nor did Doug, so his heated complaints just continued.

Shelly could hardly explain it, but he knew something was seriously amiss. Day after day Andy never let up or changed. If he did, the relief was only momentary. He chided her or Alison constantly. She was tired, and felt as if she had battle fatigue.

Shelly tried everything she knew to help Andy. She listened to him. She talked with him. She was patient. She also created a Bar Mitzvah. She tried to show him in many ways that she loved him. She dipped into the money her father had made her promise never to touch to pay expanding bills. She bought the boys musical instruments and lessons. Neither Doug nor Kristie had enough money to pay for the Bar Mitzvah, the instruments or lessons, or other special treats she wanted to give to all the kids. By the time out-of-town guests were hosted and the reception was paid for, more than $5,000 of the nest egg was gone.

But the bright side of the whole event was that Andy did remember to acknowledge Shelly in his Bar Mitzvah speech. He thanked her "for her role as his stepmother and for giving me a "Jewish home."

He said, "I came to appreciate her even if she does make me clean up my room and forced me to learn Hebrew."

Shelly felt very fortunate at that moment. Maybe he finally recognized, at last, her contribution to his life. She tried to let go of the feelings of frustration she had been feeling for a long time. Her mother would not understand, as she always predicted the worse.

But, by the time they were to go to the cabin, a few days after his Bar Mitzvah, Andy said defiantly, "I don't want to go. I am now, after all, a 'man.' I can choose not to go!"

He asserted himself. The rest of the family went off without him.

Shelly thought about the struggle on the drive to the cabin and felt she would never be able to make the connection she wanted to. Certainly not in the way she hoped he would allow her to be part of his life as a stepmother or as a friend. Andy was one of the greatest challenges she had ever met. How it was going to turn out she didn't know, but she did not want not to give up. He was defiant no matter what and she really did not know the answer.

She wrote, thought, and tried to understand the concept of "unconditional" love. She felt firmness and kindness had to be used at the same time. But regardless of her methods or attempts she could not get through Andy's tough armor. It was clear he was strongly determined not to feel good about her, or Alison, or to accept her efforts no matter what. But Shelly hoped it was a matter of time and perhaps he would realize that they were all part of the same team, and everyone was needed to pitch in.

When Shelly was with Doug at the cabin, she felt a real communion with him, and with nature... pine trees, blue jays, mountains, quiet, and clear fresh air. She forgot the city and the many pressures in her life. It was a sanctuary, their special love nest. It was really a "home" for them, because it was the first place they had bought together.

She decided to stretch the money she had a little further. She found out it was possible to purchase the lot next door. If she purchased the lot, it would ensure their privacy, and give them extra space on both sides of the cabin so the kids could spread out. She felt it was a good investment in their future.

Later, it felt good to Shelly to walk into the grove of Manzanita trees and enjoy her own special privacy in the middle of the sheltered and secluded space. She quietly watched the butterflies, hummingbirds, and deer, and was content. As she sat in the grove of trees, Shelly felt lucky. Even it if wasn't always easy, she felt she had found her family. The struggles would continue, and anyway, who said it was going to be easy? She felt stronger and more confident and kept bouncing back.

Life was, after all, a patchwork of small pieces woven together to create something larger. The whole, the summation of each part, will become whatever you want it to...sooner or later.

Chapter 21

New Perspectives

In solitude we give passionate attention to our lives, to our memories, to the detail around us. Virginia Woolf

Sometimes one has to take a risk, unknown when you start, but if you feel it's going to be a good choice you have to trust your instinct. It is best to trust your inner voice whenever confronted by difficult choices.

Two years had passed since the wedding. Doug and Shelly managed to keep things together with work, family and friends. They took a trip back to New York City.

They met a friend from San Francisco, John Lansing, who happened to know Joe Bologna, the actor, playwright and producer of "Made for Each Other." He wanted to bring them together. John was still laughing over the outcome of the movie promotion and "The Contest," and learning how his friends had gotten married. A lunch was arranged at Bardolucci's on Madison Avenue.

Joe Bologna strode in. He was open, direct, and friendly.

He listened carefully to the story, and then he broke out into hearty laughter. "How amazing!"

"Hard to believe it actually happened. We thought it was a joke! The publicity lady, whatsername, Polly somebody, said she was going to cook up something to get the promotion going for the movie. She mentioned a 'Wedding Contest,' but we thought she was kidding, and would never pull it off. It is astounding that it actually happened, and that you are the couple who won!"

Suddenly serious, Joe turned to Shelly and said, "Why don't you write the story as a script? It's a very funny situation. It's got possibilities!"

Shelly was surprised. "But, she stammered, I've never written anything like a script before. I write about childcare and about children..." Shelly's voice trailed off as she realized he was challenging her to try something new in an already crowded schedule that had not lessened.

"You're a writer! You can learn how to write a script. You start working on it, and I'll help you." He added.

She shook her head in disbelief, but inwardly she felt proud and pleased. She promised to give it some thought. Then, because she liked to be challenged (otherwise she never would have won "The Contest"), she told him, as she smiled at the idea, "OK, let me see what I can do if you promise to help."

They finished lunch, talked over the story again, and she made notes of his suggestions and took down contact information. She thanked her friend John and gave him a hug. "I will never forget this introduction." Shelly was inspired and motivated by the opportunity.

Over the next six weeks she developed an outline. She put down some ideas. She also began to write a few pages. She turned to the "Field Guide on Script Writing" and decided to give it a good try. It was almost impossible to write during the day because she was working on articles, a book on finding childcare, reviewing manuscripts, going to meetings, dealing with housekeeping, and being a doctor's wife, a mother, a stepmother, a friend, a daughter and daughter in law and a good neighbor.

Sure, she would write a script with one hand tied behind her back, but she also had to mix cookies, and there were no hands free. Doug, meanwhile, was as deeply involved as ever in his work at the hospital. He wanted things quiet when he came home at night. But they rarely were.

So they decided to take a weekend off and return to Carmel, just the two of them. They had a lovely quiet weekend walking, talking, dining, and being romantic. A trip like this was rare, and time alone with Doug was precious. She did not feel he was totally over the hill when it came to romance. There was a glimmer of hope left, and she tried to fan that glimmer every chance she could.

When they went to the cabin with the children it was calmer and more peaceful. Over the next month, Doug's travel schedule increased. He was away from home more often. Late at night after the kids were in bed, Shelly began working on the script. It gave her a challenge and something different to do.

She really didn't know exactly how to go about it even with "The Guide" at hand. But, as she began to write, the story began to unfold. She surprised herself. "The Contest", the wedding, and the circumstances were relived again from a whole new perspective.

On Tuesdays at the sauna, she met with Carol, Melanie, sometimes Pat and any of the other girlfriends who wanted to come by. They almost always talked about their usual topic: men. They discussed the pros and cons of marriage or dating, the problems they faced juggling their careers and the men in their lives. Each of the women had her own situation to work out. It was fun for them to compare notes.

"He now goes to sleep watching TV."

"Hard to get him involved in what I like to do."

"There is so little free time to do things together like we did when we dated."

"He snores, and keeps me awake just when I am trying to go to sleep."

"The kids are so demanding."

"We hardly have time or energy to talk during dinner."

"Sex is not fun anymore."

"Sex? "   "What's that?"

They all laughed.

Shelly continued to work on the script late at night when everyone was asleep. She put out the cups and cereal bowls before she fell asleep near dawn. The script was something new and interesting to write, but she wasn't confident at all about how to do it. She tried her best to get the story to fit the plot form, but it spilled over and was unwieldy.

Toward the end of that year, Doug was invited to participate in a conference in Caracas, Venezuela. His travel costs for the trip were to be covered and he received an honorarium. He invited Shelly to go. She was excited about the idea of a taking a long trip together. They spent three weeks traveling throughout South America, seeing Buenos Aires, Caracas, Iguaçu Falls, and finally they went to Machu Picchu.

The trip to Machu Picchu was an extraordinary experience for Shelly. She gazed out over the ruins and imagined the ancient civilization that had been there. She was in awe. Her problems at home seemed for the first time miniscule. The dimensions of her life dwarfed in comparison to the magnitude of the ruins of the Inca's ancient civilization and their sacrifices. She could not imagine how the huge carved rocks got there.

From the anthropologist she met on the train, she discovered that there were other hidden cities far off in the distance that were almost impossible to reach as the train only went as far as the mountain they were on. The anthropologist and his girlfriend asked Shelly and Doug to go with them to visit another ruin. He had a Jeep parked at the next village. They returned on the train and got off at the next stop and then drove in the Jeep deep into the mountains along a narrow road that was just as wide as the Jeep. The sharp drop on one side was frightening. Shelly held her breath during some of the curves. When they finally reached the quiet village, they walked past the church, behind the graveyard, and up a little winding path.

There, in the late afternoon sun, was another magnificent ancient city. The stones were rose pink as seashells, and were the same huge size as those of Machu Picchu. It was an incredible sight, hidden from outsiders, an ancient rose pink stone city!

Shelly knew at once that trusting her instincts led her to this place. Doug had not been sure about the decision and, of course, was now delighted. Sometimes Shelly thought one has to take a risk, unknown when you start, but if you feel it's going to be a good choice you have to trust your instinct. Shelly tried to remind herself of that trust of her inner voice whenever she was confronted by difficult choices.

The trip was exciting for Shelly. It opened up possibilities she had not allowed herself to think about for years. She enjoyed being away with Doug. Yet, he seemed tense, preoccupied, and distant, even while vacationing.

She noticed on returning that Alison was quieter than usual, seemed easily upset, and continued to frequently wet her pants. She was concerned about Alison. She tried everything she knew to comfort her. She did not know what else to do to turn things around for her. She comforted her and held her close. Alison was not able to tell her mother that the boys had molested her again. She was fearful they would hurt her. She grew quieter.

When they got home, and Shelly thought everything was fine, she continued working on the script late at night when it was quiet. She finally completed half of it. She sent the draft of the script to Joe Bologna in New York.

While waiting for a response, she worked on other writing, especially "The Journal" about her life with Doug and the children. She shared more about how she was adjusting to the children, their high noise level, and the increasing complexity of activities. The boys were playing music (drums, with a full set, and electric guitar) and that added to the cacophony of sounds within the house.

The sauna, Golden Gate Park, or Charles and Peter's house were the only places she could safely retreat. The sauna time was her relaxing respite. When she got back from the sauna, she always felt she could manage to do whatever was required of her. Walking around the Lake was relaxing and helped her to keep in balance. And of course Charles and Peter were always perfect for a new perspective.

She continued to work on the script in bits and pieces, when everyone else was asleep. She wanted to get it finished. She was content to write about how she won "The Contest" and how they happened to get married. What was once far-fetched had indeed become a very clear reality; yet winning "The Contest" was still amazing. She won a wedding, and everything that went with it, but she still had plenty to cope with. Life was not a game.

Chapter 22

Petals Fall

As a matter of fact, life was a daily contest.

"Petals keep falling down with tear drops
as silently with no sound
And all they do is keep up all the mocks
so why do the flowers have to die?
And why do people have to make others cry?

You keep killing me
Bringing me down
Falling like a petal with no sound
And die away into the ground
But all these reasons we found
To grow back once more
And to see what new tricks are in store
To die and disappear into the ground" ...Zanzami

Shelly was in the middle of working on a new childcare article when the phone rang. It was Joe Bologna calling from New York City. He had gotten the screenplay draft.

"Kid, I like it! It's good! It's got possibilities. How much more have you got finished?" he asked her.

When she told him, "I have about half done, and I am doing it as fast as I can."

He said, "Terrific! I'll be going to LA in a couple of weeks. As soon as I settle in, you'll come down, and we'll go over everything. Good work. Keep it up!"

Shelly hung up the phone. She took a deep breath. She was thrilled.

It was April, the beginning of spring…a new beginning. She could feel this was a great opportunity, an exciting new challenge. She believed she could be creative and actually create the whole script if she stuck with it. Her other "serious" work would get done later. There was plenty of room to grow as a writer. She wanted to learn to write in different styles and she was willing to try and give it her all. Shelly had completed several childcare articles, and then a book of poetry: Petals.

Shelly had been writing as she could, and working on the poetry book for several years. She learned what it takes to lay out the text, insert illustrations, get bids and go through printing. She sent it out as a gift to friends and family. She included the poem she wrote about Doug and their wedding day. Her heart was full of sonnets and love poetry. She was inspired by Elizabeth Barrett Browning, Edna St. Vincent Millay, and Walter Benton—their inspirations of romantic illusions merged together in her heart, as her feelings remained loving and strong for Doug and the children, despite the many challenges.

Shelly believed that love would overcome all the challenges and issues. She was determined to not be overwhelmed, except that at times she felt like her strength ebbed instead of flowed.

She continued to talk with specialists across the country in interviews about their childcare experiences. They presented their views and she compiled them into a series of books containing the details on how to create good childcare services. She also worked on a guide to help parents find good childcare, but as she could manage a few hours late at night she continued working on the script.

A month passed. Joe Bologna phoned her again.

He said, "Hey kid. I'm now at 20th Century Fox. You should plan to come to Hollywood as soon as you can so we can talk more about the script."

Shelly was excited as she made arrangements to go to Los Angeles.

Doug seemed genuinely pleased for her and proud of her accomplishment.

Shelly flew to Los Angeles.

She met with Joe in his office at 20th Century Fox. They talked for several hours about the script. Then they went to lunch in the Commissary. She felt very happy discussing the script with him. Joe made many constructive comments. She listened and made lots of notes. She felt confident now that she would be better able to get back to completing it. She was glad to be working on the script again. She felt that somehow everything had come together in whole new ways she had never dreamed possible.

When she got back to San Francisco that night, she was joyful. She told Doug the news. He was very happy. He was however slightly concerned,

He said, "What about the publicity of a possible movie? I am not sure that is wise."

Shelly replied, "There is nothing to be concerned about. We have nothing to hide, and besides, all the names would be changed to protect the innocent."

They laughed.

Then Shelly said, "Let's have a party to celebrate the script, and possibilities ahead. Let's make it a Sabbath gathering with all of our close friends."

He nodded and smiled thinking of the food, camaraderie, and music.

Shelly said, "I am certain I can pull things together easily. I will start by calling people tomorrow."

During the next two weeks, Shelly found herself caught up in her busy routine, making phone calls plus writing, working with the children, doing housewifery, mothering, and the many other things that were needed to be done by a good Jewish mother. Whenever she had a few moments, or late into the night, she worked on the changes that Joe had suggested on the script. She liked the new form of writing and it challenged her. She was happy and preoccupied. She fixed breakfast and the sandwiches for lunch for the children before she went to bed, sometimes only for a few hours. She was tired, but greatly energized by the new writing project.

A few days before the party, Melanie called to tell her that she and Jake were going to announce their engagement. Shelly was thrilled. Shelly suggested they announce it Friday night. She would get champagne to celebrate. They laughed at the thought of another wedding.

Shelly said, "See, that's what happens when you catch the bridal bouquet. You get the gold ring. Now that we've had one wedding, we know the routine. The girls saved their baskets and will throw rose petals for you, if you ask them."

Melanie was in love with Jake and getting married seemed perfect to them anytime, with or without rose petals.

She continued to call friends.

She decided to call the ex-wife of a close friend of hers from Washington. Ken Foley had written her several times and suggested Shelly and his ex-wife, Karen, should get together. Then he called to say hello and added.

"I am sure you will like each other. You have so much in common," he said cheerfully over the phone.

So Shelly called and asked Karen to come, giving her directions to the house.

Dozens of people were invited. It was going to be a "potluck" dinner, one of those wonderful events where everyone brings their special dish, plus their favorite wine. Everyone was going to come, so there would be plenty of food, dessert, and wine. She could relax and focus on making a huge pot of chicken soup and matzo balls, her specialty.

Friday night came. All the guests arrived. There was a great buzz of talk and laughter. Music filled the crevices. Everyone was having a wonderful time.

One of their friends, an artist, came with a statement about the Sabbath, in the form of a scroll, beautifully hand-decorated with butterflies drawn around the border. He read it aloud after Shelly lit the candles.

Come let us welcome the Sabbath in joy and peace.
The rightness of the Sabbath light shines forth
to tell that the divine spirit of love abides within our home.
In that light all our blessings are enriched,
all our trials softened.
At this hour, God's messenger of peace
turns the hearts of the parents to the children,
and the hearts of the children to the parents;
strengthening the bonds of devotion to our beloved homes.
We thank thee, O Lord, for the blessings of the past week,
for light and health and strength and love and friendship
and for that happiness that has come to us out of our labors.
We pray that we may be worthy of thy continued favor
during the week to come and that we may be able to
greet the following Sabbath in joy and thankfulness.
Praise be thou, O Lord our God, King of the Universe,
who causes the earth to yield fruit for all.
Amen.

Everyone chimed in, "Amen!"

Shelly and Doug blessed everyone; Doug and the boys blessed the wine; and then their friend David blessed the bread and passed it around. While people were enjoying the Challah, Jake announced his engagement to Melanie and everyone responded, "Mazel Tov!" Then they all went to the table to start the feast. The plentiful potluck meal flowed out over the table and was followed by some other warm and beautiful statements.

People ate and talked, and when they felt like it went in and out of the hot tub. Singing and rejoicing filled the night air. Shelly was busy being the hostess, moving around greeting and talking to everyone.

Karen arrived in the middle of the prayers and slipped quietly inside. Shelly saw her and welcomed her and introduced Karen to Doug. Then she got busy with children, guests, asking David to pour more wine, Jake to help cut more bread, Melanie to help serve more food, while she focused on serving more chicken soup and being sure each bowl had a good sized matzo ball floating in it.

She noticed Karen and Doug in animated talk throughout the evening. She was an attractive woman, slim, dark, exotic looking. No wonder Ken, her friend in Washington, had been attracted to Karen in the first place. Shelly didn't pay much attention, but continued being the perfect hostess.

Everyone enjoyed the chicken soup, and devoured all the food that each one of them had brought to share. The evening was very congenial

Later some of the friends got together to sing and play old favorite songs around the piano. Andy played guitar, and the other children played a variety of percussion instruments.

Finally, as some of the guests were leaving, Shelly found herself chilled as she stood outside the house saying good-by. She went upstairs to get a sweater.

She approached the bedroom to find Doug standing there in the doorway with Karen. They followed her inside and he closed the door to the room. Suddenly he said, to Shelly and in front of Karen, in a very casual yet matter of fact way,

"Shelly, this is not easy, but I have to tell you the truth. I was enjoying getting to know Karen and talking to her this evening. I have asked her to go with me to the cabin for the weekend. I hope you don't mind."

Shelly looked at him and tried to hide her shock. The room rocked, and she didn't believe what she was hearing. Was this real? It felt as if he had just punched her hard in the stomach Shelly looked at him and tried to hide her shock. Somehow she was able to hold back her emotions.

She thought, "This is a test! This is a test! Do not react! Stay perfectly calm. Respond in a 'New Age' way, be tolerant, be understanding. What would Werner say in response to this news at this moment? Do try to be patient. Try to respond to his outrageous statement in an understanding, civilized, conscious way."

Did she have a choice?

After a few moments, she finally replied, "If that's what you need to do." Her voice was barely audible.

She turned to get a sweater and not show her feelings. Tears filled Shelly's eyes. They could not see her eyes as they were looking at each other instead. Karen smiled at Doug. She thought him to be very open and honest. Shelly was not told about his plans or the change in the rules of their marriage. Doug had told Karen he was in an "Open Marriage," so she did not know at that moment that anything was amiss and was very impressed at how understanding his wife was when he told her of their plans Doug was very calm and deliberate. Karen thought he was considerate, upfront, sharing what he was going to do, and not sneaking behind Shelly's back. Karen made a mental note about how to handle frankness in an "open marriage."

Shelly was stunned. She couldn't understand why Doug had chosen this time, this way, and this night, the Sabbath of all the times, to confront her and to do it in front of this stranger. He decided to experiment, to test himself and their marriage. Why now? When everything seemed to be so perfect.

The reason was not clear. Did it absolve him of guilt to tell Shelly openly about his plans so there could not be any confusion in anyone's mind about his intentions? Shelly was overwhelmed with emotion, confusion and pain.

Was truth supposed to hit you between the eyes? Was your head supposed to crack open and the truth pour in? Did Doug expect Shelly to babysit the children? Did he expect to leave her alone while he went with another woman, a stranger, to their sanctuary, their cabin, her special place, for a weekend? Did he think she would be able to just casually handle the sudden decision? Or, did she not fully understand what he really wanted? He wanted his cake and freedom, too. He wanted something new, an "Open Marriage," but he forgot one small detail, to clear this sudden change and discuss it privately with her first. Did her feelings not count?

He forgot about their commitment and vows with her. He never discussed the issue of "Open Marriage" with her to prepare her for his change in heart. Nor did he discuss how they were going to handle feelings—hers and perhaps his also. Was he giving her permission to try her wings and fly the coop without him? Shelly was very confused. This was not in her plans, or scheme of things, and certainly not at that moment when she was focused on paying tribute to their wedding and writing about "The Contest".

Doug was not careful about the decision or the timing. He did not consider how his wife was feeling about the change nor did he seem to care. He was thinking only of himself. He decided he wanted to be free to experiment. He believed all he had to do was to decide what he wanted to do, and in this case, the other person, his wife, Shelly, did not like or want or accept his choice, that it was her problem, not his. After all he took EST and that is what he got. His choice was first and foremost. If she did not like it the response was her problem.

Her thoughts slipped away, evaporating silently in the night's darkness. Shelly felt a void, an extreme emptiness inside. She was not prepared to handle the abrupt news. She had to make a real effort to hold herself together, and to not disintegrate right in front of them. In her mind she replayed what had just happened. She thought perhaps there might have been another reaction (yet for only a split second in her mind), another, different scene played out with decidedly different results.

She thought she might have said instead,

"You bitch! I invite you to my home and now you want to go with my husband! To our cabin! Our sanctuary! How dare you? You haven't even asked me anything about me at all since you arrived. You spent all night captivating and teasing my husband. You did not even bring food to share. You are like the wicked witch of the East. You want my ruby slippers? You did not even ask if you could help clear or wash the dishes. You're not a girlfriend. You're a witch. Get the hell out of my house! Now! And stay away from my husband! Find your own man! Don't try to destroy us, push us apart, or break the sanctity of our marriage! Get out now!"

But, Shelly despite the powerful flash in her mind, remained silent. The words of retort did not come to her lips as she was totally censoring her full expression and feelings. She was in shock, and not able to respond. She looked well beyond Karen.

To Doug, in her mind she wanted to say, but could not say out loud,

"Doug, what is wrong with you? What have I done? Do you think I deserve to be treated like this? How could you? Why are you destroying our marriage tonight, now when everything we have worked so hard for has finally come together? Our relationship will never be the same! I'll never be able to trust you again. How could you be so stupid, thoughtless, selfish and so cruel? Did our wedding vows, taken twice, mean nothing to you? Did I ever agree to an 'Open Marriage'? If so when? I don't remember that discussion! Who do you think I want to be with? Do you think I want to do the same thing as you and leave you with the children and go to the cabin with a total stranger? Are you out of your mind? Why would I ever want to be married to you now? You have abused my love and trust. I no longer want to be your wife. This is the final straw."

But, Shelly's heart hurt and she held back the deeply hurt feelings and thoughts that welled up inside her, all wrapped in tears. She remained quiet. She was too full of pain. Words stuck in her throat. She did not want to think, or say, the word "divorce." It was all an avalanche that came pouring down on top of her head as she was being buried alive by her emotions and fears. Could this really be happening now?

She turned to get her sweater and left the room. She remained cold even with the sweater on. She just got busy. She cleaned up as best as she could after the party. She wondered if anyone else heard the break that happened inside her heart.

Karen slipped out of the house.

Later when she entered the bedroom Shelly saw that Doug was asleep. She did not want to be next to him. She took her robe and slept downstairs near the fire.

Early the next morning Doug left for his week-end with Karen. Just before he left the house he walked over to the sofa and looked over at Shelly, still asleep, and left quietly.

All that day Shelly felt numb and cold. Shelly went through the motions that were necessary. The children were busy. That evening, the children finally asleep, Melanie and Jake came over. They were welcome and good company. Breakfast at Tiffany's was going to be on TV. They could watch Audrey Hepburn party and then search for her cat and cry.

Shelly had trouble telling them what had happened. They tried to understand. A tough role for them to be in, and it was totally unexpected. They thought it would be a usual evening, and it wasn't. They did the best they could and tried to cheer her up. They were happy themselves, and they thought Doug and Shelly were, the ideal couple. It sure looked that way to them. They were sure it was but a temporary strain on what otherwise was a perfect blendship.

Shelly heated up "some even-better-the-next-day" chicken soup from the previous night, and put the pizza in the oven to get warm. Melanie and Jake chatted as the food heated up. Outwardly, Shelly tried to be good company. She was happy they were engaged, it was just hard to express that through the pain she was feeling. Shelly never expected her own marriage to crumble and fall apart all in one night just when their relationship was moving ahead.

During dinner, Doug called from the nearby town of Twain Harte in the Sierra Mountains to tell Shelly,

"You are wonderful," he said. She was confused. Then he added, "Shelly you are so understanding! I am so grateful that you have given me the 'space' I need. I might be able to quit smoking now!"

She listened to his New Age, EST-inspired, "Bullshit." She simply and barely audible said, "Good for you."

She then went to the bathroom and cried, washed her face, and returned to her company. The children were asleep. Melanie and Jake were holding hands and crying while Audrey was searching for her cat in the rain. Shelly made some tea. She hurt inside where no one could see.

Later, Shelly said goodnight to Melanie and Jake. She watched them go off hand-in-hand to spend the night together, warmly content. She was sure they would make it in life, together, and what happened to her would never be an issue for them.

The house was quiet.

Shelly went to the back of the house, took off her clothes, and entered the hot tub. She looked up at the moon.

The searing pain inside her matched the temperature of the tub. She perspired without a drop of water forming on her numb forehead.

"Alone."

Suddenly, the moon was eclipsed by clouds. Even in the hot tub Shelly felt cold inside. Her tears fell down to the steamy water. Shelly remembered the script for "The Contest" and with it her hopes, and all the changes she had made in her life. She wanted one thing, and apparently she was mistaken. Doug wanted something else.

Her thoughts came crashing in on her. She remembered her love and commitment to Doug. She could not understand how he had forgotten, and all of what they had for a fuck and a fling, or is it a fling and a fuck? Whichever came first, it was not her cup of tea. He acted as if everything would be exactly the same. He expected her to accept his actions with understanding and no complaints. She was confused and hurt too much to think clearly.

Flashes of memories passed her as the clouds covered the moon overhead. Memories interlaced with moon glow in a torrent of emotional separations and reunions, lost pregnancies, financial struggles, Alison's struggles, kids struggles, and all the family and friendships they had shared. She thought of their time together, time alone, joys, laughter, songs, and all the struggles. The sacrifices were all part of what one had to do if you loved "unconditionally," but she did not know that there is always one who loves more and that one is always more vulnerable. She thought of her responsibilities, parents, brothers, sisters, and the whole family. She recalled trips here and there. Life before was a blur of actions that were piled up like so much laundry. She could no longer sort it out. The love she held for Doug for so long and for so many nights apart and together disintegrated silently inside her. Her heart felt like shattered glass, frozen in the middle of winter and covered over with snow.

We had it all, she thought. My life with the man I have loved has frozen in the night air. He's no longer mine. He no longer wants what I want. We no longer have a sacred circle. Our vows have been broken. There are no repairs for broken vows, invisible scars, or a broken trust.

Finally, and most painfully, she had to admit, "My mother's premonitions have come true." Infidelity is, after all, a broken commandment. Her tears continued to roll down her face into the water of the hot tub as she looked up sadly at the moon. She saw at once all the moons she had shared with Doug passing by rapidly like they were ducks in a shooting gallery. She held the gun, and as they passed by, she shot each one of the moons down. Her mind was full of broken pieces of moon. Her heart felt as cold as a moon crater.

She was alone.

She left the hot tub. She went upstairs. She carefully took her many months of hard, all-night work on the script of "The Contest" from her desk. Slowly, she walked back downstairs to the fireplace. Then, Shelly very slowly fed the entire manuscript, systematically, one page at a time, into the fire. She sat watching the papers curl and burn. Her tears stayed mainly inside. One escaped rolling softly down her cheek, but that one tear was not sufficient to stop the incineration of her dreams in front of her, or to quench the burning flames inside her that were unable to melt her deeply frozen heart.

The paper burned.

The sky darkened.

Everything was silent, except for the conflagration in the fireplace.

The fire burned, crackling, sputtering, until all the love represented in the nights of writing found on the papers disappeared, swallowed up in the hot flames. Shelly was alone with fire and her pain. She could not sleep. She was exhausted and felt cold. Shelly's heart was silent.

Her heart burned. The fire burned her cherished memories. Everything was consumed by flames.

Fire cleans and purifies, but pieces that are charred cannot be put back together again.

Shelly tried, for the sake of the children, but she could not bring herself to feel the same way toward Doug. The connection she had held for so long was burned She thought she had to try all she could to make things work out. But, she only felt empty inside. Her heart did not beat the same way. She hurt all over. She could not forget his betrayal or forgive him for changing things so abruptly, and she could not understand how insensitive and cruel he had become. He changed everything between them and she was not a willing partner in that change.

She had to change herself. Whatever she tried did not change the circumstances and the event that transformed her trust and finally broke her heart. Many things came together, erupting into a crescendo and crash that shattered their marriage. Shelly and Doug went through a very painful divorce.

Doug, the man she left everything for, turned out to be, a serial murderer, the killer of love, romance, commitment and marriage, a killer in disguise. A hunter of the heart: Wife one, two, three, and then on to the next victim.

The butterfly folded her wings.

Epilogue

Time magically shifts away from that terrible night, the fire, pain, the end of her marriage, and returns to New Year's Eve in North Beach many years later. For a moment time passed quickly just as the ball drops on Times Square counting the few remaining minutes left of the old year.

Shelly did recover slowly from that night of burning flames. "The Contest" script was gone and with it all that was left of their marriage. Those were days before computers, copiers, and back-ups. The fire abruptly finished her fantasy. Shelly's fairy tale—love, wedding, and marriage forever fulfilling were in the past. Her dreams burned in that fire. She would lose all her material possessions in another fire years later and find again that she would continue and survive, but that is another story.

Shelly found herself on New Year's Eve at the Caffé Trieste alone and ready for another year to begin. The last person she expected to see that night was Doug. In a short time he stirred up the past just as he stirred his coffee. After he dropped her off at her apartment she thought of what she had been through from their first meeting, and their entire relationship, the children, "The Contest," betrayal, and beyond.

New Year's Eve in North Beach was very quiet.

Shelly stayed home, with her vivid memories, thoughts about her life, before, with, and without Doug. She thought about all the other New Year's Eves. Time passes so fast. Finally she was able to see the whole tapestry, holes, wrinkles, threads and all the spots worn thin.

She remembered: "When you're weary, feeling small, when tears are in your eyes, I will dry them all; I'm on your side...like a "Bridge over Troubled Waters"... As she hummed the melody water gushed from her eyes. Shelly never thought she would be a victim of love twice. She wanted to be shot by cupid, but instead was shot in the heart by a heartless hunter.

She woke up from her memories and realized that although her dreams had been shattered and burned, she knew her life was not over. She would find true and lasting love one day. She looked back and realized all that she had been through was the stuff of memories like kindling crackling in the fire.

Shelly had the thought about starting a new business—"A Used Husband's Exchange"—like a Dun & Bradstreet service, that would warn women before they got involved with men who were abusers, addicts, adulterers, closet homosexuals, drunks, emotional wrecks, gamblers or drifters, lazy, liars, losers, sexual felons or perverts, thieves, and otherwise high risk or dangerous men. But, instead she just laughed at the thought and realized she was not going to do it. But, she thought someone should do it.

She thought back about the years before Karen appeared in her home, of the children, of the pains, of the pleasures. It was a lot for her to handle. She saw how naïve she was and how determined she was to give it her all. Saving the marriage was not possible. She struggled with her conflicts and mixed messages to try to make things better, but she could not save what was not hers alone to save. Marriage, as any relationship, partnership, or peace treaty, takes two in agreement to make it work well. Even disagreements can be handled, if both are willing and work out the details.

After the divorce, Shelly and Alison moved far enough away, but there was not enough space she could put between painful memories that haunted them both for a long time.

Doug's marriages could not ever last because ultimately she realized he was a vampire of love…a killer of love slyly on the loose: He left the corpse of love, lifeless and drained. Nothing was left to touch after he sucked dry, the blood, spirit and energy of love. He was after all immune to taking responsibility or feeling anything was amiss by his actions. His one night stands occurred one night after another in rapid succession just because he could and he enjoyed seduction and his partners were only interested in the pleasure of the moment.

Shelly had to escape from pain, a broken heart, bruised soul, misplaced and painful memories, and deeply hurt feelings. She was in pain most by just thinking her mother was right after all, and that she could not see what her mother knew better than she did long before. Shelly realized "being alone" was just another part of life. She was content to stay alone for a long time after the divorce so she could find her own way to heal and again gain her inner strength. She was beginning again. She needed a steady transfusion of life. Over time, her body, heart, and spirit healed until finally the wounds were not perceptible.

Alison also finally healed. It took a lot of time, understanding, and patience. She was an adult well into her late twenties before she admitted to Shelly what had happened to her when she was alone with Andy and those other boys' years before. The tortured emotions she felt and her painful experience haunted her dreams and erupted in her erratic behavior for a long time. She might have been scarred for life, but she finally released the painful memories. She had to fight for her dignity. She won. Time itself is merciful, after all, and the mind is a powerful healer even if nothing was the same ever again for either of them.

Shelly was alone on that New Year's Eve, in North Beach, but her heart and mind were full. It was strange to see Doug again. He seemed his same old self, but she had greatly changed.

She knew by how he acted then, and before, that he was not at all remorseful. He never understood the impact or meaning of what he had done. He never said he was sorry for what he did to destroy their marriage. He never thought there was anything wrong. He was so far up on his pedestal, that he never had to look at his actions, his behavior, or take any responsibility for his actions. He simply blamed her for whatever went wrong. After all, he could never do anything wrong. He was perfect. If you did not like his actions or what happened, it was your problem, or so he thought. Shelly finally smiled again as she thought of that plaster pedestal and how fragile was that perch he was placed on. One day he would find himself sitting alone and no one would even care.

Finally it dawned on Shelly.

What she should have said when Doug announced his sudden betrayal to her in front of Karen, the stranger he chose to take with him to their sacred place, the cabin in the mountains, the sanctuary softly surrounded by pine trees—the place she did not want to ever return to again. The thought did not cross her mind until that moment, years later, and having the time to gain a new perspective by reliving the whole saga again. She finally said out loud for the first time the words that would not come before (because she did not know how to respond to him, could not think what to say, or how she could handle at that moment what was required for her to carry out the words):

"Right, Doug, thank you for telling me about this abrupt change that you decided to be the agreement for our marriage, changing the rules of sanctity, and deciding this without giving me a chance to think about how I feel. I am clear however that if you go away for the weekend to the cabin with Karen, you must know before you leave that, I will not be here when you return!" Then she thought she might have just turned and walked out of the bedroom and began her move.

Would that courageous response have saved her years of anguish and pain? She would not have instead turned the pain inside and heaped it on to herself. Those words would have saved her tears, wasted time, and botched trials by fire.

She wished she had said, "I will not agree or give you permission! You have just changed the rules. I don't want to continue to live with you under the circumstances. We did not agree to this kind of marriage, and after all at this moment I do not have the same situation or rights, or do I? " Now she could not turn back the clock. Her mistake of silence was taken by him as her readiness at acceptance. The mistakes were in the past. She made some too and suffered. There was nothing left to do except to gather oneself up. Be strong and move forward, one step at a time. So Shelly got up, and took her first step towards a new freedom. She turned on a record, and sang along with Billie Holiday…

"…Love is just like a faucet,
It turns off and on.
Sometimes when you think it's on,
It's turned off and gone…"

Shelly then poured herself a small glass of brandy. The New Year had almost arrived.

She remembered the first time she and Doug kissed, to Roberta Flack's First Take, the words filled her mind:

"The first time ever I saw your face…the moon and sun rose upon your face…"

She smiled at the thought of how naïve and needy she was. Shelly made a hopeful toast to herself and her future. The past was past, not quite a dream yet, but now she would turn pages and not burn them. She loved herself. Perhaps for the first time finally, she felt she would survive, and life would be good again. She would manage to ride the waves even as they crashed beneath her feet. "The Contest" was a chance to win, lose, and win again. The game was over. She did not win the "prize." "The Contest" cost her everything—job, money, security, house, cabin, time, time with Alison, end of the relationship with Molly, Andy, Ross, babies, family, friends, and much more. Her self-confidence and self-respect had been shredded. Her life dreams, like kindling, burned in the fire of lost time. Most of all, her romantic illusions were gone. But, in their place, finally, she had found herself, and the right pathway out of the maze and deep soulful sadness she had felt for so long.

The story of "The Contest" was not "Let's Pretend!" But it was a story, you may have even heard before, or even lived some portion of …the story of warm dreams turned into ashes.

We never know who the winners of contests are, except by reading snippets of paragraphs in the newspaper. That is, of course, insufficient. No one knows any other situation by just looking from the outside in. But, that is not quite the end of the story. She thought of another song that touched her heart, "The Rose."

"It's the heart afraid of dying…that never learns to live. ..

But, the seed that lies buried under the winter snow, with the warmth of the spring sun's love…will someday become the rose"

Shelly's life unfolds on new wings in the next chapter that brings her courage and conviction. Her butterfly heart takes flight again.

Love is "The Contest." Often, we win, but winning can also be an illusion. Still we want to play. Unless we enter "The Contest" we will never know if we can win, yet, we might lose. It's not just that we play the game. Ultimately, it's how well we play that counts. Sometimes love works out, exactly as it should, while sometimes it brings heartache and disappointment. That is, after all, how life plays out.

Winning "The Contest" was neither the be all nor the end all, but only a chance to play.

After "The Contest"

What lies behind us and what lies before us are small matter compared to what lies within us. ...Ralph Waldo Emerson

Shelly Stern, in 1980, after the divorce, was again on her own. Her daughter went to live with Arnold, her father, in Washington, DC. Shelly healed, found herself, and continued working. But then she lost all her possessions in a five-alarm fire that destroyed her home and office. She began again; Alison returned to live and work with her and together they created a special place to benefit children until the Loma Prieta earthquake of 1989 forced the place to close. Shelly moved, adopted a cat, and a year later unexpectedly met the perfect partner who was also living alone with a cat. The cats adjusted to each other. They all live happily together.

Doug Fine continued his medical career in San Francisco for many years. He married again and it ended again in a divorce. He lives in the same house, and still thinks he is perfect.

Flora Sanchez, the first baby sitter, continued caring for children and enjoying her new found freedom in Washington, DC.

Nick Gilmore never married, but moved to the New York City theatre scene.

Julie Darnell left the government and is now running a B&B in New England.

Gert, Maria, Bob, Glenn, and the others involved with Childcare and Head Start stayed involved for as long as possible. Marv left the government and became a college President.

Shelly's sister Elaine and husband Matt remained married.

Rhonda, Shelly's girl friend who she grew up with in New York, and her husband remained faithful and true to each other throughout their long and happy marriage.

Penny Watermark still lives at the Sonoma Ranch where she still welcomes guests.

Dr. Roy Fairfield lives on the Maine coast with his loving wife of 70 years and recently a library of Maine History was dedicated to him.

Herb Stone, the Rabbi, was divorced from his wife, married and divorced again. His son is, happily married with a new baby.

Pat moved away and divorced.

Kristie, Doug's ex-wife, never remarried and remained bitter until she died.

Nora Jones went to SF Community College where she studied to be a health worker and enrolled her daughter Ginny in the school's childcare center.

Nora's daughter Ginny learned a lot in childcare and from her loving mother.

Melanie Schwinn and Jake were married, and after having a child together were divorced.

Alan Rowan the photographer provided excellent photos of the wedding and continued doing photos.

Steve Hanan, Shelly's friend, and singer at the wedding went on to Broadway to appear in "Cats" and in other shows.

Doug's kids Andy, Ross and Molly are grown and made many of the same mistakes their parents and stepmother made. Doug's sister Lucy and her husband divorced.

Charles and Peter were married at City Hall as soon as San Francisco's marriage law changed.

The Jankofsky's remained together despite infidelities.

Eileen and Paul who shared the Mi Wuk cabin were divorced and married others.

Shelly's mom Jeanie continues to give her accurate advice at the ripe age of 96. She is always right.

Hal Slate another friend at the wedding opened a club called "The Cauldron" and later died of AIDS.

Betty moved to New York City and continues sex therapy workshops.

Alison recovered from her trauma with therapy and support from her mother, father and stepmother; she later eloped, had a son, and divorced. They live in Nevada.

Chronology of Richard Nixon's Career
and "The Contest"

1947

Richard Milhous Nixon's political career begins. He is elected to the US House of Representatives. Shelly attends grammar school in New York City.

1952

Nixon elected to Senate. Selected by Eisenhower to be running mate as Vice President. Shelly attends high school.

1960

Nixon loses election to John F. Kennedy. Shelly graduates from College in New York City and begins living in Washington, D.C. Shelly marries Arnold.

1962

Nixon runs for Governor of California and loses. Shelly and Arnold remodel and move into their new house in Washington, D.C. She attends George Washington University for her Master's Degree.

1968

Nixon elected President, defeating Democrat, Hubert H. Humphrey to become the 37th President on January 20, 1969. Shelly and Arnold gave birth to Alison (1966)

1970

At The White House Conference on Children Nixon promises to support children. Then, despite bi-partisan passage of legislation in Congress, he vetoes the first major childcare bill that would have created quality childcare services. Divorced from Arnold Shelly raises Alison alone. She meets Doug. They attend the White House Conference along with 4000 delegates.

1971

June 13- The New York Times and Washington Post begin publishing the Pentagon Papers – The Defense Department's secret history of the Vietnam War. Shelly makes a decision to leave Washington to attend graduate school in California. September 9- The White House "plumbers" unit -- named for plugging leaks in the administration, burglarizes a psychiatrist's office to find files on Daniel Ellsberg, the former defense analyst who leaked the Pentagon Papers. Shelly attends graduate school in San Francisco. She writes about the politics of childcare.

1972

May 28- Bugging equipment is installed at Democratic National Committee headquarters at the Watergate hotel and office complex in Washington, D.C. Shelly enters "The Contest" and wins. She and Doug are married with their four *children attending. They go on the honeymoon together as a family because at the last minute no babysitter is available to care for the children; June 17- Five burglars are arrested during a break-in at the Watergate. One of them, James W. McCord, is Security Director for Committee for the Re-election of the President; June 19- Former Attorney General John Mitchell, head of Nixon re-election campaign, denies any link to operation; August 1- $25,000 cashier's check earmarked for Nixon campaign ends up in the bank account of Watergate burglar; August 30- Nixon claims White House Counsel John Dean conducted an investigation into the Watergate matter and found no one from the White House was involved; September 15- First indictments are made against burglars; September 29- Washington Post reports John Mitchell, while serving as Attorney-General, controlled a secret fund used to finance widespread intelligence gathering operations against the Democrats; Oct 10- FBI agents establish Watergate break-in stems from massive campaign of political spying and sabotage conducted on behalf of the Nixon re-election effort; November 11- Nixon is reelected in one of the largest landslides in American political history, crushing Democratic nominee, Sen. George McGovern.*

1974

Watergate scandal unfolds. Next eighteen months dominated by damaging revelations and legal fights between White House, Congress and the Supreme Court. Nixon faces impeachment by the U.S. House of Representatives. He resigns on August 10, 1974, the first U.S. President ever to do so. Shelly and Doug listen to the event on the radio, celebrating the news far from Washington, D.C., in the Sierras among blue jays, pine trees and looking at the mountains while the children play. Nixon writes a number of books and travels. Shelly continues to work to improve conditions for children and families. Shelly enters "The Contest" and wins. They marry and take the children on their honeymoon as they are without childcare. Everything is challenging, but they work things out. Then after a few years of juggling their blended family and careers suddenly and without warning there is a shattering change. Shelly and Doug are divorced.

1994

Nixon dies. Funeral is held on April 27 at the Richard Nixon Library, Yorba Linda, California. Shelly and Alison recover. Shelly struggles to continue to work in service of children and families.

2009

Shelly often wonders why the United States of America still does not have a comprehensive quality childcare program in place for all of its children along with full healthcare benefits. Alison grown up, with a child of her own needs childcare to attend school to upgrade her skills.

LaVergne, TN USA
17 March 2010
176362LV00001B/3/P